UNMAGICAL

UNMAGICAL

JENN LESSMANN

UNMAGICAL
Published by FARMER'S DAUGHTER ARTS, LLC
Copyright © 2023 Jenn Lessmann

This book is a work of fiction. Names, characters, businesses, organizations, places, events and incidents either are the product of the author's mind or are used fictitiously. Any resemblance to actual persons, living or dead, events, or locales is entirely coincidental.

Cover Design by Get Covers
Editing by Sharon Stogner

ISBN: 979-8-9893324-0-3 (Paperback)
ISBN: 979-8-9893324-1-0 (eBook)

For more information visit: **www.JennLessmann.com**

For my parents, who always believed in my gift.

March 14

Beginning, Innocence,
Freedom

1

You don't have to kill him. Even though you would be completely justified. Smile, and let him go. He's just another customer. Just keep smiling.

"Got that, Cate?" my brother asked. He winked.

I was pretty sure I could get away with it. I wouldn't even have to hide the body. I could make it look like an accident — a terrible, terrible coffee-related accident.

Slow breaths, in and out. Smile. Mark the paper cup. Smile. Pass the cup and call the order.

At the bar, my partner released a frustrated sigh when he recognized the customer.

My brother, Thomas, had been our last order every night for the past week. You'd think our shared blood and birthday would foster some level of empathy, but twenty years in, we had yet to develop anything resembling a mystical twin connection. My mother swore we were related, and I had to take her word for it.

I dropped the smile as I turned my back on him to lean against the counter, but his shining blond reflection in the drip coffee server grinned back at me. I rolled my eyes and tucked a loose hair behind my ear.

Thomas tugged on my ponytail. "Nice color. Subtle."

"Thanks," I said, ignoring his tone but hoping he wouldn't miss mine. I turned to give him my very best customer service smile. *Buh-bye now.* Tossing my hat on the counter, I retied my hair, pulling the faded purple strands out of my face and resolving to pick up some new dye on the way back to the dorm.

"Quad espresso brevé extra-hot caramel macchiato... drowning in caramel sauce and buried in whipped cream," Brian called from the other side of the bar. Thomas practically skipped around the service station to collect his sugar bomb. Brian watched with a mixture of awe and horror as my brother slurped it down. "Your teeth are going to fall out of your head."

"They'll grow back." He flashed the original pristine set. Somewhere a tiny bell chimed. Brian didn't hear it. My brother and the stupid risks he took for humor. "This is decaf, right?" Thomas asked, pushing his luck.

So completely justified.

Brian blinked and shook his head. When Thomas shrugged, the barista started taking down the espresso machine, apparently ignoring the preternatural sparkle of his customer's teeth, except that now Brian was humming "Blinded By the Light." Thomas's influence could be unintentional, but something about the way he watched Brian work made me nervous. He was playing a game, and sometimes he didn't know when to stop.

"Cut it out," I grumbled, rubbing my temples. Brian went quiet, but I glared at my brother.

"What?" he said. The faint shimmer that had started to surround him faded. Luckily, I had yet to meet anyone outside our hometown who would recognize a magical glamour if they saw one. Mundanes just weren't expecting to see anything they couldn't explain away with science.

"He's good," Thomas said, walking back to the register. He inhaled the steam from his coffee and glanced back at Brian. In a low voice, he said, "Does he know...?"

Keeping my back to the bar, I whispered, "He's mundane."

"What a thing to say!" Thomas clutched imaginary pearls.

I rolled my eyes. "We met in class. He got me the job here. The closest thing he's seen to real magic was when we did *Into the Woods* last year. Besides, there's nothing to tell."

The register blanked out, the screensaver showing the date and time: March 14, 9:56pm. We could lock the doors in four minutes.

"Why are you still here?" I asked. "I thought you decided to go back without me." I started pulling trays of leftover pastries out of the display case and covering them.

"And miss all this fun?" He balanced his steaming cup on two fingers. It sat there, like magic, until it didn't. Then it was a sticky caffeinated mess dripping down the front of my counter. I grabbed a rag and threw some paper towels on the floor. As I imagined some creative things to call him that wouldn't also insult our supportive, oblivious parents back home, he leaned over the puddle. Glancing at Brian, who had produced a pair of earbuds and was silently dancing his way through closing the bar with his back to us, Thomas dropped his voice. "Why don't you just, you know...?" And he snapped his fingers.

His cup reappeared on the counter, freshly filled and steaming. He'd even gone so far as to put a lid on it this time. He pulled a stirrer from the cube by the register and chewed on it thoughtfully. For a moment, he seemed genuinely pensive. He took his cup and sat on the arm of an overstuffed chair.

"You know why." I glanced at the security camera in the corner of the store. The blinking red light had stopped blinking almost the moment he came in. My dad would have some kind of explanation about how magical energy affects electrical signals, but mine had never been strong enough to interfere.

"Impossible. Still Cate-the-Cursed?" he asked, invoking my least favorite childhood nickname. Was he trying to make it easier to say goodbye? If I had his Gift, I'd have him singing along to the coffee shop playlist. Jack Johnson's "Home" would have gotten him moving in the right direction.

Of course, if I had his Gift, I might have considered going with him.

The café was empty. Brian went on dancing, dumping the grounds and slamming the drawers back into the espresso machine. Since Thomas had cleaned up his mess, I returned to the pastry case. Instead of being grateful I didn't have to pick up soggy paper towels and relieved that Brian didn't see Thomas's magical display, I gritted my teeth to keep from telling him off for putting us in unnecessary peril. It wouldn't be the first time we'd had that conversation, but reminding my brother not to do magic in front of a mundane, while standing a few feet away from said mundane, seemed counterproductive. Plus, I would probably just sound jealous, which I definitely... was.

"Thanks for stopping by," I said. "Have a good evening. Safe travels."

"I'm sorry," he said. "You know it doesn't really matter. To any of us. "

I was saved by a phone ringing from the backroom.

As much as I'd have loved to get into a deep philosophical discussion about my crushed dreams and failure to live up to familial expectations, I was relieved to have an excuse to walk away. I stacked the trays and headed for the cooler in the back. My cell was ringing in my coat pocket. Quickly stowing the trays, I grabbed my denim jacket from the peg on the wall and pulled out the phone, but I didn't recognize the number. Tapping *Decline*, I dropped it back. By the time I came out, Thomas was gone.

I chewed my lip. What if that was the last time I saw him? I shook off the guilt. We had a few days left before anyone expected us to come home. There was no reason to believe Thomas wouldn't be here again tomorrow night, continuing to make my job difficult. If he wanted to change my mind about going back with him, he needed a new approach.

Brian had finished with the machines. He pulled his cash drawer out of the register and took it to the back to count out. "You want to get the floors and doors?" he called. "I'll get the trash."

"On it." I grabbed a broom and headed to the front to lock up. With the door locked behind me, I surveyed the empty café. It wasn't too bad. There was a little bit of a mess around the biggest table. I remembered a mom sitting there feeding her toddler bits of a giant cookie to distract him while she worked on a laptop. She'd cleared the trash, but there were crumbs everywhere. Then there were some rings on a table in the corner where a guy had sat with a newspaper all evening, taking full advantage of the free refill policy.

I took a deep breath and closed my eyes, imagining the broom gliding around the room on its own, *Sorcerer's-Apprentice*-style, while the rag flew around, erasing the last traces of messy customers. Of course, when I opened my eyes, none of that had happened. It had never worked. Never would work. But, just to be sure, I glanced through the dark windows before I tried one last thing. There was no one there. I focused on the crumbs under the table. "Disappear," I whispered and snapped my fingers. *Nothing.*

When Brian came out with the trash bags, I'd swept the crumbs and all of the other dirty residue on the floor into a neat pile by the back door. He held the last bag open while I dumped the dustpan like any other completely normal service employee. As far as he knew, that's exactly what I was, and it wasn't far from the truth.

I'd been away from home for two and half years, and Thomas's cup trick was the first real magic I'd seen since I walked through the invisible Gate that hid our community from the mundanes.

It hadn't been particularly hard to blend in. I might as well have been mundane myself. I didn't have the Gift. I could fake it well enough (I was majoring in Theater), but nothing I could do came close to my brother's power. And he wasn't even the strongest in our family. In a few days, I'd have to permanently decide whether or not I would go back, but I didn't see why I should. Nobody needed me there. I wasn't like them.

"Just the way you are..." Brian sang, picking up the trash bags. He stopped outside the door and did a little spin, tipping his hat to the side. Although the café baseball cap wasn't a fedora, and Brian's skin tone was a little darker than the singer's, it was a pretty good impression. He winked before heaving the bags off the sidewalk and shuffling down to the dumpster. I stood, holding the door for him, reminding myself that he couldn't read minds, so the song choice was more likely a sign of his appreciation of Bruno Mars than a secret message for me. Still. The coincidence made me smile, the first real one in a while. *Thanks for the pep talk, universe.*

Later, I grabbed a box of Ultra-Violet Conditioning Color for Dark Hair from the drug store next to the café. It wouldn't be a permanent change, and the hall bathroom would smell extra-minty for a while, but when I saw vibrant purple streaks in my hair, somehow, I would feel more in control of my life.

Thomas could probably pull off a glamour and get the same effect in half the time without the mess, but he never had. Maybe it never occurred to him, even though lots of our friends and neighbors back home had unusual hairstyles or otherwise embellished their appearances. Somehow the easy things never seemed as important as the ones you had to work for.

I stayed up for an extra hour to color my hair and avoid my thoughts. Then I lay awake all night worrying about a decision I thought I'd already made. Thomas would go home, and I would stay here. It was safer that way. For everyone. Better to be here, finishing my degree, where I could get a job that didn't require magical aptitude. And my family was better off without me carrying a curse around.

But curses weren't real. Not if you didn't believe in them.

Which I didn't.

My brothers didn't mean it when they called me Cate-the-Cursed. It was just a thing obnoxious older brothers said. Teasing me for years of coincidental bad luck, lack of talent, and being a burden on my family of Gifted witches. They didn't mean it. Brothers just say things. Stupid, hurtful things.

They were just playing.

But what if it manifested...? What if I started to believe it, and I manifested it? Impossible. All attempts at the Craft aside, it never came when I called. Not even when I was centered and physically sitting in the sacred spaces back home. I was a walking magic-free zone. No magic, no curses.

Right?

March 15

Sacrifice, Waiting,
Uncertainty

2

The next morning I seriously considered staying in bed. My roommate was almost certainly sitting in an upper-level science class. I could stay under the covers and tell myself that no one would miss me if I skipped my 11:00am *Theater History* class. That was one of the greatest and most dangerous things about college. You were in total control of your own schedule. Nobody woke you by throwing pillows at you or dragging you out of bed by your feet. Nobody called your name — repeatedly — from down the hall, urging you to get dressed and "Greet the day!" Whatever plans had been made, whatever work needed to be done, whatever expectations were in place, you put them there.

I twisted a newly-purple strand of my hair.

I did this. I made this commitment. I would face the consequences.

Ugh. I hated consequences. As usual, my sense of personal responsibility won out over youthful rebellion. Besides, I chose these classes for a reason. I liked them, and I didn't want to get behind.

In a few days, it would be Spring Break, and if I wanted to,

I would have just enough time to go home and formally say good-bye before I came back for exams. I could still get in and out before my birthday on March 21. Probably.

It was a risk though. If I stayed a minute too long, the Gate would trap me inside with everyone else who'd chosen a magical life. Except that I hadn't chosen it. Or it hadn't chosen me, which amounted to pretty much the same thing.

The seventh Corey child, only daughter of a seventh son. Destined to wield great magic, successor of the Gatekeeper, I was a mistake of fate. A mundane in witch's clothing. And I'd be stuck there, a failure with no Gift.

No, I wasn't going back. These second thoughts were normal. Fear of the unknown shouldn't hold me back. In the mundane world, people leave home after college all the time. *So long, don't forget to write. Keep moving forward. Get up, and get going.* Staying in bed and feeding into the negative energy would only make it stronger.

I stopped at the University Center on my way to class to use my meal plan points for coffee. I might have developed a slight addiction while working at the café. I still preferred chai, spicy and steaming, with extra cinnamon, stirred clockwise, three times, like Mom prepared it for protection back home. But the UC didn't have the selection of the café, and part-time pay didn't quite cover my habit. The café wasn't exactly on the way to the theater building anyway.

I checked my mailbox in the UC basement before I headed out, even though the box would be mostly empty, as usual. Some of my classmates had subscribed to magazines or signed up for newsletters just to have a reason to check their mailboxes, but I hated the idea of all that wasted paper. Snail mail wasn't such a novelty to me. Plus, I'd completely embraced their digital culture. The other students here grew up with it, but there weren't any cell towers or internet back home. When I first discovered the reach of online services out here, I was almost sure it was some kind of magic (except that it worked for me).

There was only ever one envelope in my mailbox. It'd be small, almost square, and made of rough blue paper, the same as the one I got last week and the week before, going all the way back to my freshman orientation. When I opened it, the note would be short but thoughtfully written in my dad's angular handwriting. I would wonder, again, how his students ever understood the comments he left on their papers.

He'd tell me not to worry, that things at home remained unchanged. He'd include a funny story about one of my older brothers (maybe some news about Caleb's relationship with Elspeth or Benjamin's training with the Watch). He'd tell me my mother missed me but wished me luck on my upcoming exams. He might include a stone, or a dried herb from her to use when setting my intentions, even though I'd told them I wasn't following those traditions at school. He'd remind me my birthday was coming, and he knew I would "make the right choice when the time came." I'd roll my eyes, but I'd keep the note. It would go into the shoebox in my dorm closet with the others. I'd write back in a few days, dropping my letter in the box outside the café on my way to work.

My mailbox was empty. I frowned, closed the box, locked it, and stepped back to make sure I'd checked the right one. I opened it again. Still empty. I looked up at the huge wall clock above the bank of mailboxes. The mail was delivered by 10am each morning. It was almost 11am. I reached into the box blindly and felt the sides in case the envelope was somehow stuck. I even used the flashlight on my phone to get a better look. But it just wasn't there.

I went to class, but I would have to get the notes for *Theater History* from someone else because I spent most of the next hour trying to remember a time when my dad's letters had skipped a week.

I'd check the box again tomorrow. Then I'd go to the guy at the package window and ask him to check the lost letters bin. It was probably just delayed. Or misdelivered. It was probably sitting in someone else's box. That person would be super excited to get a real letter and then terribly disappointed it wasn't for them. They'd feel so much empathy from this roller coaster of emotions that they would immediately turn it in to the postal counter and demand to watch as it was delivered to the rightful box. The postal employee would be annoyed but ultimately deeply apologetic for the confusion.

Or the person who got my letter by mistake would shrug and toss it in the trash.

Or they'd be one of those people who never checked their mail because they only got junk mail, and who needed it anyway?

And my dad's letter would sit in their box until they graduated.

But all that would be fine because I'd get a new letter next week, and my dad would want to know why I hadn't responded to his last one. I'd write to remind him that if Queen's Creek were an open community, I could just call him, and we wouldn't have to wait a week to communicate. He'd send me an annotated treatise on our town's archaic, magical security system and the explicit conflicts presented by the interaction of magic and technology throughout history. And then I'd laugh as I wrote him back in text abbreviations and hand-drawn emojis.

But really, it would most likely turn up tomorrow, and I would have obsessed about my bad luck for nothing. Again.

I tried to put it out of my mind. I was at the mercy of the post office. It would come when it came. I had to be patient.

I had to do something.

It felt like something was wrong, and witches had to trust their intuition, right? Even cursed witches, who had no Gift. And there was something I could try, if my skills held up. There was a reason witches said they *practiced* the Craft.

I'd told my parents I wouldn't practice at school, but that hadn't stopped Mom from packing a disguised ritual altar in with my bathroom caddy and shower shoes. I hadn't seen any signs of the witch hunters my parents were so concerned about, but it was better to be cautious. Just because I hadn't seen them, didn't mean they weren't watching.

So, before I pulled the tin mint box out of my desk drawer for the first time since I'd moved in, I checked to make sure my roommate was gone. It didn't take long. The dorm only had space for two desks, two dressers, and a bunk bed. She must have still been in class. I locked the door. My altar cloth was in my sock drawer, wrapped around the composition notebook I used as both a diary and my book of shadows. I spread the cloth out on my desk, popped the lid on the tin, and laid out the contents. I had the elements represented by a small shell, a feather, a narrow selenite wand, and a tea candle. Two tiny vials held sea salt and black salt. A pack of matches also hid a bay leaf and a sprig of rosemary. A tiny bell. A piece of chalk. I grabbed a bottle of water from the mini fridge. It would have been better if I'd charged it under the last full moon, but *sourced from a natural spring in the Blue Ridge Mountains* would have to do.

When my materials were ready, I invoked the goddess and her consort. For things that were lost, I sought them in the forms of Ichnaea and Hermes. The Greeks were great at specializing their spiritual guidance. To attract my lost letter and help it find its way back to me, I performed a spell I'd read hundreds of times before. If I were a Gifted witch, I could probably have waved a hand and made it appear on my desk instantly. The Craft would require a bit more time.

Growing up, I'd seen lost rings turn up in plain sight on the bookshelf hutch of my desk. Missing books appeared in a closet I'd already searched. Once, I went down the hall to the bathroom, and the missing object was on my desk when I got back. Lost things wanted to come home. Sometimes they just needed a little help.

Pulling out the last letter from Dad, I tore off the piece with his signature and put the rest away. I drew a sigil on the back with the chalk. There were a few that might have worked in my book of shadows, but I used the one I could do by heart, a pattern that used circles and arrows to represent a return. I set out my elements on the corners of my altar cloth to focus the energy. The salt and the bell could stay in the tin. My oversized tea cup came down from the shelf over the desk and was filled halfway with spring water.

Holding my hands above the water, I charged it with my intentions, visualizing my letter finding its way to my mailbox. I imagined opening the box tomorrow morning and seeing the envelope waiting inside. Calling on the goddess and her consort one last time, I held the marked paper over the cup of water and lit it with my matches. I held it until it burned most of the way down and then dropped it in the water. It swirled and floated as the flame went out and the paper dissolved.

The spell was a request, a cry for help from the universe since I didn't have the power to draw my letter to me. All that remained was to wait for an answer.

3

When Thomas reappeared at the café, I managed to hide my relief. I should have known he wouldn't go home without me. I wasn't ready to see him go, but I didn't want him to think I needed him like I did when we were kids. At the very least, he wasn't likely to drop out of my life forever without an emotional good-bye tour. He wasn't exactly subtle in making his impact known.

Brian had been singing a homecoming playlist for the last few closing shifts. What started with jams like Bon Jovi's "Who Says You Can't Go Home?" devolved into mournful nostalgia like "Homeward Bound" and "Country Roads." Now, he was counting out his cash drawer in the backroom, belting out a slightly more urgent "Take Me Home Tonight."

My brother's magic couldn't control people, but he did have a talent for influence. The goddess' gift didn't even have to work that hard at it. He invoked the element of fire and warmed everyone around him. Especially around artists and musicians, anyone with a spark. Somehow they just got inspired by whatever intention he set. It wasn't hard to guess what he intended now. I ignored both the music and the muse.

Well, I tried. I sprayed down the inside of the pastry case until my brother's face was no longer visible on the other side.

"Cate," he said.

"We're closed," I said, shutting the case and stacking the dirty pastry trays. I dropped the rag on top, but it slid off when I lifted the pile.

"Hey. Just wait a second. Please." He picked up the rag, wiping a stray drop off the counter.

I stood halfway through the door to the backroom, balancing the heavy trays on my knee. Brian came out with his empty cash drawer. He raised his eyebrow when he saw my brother, but when I shook my head, he just shrugged and went back to work. After locking the empty drawer back in the register, he winked and made a show of turning up his music so he wouldn't overhear our family business. Then he started breaking down the machines.

I shoved the trays on the counter and crossed my arms. "What do you want? You keep coming in here, throwing your magic around, acting like it's no big deal. Like there aren't hunters out there watching for any sign of a Gift. Maybe it's all a game to you, but what's going to happen if they find you? Do you want to end up like Duncan?"

"Look, I didn't come here to fight..." Thomas said.

I tried to keep my voice low, but my brother's innocent act set my teeth on edge. "Seriously. If they find you, it's not just you you're putting in danger. What if they follow you home? Queen's Creek has enough problems without being revealed to the entire mundane world."

He held up his hands. "Will you give it a rest? That's why I'm here."

I waited, tapping my fingers on my arm.

Thomas sucked in a breath and ran his hands through his

hair. When he released it, it bounced right back. "I went home."

"When?"

"Yesterday. After I left here, I tried to… It doesn't matter. It didn't work. So I went home. But there's something wrong with the Gate. It's glitching or something. Alice told me to bring you home." He knotted his fingers in his hair again.

My blood turned to ice. The Gatekeeper wanted me home. The witch responsible for the boundary spell that protected our hidden hometown, who alone decided which of us could leave, was calling me back a week early. Never mind the fact that I didn't intend to go back at all. "But our Wakening isn't over yet."

The clock on the register ticked over to 10pm. Three separate timers went off. I jumped. *It's not a sign. It's just closing time and old coffee.*

Thomas's phone rang.

He paused just a second before answering it. "Sorry," he mouthed, stepping away.

Brian locked the front door while I scrambled to pull timers off the coffee servers. We were supposed to dump the urns and brew fresh coffee every thirty minutes, but we didn't usually set a timer on the last batch.

One of us flaked. So much of the closing routine was muscle memory now. One of us punched the reset button without thinking.

There's still plenty of time. Loads of it, actually. The Wakening deadline only matters if you want to live inside the Gate. And I don't.

To illustrate how unbothered I was, if only to myself, since Thomas had his back to me, I picked up the pastry trays to finish cleaning up. Brian grabbed a broom and swept the far side of the café.

"Hey, Adam," Thomas said, turning. "Yeah, yeah, she's

here."

He looked up, signaling me to wait.

I shifted the trays in my arms. *How did Adam get a phone?* As far as I knew, my brother's friend had ended his Wakening months ago and gone back to Queen's Creek.

Thomas shrugged. "No, not yet. I think maybe tomorrow.... What? No..."

I glanced over my shoulder, gauging how quickly I could get to the back sink. The trays were getting heavy.

Thomas slapped the counter a few times to get my attention. I raised an eyebrow. He shook his head, still listening. His eyes widened. "No. Just wait. Hold the Gate. Tell Alice we're on our way."

"What do you mean, 'We're on our way'? I told you I'm not ready. And if you think—"

"Dad's missing, Cate." He dropped the phone into his back pocket.

"What?" I almost dropped the trays. "Hold on, let me just —"

Brian came to my rescue without missing a beat. A minute later, the trays were safely in the washer, and he was singing loudly in the back room, probably simultaneously finishing the dishes.

"Dad's missing?" I grabbed the rag and rinsed it in the sink behind the counter, my hands moving on their own. My stomach twisted. How long had he been gone? *My empty mailbox.* There had been no results from my spell yet. Dad had never missed a letter before. *Why now?*

Thomas was still talking. "Uncle Giles says he crossed the Creek."

I didn't know how to respond. It wasn't possible. None of this was possible. I blinked. "He did not."

No one crossed the Creek. It was practically suicide. The enchanted border around our community was impenetrable.

Unless you went through the Gate. Which you could only do during your Wakening like Thomas and I had. Dad's time was well past. He made his decision before we were born. Once made, it was permanent.

Thomas raised an eyebrow. "You don't believe Uncle Giles? Or you don't believe he said that? Adam was pretty clear."

"I don't care who said it. Dad did not — would not — cross the Creek."

Giles wasn't actually related to us, but the lead investigator of the Watch had always been close with our family. He and our father grew up together. He was training our brother, Benjamin, to join the Watch as a detective. I'd never liked him, so of course, Thomas loved him.

Still, I couldn't believe he would lie about this. If Giles said Dad crossed the Creek, he believed it. I just didn't understand how he could be so wrong.

"We have to go back, Cate," Thomas said.

He wasn't listening to me. I wanted to scream, but I heard Brian turn off the water in the backroom. My voice came out tight and low. "You know he didn't cross."

Thomas stared at me, and I wanted to smack the pity out of his eyes.

He put his hands flat on the counter and leaned toward me. Slowly, his right hand reached for mine and covered it. "Uncle Giles is closing his investigation. The Reading is tomorrow night, after the Last Light ritual."

I shivered. A formal investigation by the Community Watch couldn't be closed until it was solved to the satisfaction of the entire community. He'd have to prove his theory, whatever it was. "He thinks he's solved it?"

"That's what it sounds like. Get your stuff. We have to go back for the Reading."

"There's not going to be a Reading. I dissent."

"You can't dissent from here."

Thomas had a point. My brother had been trying to get me to come home with him all week. None of his arguments had been this compelling. I'd put off telling him my decision, but this wasn't it.

I hesitated. What if we couldn't find Dad before our birthday? How long could I risk staying? *I'm not ready.*

"The Reading won't wait for us. We need to go now." He was so sure and so insistent. I walked with him to the store's exit.

"You go. I'll catch up." I unlocked the door and pulled it open for him.

"Cate—"

I held up a hand. "Just go! I have to close up." I needed him gone before I broke. *Focus on the things you can control.* "I can't just disappear. There are things I need to do first. I'll be home before Last Light tomorrow."

My mind whirred with possible explanations for our father's disappearance, the consequences of leaving school early, fears about going home and getting trapped forever (or not getting back in time), and the usual irrational anxiety that somehow this was all my fault. My curse.

Focus on what needs to be done. Our father was missing, not dead. It was too soon to mourn. The Reading had to be stopped.

Thomas paused in the doorway. "If you're really going to dissent, you have to be inside before the sun sets tomorrow night."

He was trying to help, but his patronizing tone fueled my frustration. He beat me into the world by two minutes and enjoyed playing the big brother role a little too much. I had enough older brothers to protect me. My twin was supposed to be beside me, even if I pushed him away.

"I'll be there," I said. "Tell them I'm coming."

I closed the door, locked it, and pulled down the shade before he could argue. A spark of light around the edges of the door marked his departure.

Let this be the right choice. I'd take the long way home, but there was no reason to slow Thomas down.

As I turned around, Brian came out of the back office with the last bags of garbage.

"You okay?" His earbuds dangled around his neck, but the music pulsed from across the room.

"I have to go home." *I wish I could tell him everything.* He'd never understand the crazy choice I was being asked to make; to spend the rest of my life living with my magical brother in a magical kingdom where I could do no magic myself or to stay here, finish my Theater degree and try to make practical magic on stage.

"Yeah, me too. Let's dump this so we can get out of here."

"No, I mean. I have to go home. I'm leaving school tomorrow."

Brian dropped the bag. "Are you okay?" he asked again.

Tears tickled my cheeks. I hadn't felt them coming, but I couldn't stop them now. Brian took a few steps toward me but moved like he was approaching a bomb. I froze, and when he embraced me, it was possibly the most uncomfortable moment of my life. I turned my face to the side to avoid crushing my glasses against his chest. Instead, they slid up my forehead. I started to giggle at the absurdity of it all.

"Umm... are you...?" Brian started again.

I pushed him away. My glasses had fogged up, so I used the distraction of cleaning them on my apron to get myself together. "I'm okay. Thanks. I'm sorry. I didn't mean to..."

There was a wet spot on his shirt, just above his heart. From the heat on my face, I was sure I'd gone bright red. If Brian was blushing too, his dark skin masked it. I looked away.

"Do you want to talk about it?" he asked, but his eyes followed the headlights of passing traffic, and I knew he was waiting for his ride. I grabbed the garbage bags and headed out the back door.

"I'm fine," I said to the night air. I almost believed it.

March 16

Change, Chaos,
Revelation

Manifestation,
Resourcefulness,
Inspiration

Strength, Courage,
Compassion

Control, Willpower,
Determination

Creativity, Charm,
Romance

4

I knew he'd watch me walk to the dumpster and back. Late-night safety protocol. It was his turn to take it out, so I should've been the one standing guard, but I needed to walk in the fresh air to pull myself together.

I swung the lid open and let it slam against the back of the dumpster, terrifying what sounded like a couple of rats or a small stray cat. The first bag went in. The second was a swing and a miss. It smacked the edge of the dumpster, snagged, and dropped a few cups on the ground. I shoved the rest of it over and bent to pick up the debris. For a second, I stopped.

Brian was still watching, but I had my back to him, and the alley light was not great. I don't know what made me think this time might be different, but I needed a sign. I focused on a cup that landed close to my foot.

"Rise," I whispered. I imagined energy forming around my words, floating down to the cup on the ground and lifting it, weightless, into the air. I wasn't even asking it to teleport like Thomas's did yesterday. Just a slight movement that could have been the wind. I focused, breathed, and snapped my fingers.

Nothing. Nada. Zippo.

What was I thinking? I wasn't going to suddenly grow into my magic. Certainly not in a dramatic moment, just because I needed it. But going home would have been so much easier if I did. Especially now. Whatever happened to Dad, there was unlikely to be a mundane answer, and finding him would almost definitely require more magic than lifting a cup.

A glance over my shoulder showed Brian bopping to whatever blasted out of his earbuds, basically oblivious to anything happening in the dark alley. *Safe.* He might not be a great lookout, but at least he missed my experiment. I sighed and bent to grab the cups, stacking them and tossing them into the dumpster by hand.

Before dropping the lid, I mentally expelled all of my negative energy into the garbage. It might have been more psychological than magical, but it worked. When I turned around, I felt lighter. I smiled at Brian.

"Thanks," I said, coming through the door he held for me.

As we were getting our stuff and locking up, I gave him the abridged version of Thomas's news, edited for general audiences, of course. No magic, just Serious Family Business.

"So, I guess this is goodbye," I said when we were back on the sidewalk. I was already planning my next step. *Don't want to get stuck in this one and start crying again.*

I was probably going to lose my job. They frowned on unexpected absences. *But it's a family emergency. I'll send the manager an email before I pack up my laptop. Should I pack my laptop? There's no internet back home.*

I filed through a mental inventory of the stuff waiting to be packed in my dorm. It was amazing what you could accumulate in a few years, even in a 12x12 cinder block box. There was no way I could carry it all. My roommate was about to get a major donation.

"I'll see you in the morning," Brian said.

"What?"

"Tomorrow. I'll be there at eight." He locked the store and pocketed the keys.

"Brian, I'm not going to have time. I have to—"

"You're not going to do this alone. I'll see you at eight."

He was making this harder. "I won't be alone. My roommate will be there."

"She's not going to skip her classes to help you pack," Brian said, and he was right, obviously. Again.

"But you will?" I asked, even though I knew the answer.

"Tomorrow. At eight." His girlfriend pulled up, and he got in the car. As usual, she offered me a ride, and I declined, as always, although I wasn't sure how she heard me over the music that poured out of Brian's open door. The Bluetooth had already connected to his phone.

I had no interest in third-wheeling my way back to campus. If we were any farther, I'd have taken the L, but we were between stops, and I'd rather walk anyway. I fell in with the other pedestrians, mostly couples and small groups just starting their night. Something about walking in a stranger's footsteps always felt safe. Besides, I was pretty sure my hat head and sour milk smell would deter any unwanted attention.

The walk back to campus gave me a chance to think about what it meant for me to go home now. Brian and I had been working the closing shift at the café ever since we met in stagecraft. He was the one person I'd considered telling my secrets. He knew I grew up in Virginia, and my hometown was too small to find on a map. He knew I never felt like I fit in there and that I'd been much happier in Chicago, even though it was a rough adjustment at first. He was shocked by how little I understood about technology. He still teased me about how I typed, using just my thumbs, index, and middle fingers on the keyboard. He probably imagined me on an old family farm or a cabin in the woods. He wouldn't be too far off, although Queen's Creek had more than a few traditions that might have surprised him.

That said, I'd adapted pretty well to city life. I liked it here. It didn't matter so much when I first left home, knowing I would probably be back in a few years. But as my 21st birthday moved closer, I started considering how I could survive outside the Creek. If I didn't go back, I'd be on my own.

No one in my family had emigrated in the past two generations. Thomas was taking a risk in coming back for me with less than a week left. We'd always known what his decision would be. His Wakening was more like a vacation than a choice. I'd been less sure. I purposefully avoided looking up my peers after we crossed through the Gate so this decision would be mine alone, but now I wondered. Some of them would have gone back already, but I wouldn't know who did unless I went back inside.

Until I went back inside. Because I was going back, and the odds of getting back out again were slimmer than I'd like. There was no use pretending I had a choice anymore or wondering what a life outside the community could be like. *A life of total independence and no expectations.* I had to go back and keep my father's best friend from essentially declaring him dead. I didn't know what Giles had that made him so sure that Dad crossed the Creek, but it couldn't be true.

When I returned to my room, the dorm was dark, so I used the light from my phone to find my laptop. My roommate, Nyla, rolled over to face the wall. It was hard to tell if she was awake in the top bunk. In the cool glow of the screen, I used most of my coffee earnings from the last three months to buy a flight home, nonstop Chicago to Richmond, one-way, first available, any seat, no checked baggage.

Can't wait for all the extra security attention I'll get with that one. But I could barely afford one flight. I had no idea how I was going to manage the return.

Messages went out to my store manager and my academic advisor. Before I climbed into my bunk, I typed a message to Nyla, explaining that I'd had a family emergency. It was mostly true. I scheduled it to send in the afternoon. I didn't want to answer any questions in the morning. She'd see it after I was gone.

Shfting under the covers, I had a feeling I was about to spend the next few hours staring at the bottom of Nyla's mattress and imagining all of the terrible things that might keep my father from writing to me. Things that would keep him from contacting anyone to let them know he was still there. Luckily, worrying about worrying was apparently where my brain drew the line because I was gone as soon as my head touched the pillow.

After what felt like a minute, I jolted back awake. *What is that noise?* Groaning, I dragged the pillow over my head. My roommate was usually so quiet in the morning. Last week, if I hadn't seen the familiar lump in the top bunk each night when I came home, I couldn't have been sure she was still living here. The noise continued. Pounding like a heartbeat.

Ohhhh. Damn. It's the door.

Go. Away.

I rolled over and looked at the clock. It was blurry, but I could just make out the big red digital numbers about six inches from my face: 8am.

Brian.

I sat up too quickly and smacked my head on the top bunk. The fact that there was no response from above confirmed that Nyla had already left.

"Just a minute," I called, grabbing my glasses from the dresser by my bed. I pulled myself out of my cave and threw on some clothes. When I opened the door, Brian stood there with two paper coffee cups and a smile. His earbuds buzzed around his neck, and a couple of boxes lay on the floor in the hall behind him.

"Good Morning, Sunshine." Brian handed me my liquid breakfast. I sipped my chai and closed my eyes. We spent the next two hours sorting through my stuff. Brian put his earbuds in, and we did the work mostly without talking. *Thank you.* I didn't want to talk about it. I didn't want to think about it. *No time for an emotional breakdown today.*

When we were done, I had a backpack full of essentials to take home, a stack of donations for my roommate (mostly school supplies and snacks), and two boxes Brian promised to hold onto 'until I got back'. I hadn't told him the odds of that happening, and I felt a little guilty saddling him with my crap, but I was also kind of hoping I'd get the chance to reclaim it.

After I go home, prove that my dad's not dead, and escape back through the magical portal. In five days or less.

We carried the boxes down from my third-floor hall and shoved them into the overstuffed trunk of his girlfriend's car. When he hugged me this time, I didn't giggle, and when I pulled away, there was no wet spot to betray me. For a split second, I wondered what would have happened if it had been his car. If he hadn't been dating the same girl since about a week before we met. Would he have driven me to the airport? Would I have asked him to come with me? I tried to imagine him in Queen's Creek.

Then I remembered his birthday party last month. He'd never have been able to see the Gate.

It was already too late for him.

5

Brian got in the car, the music blasted, and I tried to smile as I waved goodbye. His girlfriend put her hand on his knee and peeled out of the parking lot. I reminded myself that boys and girls can be friends, and I must not be jealous of my best friend's girlfriend. Our relationship had never been romantic anyway.

I revised my daydream to something slightly more probable. They were helping me move into my apartment instead of just cleaning out my dorm. It was a small place, maybe a studio, up way too many stairs, near the train. I'd take the L to the theater district and work backstage with my found family. I'd probably have to keep a side job like the café or maybe a bar. But that would be okay because that'd be where I'd meet someone to share it with. Maybe someone like Brian, who was smart and kind and understood that making art could be magical, even if you didn't have a Gift. I imagined getting tickets to the show I was working on so my parents could see what I could do.

And then I remembered why that would never happen. The idea that I might never see my dad again made my stomach tighten and then flip. I wasn't ready to lose him. I hadn't said goodbye. My skin turned cold. As my arms broke out in goosebumps, I pushed it all down, trying to quiet the buzzing in my head.

It's all been a mistake. I'm sure they'll have figured that out by the time I get home. And if they don't, I'll do it for them.

I checked my email on my phone. There was a response from my advisor. Ten minutes to get to her office. Maybe by the time I got there, I would have figured out what to say. I shouldered my backpack and headed across campus.

The sign on her door read simply: Dr. Jennings - Theatre. She was the department chair, but you'd never know it from her space. Inside, the office was dim. The professor was somewhere behind a stack of costume books, a small mountain of fabric, and what I hoped was a plaster skull from last season's *Hamlet*.

"Hey, Nora?"

Her curly ginger ponytail appeared first. Three or four pens stuck out of it. Last time it was peacock feathers. Her oversized glasses perched crookedly on top of her head, half-buried in her graying roots. The beaded eyeglass chain looped behind her ears and trailed down her back. She stood and smoothed her long skirt, popping her collar.

"Ah! Cate! So good to see you! Thanks for coming," she said. She gestured to the only visible chair in the room, realized that it was covered in papers, and gathered most of them up.

I perched on the edge and pushed my backpack between my feet. "Umm, so, like I said in my email—"

"You're leaving school."

"Yes."

Nora sat behind her desk. When she realized she couldn't see me anymore, she got up and came around it. She pushed some of the mess back and leaned on the desk behind her. "It's not what I expected."

I frowned. "I'm not sure anyone expected—"

"I thought for sure you'd be the one this year. But back through the Gate you must go, I suppose."

"Well, yes, I have to..." *Wait. The Gate?*

"I heard about what happened, of course, but I think everyone was just as surprised as I was. We all thought your father would run for Speaker next year."

I didn't know what to think. She talked as if she knew what was going on at home. But how had she heard from someone in Queen's Creek? Had Adam called her too? Why would he do that? *Does the Gatekeeper have a cell phone?*

My entire worldview shook as I tried to picture the Gatekeeper — Alice, in her old-fashioned cottage with no running water — casually texting a professor halfway across the country.

Also, Nora had been advising me on my courses for the past two years. She was a gifted artist and a great mentor. I'd never taken her costuming class, but her students loved her. She'd been running the theater forever. But she was mundane. *Wasn't she?*

She sighed. "You're confused. We're pretty far from the Source here, but surely you don't think we are entirely without magic? Or that I don't have contacts in our community?"

She waved a hand and a stack of bangles clanked on her wrist. For the first time, I noticed the engraved patterns on some of them looked like runes.

Well, shit. She's a witch. She knew where I came from, and now she would realize something was wrong with me. I hadn't expected to run into someone familiar with magical practices on the outside. I'd heard about people who managed to keep practicing the Craft outside of the community. But most of the witches with any kind of real Gift went underground after Salem. They formed small, local, hidden communities like mine to hide from the persecution of people who feared their differences. The Wakening period gave us some connection to the outside world, but ultimately, those with the Gift usually came back, and those without it didn't.

Going home now, before my birthday locked the Gate, meant going back to being constantly on guard. If no one outside my immediate family knew I couldn't do magic, I could avoid those looks of pity and disappointment, that feeling of being less than.

Unless it was too late. If she knew what I was supposed to be and realized I didn't see her for what she was... I was out. I'd be a sad weirdo at home for the rest of my life.

I had to convince her I knew her secret. That I had recognized her power before she mentioned it. But even I knew my effort was weak. I tried to remember exactly what she asked. Something rhetorical about my assumption that she didn't have connections.

"Umm, no. Of course you would have heard, I just—"

She blinked and pulled her enormous glasses down on her face. They caught in her hair, and she snapped her fingers before they came free. Her eyes were bright as she read me.

"Well," she said, pushing the glasses back up on her head, "I wondered why you never said anything, but, you know, I'm here to advise, not to pry. If you don't want to talk about the Old Ways, I won't push. I thought you'd decided to emigrate. You seemed so at home here, so connected to your mundane studies. Summer courses, a full load plus extracurricular hours in the theater, and all that." She paused and rubbed her eyes. "But that isn't it, is it? It's not that you planned to deny your magical heritage at all. You—"

"I don't have any," I finished for her, surprising myself more than my advisor. It was a relief to say it out loud. "Magic, I mean. I have the heritage. Just no natural magic. To speak of."

"But you're going back." There was no reaction to my confession.

"My father—"

"Crossed the Creek," she said. It hung there.

I stood and picked up my bag. I wasn't going to argue with my academic advisor, but she didn't know what she was talking about. Witch, or no witch.

"But he wasn't alone," she finished.

"What?" *How could she possibly know that?*

"You need to talk to Alice." The professor pushed off the desk and slid her hands into the almost invisible pockets of her patchwork skirt.

Alice had held the Gatehouse longer than anyone in the community could remember. She guided everyone through the Wakening when their time came. I spent three days with the Gatekeeper before she decided I was ready to explore the mundane world and make my choice. Three days of testing and meditation that left me more and more confused. It was a relief when she set me free.

"I have," I said.

Nora squinted and pursed her lips. "You've spoken with her? About your father?"

"Not exactly." How could I explain? I didn't trust the judgment of the one person my entire community looked to for guidance. I didn't want to ask her what happened to Dad because I was still angry about the weight she'd laid on me. "When I left..."

"What did she tell you about your future?" Nora asked, once again responding to things I hadn't said.

I bit my lip. Maybe she said the same thing to everyone. Maybe I'd been taking this too seriously. Maybe it was a test.

Nora waited.

"She said that I was the next Gatekeeper."

Nora blinked. "Interesting," she said, pulling her glasses down again. This time she walked around me, tilting her head to the side the way she sometimes did during a costume fitting.

"It's not true!" I insisted.

"Mmmm, hmmm..."

"Nora!"

"Sorry, what? No, of course not. But maybe... why not, exactly?" She paused in front of me, tapping the frames of her glasses.

"I have no Gift," I reminded her. This fact alone disqualified me from the position. Gatekeeper was a job for someone with strong natural magic.

"But you are the seventh child of a seventh son."

"And his only daughter." I should have been the strongest witch of my generation. Stronger than we were likely to see in three generations. Chosen. But somebody chose wrong.

My phone buzzed. A notification for my flight. I needed to be on this plane. "I have to go. I'll... call you."

It was a stupid thing to offer since we both knew there was no cell service inside the boundary of Queen's Creek.

Nora was searching for something on her desk. "No, you won't," she said. "But that's fine. It's as it should be. After all, it's almost Spring Break. I'll file your papers for a leave of absence, just in case. But do try to get back in time for exams."

I watched her shift through the stacks of paper and ephemera. I wished I had her hope. I wanted to graduate. I wanted to take that degree and join the unemployable ranks of liberal arts graduates struggling to make ends meet without giving up on their art. It might not be a practical or financially sound choice, but for once, it would be my choice. My success or failure would be about something I did instead of something I wasn't. But I was about to drop out of the known world, not just the university. *It's impossible*. I had to tell her she was wasting her time looking for the form.

I wasn't quick enough.

She breathed an almost inaudible "Ah ha!" and smiled. "Just one thing..." she said, straightening. She pulled a tarot deck from a pile of art books.

"Oh, umm, thanks, Nora, but I have my own." I pulled my backpack over my shoulder.

"Not like these."

My hand was already on the door. "I'm sorry. I don't have time—"

"Just one," she said. "Cut."

I broke the deck and handed it back to her. She pulled the top card. She barely looked at it before nodding.

"This will help," she said. "Take it with you. When you need it, you'll know."

I didn't have time for questions, so I held out my hand. She took it in both of hers. A rush of energy woke me up more than the cup Brian brought that morning. Suddenly I couldn't imagine disagreeing with her. *A charm?* Shoving the card into my back pocket, I turned to leave. At the last minute, I stopped.

"Thank you," I said to the door.

"Be well," she whispered.

6

On the train to the airport, I stood for three stops until a seat opened. I practiced my surfing stance and tested how long I could go without grabbing the pole. It wasn't long. When I sat, I remembered the card in my back pocket. It was a little creased. I smoothed it against my leg. The heat it was radiating before had dissipated. I flipped it over.

A young woman in a long white dress embracing a lion, her wild red hair escaping its braid and blending with the lion's mane. Something in its wildness reminded me of Nora. A ribbon woven through her braid formed the symbol of infinity across her forehead. *Strength*. It was beautiful, but there didn't seem to be anything special about it to explain what I felt when she took my hand.

Maybe Nora transferred more than just the card to me. If it had its own magic, I might be able to use it. You didn't have to be Gifted to work a charmed object. In literally none of the stories did a powerful witch get the magic lamp, ring, spindle, or whatever. It was always a mundane street rat, a hobbit. Okay, sometimes it was a princess, but she couldn't do magic on her own. Was that what Nora meant when she said it would help?

Do not get excited. But. My own magical battery! Anything that might undo my Cate-the-Cursed status. For a second, I imagined a triumphant, prodigal return instead of an angsty internal kicking-and-screaming. I'd be the hero they wanted me to be. Dad would be so proud.

Right. Manage expectations. But if it worked... if I could pretend, for a while, to be just like everybody else back home... maybe going home wouldn't be so bad. Maybe I could help. I looked at the card in my hands. I'd never know unless I tried. It felt like magic. I just had to unlock it. Maybe.

I put my hand over the image and closed my eyes. I visualized Nora's office. I tuned out the sounds of the other passengers and lost myself in the sound and sway of the train. I concentrated on my breath, in and out like waves on the ocean. A minute passed. Two. Nothing. I sighed and opened my eyes. *It would have worked for Thomas*.

The person in the seat next to me shifted. She probably thought I was some kind of psycho. I yawned. Maybe I was just an exhausted college student who pulled an all-nighter? It was kind of true. Whatever she thought, she got off at the next stop. When I had the bench to myself, I popped my phone out of its case. Laying the card inside, I squeezed my phone back in on top of it. Whatever use Nora thought this would be, apparently, now was not the moment of need.

I couldn't really experiment with the Craft on the plane, so further testing of the card would have to wait until I was closer to home. It might be stronger nearer the Source anyway. My last-minute ticket had me boarding in the final group and sitting in a middle seat near the back. I shoved my phone into the front pocket of my backpack, pulled out a novel, and squished the bag under the seat in front of me. It was hard to focus on the book though. I kept thinking about Nora's card, and graduation, and my birthday, and Dad.

The guy in the window seat spent most of the flight watching a movie on his phone with his earbuds in. It must have been some kind of comedy because every ten minutes or so, he laughed so hard his elbow shook the arm of the chair.

The woman on the aisle had amazing legs. At least, she thought so. She kept stretching them out in the aisle and then acting surprised when a flight attendant couldn't get by. "I'm so sorry," she said each time, gingerly folding them back under the seat.

This was how I knew for a fact that natural magic had failed me. Anyone else in my family would have booked the last available seat in an exit row or been spontaneously upgraded to first class because the flight was overbooked in economy.

When the plane started to shake, I was more annoyed than afraid.

Ms. Legs grabbed the armrest, and her acrylic nails dug into my arm. The Laugh Track startled so hard he dropped his phone. He reeled it back in by the cord attached to his earbuds, apologizing again. My knee tingled where the phone had smacked it on the way down.

On the next bounce, I grabbed the seat in front of me to keep from hitting my head on the secured tray table. It was like the clouds were filled with speed bumps. The plane tilted to the side, and it was my turn to apologize to the Laugh Track. I braced myself to keep from falling into his lap. My seatbelt was a joke. I suppressed a nervous giggle when the seatbelt sign dinged on. My stomach tensed from the challenge of staying in my seat.

An announcement was made, but I missed all the words. My ears were drowning in the air pressure. The passengers were all talking, searching, mumbling, fumbling with air-sick bags. I put my head down in my lap and tried to will the acid in my stomach to stay there. The plane dropped, and my stomach went with it.

Before I realized what I was doing or why, I was hugging my overstuffed backpack, and my hand closed around the bulge where my phone strained against the pocket. I gripped it like a ripcord that could pull me through space and time and set me gently on the ground. Another bump pushed my face into the nylon. The zipper scraped my nose. I held my breath, silently calling on the goddess in all her forms. *Maiden, save me. Mother, protect me. Crone, show me the way.* My heartbeat bruised my eardrums.

Stop! My hand burned. Fire thrilled up my arm and lit up my chest. Everything went white and warm and quiet. *Please, just get me through this.* The blood whooshed in my ears, deafening me. Like the ocean breaths I did on the train but so, so much louder. I swayed, trying to ride it out like the curves on the tracks. *I really might throw up.* I gritted my teeth. Other sounds started to compete with the waves in my ears.

Before I opened my eyes, Ms. Legs whispered the Lord's Prayer. The Laugh Track was crying. Another announcement.

Ding. "Sorry about that turbulence, folks. Looks like we're through it now, though. Should have you on the ground in about 35 minutes. Flight attendants, prepare for landing."

Applause.

My eyes refused to focus. *Too bright.* My breath caught when I tried to release it. My lungs burned. My fingers froze. I had to consciously relax each one to separate them from my backpack. I blinked.

People were laughing, shifting in their seats, going back to whatever they were doing before we almost plunged to our deaths. Some of them started gathering their things. *Landing already?*

I dug out my phone, confirmed that we'd been in the air

for the two shortest hours of all time, and slid off the case. When I flipped the card, the girl and her lion were gone. The figure was still draped in white, but he was also cloaked in red. Four tools lay on a table in front of him, magical resources. The infinity symbol floated above his head. *The Magician.* A card of determination and skill. My breath slowed. Nora's deck was not like mine.

I checked the time again. It really didn't feel like a two-hour flight. Another theory started to form about what this card could do. *Can I skip to the good part?* It was worth a try. I closed my eyes and gripped the card. I wished to be safely on the ground. I counted my breaths.

Nothing.

I guess it's no longer a moment of need.

I carefully slipped the card back into its hiding place, considering the message it had given me. The Magician with his tools. I still didn't know what awaited me on the ground, but I was more confident that I had what I needed to face it.

7

Thomas was waiting for me when I got off the plane in Richmond. He leaned against a wall, tapping his foot as I came up the ramp from the terminal. When he saw me, he jumped and ran. The security officer gave a warning grunt (clearly not the first one). Thomas hit the brakes before he accidentally crossed the invisible line between the lobby and the gates. He windmilled his arms to balance his slender frame before he crashed into anyone. Landing on tip-toes, he shifted anxiously from one foot to the other. I walked a little faster.

"So, how's Alice?" I said.

"You're late." He waved at the security guard, who gave him a begrudging thumbs up and went back to watching the ramp.

"It was the earliest flight they had."

He ignored my question, but before I could follow up, he grabbed my hand and dragged me through the airport. I pulled free and matched his stride, my legs just as long as his. Our twin frames bobbed through the concourse, easily outstripping passengers laden with heavier bags and rolling suitcases.

"Come on, the car's over here." He turned past the baggage claim carousels.

The terminal seemed less crowded than usual somehow. When we got through the sliding doors, a silver CRV waited exactly where airports always announced cars should not be. Thomas got in on the passenger side. The doors were unlocked, and the engine was running. I didn't ask how he got it, considering we were both low on cash and underage for car rentals. I tossed my bag in the back and took the driver's seat.

My brother knew how to drive but didn't get much practice. It was safer not relying on his luck to get us home safely, no matter how reliable the magic behind it was. When we were on the road, I took another shot at getting answers.

"What did Alice say?"

"She wants to talk to you," he pouted.

"Me? Why?"

"You would know better than I would. She only wants to talk to you." He stared straight ahead. The sunlight flashed on his hair.

When we were little, I occasionally got extra attention from Mom's friends ("Oh, Sarah! She looks just like you! It's so nice that you finally have your little girl after all those boys!"). Thomas would pout then, too. It never lasted. He seemed to glow whenever he felt ignored. No one could help but notice him then.

I rolled my eyes. "Take it down, Sparkles. I don't know why she wants to talk to me."

"You don't have any idea?" he asked, but it sounded more like an accusation. First-born twin still made him sixth-born son. He'd missed out on Special status by two minutes. It bothered him, and sometimes he let it show. *You want my impossible destiny? Take it.*

"Maybe she wants us there together?" I tried. "If she

knows something about Dad..."

"She knows something."

I didn't ask how he was so sure. "What do you think it is?"

"I didn't get a chance to find out. As soon as she said she wanted to wait for you, Adam kicked me out of the Gatehouse. He's taking this new Guardian job a little too seriously if you ask me."

"Wait, they made Adam the Guardian?" I asked, but it made a certain amount of sense. It explained how he could've been home to know that Dad was missing and still been able to contact Thomas. The Guardian held the border. He'd be the one person who could communicate with the world outside.

Adam and Thomas had been friends since we were kids. It would have been hard not to be friends with Giles's son, thrown together as often as we were. Still, Adam made it easy. He got along with all of my brothers and became just another member of the pack. They were like a pile of puppies, always tumbling over each other in the yard. It was impossible to stay out of their way. Not that I wanted to. The games they made up were always exciting, usually magical, and sometimes a little dangerous. Mom was constantly begging them to be more careful around me. They rarely listened. I was grateful.

But Guardian at the Gate was an honored position. It was a sacred role that came with a lot of responsibility. *What else has changed?*

Thomas huffed. "I guess when your dad commands the Watch, you get to skip a few of the tough assignments. Wait till you see him. You won't even recognize him. He's doing this voice... and the test I had to do—" He broke off.

"What?" I risked a glance at the passenger seat. He was looking out the window.

"That's our exit. You're going to—you missed it," he offered helpfully. He was right. I'd missed all of the signs. I took the exit for Busch Gardens and turned around, heading back into the Historic Triangle. I swerved to the right just in time to see the exit for Colonial Williamsburg on the second try.

Thomas grabbed the dashboard. "You're gonna miss it again."

"Chill. I've got it," I said, shifting over. The streets became increasingly narrow as we passed the tourist traps and hotels. I drove past an elementary school and the humane society and took a deep breath as the trees began to close in around us. *Almost home.* There was a turnoff behind the electrical substation that most people didn't notice. Except that today, signs warned of an upcoming construction project. "Thomas?"

"I see it."

"Was that there—"

"I didn't take the road. Slow down."

Right. He blinked in. Probably landed right on Alice's doorstep from the café.

As we came around a curve, the road unexpectedly opened up. I was distracted from my petty sibling jealousy by the development that had happened while I was gone. They'd started to clear the trees. Great piles of red dirt and wide spaces were carved out of the forest. Civilization was closing in.

A moment later, we'd passed the construction, and the foliage reached out for us again. Shadows danced across the dashboard. The light twinkled and flashed where it broke through the leaves. We were almost at the Creek. I sped up again. The paved road ended, giving way to dirt and a little gravel. It dead-ended in a small clearing. We ditched the car. I grabbed my backpack, and we hiked through the woods. What we could see of the sky started to turn pink. Thomas could've hopped ahead. I'd have been on my own to get to the Gate before Last Light. No doubt it occurred to him as we pushed our way through the undergrowth, but with a few expletive exceptions, he was silent.

A few tiny lights appeared as we got closer to the Gate. Too big and too erratic to be fireflies, the will-o'-the-wisps fed off of the magical energy that powered the boundary spell around Queen's Creek. The coven tolerated them since they distracted most mundanes, leading them into the woods away from our community. I kept my eyes on the trail, placing my feet in Thomas's footprints until the Gatehouse came into view.

"There!" I was more excited to see the cottage than I thought I'd be. It looked like something out of a fairy tale, small, crooked, covered in carved gingerbreading, wooden ivy blending in with the real stuff as the forest reclaimed the space. The Gatehouse backed onto a narrow branch of the actual Queen's Creek. The tributary wound its way around the entire community that took its name, a natural barrier enclosing the Source. Occasionally mundane children got lost in the woods and stumbled across it, but who would believe Hansel and Gretel when they walked back without any candy?

Adults didn't see it at all. Hardly anyone came this deep into the woods, and when they did, all they saw were more trees, as if the Creek reflected the forest back at them. They could walk for hours and end up right back where they started unless they followed the wisps.

I ran the last few steps to Alice's door. The sky grew darker. The night was coming too fast. I stood on the stone in front of the cottage and looked up. Clouds rolled in. I felt the thunder in my skin before I heard it.

"What are you waiting for? Come on!" Thomas shoved past me and knocked on the door. "Alice? We're here! Open up!" He was about to knock again when the door opened, flooding us with sunlight.

On the other side of the Gatehouse, all of the windows were open. Sun streamed through the uneven panes of glass. Alice shone. The light behind her edged everything in sparkles, from her loose blond hair to her bare feet. Thomas blew by her like she wasn't there, just in time to miss the downpour that drenched me as I stood dazzled on her shadowy doorstep.

8

I imagined melting into the puddle that was dripping off my clothes. The Gatekeeper smiled, and I wondered, not for the first time, what she saw when she looked at me.

"Welcome back," she said. She stepped to the side to allow me to enter. The darkness closed in behind me, but the first step across the threshold washed me in light. Inside the Gatehouse, time stopped. It was Alice's 21st birthday every day and always had been. It was warmer than it was outside. I felt as though I'd just woken up from a nap, which was to say, sluggish and grouchy. I dropped my bag on the floor and fell into Alice's only chair. As she sealed the door I'd just come through, I saw the view that she saw every day. Afternoon sunlight streamed in through the front windows, even though I knew that if we opened that door, the sky was falling on the other side.

"What happened?" I asked.

"You would do better to question the Guardian," she said. "But first, remember that you have a gift."

I was about to insist she tell us what she knew or maybe say something snarky about the authenticity of her Gatekeeper vision when I realized she was looking at my bag.

The front pocket was lighting up. Another notification on my phone. Last Light. I pulled out the phone and silenced the notification. I was about to put it away when something in Alice's eyes stopped me. Nora's card pulsed in the phone case. I remembered what Nora had said. And how Thomas had said Alice would only talk to me.

"What do you know?" I asked softly, gripping my phone and wondering if it was the electronic battery or Nora's gift radiating heat.

She shook her head. "We will have our time. For now, the time is yours."

Goddess help me.

She guided me to her small bedroom, and I left Thomas leaning against a wall by the window. He wasn't used to hiking like we did today, and he stared out at the trees like they owed him something. As she closed the door between us, Alice offered him something to drink.

There was only one piece of furniture in this room, and I felt strange about sitting on Alice's bed, so I knelt on the floor. I pulled out the card without looking at it and held it in my hands. It was still warm. When I uncovered it, I was faced with a woman in a blue robe seated in front of Persephone's shower curtain, her pet moon at her feet. *What will the High Priestess tell me?* She was a representation of intuition, an archetype of sacred knowledge. I was sure she was standing in for Alice at the moment. Who else did I know more aligned with mystery and feminine spirituality? The card was telling me to trust her, but I needed more to go on.

Hopefully, the natural magic of this space would support a practical spell. I put the card on the floor in front of me, adjusted my posture, closed my eyes, and invoked the goddess. "Where is my father?" I asked the card. I focused on this one question, listening to my heartbeat, slowing my breath. "Where is my father?"

My eyes prickled with tears that refused to fall. My breath caught. My face burned. I gasped and opened my eyes. The card had changed again. A great stone tower struck by lightning. Two figures falling head first. *Shit. He's really done it. He's gone.* There was no other card that so clearly depicted destruction and chaos. The kind of sudden change that came with the unexpected, unexplained death of a loved one.

Everything had changed, but nothing was different. The light from the open window warmed the room. The air blew in gently, rustling the lacy curtains. Birds had some kind of argument just outside. The heat in my cheeks spread behind my eyes, and they burned. My chest refused to expand. I had a headache at the base of my skull. *I should go back out and talk to Thomas. I should make Alice talk. Somehow.* As if anyone could've made the Gatekeeper do anything. *I should get out of here.* I needed to find Giles and find out what he knew.

I didn't move.

I reconsidered the card. Destruction and chaos didn't have to mean death. Disappearing could cause plenty of disruption, maybe more. The unknown was terrifying. I looked at the tiny figures falling through the sky. What if they're all jumping to conclusions? That might have been an unprecedented interpretation of the card, but how could I avoid making the same mistake? I started to question everything I knew.

Dad was missing, and no one could find him (Thomas said).

He wasn't alone, or he wasn't alone when he disappeared (Nora said. But how did she know that?)

He crossed the Creek (Giles said. But I still didn't know why he thought so.)

Just because Dad was gone didn't mean he crossed the Creek. Or if he did, it may not have been voluntary. Nora said he wasn't alone. Two figures fall from the tower. How did she know? My feet slid out from under me, and my knees drew up to my chest. The card fluttered to the floor. I wrapped my arms around my legs, taking comfort in the pressure. I closed my eyes and tried to squeeze out the tears. It didn't work. They just burned. My feet tingled as the blood flow returned. I still couldn't breathe.

Why was this happening? He was fine when I left. We were happy. He was excited about my Wakening. He was the only one who understood my choice. Or the fact that I hadn't made it yet. I loved my mother, but she wouldn't understand. I talked to her about everything, just not this. This is too... real. Dad understood. I was sure he'd felt the same way at my age. He'd always been interested in the world outside. He was the one who helped me apply to college. Why would he do that if he didn't feel there was a life out there worth living? We never talked about his Wakening, but I knew coming back was complicated for him. I was less sure that I wanted to make the same decision he did.

I tried again to release my breath, but it came out as a cough. I sucked air in through my nose, but it had nowhere to go, and it caught. I swallowed hard. The pressure of my knees on my forehead started to balance out the tension in my neck. The tears finally worked their way out.

After a while, the beat in my ears settled to a regular rhythm, tick-tock-tick-tock. My chest loosened up. I tried to crack my neck, but my head rolled awkwardly above my stiff shoulders. The knock at the door sounded like an explosion. My heart was suddenly in my throat.

"Cate?" Thomas called. "What are you doing in there? We should get moving... the Reading..."

I looked out the window. It was still brighter than before we came into the Gatehouse, but night would fall here soon, too.

I took one more ragged breath and pressed the heels of my

hands to my eyes. "I'm coming. Just give me a sec." In through my nose, out through my mouth. Just breathe. I shoved the card back into my phone case and stuck the whole thing in my back pocket. Pushing off the side of Alice's bed, I stood and shook out my legs.

When I opened the door, Thomas was there with an uncharacteristically concerned look on his face. I didn't know what to tell him. I still didn't really know anything, but I didn't want Giles ending the search until the answers were more clear. I had to dissent. I tried to smile, but I knew I must look gruesome with my face puffy and red from crying. "I'm ready."

Although Alice had welcomed us into the Gatehouse, we still had to pass the Guardian to officially enter the community. It was a formality, but Adam would be waiting on the other side of the Creek with some kind of test. I hoped he was ready to talk. He may have been the last person to see my father. He was almost certainly the one who told the Community Watch that Dad had crossed the Creek. The Guardian reported directly to the Watch, even when the Guardian wasn't also the only son of the community's lead investigator.

"You have everything you need," Alice said as if she'd seen the card I held on the plane. The well-equipt Magician.

"Does it matter?" I asked. What good did it do me to have a magical card if I was too late to change anything?

"That will be up to you. As always. We will talk when you return. We have many things to discuss."

I sighed. Thomas rolled his eyes.

"See?" he whispered, "Cryptic and irritating."

"She can hear you," I reminded him.

He looked at her over my shoulder and immediately flushed.

She was definitely watching.

"Sorry," he told the Gatekeeper, his hand on his chest.

"Your road is in front of you," she said, pointing to the door.

"I do believe she's kicking us out," he said to me, wide-eyed and mocking. "Again." He should've shown more respect to the Gatekeeper. She was probably a hundred years old, even if she didn't look much older than us.

"Thank you, Alice," I said, grabbing my bag and transferring my phone back to the front pocket. She didn't answer and didn't follow us — just stood in the middle of the room with her hands clasped gently in front of her, smiling like Mona Lisa.

9

I pushed my brother out the door and into the sun. The light hurt my eyes, but it was nothing compared to the flare I saw when Alice first opened the front door. We were standing on a small stone step. The Creek lapped the edges and threatened our toes. Ten feet away, on the other side, the Guardian waited. Adam was taller than I remembered. It might've been the mask. His face was disguised behind molded leather shaped like a wolf's head, the symbol of the triple goddess painted across the forehead in white. Waxing moon, full moon, waning moon. The Maiden, Mother, and Crone. He stood at the beginning of the path that led through the last edges of wood before the way opened up to the homes of our family and friends.

"Hey, Adam," Thomas waved. "What'd ya do with the bridge?"

Adam didn't respond. The Guardian took a step forward, still keeping a few feet between himself and the water.

"Why have you come?" he called across the water. It was Adam's voice, and it wasn't. There was an echo and a depth that wasn't there when we were kids. But I hadn't seen him in a while. And there was the mask.

"Again, really? Wow." Thomas straightened, cleared his throat, and started over with a more formal tone. "I, Thomas Corey, come to complete my Wakening, to mourn my father, and to take my place in my mother's line."

"The Water Test begins. Take the first step, Thomas Corey."

"Seriously? I just... Yesterday... You know what, never mind. I could use a bath after the night I had," Thomas said. Before he'd made up his mind, he walked out into the Creek. No. He walked "on" the Creek. My brother thought he could walk on water, and he did. Witches always float. Thomas took one more step to dry land and tried to give Adam a high five. The Guardian left him hanging. I smirked. What had the test been yesterday?

"Why have you come?" Adam called across the water.

I didn't know how to swim. I shifted my bag to both shoulders.

"Why have you come?" asked the Guardian.

I considered turning around, telling Alice it was all a mistake, and going back to Chicago. The fact that I probably couldn't swing another plane ticket crossed my mind. I didn't think I could handle another bumpy flight anyway.

"Cate?" Thomas sounded concerned. He was maybe, finally, seeing this from my perspective.

"One minute." I needed my new security blanket. Nora's tarot card had gotten me through the turbulence on the plane. Maybe it would help me face this challenge, too. I waved a little and took off my bag again. There was no room in front of me, so I turned my back to the Creek and squatted. I pulled the phone out and held it up. One bar. This phone would be useless on the other side of the water. I hoped the card wouldn't be. I pulled it loose and shoved the phone back into the bag.

"Why have you come?"

Goddess, what is his hurry? Does the Guardian of the Gate have better places to be? Adam really had changed since taking this job. I stood quickly to tell him so but slipped on the wet stone as I turned around. My feet came out from under me, and I sat down hard. I lost my breath but held onto the card.

"You okay?" Thomas called, trying not to laugh. I wanted to punch him in the face.

I pulled myself up, dusted myself off, and straightened my back. Answering the Guardian, I gave my formal, stupidly ironic, full name: "I, Hecate Corey, come to complete my Wakening, to locate my father, and to find my place in my mother's line."

It was mostly true, even if I intended to formally end my Wakening on the other side of the Gate in a few days. I took the first step.

"No!" Thomas yelled, but there was a swirl of light and the water rushed over my head.

In retrospect, I should have waited for the Guardian to confirm the test. In the second before the water overtook me, I tipped my head back and gasped for air.

When I walked across the bridge two and a half years ago, I'd never have guessed how deep it was. Adam hadn't been the Guardian that day. He'd been too young. How long had he held the position?

Maybe I should tell him he's doing it wrong. You're not supposed to kill people when they come home. Why does my head hurt so much?

My chest burned. The bubbles stopped flowing out of my nose. I tried to suck them back in, and my sinuses exploded. The card floated by. Maybe I imagined it, but it looked like it was rolling on golden wheels, pulled by a mismatched set of sphinxes. I reached for the charioteer's wand. Willpower. Determination. *Don't give up.* Just out of reach.

Wait.

Everything went blurry. The water stopped swirling

around me. It was so dark. The chariot morphed into the tower card I'd seen in Alice's bedroom. Two figures still fell from a high window. This time they had my brothers' faces. Matthew and Gabriel, the oldest of my siblings, plummeted through the sky. The tower disappeared, but their bodies continued to fall. I saw them like a memory, slipping into the same Creek that held me under. Sunlight flashed on the surface, and they were gone.

What happened while I was away?

My father's face rippled above the water. He cried out, reaching for me. I felt myself rising to the surface, the water streaming away.

I woke up in the grass. My head rested in Thomas's lap, my hair dripping over his legs. His face was a near-shapeless blur above me. When I opened my eyes, he helped me sit. He handed me my glasses, and when I put them on, the lenses were inexplicably dry and clear. I was so dizzy that I almost lay right back down, but I managed to catch myself.

Thomas stood. He screamed at Adam. Lots of angry words that blurred together. He was so loud. Everything was too loud and too bright. The Guardian stood aloof, impenetrable behind the mask.

My stomach heaved and the contents spewed over the Guardian's shoes. Some kind of charm dissolved the mess instantly, cleaner than the café floor after Thomas's coffee accident.

"Did I pass?" I asked, my head between my knees.

The Guardian's voice echoed in my ringing ears. "The water test is complete. The witch floats."

"You almost drowned, idiot," Thomas said. "I think you have a concussion. There's a bump on the back of your head the size of a small bird."

"You mean an egg?"

"No, like, the egg hatched, and the baby bird came out, ate

some worms, grew a little, and is getting ready to fly."

"Neat," I said before everything went dark again.

10

Cate? I need you to open your eyes."
"Come on, Cate. We've got things to do."
"Don't be like that."
"Like what?"
"She's hurt!"
"I know. I was there."
"If you could both just... "
"You're right," my mother said. "I'm sorry. Come on, Thomas. Elspeth needs room to work."

They continued to bicker as their voices faded away. Still, better safe... Keeping my eyes closed, I explored the room with my other senses. Floral scents, chamomile, lavender, daisy, primrose, and something sour underneath them. I tasted garlic, turmeric, and herb-infused oils. Glass clinked. Drawers opened and closed. One stuck. The mattress under me was stiff but comfortable. The sheets were thin and rough.

"You can quit faking now," the healer whispered. "Or don't. I'm happy to go on pretending you're unconscious." She waited. "It's a little weird though. Your aura is practically screaming." Another drawer opened and closed. "There it is. Okay, do whatever. I'm good."

A chair scraped the floor and creaked as she settled into it.

In through my nose, out through my mouth. My pulse attacked the backs of my eyes. The baby bird behind my head chirped. He didn't like it when I looked up, so I rolled my head to the side. I peeked through my eyelashes. My childhood friend, Elspeth, was reading a novel. No, she was reading *The Scarlet Letter*. Ugh.

Elspeth had wanted to be a healer for as long as I could remember. She started training under my mom when we were twelve. Mom was disappointed that I didn't follow her, but it was better this way. I was never going to be a successful healer. I had no patience for that level of the Craft. I could have spent my whole life studying and never developed the skill Elspeth learned her first week.

Plus, Elspeth had the Gift, and she was happy here. After her brother, Duncan, disappeared during his Wakening, she'd never gone on one of her own. She still refused to talk about it. It was as if the outside world didn't exist for her. And why should it? She was just starting to take her own patients when I left, and now it looked like she was leading the practice.

"What'd you say?" she asked, without taking her attention from the book. She looked completely comfortable, posed like an old painting. She leaned into the wooden chair, her legs crossed at the ankles under a long, aproned skirt, the book in her lap, her dark brown braid trailing over her shoulder, almost brushing the pages.

It was stupid to ask how I got here, but I did it anyway. The words slurred on the way out. I sounded like I'd been drinking for the past three days. I tried again, and it might've been worse. "Nev...er... mine..." I sighed.

"You're going to be fine," Elspeth said. She didn't get up, but she put a finger between the pages of her book and threw her braid behind her as she turned to face me. When I looked into her mossy brown eyes, my breath slowed. The pain in my head subsided a little. She really was as good as they said. Caleb was lucky. She smiled. I couldn't remember if her empathic abilities included the transfer of thoughts.

"See?" she said. "Better already." She drew an invisible X on the page with her finger and put the book on a side table. She brewed something stinky over a small green flame on a workbench beside the cot where I was recovering.

"It won't take much," she assured me. She adjusted the strap of her tank top as she stood. Pulling a ceramic cup from a shelf, she used an earthenware ladle to dip out some of the liquid. "Inhale before you drink. It needs to mix with the air." An elemental potion.

I pushed myself up slowly and took the cup in both hands. I was a little dizzy, but it started to dissipate as I leaned into the steam. I closed my eyes and breathed deeply. It was bitter but also minty? I peeked out at the healer. She'd already gone back to Hester Prynne.

"Be careful," she said to the book, "it's hot."

I sipped from Elspeth's cup. It might've been mostly unsweetened tea. Maybe rooibos. It had an odd cooling effect going down. My head started to clear.

"The swelling is going down," Elspeth said, "But Thomas was right. You do have a concussion. The tea will help with the symptoms, but you aren't healed. That will take time. You got a little.... scrambled."

She didn't ask what happened or how I felt now. My brother must have filled her in on the former, and her empathy answered the latter.

"What happened?" I asked.

She frowned, reaching to check the bump on the back of my head.

I waved her off. "No. Not to me. Not today. While I was gone. Did something happen to Matthew and Gabriel? Adam told Thomas Dad was missing, but—"

She felt my head anyway, gently touching the injury before testing my temperature with her wrist on my forehead. "I don't want you to panic. It would be bad for your recovery."

"Well, I wasn't going to, but now I am. I had a vision in the Creek. They were falling."

She sighed. "Caleb hasn't heard from them in a few days. They didn't check in with anyone after what happened with your dad. I think your mom is covering for them, but I don't know why."

"Could they have… Does Caleb think… Were they with him? With Dad, I mean?"

Elspeth closed her eyes, but they moved beneath her lids. Her eyelashes fluttered. "It's hard to say. I don't feel them in the village."

My eyebrows jumped. Her Gift had grown since I last saw her. "Can you usually? Feel their presence when they aren't here with you?"

She opened her eyes. "Sometimes. If I focus. It's easier when it's someone I have a connection with."

"Like Caleb?"

Elspeth shrugged. "Or your mom. Being her apprentice. But sometimes I can follow a path. I'm connected to her. She's connected to them. I can sense Jonathan closing out at the library, and Benjamin's at the Watch Tower already."

"But it's not working with Matthew and Gabriel now?"

"No," she said. "But I don't know what that means. It might not be anything."

Or it might be everything.

"What is Giles going to say at the Reading? What are people saying about Dad?"

She tilted her head. "When was the last time you heard from him?"

"I got a letter last week." This week's missing letter made me pause.

"Did he say anything strange?" She picked at a loose thread on her skirt.

"Like what, El? He didn't say anything about planning to dive into an enchanted waterway if that's what you're asking. You're as bad as Alice. Just tell me what happened."

With what appeared to be a great effort of patience, she said, "I don't know what happened. That's why there's going to be a Reading. So the Watch Commander can explain it to us."

"But you have some idea. Come on. You haven't felt anything strange around the Commander? No vibes coming off my dad the last few days?"

"He's been stressed," she said. "Both of them, honestly. Things have been weird all over Queen's Creek lately. It started before you left, but it's just gotten worse."

"The glitches?" It was one of the reasons my parents had encouraged Thomas and me to leave as soon as the window opened for our Wakening. Magic was unstable. Spells didn't work the way they should. Even Gifted witches couldn't predict the way energy would respond to them.

The Speaker had said there was nothing to worry about. It was just the end of a cycle. The Gatekeeper needed to be replaced. *Like an old battery.*

Alice's time had almost run out, and as she weakened, so did the boundary spell that hid the community and regulated the flow of magical energy. Someone had to take her place, but it couldn't be me. Her chosen successor was a magical dud.

"It's not your fault."

"Don't read me, okay?" Perils of befriending an empath. No emotional crisis was secret. It probably showed on my face anyway.

"Take care of yourself, please? I don't want to have to tell Caleb that I couldn't save you." She said it softly and looked up through her lashes to make sure it landed.

I got it. We were family now. My mother had practically accepted her as a surrogate daughter before I left. I swung my feet off the cot and stood. *Too much.* I sat back down with Elspeth's help.

"I'd tell you to take it slow, but you're... you." She smiled. "Just try not to run? And don't hit your head again. I might not be able to bring you back."

I pushed off the cot at snail speed. This time I managed to keep my balance.

"You could rest a while longer," Elspeth said.

"Thanks. But I have to go. The Reading..."

"Is about to start," she finished. "You should take the shortcut. I'll distract them." She gestured to a doorway half obscured by a soft green curtain. It was on the opposite side of the small room from the door my mother and brother took. I raised an eyebrow. She nodded and handed me my backpack.

"Go," whispered Elspeth just as I heard my brother's voice outside the door. He was still arguing with my mom. It sounded like she wanted him to stay out and let me rest until it was all over, but he was insisting on talking to me first. *Thanks, Thomas, but I think I'll skip the argument.*

I slid past the curtain and fumbled through Elspeth's dark storage room, choosing not to recognize some of the more unusual ingredients for healing potions. *Was that an actual bat's wing?* I grasped the back door handle just as the front door opened.

11

The path behind the healer's cottage was covered in soft moss. The trees arched across the path, so the branches on either side wove together in an unbroken canopy. Judging by the dappled shadows at my feet, I was running out of time. I had to get to the Watch Tower.

The stone building was geographically at the center of town, but that area would be mostly empty by this time of day. The market that opened in the square below the tower would be closing for Last Light. People would be walking, rolling and (in some eccentric cases) flying home, following one of the other two paths like this one that radiated out and then curved through the woods.

A lamp flickered through the trees on my right and then went out again. One of Elspeth's neighbors was preparing for the evening ritual. I took a breath and quickened my pace.

Cautiously.

"I dissent," I said aloud, announcing myself to the empty path. Practice might loosen the knot in my belly or the chains across my chest. "I dissent this reading. In the case of the disappearance of Marcus Corey, I, his only daughter, dissent the findings of the Watch."

"You shouldn't come to the Reading."

There was a shadow moving through the tree line. A wolf broke through. A man in wolf's clothing. The Guardian pushed his mask up, revealing a pale, freckled face. Strawberry blond curls stuck to his forehead.

"What do you know, Adam?" I asked. "Or are you just following me to finish me off? The near-drowning wasn't enough? Way to bring back the old ways. A real vintage witch test. You know, I could have died. I still might. I have a head injury that—"

"Enough. You think this is a joke? Your father was a threat to all of us." Adam's neck was red, and the flush started to creep up over his chin.

"What are you talking about? He was beloved." It was Dad's favorite joke. *I'm much beloved*, he'd answer anytime we questioned how he could get the influence he needed. Nora wasn't the first to suggest that he should run for Speaker, but Dad had always had some excuse not to.

"You've been gone a long time." The flush rose up his cheeks. "Things change."

"I guess they do. I would have expected more sympathy from my brother's friend."

Adam flinched, his hands tightening into fists at his sides. He looked down. "Where are your brothers, Cate? Have you heard from Matthew or Gabriel?"

Elspeth wasn't the only one who'd noticed they were missing, then. Did he suspect they had something to do with what happened to Dad? *Did they?*

I took a step back, away from him, closer to the tower. "I don't know what you think you know, but my family isn't hiding anything. My dad had some kind of accident. There's no way he crossed the Creek. If your father thinks—"

"He was his best friend! Do you think this makes him happy? Stay away from that Reading. You won't like what you hear." He pulled his mask down before the blood rose past his eyes. I tensed for an attack. Then he disappeared back into the woods.

I could've followed him. His route was probably more direct than the winding path. But he was already out of sight, and with my luck, I'd get lost, and I had no red cape or bread crumbs to help someone find me later.

Get moving. Others would crowd the path soon, and I wasn't ready to make idle conversation as we walked to my family's destruction. If I was too injured to run, I needed to maintain a steady pace.

But first, I had to check something. I pulled my bag around and shoved my hand in the front pocket. A knight in shining armor on a white horse held up a golden goblet. I almost laughed. Passion and creativity. A new romantic relationship. *Well, that's a mistake. Nice try, Nora.*

I turned the card face down and held it out in my palm. I covered it with my other hand and tried to set my intention, but now all I could think about were Adam's intentions. What did he care if I went to the Reading or not? He almost killed me, and the warning I just received was more threatening than compassionate. Still, I was more intrigued than afraid. I took a breath and closed my eyes. *How should I respond to his warning?*

The card grew warm. On my next exhale, I opened my eyes. I hesitated for just a moment before I uncovered the card. It flipped face up. The knight of cups was insistent. Before giving up, I remembered that there was another way to interpret this emotional card. *I should trust my intuition.* My heart said to keep moving.

The Watch Tower glowed as the sun dropped into its shadow. Bells rang from five different directions. The Reading would begin when the ritual closed. I needed to be within the sacred circle before the casting began. A slow breath steadied my head, and I pushed myself up the three stone stairs. Touching the rune on the rounded wall as I crossed the threshold, I gathered strength from the familiar traditions. *Lavender and rosemary.* This doorway had already been smudged.

The gathering room of the Watch Tower was a circle within the circle. Four doorways led in from the outer hall, one each for north, south, east, and west. The entrance I came in was halfway between the south and west doors. *The first choice.* I silently asked for guidance and stepped through the one to the south. Its cardinal direction aligned with action and inspiration but also expressed a desire for connection. No one inside noticed, but I took the step through the threshold purposefully, focusing on my intentions. *May my actions tonight connect me with my family and community and inspire them not to give up hope.*

Inside the gathering room, a small crowd ringed the central platform, where five people formed the points of a star with the sixth participant and an altar at the center. Each of the six held a lit taper in front of them, their eyes closed as they hummed a low tone. Witnesses stood near the platform, eyes closed in meditation. Others waited off to the side, holding whispered conversations.

The altar was covered in a green cloth and laid with the ritual tools, just like the Magician's card. The Mother stood behind a large candle facing the east door. It was my mother. Last Light was lit in every home at the same time by Maiden, Mother, or Crone. The women of the community took turns lighting the sacred candle in the Tower. I shouldn't have been surprised to see Mom up there. Of course she beat me here.

No shortcut walking path can beat magical transportation.

Thomas faced her at the top of the pentacle, his head bowed. In that position, he represented Youth, the male counterpart to the Maiden. He seemed to feel me watching him and looked up for a moment. I raised an eyebrow. He'd never been much of a spiritual leader, although everyone eventually took a turn in the ritual. He shrugged. Not a planned participation on his part, then.

Did the Speaker choose them purposefully for the ritual, or did my mother volunteer them tonight? Participating in the trance-like ceremony might have been a welcome distraction.

Next to Thomas, a girl I didn't quite recognize represented the Maiden. Her eyes were open a sliver, but she was entirely focused on the flame of her candle. Something was familiar about her, but the time I'd been away had been transformative for some of the community's younger members.

Adam, unmasked, stood beside her as the Warrior, counterbalancing the Mother in the ceremony. A little on the nose for the guy who spends his days protecting the Gate, but ritual symbolism didn't always have to be obscure.

Beside him stood an older woman in a purple cloak. Mrs. Kirk had been elected our community's Speaker before I left, and as the ritual's Crone, she led the Last Light ritual each night. Afterward, she'd represent the entire Coven, our governing body, when she heard the Reading from the Commander of the Watch. I'd never really thought about our leadership before. But remembering something Nora said, I wondered if the Speaker hoped to serve another term. Did she have any competition now?

I studied the lines on her face, but without my brother Benjamin's Gift for vision, I couldn't read anything from it. My brother Caleb might hear something in the tone of her humming. But I only noticed it was slightly louder than the others, as it should be since they were following her lead.

Detective Giles Parker filled the masculine elder position of Sage, closing the inner circle. *How ironic.*

Twenty or so witnesses formed the outer circle. The number was high for a regular Last Light ritual, even though the community's safety depended on what happened there.

These vultures have come to hear the reading of the investigation report. They'd tell each other they came here out of concern for my father or support for my mother, brothers, or me, but they didn't. Crossing the Creek was unheard of. This was the most exciting thing any of them had witnessed in their lives.

A few of my father's colleagues from the school stood in the crowd. At least two of them would be promoted. Someone would need to find a new alchemist. A few of his teenage students pretended to pay attention to the ritual while they murmured and conjured small illusions. *What will happen to their scores this year*? One of them giggled as another made a tiny purple frog appear to explode on his friend's shoe, oblivious to the tension in the room. The tutors ignored them. Their parents talked among themselves.

My neighbors stood at a distance, the only ones who seemed genuinely concerned. Mrs. Gosnall wore a sachet around her neck that matched a cloth tied around Mom's wrist, a charm for comfort. *Thank you.*

Irrationally, I wished Brian were here. Or Nyla. It made no sense. I should've been glad no one was here for me. *What would I say to them?* This way, I could focus on what I had to do. I had to get the timing exactly right. Making it inside before the casting locked everything down had been key, but I was still too early for a dramatic entrance with my one line: I dissent!

I had to be careful. They'd expel me if it looked like I would disrupt the ceremony. Then I'd never find out what happened to Dad. I needed to end the Reading, not the ritual.

12

At home, the Last Light ritual took less than five minutes, as someone in each house lit a candle on their altar at the same moment. Officials here in the gathering room completed the rest of the ritual to reset the charms that hid the community from the mundanes. The practice fueled the magic that powered the boundary spell on Creek. For hundreds of years, our community had followed the steps of this ritual for protection.

The Reading would start when they finished.

The momentum that brought me here crashed. The idea of possibly waiting hours to act made my already aching head throb. I shoved my hands into my jacket pockets to hide the shaking.

As the witnesses spread out to cast the circle, I tried to blend in. *Nothing to see here. Just an ordinary grieving daughter. Certainly not here to disrupt anything or add chaos to this finely maintained social order.*

That's what magic was, after all, directing energy to bring order to the chaos of nature. I considered wiping a tear for effect and almost managed it when I stifled a real yawn. Even with the short flight, it'd been a long day, and it wasn't close to over yet. I glanced up at the platform to see if my performance was going over.

Giles had been facing me when I came in, his eyes open when everyone else's were closed. He lowered his head when he saw me looking. My mother hadn't even noticed my entrance. She was under the influence of the candle, letting it soothe the rough edges of her grief. Thomas swayed a bit, too. He'd always devoted himself completely when given this kind of responsibility. It was rare enough. I stood shoulder to shoulder with neighbors I'd never spoken to and closed my eyes, joining the hum that vibrated through the collected coven. My mother invoked the goddess, her consort, and the moon.

As the chanting began, I opened my eyes again. My mother lifted her candle and called the quarters, facing each direction in turn—the Air in the East, Fire in the South, Water in the West, and Earth in the North. She touched her taper to the candle on the altar and traded places with the Crone.

Mrs. Kirk had a deep, raspy voice from years of herbally-enhanced conjuring. She wore her wiry gray hair in a loose bun on top of her head to help keep the pointy hat in place during ceremonies. She had a reputation for bluntness and a history of decisive action.

Before being elected Speaker, she served the community as Librarian, the keeper of the grimoire. Our entire culture, past experiences, past lives, and present spells are contained in its delicate pages. The library held other books, of course, but no others with leaves supposedly composed of fairies' wings and bindings of trolls' tears.

Standing behind the candle, she raised her arms to quiet the mystical noise. The chants subsided to a low purr. Elbows out, she flattened her hands above the flame. The light changed yellow to blue to purple to green to glittering gold.

The rest of the ritual was performed as rote, meticulously

and too slowly for my nerves. When the young pages of the community passed the cups for the final benediction, I almost splashed the wine in my hurry to get this over and done.

Mrs. Kirk raised the chalice at the altar. "As above..."

"As above," repeated the crowd, glasses high.

"...so below," finished Giles, drinking from the chalice she passed him.

"So below." I drank my small serving of wine in one gulp.

The pages returned to gather the cups, and people started to murmur. Thomas put his hand on Mom's back as they stepped down from the platform. The other participants followed, shedding their holy personas as they joined friends and family in the crowd. Only the Speaker remained by the altar, but her posture relaxed, releasing the Crone.

My brothers moved to find each other, but I took a few steps to keep people between us. They might not try to stop me, but I couldn't risk it.

"We gather in this Last Light of the day to protect our community. We ask for security for our border and guidance for our leaders. May tonight's Reading bring us peace." Mrs. Kirk held my mother's eyes for a moment, and their breaths aligned.

A single, painful tear rolled down my mother's cheek, but her breath was calm. Mrs. Kirk looked at my brother next, but he avoided her gaze, his eyes glistening as he stared into the candle. She smiled, offering consolation that somehow did more to make her seem strong than it did to lift them up.

This was why she selected my family. She wanted to show our community she had control of the situation, a benevolent grandmother soothing frightened children.

Maybe Nora wasn't the only one who'd thought my father could replace her.

The Speaker silently checked in with the Maiden, the Warrior, and the Sage. Then Giles nodded. She found me in the crowd.

My eyes burned. The smoke. My allergies. My anger. Her breath. My heart raced, and my chest tightened. I looked into her eyes, shining even at this distance. The irises bloomed like sunflowers, yellow-gold overlaid on green. My breath slowed, and my body relaxed, warm, a little dizzy.

No. I clenched my fingers until my nails dug into my palms. I gritted my teeth, holding my breath and my anger. She'd get no endorsement from me. Before I pulled back my gaze and stared at the floor, she frowned. She didn't like to lose.

Mrs. Kirk allowed herself only a moment before her eyes lifted back to the assembled audience. She flicked at a wrinkle in her cloak before smoothing it down.

She smiled at each of my older brothers in turn, testing their response to her eye contact. Jonathan bowed his head but met her eyes, stoic as ever. His wife stood beside him with their two girls. They were so much taller than I remembered, right at that age when little kids became big. Benjamin's gaze roamed over the gathering, so intent on catching any sudden movements that he almost missed the Speaker's attention on him. When he finally felt her stare, he froze. Caleb stood with his arm around Elspeth. The Speaker caught his eye, and he stiffened. Elspeth rested her head on his shoulder. Her touch melted something in him, and he bent to kiss the top of her head.

There was no sign of Matthew or Gabriel, but Mrs. Kirk didn't seem surprised. Instead of searching the crowd for them, she squared her shoulders and faced the assembly as one. *What did she know that Adam didn't?*

All of this happened in the span of seconds. No one in the crowd noticed.

"Friends," Mrs. Kirk finally called in a voice just loud enough to capture the attention of everyone in the room. "I am grateful to see so many of you in this evening's Last Light, but I know that other business calls you here. One of our own has been lost. In times like these, we look to the Watch."

Giles inclined his head.

Business. My father was not a missing file. My missing letter came to mind again. *Had he even written one this week?*

Before Giles could speak, she continued, "And we will hear the Commander's Reading, but first, I'd like to address something that concerns us all."

Murmurs ran through the crowd.

She raised a hand and waited for silence. When the crowd stilled, she clasped her hands in front of her and straightened her posture. "We all know that Queen's Creek is in danger. Our magic is unstable, and the mundanes move ever closer to our borders. Tonight, as always, we come together to protect our community. The spell we cast in the Last Light ensures a new day, safe from those who do not understand our ways. But soon, it will not be enough. The boundary spell is failing."

People around me gasped. A few of them called out panicked questions to Mrs. Kirk.

So, what Elspeth had told me was true. It sounded so much worse coming from the Speaker.

She raised her hand again, ever the patient caretaker. Her voice cut through the noise. "Fear not, friends. We knew this time would come. It has come many times before. There is but one way to revitalize the spell and maintain our Gate. It is time for a new Gatekeeper."

My fists clenched, nails biting into my palms.

The woman beside me brought her hands to her mouth, eyes wide. Her husband rubbed her back.

Mrs. Kirk continued as if she had not just raised the collective blood pressure of the assembly. "Our dear Alice has already made her selection. Our new Gatekeeper's Wakening delayed the transition, but luckily, she has returned to us, although it pains me that it is under such dark circumstances."

Shit. Shit. Shit. A glamour spell would have been amazing right then, but if I could pull that kind of power, I wouldn't have needed it.

The Speaker's eyes bored into me. Suddenly the space between me and the neighbors around me widened. They all turned, following Mrs. Kirk's line of focus. She smiled.

My face blazed. My legs liquified. I tried to turn invisible by force of will. My head pounded. *I'm going to throw up.*

"Hecate Corey, you have received the Keeper's blessing. You are her chosen successor. Will you accept?"

My stomach knotted around all of my fears, sending acid to burn holes in my throat. I coughed. I couldn't accept. Didn't she know that? My Gift wasn't just late-blooming. It was fallow. I tried to find my mother in the crowd. Let one of my brothers say something about their cursed little sister. My vision contracted to a pinpoint, and the sound of the blood in my ears drowned out the voices around me. *No. No. No.*

My mouth worked on its own, but my voice scraped my throat. "I cannot."

The crowd faded into a blur of color and jumbled sounds around me. Mrs. Kirk's face alone remained in focus, lips pursed and eyebrows drawn.

"But you must. There is no other way."

There's always another way. We'll find it. Something my father had said when he'd sent Thomas and me away. Even though it was dangerous outside. Even after what happened to Duncan. He'd known something then. Something was wrong with the magic in Queen's Creek, and I didn't think the Gatekeeper could fix it.

Any Gatekeeper.

I cleared my throat, forcing the bile back down. Her plan wouldn't work. Maybe she didn't know. Someone had to tell her. "You're wrong. My father—"

"Your father nearly destroyed the boundary spell with his experiments." Her mouth tightened. "I'm ashamed to speak ill of the dead, but he was foolish in this. He risked us all."

"He's not dead," I whispered.

Her eyes lifted, taking in the rest of the assembly. On her next breath, her tone softened, her head tilted gently to one side, and the grandmotherly demeanor returned. "Perhaps we have gotten ahead of ourselves. I have pushed you too soon. Let us take a short recess and then we will hear the Reading of the Watch Command so that you may be satisfied with what so many of us already know to be true."

13

rs. Kirk waved to the pages, who circulated quickly through the room carrying trays of small cakes and cups of spiced ale. The snacks usually came at the end of the meeting to replenish the energy expended in the ritual, but people took them gratefully. *Sugar heals more than a sweet tooth.*

Chairs flickered into existence, facing the west side of the platform. There were just enough for everyone, coming into focus as each person approached to take one. Slowly, people turned away from me, though I felt their furtive glances. Whispered conversations rumbled through the room, each small group unconsciously speaking louder to be heard over their neighbors.

"So sad… such a shame."

"You know, I saw him just the other day. Talking to himself on the path. Probably going to the Creek to do goddess-knows-what."

"He's been losing it for years, if you ask me."

"That whole family… Did you hear about the oldest boys… And what about her? Can you believe the way she spoke to the Speaker just now?"

"I do feel bad for Sarah, though. What she has to put up with…"

I stood apart, my heart racing. I had to stop this, but I couldn't find the words. Too many people looking at me. Concerned, empathetic, angry, judgmental, scared people looking to me to save their magic, to accept the role they thought I was born to play.

Had they all forgotten what it was like before I left? Had I hidden my failings so well? Or did they think a stint in the mundane world brought out buried magical reserves? I didn't have it, but how did you prove a negative?

I crossed my arms, rocking in place, breathing through my nose. I concentrated on staying upright and keeping my lunch down. Goddess, my head. *Just don't vomit in the middle of the gathering room.*

My family quietly claimed the ethereal chairs closest to me, pulling their seats more fully into this dimension from wherever they'd been stored. Benjamin sat next to Caleb and Elspeth, leaning forward, elbows on his knees. When I didn't sit, Jonathan looked up from his place behind Caleb and immediately stood. "Cate, take my chair."

His wife smiled, patting the empty, but now solid, chair beside her. Their girls twisted around in their seats to look at me, big eyes blinking.

"No, thanks." I wanted to be ready. I couldn't sit, couldn't calm down, or I might chicken out.

"It's fine, I'll get another," he said, reaching for something that only half existed.

"No, thanks."

"I insist—" he started.

"You know, I'll stand, too," Thomas said, appearing behind me. "We can see better from over here." My heart followed my twin a few feet away, behind a row of comfortable strangers.

I put my hand out, and he squeezed it. One. Two. Three. I squeezed back. Four. Five. Six.

Thomas grabbed a cup of ale from a passing page and pressed it into my hand. As soon as it touched my lips, warmth flooded through me. I took a slow breath. *I can do this.*

"You ready?" Thomas asked. "Whatever they have to say, we have to hear it. If you still want to dissent—"

"She's wrong. You know she is."

I swear, he looked down his nose at me. *Do not "oh, honey" me, Thomas.*

"Maybe. But I don't know that for sure. And neither do you."

"Are you kidding me right now?" All the warmth I'd gained from the ale centered itself in my face.

He grabbed his own cup and took a steadying sip. "Is this about that thing she said about the Gatekeeper? We'll sort that out. It doesn't have to be you. They'll find someone else."

I narrowed my eyes at the Speaker, who was returning to the platform. "She's not looking for anyone else."

"She'll have to, okay? But right now, let's focus on one thing at a time. We're here to find out what happened to Dad."

I nodded and turned back to face the altar, where Mrs. Kirk stood with her arms open, inviting everyone to return to the meeting.

"Detective Parker, please advise us of your findings and read your determination into the record," she said.

It's about goddess-be-blessed time.

"Good evening," Giles began. "It is with great sorrow that I relay the results of my investigation. Marcus Corey was my first friend, as he was a friend to many of us here. He was a trusted advisor, a beloved professor, and a gifted alchemist."

My mother's face was stone, her attention completely

focused on the detective. With a last squeeze of my hand, Thomas slipped away to stand behind her chair, placing his hands on her shoulders. She reached up to acknowledge him without looking away.

I chewed my lip. *Get to the Reading. Stop talking about my father in the past tense. I can't dissent a eulogy.* I tried to stop my foot from tapping.

The detective went on to describe meeting Dad in study group and told a few stories about their youthful adventures. It all just amplified his apparent desertion in our moment of need. How could he stand there, act like he knew my father so well, and then tell all these people he killed himself? The betrayal was unforgivable. Disgusting. My stomach tightened. The waiting might actually kill me. I was getting an ulcer, for sure. *Get to the community response. Hurry.*

Someone was humming a beautiful and peaceful melody, totally ruining the escalation of my anger. It was hard enough trying to build up the righteous fury to openly object to the Watch's decision without this soothing song wrecking it. But I couldn't let them declare my missing father dead by suicide. No matter what evidence they might have.

Maiden, Mother, and Crone help me get through this.

Nora's card warmed in my pocket, and I pulled it out, clutching it at my side without looking at it. I didn't need advice. I needed patience. *Just get to the end.*

My vision blurred like it had in the Creek. Giles' voice softened behind waves of white noise. The space shrunk, growing fuzzy around the edges. What was he saying? I tried to read his lips. What evidence did he have? How many witnesses would he call? The community intercession came last. You were supposed to make an informed decision before you spoke.

I need this to be over.

The sound intensified, the waves filling the room. It

wrapped around me, my own slow heartbeat in my ears. Static made my arms tingle. The room rippled like water in a breeze. I closed my eyes.

Jolted back. *Too bright. Too loud.*

"This completes the findings of the Watch." The detective paused, sharing a glance with Mrs. Kirk.

She nodded, then bowed her head.

The music faded away. All of the sound left the room.

Silence was acceptance.

I blinked and the room opened up. It couldn't be over. They'd only started a moment ago.

"So it is, with great sadness, that I declare Marcus Corey dead—"

"No!"

"Having crossed the Creek of his own accord," Giles looked down.

"No! I diss—" I yelled.

Thomas pulled me back. "It's too late," he said between his teeth. "What are you doing? It's too late. It's in the record. You're too late."

March 17

Adversity, Isolation,
Loss

Meditation, Contemplation,
Discontent

Leadership, Vision,
Optimism

14

What the hell, Cate?" Thomas dragged me outside. The tower walls were thick enough to mute our conversation, and the one narrow window was covered with charmed glass. "What happened in there? It was like your brain left your body." He lowered his voice and rested his hand on my arm, pulling me closer and inspecting my eyes. "Is it your head? Should I get Elspeth?"

I pulled his hand off my arm and met his eyes with what I hoped was a clear-eyed glare. "I'm fine. That music... you heard it. Where was it coming from?"

"What?" He squinted, then raised an eyebrow. "What music? Are you serious? What happened to you? Maybe you should lie down. That concussion—" He touched the bump on my head.

I brushed his hand away. "Stop it. Are you going to stand there and pretend you didn't hear someone humming during the reading?"

"What?"

I'm going to hit him. I'm going to give him a bump like mine, but right between his stupid eyes. "Someone was using music magic like Mom does."

"Are you sure?"

My fists tightened. *How could he have missed it? He's lucky he's so pretty. This is how the universe finds balance. It wouldn't have been fair to give him brains and beauty.*

Then he finally asked the logical question, and I had to reevaluate my position as the smart twin. "Who?"

"I don't know," I admitted. "It was like something glitched. There was music, and then this whooshing noise, and then it was over. One minute Giles was talking about the good old days. Next, he's thanking Adam for his testimony. I never even saw him step onto the platform."

Thomas stared at me.

I crossed my arms.

"Tell me it didn't happen," I said. "Go on. Tell me that it's impossible, standing near the Source of natural magic, for someone who is probably descended from twelve generations of witches to distract me like that."

"I don't know. I'm telling you, I didn't hear anything. I was listening to the Reading."

I glared at him. "Why didn't you do anything? Why didn't you stop them? Why didn't you dissent?"

"What? You really didn't hear any of it, did you? There's nothing to dissent. The evidence—"

"There is nothing they could have said that would make me believe Dad crossed the Creek. I can't believe you do. It's the whole reason we came home. You should have stopped them when I didn't."

He shook his head. "That's why you came home. I came to hear them out. I'm sorry about whatever happened to you in there, but I didn't know what you were doing. You hit your head. A thing like that could change your priorities."

I rubbed my face. My head throbbed, but I'd never heard of a concussion causing auditory hallucinations. Someone had been humming that song. The ritual came back to me.

There had been something about the Maiden. The way her lips moved when she stared into the candle. Where had she been sitting during the Reading? I pictured the layout of the room, put myself back there, and I knew. I grabbed my brother's arm.

"Thomas, the Maiden, it was her. I don't know why she did it, but she did this. She distracted me when I could have stopped it. Why would she do that?"

"How should I know?"

"You were in the ritual with her."

"I didn't choose that. Look, we got here, and Mrs. Kirk called out the names. I don't know why she chose us to stand up for Youth in the ritual. I guess she didn't trust the, you know, actual *youths*." He said it like he was a year away from yelling, *Get off my lawn!* in some sitcom suburb, rather than only a couple of years past being the youth in somebody's yard himself.

"Did she say anything to you?"

"Who?"

I took a deep breath and gave him a minute. I pushed up my glasses.

"Shiri?" he guessed. "No, like... no. She didn't say anything. I mean, what do you think she said? 'Hey, nice to see you. I'm gonna put a whammy on your sister later, cool?' No. Nothing like that."

The name felt familiar, but it didn't match the girl from the ritual. I peered in through the window. The young woman representing the Maiden stood out, even among a crowd of people who had the skills to alter their appearance however they chose. Her long hair was pulled away from her face, but the dark blue-black tendrils transitioned to pink, then orange, then red as they fell down her back like a sunset, ending in bright yellow near her waist. Leather cords secured the loose ponytail.

"She didn't say anything? To anybody? Where did she come from?"

"I don't know. I guess she came with her grandmother? I didn't really see her around anybody else," he said.

"Her grandmother?"

Thomas looked at me like I might pass out again.

"Mrs. Kirk?" he said slowly, as though it was the most obvious thing in the world.

"She's the Speaker's granddaughter? You didn't think that might be important?"

Thomas peeked over my shoulder. "I mean, she's taller and her hair is whatever... but it's still Shiri. You used to babysit her."

I tried to picture her a few years younger, with a more natural hair color. Childlike innocence. *Maybe.* When I was fourteen, I'd spent a few nights a month entertaining a sweet nine-year-old kid while her parents went to coven meetings. I turned back and leaned on the windowsill, remembering a little girl in yellow braids, singing when she wanted something she knew she wasn't allowed to have. My head throbbed. "Was she a blonde?"

"Yeah."

I rubbed my eyes, then pushed my glasses back into place.

Queen's Creek was not that big a town. I'd been distracted by music. It couldn't be a coincidence that the Speaker's granddaughter was a siren.

Thomas shifted his weight. Tilted his head. Tilted it the other way, like a puppy trying to work out which hand had the treat. *Maiden-mother-and-crone, why is this my life?*

"I'm going to get Elspeth. There's something really wrong with you. You must have hit your head harder than we thought." He backed away from me toward the door. "Just wait here, okay? I'll be right back. I'm sure she can fix... whatever this is."

"Will you hold on a minute? I'm thinking." *What was the Speaker's granddaughter up to now? What were they trying to hide?*

He raised an eyebrow.

My jaw tightened. "She did something to us. Don't you want to know why?"

He sighed. "If I promise we'll talk to Shiri, will you let Elspeth look at you first?"

Maybe she should. I sounded insane. *Just because you're paranoid doesn't mean they aren't out to get you.*

"You promise?"

He took a long breath before he answered. "You really didn't hear any of it? The Reading. The testimony. Giles's conclusions."

"Nothing."

"He's gone, Cate. Dad went into the Creek, and he didn't come out."

"But why? Why would he do that? It doesn't make any sense!"

I searched his eyes for any clue that he felt what I did. He looked away, biting his lip. He stared into space for a moment. *Now who's losing focus?* I followed his gaze. He wasn't flaking out after all. There was something there, a white dot falling slowly in a chaotic path past the tower's window. Another spot danced around it, a duet that became a flash mob. As a thousand specks drifted past my bare arms, I blinked, and they caught on my glasses. I blinked again, and they slid down the lenses to melt against my hot cheek. They rolled down my face like tears. Maybe they were.

When Thomas looked at me, there was no question. The tears traced lines down his face, catching at his nose and the corners of his mouth. We stood silently together in the strange spring snow. Somehow I didn't have to check Nora's card to know it showed the five of pentacles, the card of loss.

15

When we composed ourselves enough to go back inside, the snow had crystallized in our hair. It twinkled in the candlelight. I felt it dripping through, cooling my scalp. Thomas ran a hand through his hair and the melting flakes smoothed his flyaways. It might've been magic, or it might've been the water reactivating his hair gel.

Our family and neighbors milled around the gathering room, catching up and finishing their snacks. A page walked by with a tray of drinks and more cakes. I grabbed the snack, but skipped the wine. Someone else could toast Persephone, Mother Earth, or Freya tonight. I was confused enough.

Thomas found Elspeth with Caleb on the far side of the room.

She put a hand to my head and frowned. "Let's go to the office. It'll be more private."

The Speaker's office was in the Tower behind the gathering room where the Reading took place. A metal name plate sat at eye level on the open door. Inside, two receiving chairs faced a large desk in front of a wooden cabinet.

Thomas lit candles in the sconces around the room, and

Caleb pulled one of the chairs out and gestured for me to sit. Elspeth peeked out the door before softly drawing it closed.

The change in elevation made my head spin a little. I gripped the arms of the chair. *I knew sitting was a bad idea.*

"She's having blackouts," Thomas said. "And I think she's hearing things."

"I'm not hearing things. I heard music. Because Shiri was humming."

Thomas looked to Caleb for support, but our older brother frowned. "You heard that?"

I'd never been so grateful for a brother's Gift. Unlike Thomas's fire-based magic, Caleb's aligned with the element of air. He felt its vibrations, even the smallest movements, like a whispery voice in a crowd.

"What did you hear?" Elspeth laid a hand on the side of Caleb's face.

He smiled, holding her hand in place and looking meaningfully into her eyes. Something shimmered between them, and she nodded.

"Definitely humming," she told Thomas after a moment, breaking her empathic connection with Caleb.

"Well, I didn't hear anything." Thomas glowered at Caleb like he was keeping secrets. Our gentle older brother just shrugged.

"I swear, if you start sparkling again—" The threat died on my lips as I realized I'd have to stand up again to reach him.

Elspeth sat in the chair beside me, leaning forward to examine my face. "So, you heard the siren song. You probably shouldn't have. We didn't. But we'll come back to that. You heard it, and then what?"

"She was humming, and then… I don't know. I blinked."

"You blinked?" Elspeth's inflection made it clear she envisioned the more magical use of the word than just clearing my eyes.

My brothers looked at each other. They'd probably blinked to the Watch Tower earlier. Traveling by magic used an unnecessary amount of energy when you could just walk, but if a witch was Gifted with a strong connection to the Source, and if they were running late, or had a long distance to travel, or weren't very patient, it might be worth it. It wasn't something I could ever do.

"Not like that."

"Like what, then?" Thomas leaned back against the doorframe, crossing his arms.

"I don't know. I blinked. I closed my eyes, and when I opened them, things had changed."

"What does that even mean? *Things had changed*?" Thomas's impression of my voice was not flattering. I leaned forward against my better judgment.

Elspeth rested a hand on my knee. "Maybe one more time."

"Third time's the charm." Had I said that out loud? I huffed and sat back into the chair, staring at the ceiling.

"This has happened before?" Elspeth asked.

"Twice. On the flight out here. It felt like the plane was going to crash. I closed my eyes, prayed to the Three to get me through it. And then when I fell in the Creek, before Thomas pulled me out. I saw Matthew and Gabriel, but they weren't there. Not today. And then just now. All three times, I was dizzy, and my heart raced like it would burst. I couldn't breathe, and when I opened my eyes, it felt like there was a hole in my memory. Like everyone else experienced something that I didn't remember. But I swear I was there the whole time."

"You fell in the Creek?" Caleb's eyebrows flew up.

"Only for a second," Thomas said. "That's how she hit her head. Adam's stupid test. I pulled her right out again. She probably had a panic attack."

It wasn't a panic attack.

Elspeth felt my head again. "Maybe. You said you closed your eyes, and when you opened them, everything was different? Like you missed something, skipped ahead?"

That was it exactly. "Yes. I panicked. I don't deny it. But then it felt like I just skipped past the scary part, and when I opened my eyes, everything was okay."

"That sounds more magical than medical." Caleb sat on the Speaker's desk, looking from Elspeth to me. "Maybe your Gift is finally starting to show."

Part of me wanted it to be true. So many things would be so much easier if I just grew into my Gift like everyone expected me to. At the same time, if I had a Gift, there would be consequences. Chosen-One-level expectations. A future in the Gatehouse instead of Chicago. *I hate consequences.*

Nora's card felt like it would burn a hole in my pocket. Of course. It made so much more sense. It wasn't me. It was the card. I asked for help, and the card answered. I'd been so stupid, carrying around a charmed object I didn't understand.

"El, there's something I should show you."

I shifted to take it out, but Elspeth held up a hand. Her fingers tapped at the air between us like a mime testing the strength of an invisible box. Then she sat back and folded her hands in her lap. "There's something there. Do you mind if I scan you?"

I shrugged. She'd find it on her own.

She bit her lip. Squinted. Brushed her hair back from her face. I wished I could see what she was looking for. She reached out and plucked something between us. My breath caught. Whatever she'd found had nothing to do with the card.

"It's right here," she said, "You don't feel that?"

I raised an eyebrow. I still didn't see anything. She pulled a little, and suddenly the office grew smaller. I wasn't claustrophobic, but it felt like some of the air had left the room. When she let go, my breath came easier.

"It's a binding. Like a thread wrapped around you. It looks like it's been there a long time, maybe years. You didn't know?" She looked genuinely surprised.

"What kind of binding?" I asked. "I've been gone for almost three years. I don't want to tell you how to use your Gift, but I don't feel particularly tied down."

Every witch who'd ever had a toxic relationship had practiced some kind of binding craft. You bound your friend from self-harm after she had a bad breakup, or you bound your rival to keep them from bullying you. But I'd never been a danger to anyone. Who needed to bind me?

Elspeth frowned and took a moment to follow another thread. I felt a tug somewhere deep in my chest. She grasped the thread in one hand and closed her eyes. They popped open almost immediately.

"Underneath it. There's something else. It's strong." She looked at me like we were strangers.

I shivered.

Thomas took a step closer, pushing away from the doorway, but he didn't seem to see what the Healer did. Beside me, Caleb watched her closely.

"What is it?" What was worse than a bind? What was the bind holding back? *This is it. The curse is real.* I waited for Elspeth to confirm all my worst suspicions.

"You have so much Potential," she said, and somehow it sounded different than when parents or teachers had said it in the past. No hope or disappointment, only wonder.

Relief washed over me, and I laughed at the earnestness in her wide eyes. Potential. I'd been hearing it my whole life. What good was potential that was never realized? *No Gift. No magic. No curse.*

Maybe Caleb was right about the panic attacks. That made more sense than a mysterious bind covering even more mysterious untapped potential. This had gone far enough. We had to find Shiri before everyone cleared out.

"Okay, thanks, El," I said, standing. "I'll try and live up to —"

"Just wait!" She pushed me back down. "I'm sorry. Just, give me a sec." She pulled a small pair of half-moon glasses out of the patched pocket of her skirt and put them on.

I tried to hold still as she inspected me, picking at invisible threads. Finally, she pulled off the glasses. She twisted them between her fingers, mesmerized by little flashes of light off the pink lenses.

"Well?" I asked. My brothers said nothing.

She ignored me. Her tongue stuck out a little, her brows furrowed. Eventually, she nodded, folded up the glasses, and put them away. Then she sat on her hands and looked up, making eye contact for the first time in probably five minutes or more.

"Well?" I asked again.

She smiled apologetically. "Yeah," she said, "You're cursed."

"I'm what?" *No. She said I had potential.* You didn't say that to somebody under the effects of a hexing honest-to-Gaia malediction.

"Cursed. Well, bound. Well, it's a curse that's binding you."

Thomas looked as confused as I felt. Caleb rubbed his mouth.

"You want to try again?" I asked. *Maybe she's the one who needs an exam.*

Elspeth stood and paced the room, occasionally glancing back at me as though trying to catch the curse by surprise. Thomas started to say something, but she waved him off. She came back around and stood in front of me, crossing her arms.

"There's like this... net. Threads are twisted and knotted together," she gestured at the space around me. "It's wrapped all the way around and then tied over... here," she gestured to the middle of my forehead. "Can't you feel it?"

I shrugged. I felt a lot of things. Mostly nausea. And maybe the beginnings of an actual panic attack. "What about the thing underneath..." I pointed awkwardly at myself, where she said she found something hidden.

"That's what's weird."

I raised an eyebrow. "That's weird?"

"Well, you know, this is crazy because who has a Gift like that? Except maybe Alice, but you're not— I mean, you don't —I don't even—"

"El?"

"Sorry. Look, a Gift like that, it could power the Gate."

"Alice was right," Caleb whispered.

"What? No. No. I don't have a Gift. I'm not the next Gatekeeper."

"If she had a Gift that strong, wouldn't we know it?" Thomas came around the desk and sat in the Speaker's chair.

Caleb glared at him.

"What? We're all thinking it. Something that big? You're saying she has more power than..." He waved around the room.

"She might be stronger than Alice," Elspeth said.

"And no one saw it? I'm sorry, Cate. You're my sister, and I love you, but how is that possible?"

I couldn't even fault him. Thomas was right. What Elspeth was saying wasn't possible. It had to be the card. I pulled it out.

"What's that?" Caleb asked.

I handed it to Elspeth. It was still warm. "I tried to show

you this before. I'm pretty sure it's charmed. That's where the magic is coming from. Not me."

She turned it over once and handed it to Caleb. Even in their hands, I felt the energy coming off of it. "Shield that for a sec?"

He pushed off the desk and looked around the office. The Speaker kept a small collection of crystals on a shelf behind the desk. He lifted the black tourmaline and set it on top of the card.

The heat of the card dissipated, but didn't disappear. Caleb frowned. He opened a desk drawer and dropped the card inside, setting the crystal back on top of it before he closed the drawer. Satisfied, he gave Elspeth a thumbs up.

Thomas pulled the drawer open a crack, peeking inside. When Caleb gave him a look, he closed it again.

Elspeth put her hand over my heart and closed her eyes. "Yeah, it's still there. The energy. It's not coming from the card. It's coming from you. Your Gift. This binding spell is blocking it."

"Can you remove the bind?" Thomas asked, snooping through the next drawer.

The healer shook her head, opening her eyes and dropping her hand back to her lap. "A bind like that can only be broken by the one who cast it."

"Where did it come from?" I asked. "Who did this to me? Why?"

"I don't know. This wasn't easy. It would have to be done carefully by someone who had a very good reason. But they'd have to be someone..." she hesitated before meeting my gaze. "Someone close. And someone very strong."

16

Someone with a slightly ominous list of the residents of Queen's Creek with arcane symbols next to their names?" Thomas bent over a binder he'd found in one of the desk drawers, rifling pages.

"What's that?" Caleb slid the binder across the desk.

"It's sketchy, is what it is." Thomas opened another drawer.

Caleb pushed the binder to where Elspeth and I could see it, running a finger down the page listing the Corey family names. "These are elemental identifiers. See? The triangle with the line through it next to my name? It represents air. And this one, the triangle next to Thomas's name? That's fire. These are the elements that align with our Gifts."

Sarah Corey had an upright triangle like Thomas's.

Marcus Corey, the symbol for air like Caleb's.

Matthew's and Jonathan's also looked like Caleb's but reversed. The triangles pointed down.

"Earth," Caleb said.

Gabriel had the fire symbol.

Benjamin's was the fire symbol reversed. "Water."

And next to my name, a circle. "What does that mean?"

"Spirit."

All the times Dad had excused my childhood outbursts by saying, "She's just spirited, our Cate," flashed through my mind. Had he known? Was he watching for my Gift to surface?

But it never had because someone had bound it.

"Why does she have this?" *Why does she know more about my Gift than I do?*

"Well, she's the Speaker. It's a census, right? Or, um, a registry?" Elspeth offered.

"I don't remember registering. Do you?" Thomas asked.

Caleb cocked his head toward the door, listening. Then he pulled the binder from me, flipping it closed and handing it to Thomas. "Put this back where you got it. We should get out there. They're starting to disperse."

He pulled the card out from under the tourmaline in the drawer and put the crystal on the shelf.

The young man on the tarot card looked as discouraged as I felt. The Four of Cups invited contemplation and warned against missed opportunities. But what opportunity was there in being trapped and bound?

I shoved the card back into my pocket.

Someone in the gathering room might be responsible for binding my Gift. I needed to know for sure. It was more important than ever to talk to Shiri and find out why she'd distracted me from the Reading. Who else was hiding things from me?

Elspeth touched my shoulder as she stood. "We'll figure this out, okay? But tonight, you need to get some rest."

I nodded, not trusting my words to convince her of patience I didn't have. Pushing out of the chair slowly, I let Caleb and Elspeth leave first.

"Where do you think she went?" I asked Thomas as we left the office. Although a lot of people had cleared out, small groups still clustered around the meeting room, and some students were playing around, using the event as an excuse to stay out late.

I spotted Mom talking with the Gosnalls. Caleb and Elspeth went to stand nearby. Benjamin was having an intense discussion with a member of the Watch. Well, Benjamin was intense. The Watchman looked bored. I didn't see Jonathan, but he'd probably taken the kids home to bed. They still had classes tomorrow.

To his credit, Thomas remembered his promise to help me confront the humming Maiden. He eyed the platform, where the ritual instruments were still set up. "I'd think she'd be helping Mrs. Kirk with— Oh, there she is," he nodded toward the large cabinet on the far side of the room where the materials were stored. Mrs. Kirk took a handful of candles from a young woman and stored them away. Shiri had taken off the dark cloak she wore for the ritual, but it was definitely her.

Now I could see that her hair wasn't the only thing she'd changed. She must have been going through the experimental phase where magical teens think they need to try All The Things just because they can. Her bare arms were covered in watercolor tattoos of butterflies and wildflowers. If I'd been closer, I was pretty sure I'd be able to see the wings flap or the flowers glisten with dew. Some trends last longer than others in a closed community, and motion tatts were just starting to get big when I left.

Screw it. I'm done. She's going to tell me what she did to me. And why.

I got one step in before Thomas grabbed my arm.

"Hold up," he said. "What are you going to do?"

"What do you think I'm going to do? I'm going to go over there and make her talk to me."

Thomas raised an eyebrow.

"Nicely," I added.

"Look, I'm not saying she won't deserve whatever you do. But." He raised his hands as I tried to step around him. "But," he said again, "this is maybe a situation that calls for a slightly less direct approach."

He smiled hopefully, showing his perfect teeth again. Flash of light, chimes, the whole thing. He may as well have been batting his eyes.

"You really think that's going to work on her? Pretty sure her Gift is at least as strong as yours."

"I guess we'll see, won't we?" He winked and pivoted away from me.

He caught up to Shiri as she gathered the tools from the altar. When she lifted the athamé by its black stone handle, he fell to his knees and raised his hands. She gasped.

I rolled my eyes. I couldn't hear what he said, but it went over well. She giggled. He shifted his weight to one leg, bowed his head, and put his hands on his knee. For a second, she looked confused, then she straightened, smoothed her long, green skirt, and formally tapped each of his shoulders with the flat side of the knife.

Definitely a "less direct approach." I briefly entertained a fantasy in which I dragged her out by the yellow tips of her wavy ponytail and used the ritual knife to encourage some honesty. *I would never do that, of course. Obviously.*

Shiri put the athamé back down on the altar and reached out to help Thomas up. Her shining knight planted a quick kiss on her hand, then stood, raised her arm, and spun her around. She laughed again.

The teens across the room snickered at the strange performance, but most of the adults either smiled and shook their heads or completely ignored the show Thomas was putting on. My brother had always loved to be the center of attention.

I hope he's enjoying himself. It's not going to last long. A couple of boys who had definitely already been causing trouble as initiates three years ago were up to something. Probably something dangerous and stupid. They were doing that slow, meandering walk younger guys did when they wanted to be sneaky. The slow, ducking moves that actually drew way more attention than if they just walked across the room with a sense of purpose. I looked around to see if anyone else had noticed.

Please don't be stupid and make me get involved. I won't. It's none of my business. I am not their mother. They are somebody else's problem. There. The Watchman who was talking to Benjamin was on to them. Benjamin had moved to the other side of the room, but he was watching them, too. *Good.*

Mrs. Kirk was not watching them. She was watching me. When she saw me looking, she smiled, and it almost felt friendly, except that it didn't quite reach her eyes. After a moment, she turned back to the cabinet, folding a cloak and tucking it onto a shelf. Shiri wasn't the only one we needed to talk to. *Come on, Thomas. Work your magic and get back here.*

The explosion was loud and bright, and the kid who set it off disappeared almost immediately. His friends were less skilled with their magical exits. Two of them gave up and charged the door behind me. I jumped back and slammed into a wall.

No. Not a wall. Adam. He gripped my arms to stabilize me, but he wasn't quite quick enough, and his chin bounced off the top of my head. He grunted. My teeth jarred, and I was dizzy for a second. Then I pulled myself away and faced him. He rubbed his jaw. *I hope it hurts.*

"Are you okay?" he asked.

"Shouldn't you be going after them?" I said, raising my hand to my head. The old bump was still there. My head ached, but I didn't feel any new injuries.

"I'm off duty," he said. "Besides, this is not my jurisdiction. Dad can handle it."

Giles directed Watchman Hale after the kids. The Watch Commander's hand reached out in a fist. As the Watchman took off, Giles waved his other hand across the space in front of him. A short, blond boy gradually came into focus. The back of his shirt was twisted in Giles's outstretched fist. The kid stopped squirming as soon as he realized that he was visible. Giles frowned at him, but the kid's embarrassed parents came to claim him and blocked my view before I could hear what he said.

"That was a pretty impressive glamour for an apprentice," said Adam, completely ignoring the fact that the explosive residue of the suspect's flashbang streaked the floor.

"Somebody could have been hurt," I said.

"Nah, that's more your thing."

"What is your problem?"

"Forget it," he said. "You should go home. Get some rest. It's been a long day." He started to walk away.

"Do not tell me to forget it," I said through my clenched teeth.

He stopped, but only turned halfway to respond over his shoulder. "What do you want me to say?" he asked. "I'm tired. I said my piece during the Reading. I don't have anything to add." His shoulders sagged, making his whole body seem smaller.

"Tell me," I said. "Tell me—"

Someone gently pressed on my back to get around me. I was blocking the door again. I stepped forward to allow some of my neighbors to pass. People were filing out into the early morning darkness now that the Reading was over, and the kids had been caught. On the verge of either adding to the violence or collapsing on the floor, I reached for Adam's arm, but he pulled away.

"Just go home. It's over." And then he was gone.

"No!" I yelled. I felt the edge of a memory. It wasn't something I could see, but this frustration was familiar. It was more personal than the usual annoyance at my brother's friend.

Thomas appeared by my side, Caleb and Elspeth not far behind.

Across the room, Mom looked up, her eyes pained. She was too far away to hear her voice, but my name was on her lips. Mrs. Gosnall patted her arm, and then she and her husband followed the crowd out a side door, pointing Benjamin in Mom's direction as they passed.

"Let us know if you need anything," Mr. Gosnall told him.

Benjamin nodded.

Thomas wrapped his arms around me. The pressure of his embrace grounded me. I let go of the faded memory, and it vanished completely. All I could see were the feet of people shuffling out. Raising my head to his shoulder, I took in the drawn expressions on my brothers' faces and the tears shining in Mom's eyes. The full force of my failure hit me.

"It's not over," I said into his neck. "They got it wrong. Dad would never."

"Shhh," said Thomas gently. Then he whispered, "We can talk at home. Get it together. Not here."

Caleb rubbed my back. Elspeth murmured something to him, and he nodded.

"Take it slow," Caleb said. "We'll all go together. Don't rush it."

17

The walk home was the saddest, slowest parade in history. Once we got out of the Tower, the way was mostly clear. Our neighbors had taken their own paths or blinked out. Caleb and Elspeth led the way, hand in hand. Mom trailed behind, talking softly with Benjamin.

There were a series of hugs as we passed the healer's cottage. Caleb walked Elspeth inside, telling Mom he'd catch up later. Back at my parents' house, Benjamin disappeared, probably to his old room.

"Your room is where you left it," Mom told me as we walked in through the kitchen. "I put fresh sheets on the bed, and there are towels..."

"I'll find them. Is there anything you need?" There were so many things I wanted to tell her, questions I needed to ask, but I couldn't burden her now. Not when I could see what the Reading had taken out of her.

She steadied herself with a hand on the table. "I'm just glad you're home."

I hugged her. I'd been taller than her for a few years, but she'd never seemed so small. "I love you, Mom," I whispered.

"Love you, Mom," Thomas echoed. "Goodnight."

"Get some rest," she said. She stepped out of her shoes and left them at the door before padding off to bed in her bare feet.

We were all exhausted, but Thomas led me out to the garden, past the lavender that lined the stone path from our kitchen door. I inhaled the rosemary at the wooden gate and swung the low door shut behind me out of habit to keep out the rabbits and the deer.

"You good?" Thomas asked. He snapped his fingers and the fairy lights strung over the garden twinkled, casting a cool glow over the raised beds.

I rubbed my head. "What are you even saying right now? Am I good? No. I am not good. I am cursed. Clearly. Coming back here was a mistake."

"It's not like that," Thomas said.

"It's just like that. Whenever I'm around magic, trouble follows. I was fine in Chicago. No emergencies. No injuries. I've been home less than twenty-four hours, and I've almost drowned, got a concussion, and apparently started suffering from magically-induced blackouts brought on by the granddaughter of the most powerful witch in the community. Not to mention this revelation that I somehow have a Gift I never knew about, and the Speaker of our coven may have done something to hide it from me."

"I wouldn't say she's the most powerful..." Thomas said. "I mean, a water-based elemental Gift is going to be useful in a community bounded by an enchanted Creek, but I'm pretty sure she's mostly limited to hydromancy. It's not like she..." Thomas looked at me. "Oh, you meant politically." He frowned. "Is she though? I always thought Speaker was kind of a figurehead position."

"Still not the point," I said.

"It's going to be fine."

I wished it were true.

He picked a leaf off the mint escaping its half-buried container and growing wild on both sides of our garden fence. He rolled it between his fingers, releasing the sticky scent.

The crushed mint cleared my head. *I swear to the goddess in all her forms, if Thomas is trying to use his Gift to pacify me, he will regret it.* "It's not fine, Thomas! It is not going to be fine!"

Thomas glanced back at Mom's window. Her light was out, but the window was cracked to let in the evening breeze. "Keep it down, okay?"

Ugh. Logic and empathy. Worse than magic. I hate it when he's right. I lowered my voice but didn't soften the edge. "Look, I'm glad you had a nice time flirting with that kid, but I don't have a magical defense against whatever she's decided to do to me. I thought you were going over there to help me," I said. "I guess I'm on my own again."

Embracing my moment of self-pity, I turned away from him and examined the edible flowers growing along the back of the small kitchen plot. Calendula, yarrow, and dianthus bloomed, their colors bright even under the dim fairy lights. None of them seemed affected by the snow that fell earlier. In fact, nothing in the garden was even wet.

"Save the drama for the stage, Cate. I am helping you."

"How's that?" I said, still half ignoring him. I ran my fingers over a downy but dry sage leaf. Snow in March was strange enough, beyond improbable in Virginia. Snow that confined itself to the center of town verged on impossible. And yet, when I ran my hand through my hair, I still came away with melted droplets on my fingers. I turned around and considered the way the light caught Thomas's waves. *What is happening with the weather?*

Thomas frowned. "First of all, I wasn't flirting with that teenager. Eww. I was building rapport. I just suggested that she trust me."

Right. Focus. Pick your poison. The weather is a tomorrow problem.

"Sure. You were being suggestive." It wasn't the first time he'd heard a snarky comment about his Gift, but when your brother had muse-like abilities to influence people, sometimes he needed to be reminded that his charm didn't work on everyone.

"Whatever. It worked," he said. "She admitted to casting during the reading."

"She did?" *Interesting.* There wasn't really any way to regulate magic use but most witches would draw an invisible line at using it against others. '*And it harm none,' and all that.*

Thomas's Gift skirted the taboo because he mostly inspired people to act on things they already believed in. It'd gotten him into trouble a few times.

"What did she say? What did she do to me? Why?" I asked, all of my fears coming out at once.

"She didn't do anything to you. I mean, she doesn't know why you blacked out. That's not what she was doing," he said.

"What was she doing then?" *If I could just get answers to one of my questions, I might be able to hold it together to work out the rest.*

"She was a distraction. The Speaker told her she was concerned some people might be upset..."

"Might be?" I couldn't believe how indifferent the Crone was to our family's loss.

"Right. So. She told Shiri to set a more chill mood."

"She's a DJ?" I asked, raising my eyebrows. My mother had just become a widow, the school had lost its best teacher, the community was without an alchemist for the first time, maybe ever, and all the Speaker of the Coven cared about was maintaining the mood of the ritual?

"Yeah. Umm. She was supposed to just kind of send out a calm vibe to keep people from overreacting to the report."

"Overreacting? Or reacting at all? She didn't want anyone to interfere. This has to be illegal. They can't stop us from dissenting the findings of an investigation. The whole point of having a Reading is to keep the community involved!" I needed something to throw.

"I don't think she meant to," Thomas started.

"She didn't mean to? I completely missed the most important part of the Reading, but it's okay because she didn't mean to do it?" I yelled. My hands flew out, but nothing was close enough to make contact.

"I don't think that part was her," he said.

"Who was it then? You just said she admitted it! The Speaker told her to! She must be the first teenager in history to do everything her grandmother tells her to do. Lucky us." I crossed my arms and balled my fists.

"I don't know what's going on with you, but Shiri is a baby witch. She's not that powerful. I didn't even have to push her that hard to get her to talk to me. I don't think she could fully black you out if she wanted to. And why would she want to? You saw her. She's literally a rainbow child. It's all sunshine in there."

"Then the Speaker must have done it herself. Mrs. Kirk is hiding something," I said through gritted teeth.

"No doubt," he agreed. "But what can we do about it now?"

"Now?" My head throbbed. My eyes itched. I couldn't stop the yawn that forced its way out. It was still way too early for sunrise, but the sky was undeniably lighter than it had been when we left the Tower. "Nothing," I admitted.

I looked up at the stars, so much brighter here than in the city. The same stars, but the sky here didn't glow with competing light from street lamps, buildings, and billboards.

It made them feel closer. It was kind of terrifying to see your place in the universe without the veil of light pollution. I closed my eyes, and when I opened them, I was alone in the garden.

So, I guess this was goodnight? With all the intrigue and covert efforts to find out why I missed the reports at the reading, we never got around to *what* I missed at the reading. The whole reason I came home: to find out what happened to Dad, to understand why the Watch thought he chose to disappear. I couldn't believe Thomas thought we were done here.

But I was too tired to chase him to his room and hold a whispered argument about conversational etiquette. And I couldn't ask Mom to relive it. Plus, I didn't really want to wake her up just to get into why I missed it in the first place. My glasses slipped down again. I shoved them back on my nose. Sighing, I made my way back to my old room, where I collapsed on an unfamiliar bed just as the sun pinked the sky outside my window.

Unwilling to get up to close the curtains against the encroaching daylight, I dropped my glasses on the nightstand and smashed my face into the pillow. My exhausted brain promptly produced five or ten really interesting ways I could have reacted to tonight's events if only I'd thought of them in the moment. A lot of them involved shouting at Mrs. Kirk. My favorite was when I just yelled, *Stop!* like on the plane. *We've got to be past most of the turbulence now.* I wished I could rewind it all. I'd turn the volume way up or maybe just mute Shiri for a minute. *Thomas better be ready to give a full report tomorrow.*

When I finally slept, I dreamt I was lost in the woods outside of Queen's Creek. At first, I couldn't find the Gate. I couldn't even see the boundary, like some kind of mundane. Then I stumbled, and when I reached out to catch myself, I pushed through a spiderweb I didn't see. The invisible threads stuck to my face and arms. On the other side, the Creek caught the sunlight and sparkled like the stars.

18

The King of Wands held his staff in his hand as he sat on a throne decorated with lions, a charismatic leader with a clear vision. As I lay in bed, more lost than ever, I assumed the card was attaching itself to my feelings for my father. He always knew what to do.

Did I miss the window for Nora's moment of need where it would've been useful? Could've used a better warning before the Reading. Useless Knight of Cups.

Like many kids who grew up here, I started studying the cards at a young age. First, it was a game, then a guide for meditation. Eventually, I developed my intuition enough to quickly catch the meaning behind the images and make connections to the world around me. But they'd never been foolproof in their directives. Tarot reading wasn't always magical. (Maybe that was why the cards worked for me.) The cards were a tool for introspection, prompting you to think of things from different points of view and to put ideas and experiences in perspective.

In retrospect, the Knight of Cups might have been a warning against letting my emotions guide my actions. It might have been telling me to be more active in achieving the things I cared about. Or the message might be something else entirely.

Sometimes court cards like knights and kings stood in for a person you knew. This Knight was charming and idealistic. More like Thomas than Adam. *The interpretation should be guided by the reader's intention in the moment.*

What had I asked Nora's card while standing on the forest path? I was practicing my dissent. Adam was an ass. He said... something about staying away. He told me I wouldn't like what I heard.

I'll bet I wouldn't have. If I had heard it. I grabbed my pillow and gripped it tightly in both hands. I should've screamed into it or thrown it against the wall. Instead, I mashed my fists into it and slammed it back against the headboard.

They'd pronounced Dad officially dead. It didn't matter that it didn't make any sense. That nobody crossed the Creek. That Dad was happy the last time I saw him. As far as the community was concerned, his death was in the record. *What does that mean for Mom?*

I'd been to funerals before. My grandparents died when I was young. I knew what to expect from the rituals and ceremonies surrounding the death of a loved one, but I didn't know how we moved forward now. This wasn't like when someone died of old age, the expected closing of a circle we all saw coming.

When the late morning (or was it early afternoon?) sunlight had splashed across my face half an hour ago, ending what little rest I could pull from the last hours of night, I had pulled the quilt over my head and consulted Nora's card in semi-darkness. *I don't want this. I don't want to be here. I don't want this to be my life. Why is this my life? What's happening to me? What's happening to my family? What happened to Matthew and Gabriel? Where is my father?*

It might have been too much for one tarot card.

I overwhelmed it with too many intentions, and all it could latch onto was that last thought. My father. The King of Wands.

The King of Wands was fearless and determined. He faced his problems and solved them. *Take the hint.*

I would very much have preferred to continue sulking and wondering and panicking in my room, but movement down the hall made that impossible. *Time to face today's problems.* Starting with checking in with whoever was shuffling around.

In the kitchen, Mom sat at a table that seemed much smaller than it used to be, and not just because someone had taken out the extra leaves we needed when all of my brothers lived at home. Papers and photos covered its surface. Mom leaned back in her chair, cradling a steaming mug in both hands.

She looked up. "Good morning. Did you sleep? How's your head?"

"A bit. Still a little dizzy."

"You should sit."

"I will."

I checked the stove to see what was in her pot. Last night's rest (well, this morning's rest) was as restorative as you could expect after crossing the country, running through the woods, suffering unexplainable mental and emotional trauma, and collapsing on an unfamiliar mattress just before dawn.

It's coffee. Blessed Be.

I poured a cup into an earthenware mug with a spider carved into the bottom. One of Thomas's jokes, or an artistic representation of nature's beauty by Caleb.

"It was wrong of the Speaker to ambush you like that."

"Did you know?" *About the Speaker's plans? About my Gift? About the bind?*

"I'm sorry. I should have seen it coming. But I never would

have thought so soon. That wasn't why you came home. I thought we had more time, but there's never enough, is there?"

"I'm sorry, Mom," I said.

She sighed. "For what, dear?" she asked, sipping her brew.

"I came home to stop them. I failed."

"There was nothing you could have done."

"I could have dissented." The next words came out before I thought them through. "Why didn't you? Why didn't anybody…"

Mom held up a hand. "Stop. You weren't here. You don't know what it was like."

"What happened, Mom?"

"He wasn't himself."

"What do you mean?"

She put her cup down on the table and rubbed her eyes. "It was a lot. He was working on… we were working on something together. And it didn't go as planned. He was disappointed, but he kept going. He was working all the time. I couldn't keep up."

"What were you working on?"

"I don't want you to worry," she said as if that were possible. As if I hadn't been worried since Thomas showed up at the café with the news.

"Mom…" I didn't continue because I couldn't think of any way to word how frustrating and patronizing her concern felt. *What could I possibly say that wouldn't either hurt her and make me feel like the worst child ever or make her angry and end any possibility of her explaining what happened?* I had nothing. So I waited.

"There's a problem with the Source," she told the mug.

I stared at her mug. I looked down at mine. When I looked up, she'd shifted her gaze to my face.

Click.

"The Source of magic?" My eyebrows got lost in my hairline, and my glasses slid down my nose. This was worse than the boundary spell failing. "There's a problem with the Source of magic? And you didn't want to worry me? You don't think that's something people should know? Does Thomas know?"

"We thought we could handle it," she said. "And no, your brother doesn't know. At first, we only told the Speaker. We didn't want people to panic. According to your father's calculations..."

"People are going to panic, Mom. They should panic. What kind of problem?" Just because I couldn't do magic didn't mean I wasn't affected by it. The entire culture of Queen's Creek was built around the community's connection to the Source. If there was a problem, it would impact our entire way of life.

"It's unstable," she said. "There have been... glitches in the flow of power. Especially around the Creek. We think it's affecting the boundary spell. You heard what Mrs. Kirk said, but that's just the beginning."

I pictured the view from Alice's windows in the Gatehouse. How it was pouring on one side and sunny on the other. The time shift from nightfall outside to late afternoon inside.

Had it been like that when I left? What about my test? Was it possible I hadn't screwed it up? What if the bridge glitched?

Probably not. It was more likely I ended up underwater because I took the first step before the Guardian cleared me to do it. Or, you know, because I was cursed.

"How bad is it? What's causing it?" *Don't say the Gatekeeper.*

"It's pretty bad," Mom admitted. "I don't know exactly what's causing it. Your father had ideas. He was studying energy transfers at different points along the boundary."

The boundary that ran along the Creek around the

community. The boundary that hid us from the outside world, protected us by keeping magic mostly trapped inside with people who had been trained to wield it. Except when the Gifted took it with them through the Gate for their Wakenings. Except if someone crossed the Creek.

I suddenly realized why a magic user crossing the Creek without passing through the enchanted Gatehouse was prohibited.

It should be impossible. The magic should bounce back, bringing the witch with it. If it didn't... Could someone with a strong enough Gift push through? What happened to the boundary? Was it all full of holes? Or what if... Could the magic be separated from the witch? Would the magic stay inside while the man walked free into the woods on the other side? Was Dad out there somewhere without his Gift? Did he know who he was if part of him was missing?

"What did he find out?" I asked, even as the question was overrun by a whole series of follow-ups: *if the energy dipped in certain places... would it be easier to cross? Or would it tear bigger holes in the boundary?*

"His research wasn't finished. He went to meet with the Speaker." Her tone dropped just a bit when she mentioned Mrs. Kirk, but it might have indicated disappointment or distaste.

Would Mom have supported Dad if he'd run for the position? Back before all of this.

"He needed support for more tests, but he came back raving that she wouldn't listen. She didn't believe we were at risk." She frowned. "She told him to drop it."

"But he didn't."

"No. He became obsessed. He kept trying to tell people time was running out. That the boundary would fail."

"Why?"

"I'm not sure. He became difficult to listen to after that. Angry, short-tempered. I begged him to take a break. He wouldn't listen." She paused, covering her mouth and taking a deep breath through her nose. For a moment, she closed her eyes. Then she spread her hands on the table as if she could smooth out the already buffed knots in the wooden top.

When she looked up, her eyes were full. "But I believed him. There is something very wrong at the Source. We're only starting to see the effects, but your father... he... he got too close," she said, taking a shaky breath.

"Mom."

She stood. "No. I'm sorry. I can't talk about this anymore."

19

We have to talk about it, Mom." I didn't know which questions to ask first, but this conversation was far from over.

The Source of magic was so unstable that it affected the boundary protecting us from mundanes, and when he spoke out about it, my father disappeared.

My eldest brothers hadn't shown up to the Reading where the Speaker of our community declared him dead.

And after years of believing there was something wrong with me and depending on the Craft for things everyone in my family could do without thinking, I now knew that someone had bound my Gift. Why? What did anyone have to gain by keeping my magic from me?

My mother stood silently in the doorway. She looked so defeated.

"Please tell me what happened."

"You are so like him."

"Mom."

"Really. Sometimes, you have that look. When you're puzzling it all out, but you already know the answer. The way you wrinkle your nose. That's your father in you."

"Why didn't you say anything? If you believed him, why didn't you do something?"

"And always asking difficult questions." She picked at her nails. "They sound open, but they're not. Judgmental, rhetorical questions disguised as idle curiosity."

The tension in her voice surprised me. She'd never spoken against my father. Never shown anything but playful devotion. I started to wonder who my parents were before I was born. And why I'd never considered it before. *My parents are people. They had whole lives that had nothing to do with me.*

But she still hadn't answered my question.

Fine. We won't talk about Dad. Start with the easiest to explain. "Where are Matthew and Gabriel, then? Why weren't they at the Reading?"

She looked around the kitchen, this family space disrupted by stacks of papers pulled from our bookcases and drawers. It should have been full of noise, not notes. "Come."

She led me down the hall, and we sat together on her bed. I'd been invited in only a few times before—when she thought I was about to start menstruating, when she thought I was in love with a boy, when she thought I loved a girl— otherwise, she always kept the door closed. This was a safe, sacred space, but I'd always felt awkward sitting on the soft blanket. She propped herself up against the wooden headboard, drawing her knees to her chest like a child. She waited as if she knew what I wanted to say.

The Tower. Two figures falling. My vision.

"They went into the Creek," I said. *Nobody crosses the Creek.* Except apparently, they did. Why? Where did they go? What happens now?

She nodded.

"Before Dad." My family was disappearing one by one. It wasn't supposed to be them. I was the chosen sacrifice. My life given to the Gatehouse. My energy linked to the boundary spell for the good of all. Was Mrs. Kirk right? Would it all stop if I accepted the responsibility? *There's always another way.*

She sighed and picked at her fingernails again.

"What happened while I was gone, Mom?"

"The Speaker is right about Alice. Our Gatekeeper weakens every day. She should have been replaced long ago."

"Then why send me away? Why let me go out on my Wakening when the boundary spell was breaking?" *Why would anyone bind my Gift?* I held back the hardest question, afraid of what the answer might be.

She held my hand. "It was because the boundary spell was breaking that we sent you. There's something wrong. Something more than what's happening to Alice. We couldn't allow you to be trapped in that Gatehouse for nothing. You deserve more than that."

I tried to imagine what it was like. Living alone in the Gatehouse. Seeing the community change, become more fearful of the outside. Watching the young ones dare each other to come near the Creek. Testing themselves against the rules of our community. Taking unnecessary risks.

We'd never done that. The Creek was dangerous and off-limits. I'd seen it the first time when I snuck out with Elspeth a few days before her brother left for his Wakening. Even the shimmer of the moon reflecting on the ripples seemed vaguely sinister. I hadn't been afraid, exactly, but it didn't seem like the kind of place you'd want to spend much time. *And Alice expects me to succeed her, living in those empty rooms, watching over the Creek through the enchanted windows. Not in this lifetime.*

When I looked up, she avoided my eyes. The coffee soured in my stomach. *How far would she go to keep me from becoming the next Gatekeeper?*

"Mom, what did you…"

She held up a hand. "Let me continue, or I'll never get it out."

I chewed my lip. Half-formed accusations tickled my throat, but this was my mother, and I wasn't ready to speak them. I nodded.

"The Speaker gave your father a project, something she thought could help Alice. So the boys focused on the boundary. Gabriel had an idea. He was the one who started testing the energy readings around the Creek. Something about the wisps he saw when he came in from his Wakening. More of them than there should have been. Your dad thought he had something."

It would have made Gabriel so proud. He'd always competed with Matthew for Dad's attention. Matthew's Gift for transmutation made him the perfect apprentice alchemist. He and Dad had so much in common, but Gabriel wanted it more. He'd proven himself over and over again through his studies.

I waited for Mom to continue.

"The boys went out every day, running their tests."

"What did they learn?"

"There's so much we still don't know about where our magic comes from. I wonder if the founders did. It was such a different time. Maybe it wasn't meant to last."

What was she saying?

"How many Gatekeepers have there been? How many generations have we trapped inside the Creek because we were too afraid to face what's on the other side? Maybe it's time for a change."

Fighting Freya, my mother's a secret revolutionary.

"Matthew thought we could still fix it, find a way to balance the energy. Gabriel didn't want to wait. He said the energy had already built up too much to dissipate safely."

"What did he do?"

Her eyes unfocused, searching the memory for a way to explain. She shook her head. "I don't know. Matthew went to the Creek to talk to Gabriel, but they never came back. And then your father—"

"What do you mean 'they never came back'? My brothers disappeared at the Creek and nobody did anything?"

Mom's mouth tightened. "And then your father," she said again, "went down to look for them."

And he disappeared, too. "Why didn't you report what happened? Shouldn't this have been part of Giles' investigation? They're still missing. Is anybody looking for them? At the very least, it explains what Dad was doing there, that it was an accident."

"They were breaking the law, Cate. You know the consequences."

I hate consequences.

How did you control a closed community, already locked inside a Gate? A death sentence would make us no better than the hunters. They'd have shunned her for this. Maybe worse.

If they'd found her guilty of tampering with the boundary spell, even by association, they would have bound her connection to the Source. No magic for those who didn't appreciate what we'd sacrificed to save it.

It was the life I'd always feared. Trapped in Queen's Creek without access to magical energy.

Was that what had happened to me? If my binding was a punishment, what had I ever done to deserve Queen's Creek's justice?

20

What do you mean the boundary's coming down?" Thomas asked when he finally rolled out of bed. "It can't come down."

I pushed out the chair next to me, and he sat, shoving the papers Mom had been assembling back from the edge of the table. Some of them were family records and photos: the kinds of things we needed to organize before the end of life and return to earth rites could be performed. Some were Dad's notes. We needed to talk about those pages. But first…

"Did Mom tell you about Matthew and Gabriel?"

The papers in front of him suddenly became very interesting.

"Hex-in-a-handbasket, Thomas. Anything else you're keeping to yourself?"

"I'm sorry. I should have said something last night, but you know. We were dealing with the whole "who-bound-my-sister?" problem. It seemed more urgent than giving you a status report on our missing siblings."

"But they're missing!"

"Yeah, I know. But Mom knows where they are, and she's

not panicking yet, so…"

He had a point. She hadn't reported them missing, and she wasn't mourning them. Did she have a plan to get them back? Why wouldn't she have told me?

Somebody is going to tell me what I'm missing before I completely lose my mind.

I rubbed my fingers, forcing my fists to unclench.

Starting with what I missed during my blackout at the Reading last night.

I turned to face Thomas directly. He smiled, although it took his eyes just a second to catch up. If I hadn't been trying so hard to hold down my admittedly irrational, misdirected anger, I might have been concerned by how completely he hid his pain. I put my hands on my knees and concentrated on not bouncing my legs.

"Thomas," I said.

"Cate," he mimicked, grinning.

I glared.

He shifted, composed himself, and softly apologized. "Sorry."

"Let's just pretend I missed the Reading entirely," I said. "Let's go ahead and operate as if you came to Chicago, gave me the news, and blinked back here, and by the time my plane landed, it was all over."

"Did you spend the night in the woods?"

"What?"

"Hypothetically. Are we saying you missed Last Light and didn't get into the Gatehouse until morning, or did you get there in time but just not to the Tower?" he asked, in total seriousness.

"Why does it matter?"

"I'm trying to get into the scene. If you spent the night in the woods, you're probably all stinky and grouchy, but if you got in earlier, you maybe got some rest, and you're in a much better mood right now. Or, wait, if I wasn't there, did you still wipe out on the bridge? Maybe you drowned. Oh, that's so sad. And spooky. Am I talking to your ghost?"

I'm going to be talking to Thomas's ghost in a minute. Would he be more cooperative if he were trying to finish his worldly business so that he could cross the veil? I bit my lip.

"Everything is fine. I came home, I didn't fall, or hit my head, or almost drown. I went straight to bed, got my eight hours, and now... Now, you're going to tell me what I missed at the Reading last night."

"Oh, okay, that's great." He adjusted his posture and relaxed back into his seat. He looked down, took a deep breath, looked up, and grinned. "Good morning, Cate!" he said. "Sleep well?"

Dear Mother. With enormous effort, I stopped myself from rolling my eyes. I smiled and even threw in a little yawn and a stretch. The stretch actually felt really good.

"Good morning, Thomas. Yes, thanks. What did I miss at the Reading last night?"

"So, they had me and Mom stand up for the Last Light ritual. I know it's supposed to be an honor or whatever, but it felt kind of exploitative..."

My hands returned to fists on my knees. "Wow. That does seem sort of presumptuous. I'm sorry that happened to you." *This is fine. I can play along. He'll get there eventually.*

Thomas shrugged, "Yeah, thanks. So, then they had these little cakes for the offering. Something with poppyseed, I think. Anyways, they were pretty good, much better than those moon cookies we had at the last equinox."

"Thomas," I said. "The Reading?" *Goddess of the Sea and Sky, why does everything have to be a game?* This was probably why I majored in theater. I had so much practice supporting Thomas's scenes.

Thomas reached for my coffee mug and took a sip, then

grimaced. "I was getting to that." Pushing the mug back to me, he took a breath and looked me in the eye. He dropped the character he'd been playing. "You're not going to like it," he said simply.

"I wish people would stop trying to tell me what I'm going to like. It doesn't hexing matter whether or not I like it. I need to know."

"Language," he admonished.

I closed my eyes and counted to ten.

He immediately regretted his playful tone. "Sorry. Okay. They declared him dead. I wish it weren't true, but I believe them. He walked into the Creek, and he didn't come out."

"Why? Why would he do that? And how do they know..."

"Adam saw it happen. He was on duty at the Gate. He heard something and followed the Creek to that place where the rocks are. You know, where it looks like you could hop right across if it weren't like, completely stupid dangerous to hop across a mystical defense border that just looks like a forest stream?"

"You're saying he actually tried to walk across? Why? Nobody does that. It's forbidden for a reason." *Mom said he was looking for Matthew and Gabriel. Would he risk a crossing if he thought he could find them?*

"I don't know. But he didn't make it. Maybe he slipped, or maybe he misjudged the distance." Thomas paused, taking a closer look at one of the messier diagrams in Dad's notes. "Maybe he stepped off that rock on purpose. Adam didn't see him fall. He was already going under when he got there."

"Why didn't he do anything? Why didn't he save him?" *Some Guardian.*

Thomas thought about it. "I guess he was too late. He's a Guardian, not a lifeguard. I'm not even sure he can swim. He didn't exactly jump in after you, either, if you'll recall."

He paused to make eye contact, clearly waiting for a

response this time.

"Thank you for saving my life, Thomas." Even though I wasn't completely sure he deserved the credit after what I'd seen in my visions under the water. How *had* I gotten out?

"Aww, don't mention it," he said, waving a hand. "But you're welcome."

"Mom said they were studying the energy at the boundary. Maybe he was taking measurements. Did they say anything about his equipment? Or his notes?"

Thomas examined his nails. "Yeah, we've reached the end of my report. You know everything I know. What else did Mom say?"

"She told me he was looking for Matthew and Gabriel. That they'd been doing some kind of study at the Creek. Dad thought the Source was unstable. Out of balance or something." I flipped through the piles of paper. Mixed in with Dad's lesson plans and lecture outlines, I'd found illustrated sheets covered in increasingly cramped writing and diagrams. It wasn't all easy to make out, and I might not have understood some of it, even if I could decipher the letters. I pointed at a few places where he'd circled numbers.

"These are measurements of energy, I think, and maybe dates? This looks like February something. March 20...May 1, or maybe 7... June 21..."

"Whoa." Thomas ran his fingers over a few of the papers. They came from at least three notebooks with differently-sized pages and lines. It was mostly black ink underneath, but there were also highlights, circles, and underlines in purple, green, blue, and yellow. It looked like Dad might have grabbed whatever pen or marker was at hand. He might as well have been building his own grimoire. The text was just as complex and no less mysterious.

"Yeah," I said. "It's a mess, but there's something here. Don't you think?"

He picked up a smudged sheet and looked closer. "I don't know. This stuff is pretty out there. This one is all written over. Did you see this? The paper is going yellow, but the notes on top are new. I think the base text is about an elixir. It looks like chemistry... but you're right, the new stuff is some kind of energy calculation. It doesn't make sense."

"It must have made sense to him. I wish he were here to explain it."

Thomas put the paper down on the stack I had made. "I just wish he were here."

I flattened the papers in front of me. I shouldn't have been mad. He was grieving. *I should be grieving.* Whatever happened, Dad was gone. Even Nora's card told me he wasn't coming back. The sadness was there, behind my eyes, way back in my mind, shadowing everything. But I couldn't feel it. All I felt was the anger. I needed someone to blame.

Be calm, rational.

"It might have been an accident. There's no way it was suicide."

"Either way, they found him at fault. 'Crossed the Creek of his own accord.' Investigation closed, no further justice required."

"No further investigation into the energy shifts at the boundary either." The Speaker had written off our father's concerns as a side effect of the Gatekeeper's term ending.

"The boundary has held for hundreds of years. If it is going to fail, I doubt it will happen overnight. There would be signs."

"I think it's already happening." I tapped the page in front of me, which had what looked like notes copied out of a farmer's almanac. "The glitches you told me about, for one thing. And the weather. When was the last time you saw snow here? Much less in the spring?"

Thomas clicked his tongue. "Yeah. Yeah, that was weird."

"Beyond weird."

His face cycled through several pensive expressions before he gave up and rubbed both hands through his hair. "What does Mom think we should do?" he asked with his hands still on his head.

I exhaled slowly. "She wants to forget it."

Thomas's elbows fell, and his hands slid around to cover his mouth.

"We can't leave it like this," I said.

"Maybe she's right."

"What?"

"You don't want to be here anyway," he said. "Maybe I shouldn't have come back for you."

"What?" I mean, he wasn't wrong about the first part. But that last part was insane.

Not that it hadn't crossed my mind.

If I'd never gone to the Reading, if I hadn't come home, I could have stayed in Chicago, blissfully unaware of my hobbled Gift, my family's unexpectedly increasing disappearances, and my hometown's impending doom.

But that wouldn't stop it from happening.

"So, what then? You think if you'd stayed here, I wouldn't have noticed that Dad went off the grid? I probably knew something was wrong before you did."

He raised an eyebrow.

"I didn't get a letter last week. Did you?"

Thomas bit his lip and shook his head. He sifted through the papers again. "I think he was gone a long time ago."

I didn't want to admit it, but I'd had the same thought. Especially after Mom told me how he had acted those last few weeks. Not himself. It wasn't a helpful thought. It still didn't tell me what actually happened, or where he was now. Or how to fix the problems he left behind. "We can't leave it like this," I said again, stacking the papers.

"We won't, but we have to start with Mom. First, we plan a funeral, then we save the rest of Queen's Creek. Just in time for Equinox."

Equinox.

There was something. I shifted the papers around until I came across the one I was looking for. The one with March 20 circled at the top in at least three different colors. The celebration of balance. The festival that produced more magical energy than the fireworks at the mundane's fourth of July.

Pieces slid into place. The energy imbalance. The increasing signs of uncontrolled magic. The Speaker's concerns about the strength of the Gatekeeper.

In three days, the energy from that festival would be enough to overload the boundary spell. Dad was right. It was all going to come down.

21

F amily first," Thomas said when I pointed out the deadline. "It's just a date. We don't actually know what's going to happen."

I wanted to argue. Get into a discussion of theory. Anything that would stop me from devolving into a blubbering mass of panic.

Are we still witches if we don't control the Source of magic? What's going to happen to us when the boundary comes down? But really... what is actually, literally, going to occur? Are we looking at a fizzle, pop, shimmering waves of light that fade into nothingness? Goddess, what if it's an explosion of power as all the energy tries to escape through the cracks in the invisible boundary?

I didn't know what was going to happen. I didn't know how to find out what was going to happen. There might've been clues in Dad's notes, but even Mom said he had to ask for help, and the Speaker sent him away. Whatever Mrs. Kirk knew, she wasn't going to share.

In the interest of my continued sanity and justification for Thomas's blind confidence that everything would be alright, I convinced him to help me make our own notes.

What we know: The boundary spell had been in place since

132

Queen's Creek was founded. It was part of our history lessons. In 1730, a woman named Mary was the last person in Virginia to be accused of witchcraft. *Something about using magic to find things, I think?* Anyway, this was way after Salem, and the witches here just finally decided they'd had enough. After Mary was whipped thirty-nine times for basically being a magical metal detector, the local witches moved out into the woods. Neither of us could remember what the original headcount was, but they had enough of a quorum to form an active coven. They linked their Gifts to the Source of magic and used the energy to create the boundary spell.

We continued to use the Last Light ritual to direct energy from the Source to the spell that protected us, just as our ancestors did. Our teachers loved that story. So many life lessons: overcoming adversity, teamwork, personal responsibility to community.

Nothing about what would happen if we overloaded the spell or how the spell could be corrupted over time. Not even really all that much about what the Source was, where it was, or the mechanics of how connecting to it actually worked. I knew as much about where magic came from as a mundane fourth grader knew about creating electricity. *You just flip the switch, right?*

I bet Gabriel knows. My second oldest brother had really gotten into the more science-y aspects of the Craft. He'd been teaching at the lower school in town when I left.

"Please clear the table for dinner, you two," Mom said as if we were studying homework or drawing pictures from the book of legends like we used to when we were small.

Even witches had to eat.

Thomas stacked the papers with our new notes on top and disappeared. A minute later, there was a crash from his bedroom down the hall.

"If you're going to blink in and out, you should really clean your room!" Mom called. She'd been telling him that for years.

I got the dishes from the cabinet and scooted around her while she chopped vegetables on a wooden cutting board on the counter. She stepped to the side to let me pass, but the knife continued its work on its own. By the time I reached into the drawer for the silverware, the chopping was done. She smiled as she carried the cutting board to the pan and pushed the ingredients in by hand. I grabbed some napkins and stepped out of the way as she called the salt to her with a wave of her hand, humming the whole time. The salt cellar slid along the counter until it was just within reach.

Since Benjamin got up and went back to his own place sometime while I was still in bed, and Caleb hadn't come back from Elspeth's, I set the table for three. By the time I finished, the smell of roasted chicken with onions filled the house. Mom pulled it out of the oven as I laid the last plate. She could have used a kitchen spell to make it cook faster, but it would've tasted perfect no matter when she took it out of the charmed oven. She'd timed it to allow me to participate. We hardly ever talked about it, but she'd always done this, made these little modifications in how she did things to accommodate my missing Gift. It had been a kindness, but now it worried me. *How had all of those little domestic spells cast all over the community affected the magical energy of Queen's Creek? Was it enough to crack the boundary?*

While we ate, Mom asked about our Wakenings, showing interest in our friends, my job, and my classes. She mentioned things I wrote in my last letter, sharing my father's reactions to little bits of old news as if he were going to chime in any minute. All other subjects were ignored.

Thomas played along, asking about Mom's work and Elspeth's apprenticeship with her.

Mom smiled. "Elspeth has done so well in her training. She'll be a better healer than I ever was. She has a natural affinity for it."

No wonder Elspeth had seemed so comfortable at the healer's cottage. "Mom, did you retire?"

"I'm on call," she said. "She knows how to find me if she needs me."

I struggled to imagine my mother's day without her career. *Luckily there's this oncoming apocalypse to keep her busy.*

The attempt at routine was disconcerting. A balm that drew attention to the wound. I didn't understand how we got to this place where we'd come home from our Wakening, but Dad wasn't here, and he wasn't coming back, and I still didn't really know why. I'd never expected to be back here like this. I had no intention of staying past my birthday, but maybe things were different now. If we found a way to unbind my Gift... I still couldn't believe I had one. But if I had my own magical energy, and if we stabilized the boundary... Was I needed here? Did I want to be?

After dinner, I started to wash the dishes by hand, but Mom waved me away as if I were a guest. She passed a hand over the pile, and the remnants of dinner faded away. She snapped her fingers, and they sparkled, germ-free.

"I'll put them away," she said. "You two have work to do. I need you to look through a few things. We'll need something symbolic for the blessing, something meaningful we can part with for the farewell."

It turned out that "a few things" included several boxes in the attic and more in the downstairs closets. Thomas and I agreed to split up the work for now and take turns continuing to analyze Dad's notes on energy transfers. Tomorrow we'd have to call in our brothers for reinforcements.

We had two days to help Mom sort through Dad's things before the funeral. Three days until the Equinox Festival potentially caused the boundary spell to collapse. Four days until our birthday officially ended our Wakenings. Which only mattered if Queen's Creek was still standing at the end of it.

While Thomas took a turn with the papers in the kitchen, I started in the attic, sitting against the sloped ceiling and sweating as much from the tight space as from the rising spring temperatures, still warm and humid this close to sunset. I missed the snow, even if it was a sign of impending doom.

I turned over pages and pages of my father's work, stopping occasionally when something didn't belong. Some sketches I drew as a child mixed in with notes from his most recent course. An invitation to my parents' wedding. Something old, something new. Old pictures half melted on pages of last year's research.

I gently teased them apart. They peeled like scabs. The dust made me sneeze. I smiled at the goofy baby faces of my brothers, sighed over images of my parents' early relationship. The pictures weren't in any kind of order that I recognized, although I had no doubt Dad put these together for a reason. I discovered my birth record under Thomas's but didn't find Benjamin or Caleb until halfway through the next box, buried under a stack of alchemical diagrams.

It took a few hours to clear out the small space above my parents' bedroom. When I finished, I sat back and looked at what I'd found. Sweat dripped from the hair behind my ear, and I wiped it away on my shoulder. I divided my findings into piles: things we should definitely get rid of, things we definitely needed to keep, things my mom and brothers should look at first, and things that were important to Dad.

What should I do with that last one?

I couldn't shake the stupid, insensitive feeling that they had it all wrong. Mom gave up too early. Giles didn't have enough evidence. Maybe Adam didn't see what he thought he saw.

Maybe it was me. Maybe I was going to wake up in my dorm, and when I checked my mailbox, there would be a letter from Dad. And I'd write back and tell him about this weird dream I had just because his letter was late. My eyes burned.

I remembered pulling the Tower in Alice's bedroom and the feeling that whatever happened, he was gone for good. The empty confidence of it. I sifted through the last pile one more time, dividing it among the others. I tried and failed to hold back the tears as I dropped the last of it into the first pile. I wiped my eyes and cleaned my glasses on my shirt.

Then I started again downstairs.

22

Mom lit the candle for Last Light at our household altar in the alcove behind the kitchen. It'd be dark soon.

For the first time, I questioned the ritual. Mom knew about the energy imbalance. Would working this spell contribute to the dangerous build-up of magic in Queen's Creek? Or did it still strengthen the boundary as our ancestors intended? How many of our neighbors followed the tradition as religiously as Mom did? Enough? Too many?

Maybe the answers were in Dad's notes. I'd check with Thomas if I didn't find anything in the office.

As I stood on tiptoes, edging the last box off the shelf in the top corner of the office closet, it fell. It was just as much a mess as the files I found in the attic, and I seriously considered trashing the whole thing, but some of it looked like family records, and I didn't think I had the right. The room wasn't big enough to really spread out, so I sat on the floor in the closet and flipped through it in semi-darkness, pulling out anything that looked like it might be important.

When I pulled out Jonathan's birth record, I congratulated myself on my patience. There had to be another record in the library somewhere, but it probably meant something to have the original. Matthew and Gabriel's must be in here, too. Good thing I hadn't dumped it.

My father's voice came from somewhere behind me. *Find them.*

My heart stopped. I swear, it froze in place between beats for a second or two. I gasped as it restarted. Spinning around where I sat, my foot caught on the edge of the box, and I stumbled in my rush to get to my feet. Papers slid across the floor.

Facing the empty room, I closed my eyes and tried to feel my father's presence. I imagined him sitting at the desk, and I almost smelled his cologne in the air. I listened for his voice again, slowing my breath and clearing my mind. Light and shadows played on my eyelids, but I didn't feel any closer to him than I did under the pile of boxes. *Maybe it was all in my head.*

I opened my eyes.

Two sheets of paper stuck to my bare foot. I bent and carried them to the desk. The trees outside partially blocked the light through the window, casting flickering shadows into the room. I used my lighter to kindle the lamp on the desk. Mom could have ignited it with a snap of her fingers, but I'd learned to come prepared. Independence without magic had always required a little extra forethought.

The warm light washed over my eldest brothers' birth records. It might not have meant anything, finding these documents in a pile of others, misplaced or forgotten for who knew how long in the office closet.

But two figures fell from the Tower in my vision.

Mom had said Matthew and Gabriel "went to Creek," not "they drowned."

That voice, *it was definitely my father's voice,* said, "find them."

Where were my brothers now?

I gripped the edge of the desk as my next thought roared through my mind. *Mrs. Kirk and Giles had declared Dad dead, but they hadn't found a body.*

What happened when someone fell into the Creek? Could we really get them back?

A shadow fell across the pages.

"You're doing it again," my mother said from the doorway. She mimicked my wrinkled nose.

"You said Mrs. Kirk gave Dad a project. Something to make Alice stronger?" *Had he succeeded? Could it have made him stronger too? Strong enough to survive whatever happened in the Creek?*

"She asked him to develop the elixir of life. It was the only way Mrs. Kirk would agree to let you go."

Blessed Be, he might be alive in there. His notes made more sense now. Research from all over the world pointing to the same recipe, something to extend life beyond its potential. Mrs. Kirk had wanted it for Alice. But that wasn't fair to her either. She'd already given so much.

"Did it work?" *It couldn't have.* If he'd given a successful potion to Mrs. Kirk, she wouldn't still expect me to step up. If Alice had taken it, and it had worked, that should have solved the energy problem. Unless the problem really was the Source, like Dad thought.

She shook her head. "I helped him when I could, but we weren't getting anywhere with the recipe. It was missing something."

Aren't we all? What if he finished it on his own? What if he kept it for himself?

Mom would deny the possibility. *Consequences* and all. But weren't we already facing some pretty severe consequences for whatever he'd done? How much longer could she hide Matthew and Gabriel's absence? What was she doing to get them back?

She yawned.

"It's getting late. Maybe we should go to bed. Is there anything you need?" *Please tell me. Let me help you.*

"I don't want to be a bother."

"Mom."

She just shrugged, one hand on the doorframe to steady her.

When I hugged her, I felt the distance between us more than I had in Chicago.

Later, I sat in the dark on the large bed in my old room, having fled to more familiar ground. It was not the bed I grew up with—Mom had already redecorated. Apparently, she shared Nora's confidence that I would end my Wakening outside.

She must have been so disappointed to have me back. If I'd stayed in Chicago, would she ever have told me my brothers were missing? Or would she have gone on lying to me for the rest of my life, avoiding the subject in every letter? Would she have written to me at all?

I lay back and stared at the shadows of stars on the ceiling. She'd painted over them, but when I closed my eyes, I could feel them glowing like they used to. The arrangement of the stars and planets could have an effect on the potency of some spells, so families often tracked their movements with the phases of the moon.

I liked their stories. When I couldn't sleep, the stars on my ceiling seemed to float and sing. They told me about the people who came before us and the adventures they had. In retrospect, Dad probably put some kind of nightlight charm on them to help me sleep.

Closing my eyes, I imagined rearranging the real constellations, making new ones, adding to the everlasting history in the sky. *Hey, I'm a Gifted seventh-of-a-seventh. It could happen.*

If I ever get unbound. The possibility that I might someday have a less unmagical life had never really crossed my mind. That night I dreamed of flying.

March 18

Adversity, Isolation,
Loss

Assertive, Direct,
Driven

Nurturing, Practical,
Generous

Judgement, Awakening,
Reflection

Endings, Change,
Transformation

23

D'you find anything interesting?" Thomas asked the next morning. When I looked up, he leaned on the doorframe with a few folders and notebooks under his arm.

Well, the disembodied voice of our missing father entreated me to find our suspiciously absent brothers. But Mom thinks I'm just like him, so a connection like that's probably normal, right? Oh, and I'm working a new theory that he might have survived an encounter with the enchanted border by drinking a potion that was supposed to grant eternal life to our community's ethereal sentinel.

And people thought Dad was losing it.

Pushing myself up in bed, I rubbed my eyes and put on my glasses. Nothing cleared up. "I think there's something wrong with me."

Thomas sat beside me, the folders in his lap. He squinted at me, waving one hand in front of my face and over my shoulder like Elspeth had done. But he didn't have her Gift, and he couldn't see what she did.

He squeezed my shoulder. "Maybe. But if it's the concussion, it'll heal. And if it's the bind, we'll fix it. You know you're not really cursed, right? It's just a joke. We didn't mean it."

"Doesn't seem like a joke now." I stood and took one of the files. The papers inside looked just like the others, covered in overlapping notes and strange diagrams.

He looked from me to the folder. "Because of this stuff? It has nothing to do with you. The boundary has nothing to do with you. What happened to Dad had nothing to do with you."

He stood and put the rest of the folders on my desk, flipping open a notebook and rifling the pages. "This was going on for years. These notes start before we left for our Wakening. He was obsessed. I guess it just got harder for him to hide it."

"We would have noticed."

Thomas shrugged. "We were busy."

I dropped the file back on his stack. "Not that busy."

"We were selfish assholes. What? Teenagers suck. We were awful, moody, easily distracted, excited about our own stuff. I bet there were a lot of things going on three years ago that we missed."

"What do you think we're missing now?"

Thomas drummed his fingers against his chin and then knocked on the stack of files. "A lot of it's in some kind of shorthand, and his handwriting was, erm, challenging before he started layering annotations. I'll keep working on it, but it's probably time we ask for help."

He sat on my bed, yawning. We'd had a late night and gotten up early to get some plans in place before Mom woke up.

"Mom doesn't want to talk about it," I said.

Thomas rubbed his eyes. "Yeah, I didn't mean Mom. I was more thinking of somebody a little closer to the problem."

Closer to the problem? As far as we knew, Mom and Dad were the only ones working on it. Except Gabriel and maybe

Matthew. If Dad couldn't find them, what chance did we have? Who would know more about the boundary than the people actively studying it?

Oh. Shit.

"Thomas, I really don't..."

He stood. "You have to go to the Gatehouse. Who is Alice more likely to talk to? She made you her successor. She must trust you. You were chosen for a reason. If there's something wrong with the spell that you are supposed to be the custodian of, she would know, and you have a right to know, too. No, she has an obligation." Thomas got louder as he went, pacing tracks into the rag rug on my bedroom floor.

"Shhh!" I hissed. I jumped up and stood in front of him before he could get any further. "You're going to wake her up!"

"You have to go, Cate."

I clenched and unclenched my fists. *He's right.* Because, of course, he was. I looked at the papers that were about to slide off my desk. Thomas was going to need help too.

"Fine. I'll go to the Gatehouse. But you should take those to Ben. Maybe he'll see something you don't."

Thomas's eyes narrowed. "Don't think I don't see what you did there."

I smirked. There was a time before he mastered his own Gift when Thomas was jealous of the sense-based Gifts our brothers were born with: Jonathan's strength, Caleb's preternatural hearing, and Benjamin's extraordinary sight. It was only fair that if I had to have some awkward conversations, he should too. Besides, the way Ben had been training for the Watch, he'd had a lot of practice with analysis and observation lately. *He might catch something without even engaging his second sight, or third eye, or whatever.*

Before I could say anything, soft music floated down the hall. I turned my head to listen, holding up a hand. "You hear that too, right?"

Thomas tilted his head. "It's Mom, isn't it? Sounds like... what's that sad Toni Braxton song?"

Mom loved music from the 90s, and if it were anybody else, maybe I wouldn't question the low vocals as a form of mourning, but music was Mom's Gift. Sometimes a song was not just a song. I tried to remember the lyrics, but she sang too softly for me to pick up. The melody was so familiar. Something about a lost love. "You don't think she's trying to call him back, do you?"

"Like...?" Thomas waved his hands in front of him, zombie-style.

I wrinkled my nose.

"Cate, she's sad. She's not a necromancer," Thomas said. "Yesterday, she was singing 'Dreamlover.' Old-school divas are her happy place."

The broken-hearted anthem coming from down the hall didn't sound happy, but maybe he was right. Maybe she was meditating, tapping into her divine energy to help her deal with her grief. We listened in silence for a minute, and then the music faded away. I gathered the folders and pushed them into Thomas's hands.

"Let me know what Ben thinks," I said, pushing him out so I could change. I threw on a t-shirt and the jeans from yesterday. Nora's card was still in the back pocket. I pulled it out, covering it with my hands. This time it didn't warm to my touch.

Any help here? Just tell me we're on the right track.

A couple of peeks and repeated intentions later, I had to admit the card had nothing new to tell me. Maybe I hadn't absorbed the last lesson.

The King of Wands stared up at me, as determined as he had been yesterday.

Don't give up.

24

My stomach twisted as I got closer to the Gatehouse and the hard-packed dirt gave way to looser soil and wild grasses. The chickweed and clover that the college lawn service fought back all year grew unchecked here. Same with burdock and kudzu. Mom kept most of these plants out of our garden, but she didn't share the animosity toward weeds that people with lawns seem to have.

"Weeds are just plants growing where you don't want them to," she'd told me. Then she'd shown me how to collect, label, and use them in the kitchen and medicine cabinets.

I picked a dandelion and blew the seeds for luck. Two left. Wishes only came true if you cleared the flower in one breath. My stomach didn't feel any better. I dropped the stem and approached the Gate.

"What is your business here?" The Guardian stood at his post, one foot on the bank of the Creek, one on the bridge to Alice's little cottage. No one met the Gatekeeper unless the Guardian allowed it.

"I come to speak with the Gatekeeper," I said, keeping my voice as even as I could—as if I had not vomited all over his shoes the last time we were here.

"The Gatekeeper does not see unexpected visitors." His voice was detached, betraying none of the frustration he had shown at the Reading.

I pursed my lips. The bridge wasn't wide enough for me to get past him. I imagined running straight at him and knocking him off balance like a football player, but the moment passed almost immediately. He was an imposing figure. Despite his uneven footing, Adam's stance looked stable. He crossed his arms and looked down at me through the shadowy eyes of the wolf mask.

I took a more formal posture, straightening my shoulders and addressing him with what I hoped was a commanding tone. "Guardian of the Gate, let me pass. I invoke my right as the Gatekeeper's successor."

"You do not." His head tilted to one side, the ears of his mask twitching. I'd surprised him, and for a moment, I saw my brother's friend through the glamor of the Guardian.

I glared at him.

"I have to talk to Alice, Adam." I took a step forward, but it was too soon. He snapped back to his role and barred my way. I considered threatening him. *Does he know I'm a seventh? I'll bet he does. And he doesn't know I'm bound. I hadn't known until yesterday. For all he knows, my Gift surfaced while I was away.*

I tried to remember how long he'd held this post. He wasn't here when I left. But he was here when Thomas came back. He was here when Dad disappeared. That can't have been the only time he saw him. *Maybe I don't need to get past him.*

"How many times?" I asked.

At first, it seemed like he wasn't going to answer. He stared past me and tensed his shoulders. I was only a few feet away now. I searched his eyes. He looked down for just a second.

"How many times did my father come here and ask you to let him pass?" I pressed. "Why didn't you help him?" Angry tears pricked at my eyes, and I blinked them back.

"Cate..." his voice softened. "Why are you here?"

"How many times?"

"Seven."

"What did he say to you?"

He squinted through the mask. "I gave my report at the Reading. You were there." He was angry again. *Curse that young siren.*

"It's just so... hard to believe." I didn't want him to know I was enchanted at the Reading. Not yet, anyway.

"Do you question my testimony?" His eyes burned with a righteous flame.

I rolled my eyes. "Adam—"

He took the mask off, and the Guardian slipped away completely. My brother's friend was only a little older than us, a little taller than me. "He broke the covenant."

I stared at Adam. Without the mask, I saw the child he used to be, even though he tried to seem imposing. He was angry, but underneath, he was broken-hearted. He missed my father, too.

"How?" I asked. The covenant was sacrosanct. The community had existed for hundreds of years on the strength of our secret, on the trust of our people to protect each other.

"He contacted outsiders."

"But that was part of his job," I said. "He kept connections at the college to help smooth the way for our Wakenings. It wasn't magical. It was academic."

"This wasn't about scholarships and housing."

"Then what? What do you think he did that risked the discovery of magic?" Nothing less than revealing our sanctuary and exposing the community to the people who had condemned our ancestors because of their Gifts could break the covenant.

"Your dad was doing tests on the Creek and sending messages to someone on the outside. He told me he was trying to protect the boundary spell."

I waited, arms crossed, eyebrows raised.

"He was lying."

I didn't ask how he knew. Adam's magic was grounded in the earth. Among other things, he always seemed to know when something was hidden beneath the surface. A chill washed over me. I dropped my arms to my sides and wiped my hands on my jeans. He was missing something. He had to be. The Gatekeeper would know.

"Well, I'm not lying to you. I need to talk to Alice. Please. Let me pass."

Adam closed his eyes. The air around me charged.

My scalp tingled. When he opened his eyes again, I asked, "Satisfied?"

He slid the wolf mask back over his face, standing straighter. He shifted his weight and, without moving from his post, gave me space to cross the bridge. My stomach tightened as I stepped toward the Creek, but the bridge was dry, the sun was shining, and as I passed the Guardian, he held out a hand to guide me. I wasn't too proud to take it as I stepped carefully across and stopped at the stone step. On the other side of that door, the Gatekeeper waited for me.

It's time we had that talk she promised.

The door opened as I approached. A diaphanous glow drifted out onto the water, making it glisten. It was softer than I remembered and started to dim almost immediately.

Alice wasn't in the doorway when I got there. In fact, the main room was empty. Even the walls seemed faded. The windows on the far side of the room blurred. I touched my fingers to the glass. It was raining again on the other side, but Alice's windows were charmed to reflect the view from her birthday. *It should be sunny*. The light shifted a little as though I were looking through a projection, and I saw both views.

"Alice?" I called. "There's something wrong with—"

Something fell in the bedroom. I ran. At first, the room seemed empty. Then I heard a soft moan. Alice's bare feet stuck out just beyond the edge of the bed. When I got around it, I found her lying on her side. I fell to my knees beside her, careful not to sit on her white dress where it spilled out over the floor. I didn't see any blood or other signs of injury. I reached out to touch her.

"What have you done?" Adam shouted from the bedroom doorway.

He pushed me back, gathered the Gatekeeper gently into his arms and scooped her onto her bed. He straightened her skirt before kneeling reverently beside her. His hands went to her head and heart. He bowed his head and murmured something I couldn't hear. She didn't move, but a soft sigh escaped her lips. When he stood a few moments later, he seemed to have forgotten me.

I stepped back to the doorway to get a better view of the room. Nothing seemed out of place, but then, apart from the bed, Alice didn't keep much here. Before I could move, I suddenly felt warm.

When I tried to meet Adam's eyes, they glowed red under the mask.

"Ummm... Is she okay?"

"Leave this place."

"Look, Adam, I don't know what happened. I wasn't even —"

His eyes flashed.

I backed out of the bedroom. Rain coursed down the glass on the windows that faced outside the community. Even the windows on our side seemed dimmer, like a cloud blocking the sun. I looked around, completely lost. Alice's small sitting room was starting to show its age. The fabric on her chair had faded. The bookcase was dusty. There were a few places where the rag rug had come untied.

I guess I missed those details when Alice welcomed us back because her own light was so strong. Mrs. Kirk wasn't lying about the Gatekeeper weakening. How long has she been fading?

Lightening brightened the room for a split second and then plunged it back into semi-darkness.

25

The Guardian's voice pulled me back. "When you endanger the Gatekeeper, you put us all at risk."

He stood just inside the room, Alice's bedroom door closed behind him.

"I didn't do anything! Adam, you know I would never—" I wasn't even sure how to end that sentence. I didn't understand what was happening to Alice and wasn't sure he did either.

"The Gatekeeper is vulnerable. The Gate must be protected." He sounded like he was reciting somebody else's lines. The storm outside grew louder.

"Is she okay?" I asked again. I waved my hand in front of his masked face. "Adam! Talk to me!"

I took a risk and put my hand on his arm.

He startled and blinked. His eyes cleared. For a minute, he tried to maintain the Guardian facade, but his shoulders sagged. He pulled the mask away and looked down. "I don't know."

"Adam? What's happening?"

He shook his head. "There's something wrong with her. We're not supposed to talk about it. The Speaker doesn't want people to be afraid."

"But we have to do something to help her."

"The Guardians protect her. I can make sure that she's safe. I can heal her injuries." He waved to the window, where the storm had already started to recede. "But if her turn is ending, if she's coming to the natural end of her life..." He ran a hand through his tangled curls. "No one can hold Death, Cate. She'll pass through the veil, and we'll initiate the new Gatekeeper."

I didn't like how he looked at me when he said it. I might have reminded him that I basically failed his entrance test if I'd been sure he wouldn't drag me outside and make me prove my connection to the Source again right there.

I can't be Gatekeeper. I'm not even supposed to be here.

Adam pressed a hand to the bedroom door and closed his eyes. His lips moved, and it might have been a protection spell or a prayer for her recovery.

She can't die. And not just because I wasn't ready. And not just because there was no one else.

I defy the Crone to cut her thread.

Queen's Creek had been loyal to the goddess in all of her forms. We'd followed the old ways and invented new ones to bring us closer to the Divine. Generations of women had lit the candles at Last Light, and generations of men had stood Guard at the Gate. We'd honored the Mother and protected her creations. It couldn't have been for nothing.

The sacrifice and self-imposed exile of Gifted witches were supposed to protect us. How many maidens had come before Alice? Going back to Mary after the trials, one after another, giving up their potential lives to maintain the boundary? How many more would have to serve like Persephone? Even she got to leave for a few months each year. Not our Gatekeepers. They entered the Gatehouse for the last time on their twenty-first birthday and never left it. They gave themselves over to the magic that flowed from the Source, feeding the boundary spell and reflecting it back into the community for years until their life was used up. It was an honor and a privilege. A blessing and a curse. I was cursed enough already.

I claimed my rights as her successor, but Adam was right. I didn't want it.

This was all wrong anyway. Alice would know if her turn was ending. She would prepare us.

I'm not ready.

Adam put the mask back on.

Shit. Did I say any of that out loud?

"What are you doing?" I asked instead.

He stepped back to the door. "I serve at the pleasure of the Gatekeeper," said the Guardian. He bowed his head. Then the door closed between us, and he returned to his post at the end of the bridge.

No. Mother-maiden-crone, please tell me the Guardian did not just recognize me as Gatekeeper.

I was alone in the reception room of the Gatehouse. My legs gave out, and I sank to the floor.

I should get up. Run. I'm not the Gatekeeper yet. I don't have to be. I could walk out the other door. If I open the door that leads to the forest, I can walk until I find the car at the end of the dirt road. We left the keys in it. I could drive back the way we came. Hecate, I could drive all the way back to Chicago. It'd be cheaper than flying.

I'd thank my advisor for filling out that leave of absence form. I'd get my job back at the café and get my stuff back from Brian. Would Nyla even have noticed I was gone?

It's too soon. I'm not prepared for this. An initiate should have training. They should be someone who sticks around. Someone bound to the Source and to the community and its people. Why would Alice choose someone who might never return from her Wakening? What did she see when she looked at me? Like Thomas said, there were other big families. I wasn't the only seventh in our generation. *Why me?*

I pulled Nora's tarot card from my pocket, and it warmed immediately in my hands. When I uncovered it, my shoulders sagged. I let my fingers trace the two familiar figures in the image.

The woman pulled her ragged cloak tightly around her and leaned into the wind. The second figure used crutches that dug holes in the snow. Five pentacles glowed in a stained glass window above them. This was the card I had imagined when Thomas and I stood outside the Watch Tower after the Reading. It represented a loss of faith and security. But it was part of the minor arcana and couldn't last. It told me to look for the positive, like the light glowing in the stained glass window. *Help might be closer than you think.*

I glanced from the door on the Creek side of the Gatehouse, where Adam waited at his post, back to Alice's bedroom door. Adam knew more than he'd told me, but first, I wanted to ask Alice about my father and my destiny as an unequipped seventh. I needed her to wake up. I braced myself and tried to sense her presence. She used to fill the space with light and energy. I looked for signs of it returning.

The window by the door was open a crack, and a gentle breeze played with the gauzy curtains. The delicate light on that side of the room reached across the floor but didn't quite meet the colder shadows that still blinked in the corners on the forest side of the room. I focused on where the soft light started to push past the dark. The shadows slowly rolled back. Whatever happened to Alice, she was recovering now. *Please, let her recover.*

Alice's door creaked a little when I pushed it open. She still lay on the bed, her eyes closed. Her chest rose and fell in a slow rhythm. Still alive, still linked to the boundary spell. She could have been a sleeping princess from a fairy tale, but the bare room provided no clues to her enchantment. No apple or spindle here to explain her fall. *What would happen if she didn't wake up. Without the Gatekeeper, what happens to the Gate?*

26

I came to the Gatehouse to get answers, but all I had were guesses, vague impressions, and more questions. How long would I have to wait for the answers to come to me? Until Alice woke? Until she died? What if my Wakening ended, and I was trapped here forever? What would happen when the boundary failed?

According to Dad's notes, the boundary spell was already collapsing. Adam confirmed that Dad had come to the Creek to try to learn more. But if he wasn't trying to fix it, what was his plan? And who was he communicating with on the other side? *How?*

Something else Adam said. There was something wrong with Alice, and the Speaker didn't want people to know how bad it was. How long had the Gatekeeper been weakening? Was it connected to what was happening with the boundary spell, or was it just her time? How would we know?

The grimoire.

The entire history of Queen's Creek and all of our spells bound together in one place. If I couldn't talk to Alice, the book was the next best thing. *Maybe better.* After all, the grimoire had been around longer than she had. All I had to do was get into the library's restricted section. Luckily, I knew the Librarian.

The cottage that housed our community's book collection, like its most important tome, might have gone unobserved by anyone who didn't know where to find it. The small dark structure sat back from the path, obscured by low-hanging branches and a creeping ivy that threatened to overtake it completely. My brother liked it that way. Although Mom had often assigned Jonathan the more challenging gardening duties at home, he'd never used those skills at work. I suspected he might have actually encouraged the vine.

I don't know why he bothers. Everybody has their own book of shadows. How often would they even need to come here?

Something flickered by the window. A tiny flash of light winked.

The door opened smoothly at my touch, reinforcing my sense that the neglected exterior was mostly for show. A comfortable fire crackled in a stone fireplace, and soft woven rugs trailed a path from the door to the shelves. My brother sat behind a desk under a round window. Sunlight beamed across a surface so buried under stacks of texts that they might have been structural. Jonathan sighed at the interruption and set down the enchanted quill he'd been using to take notes in a large ledger. When he recognized me, he smiled.

"This is a nice surprise. To what do I owe the pleasure?" The formal language might have sounded insincere coming from anyone else, but Jonathan had always chosen his words carefully. Even Adam had never caught him in a lie.

"I need your help."

"Is everything okay?" His eyes widened with concern, and I remembered his attentiveness at the Reading. He had his own children now, but it had always felt like he practiced on me.

It was too much. Secrets and prophecies and expectations. The headaches and dizziness that might not come from the concussion. I couldn't hold it all in. It leaked out through my eyes. My big brother's arms wrapped around me, and I cried.

"Hey, hey, Kitty. It's going to be alright." He rubbed my back and kissed the top of my head, using our father's pet name for me. Thomas would never have gotten away with it, but Jonathan had always been so much like Dad. It was a comfort to hear it from him.

I sniffled and pushed away, wiping my glasses on my shirt. "I'm sorry."

He rubbed my arm. "Nothing to be sorry for."

He waited, watching me.

I should ask about the girls. How are they handling all of this?

But I knew time was not on our side. "I need to see the grimoire."

Jonathan nodded as though he were expecting this. "It's in the restricted section for a reason," he said. "But I think we both know those reasons don't apply to you."

I didn't know what to say. *I'm so sick of being exceptional.*

"Do you want to talk about what's going on with you? Is it Dad? Or did something happen on your Wakening?"

When I didn't answer, he rubbed his chin, considering. His next words were soft, a statement of understanding rather than an accusation. "You were going to reject the call."

"It's a mistake," I said. "It can't be me."

"You want to see the prophecy." He didn't argue or try to convince me that denying my fate was futile. Jonathan had always valued reason and evidence. He'd trust me to make up my own mind. Of course, I'd want to see the prophecy. I needed to know what I was getting into. It was probably just as well he had no idea how scrambled my mind was.

Bound, not broken. Somebody did this to me, and the more I learn about the Source of our magic, the closer I'll be to undoing it.

Thank Hecate, my namesake and patron, Jonathan's faith is unshakable. I didn't have time to get into the whole End-of-the-World-as-We-Know-It thing.

He might be able to explain some of Dad's work... Not now. Let Thomas read him in if Ben saw nothing new in Dad's notes.

"Please."

Once we stepped onto the rug leading through the stacks, the entire room opened up. Literally, physically shifted around us. The rows of shelves expanded, pushing back against a wall that got farther away as we walked. People talked about getting lost in the library at school, but they had no idea. My brother led me through a maze lined with books from floor to ceiling. They stood in straight lines, organized alphabetically, dust-free, and almost begging to be lifted from the shelves.

Two or three turns later, we passed an unattended cart struggling to reshelve heavy texts on its own. It slowed as we came closer. I stepped to the side to avoid a loose stack on the floor. Jonathan mumbled something about staffing shortages and glitches and tapped the cart as he went by. The metal frame shook itself and returned to work with renewed energy.

"Just through here," Jonathan said. He ducked under an archway of antique books, his hair brushing the keystone text. The books in the restricted section filled several tall cabinets with glass doors and tiny brass locks. A pair of gloves lay on a long wooden table in the middle of the room. Jonathan picked them up, sliding his fingers into the soft cloth. Another pair appeared on the table, exactly where he'd found them. He gave me a meaningful look, and I pulled them on. They fit perfectly. The table did not produce another pair to replace them.

"Now," said the Librarian, his tone suddenly more professional than fatherly. "Rules. You will touch only the books I retrieve for you. You will touch none of them without gloves. You will not damage or alter them in any way. Nothing leaves this room."

I rolled my eyes. "I'm not going to wreck the books. I have been in a library before."

"Not like this one." He produced a brass key with an elaborate filigree handle. His eyes flicked to the front of the building. "I need to be out there in case anyone comes in. I don't have a problem with your being back here, but others might. Tell me I can trust you."

I sighed. *Like anyone will wander into the library and perform a random security check on the restricted section.* Remembering a book about a boy wizard Jonathan used to read to me, I grinned. Holding up three fingers, I recited, "I solemnly swear I'm up to—"

"Cate." My brother was not amused.

I held up both gloved hands, no fingers crossed. "Nothing. I'm up to nothing. Or, you know. Good. Only good things. I'm here to learn about the Gate, the Gatekeeper, and the Guardian. How to keep us all safe. Good things."

He shook his head. Somehow I always reverted to his annoying little sister when we spent any time together. Mischievous and immature. But I wasn't lying. My motives were clean this time.

"Please," I said again, standing as straight as I could. "You can trust me."

He exhaled sharply and turned to unlock one of the cabinets. Lifting out the enormous grimoire as if it were a paperback, he set it on the table in front of me and relocked the cabinet. "Damage nothing. Alter nothing. Take nothing. And come see me in the front before you leave."

"I promise. Thank you."

"If you want to talk, I'm—"

"I know. Thank you. I promise to come to you first if I have questions."

Something shifted in the front of the library. I tried to remember if Jonathan had a cat.

"I'll be right out front," he said, closing the door behind him.

I shot him a thumbs-up and immediately regretted it. *Goddess, why am I such a dork?*

She didn't answer, so I focused on the book. The cover protested a little as I heaved it open. Any question that Jonathan had used his Gift when he lifted it down vanished. I pulled a chair from the other side of the table. There was little chance I could lift the book easily, but the chairs in this room were the cheap folding variety, probably aluminum. Why outfit a space no one ever visited?

Despite its weight, the cover bent a little in my hands, more delicate than it looked. *Fairy wings and troll's tears. Sure.*

It would have been cool if there'd been some kind of choral outburst or ray of light that shot out of the book when I opened it, but it really was just a text. *A really old text, compiled before printing presses came to the New World, apparently.* The whirling calligraphic text bled through the thin pages from one to the next, making words that were already difficult to read all but indecipherable.

Groaning, I peeled back the pages a few inches at a time, moving from the original book to more modern appendices. *Some kind of index would be nice.*

I almost said it aloud, just in case the magic library needed an extra hint to help me out. I pictured the pages flipping by on their own, fanning my face, my hair flying back until the holy book landed on the exact page I needed. But, of course, nothing like that had ever worked for me. Why should it start now? Just because I knew why it didn't?

Lady Libertas, I will break this bind, and then I will find the person who did it, and they shall know my wrath. I pounded the table with a fist for emphasis.

Nothing. If that didn't rouse the book, I couldn't imagine what would. I settled into the chair, mentally preparing myself for a long, slow, frustrating afternoon with the impossible book.

"You shouldn't be here."

27

Jonathan, you had one job. But of course, my by-the-book brother would never have stopped the Commander of the Watch from going wherever he wanted. *Could have warned me though.*

"I have permission," I said, turning my back on the grimoire to face Giles. Maybe he wouldn't notice what I was reading. My confidence in my awareness on the whole who-knows-which-secrets front was a little shaky.

When I left Chicago, I'd been intent on finding Giles, confronting him, and demanding he keep my father's case open. Now, I just needed him to leave me alone. He'd given up on learning the truth, but I hadn't.

He scratched his chin, fingers digging into his graying beard. "Adam told me what happened."

I bit my lip. *When?* Was he talking about Dad? Or Alice?

"You should be resting," he said.

Oh, right. That. My hand came up to the bump on the back of my head. It had subsided, mostly, but it still stuck out enough to keep my hair from lying flat. "I'm okay."

He stood in the doorway, holding it open with his heel. His eyes flicked from me around the room. Something he saw made him uncomfortable. "Why don't you come with me back to your mom's house? You have a lot of people around here worried about you. Let us take care of you."

"I can take care of myself, thanks." I crossed my arms and leaned back on the table, hopefully making my intentions clear.

He nodded, but his focus was still somewhere in the room behind me. "I'm sure you can. You're a very capable young woman, but these are difficult times. It isn't safe for you to—"

"Oh, hey, Uncle Giles. There you are. I have those records you asked for." My brother's muffled voice came from the stacks behind the Watch Commander.

"What's not safe?" I asked.

Giles finally met my eyes. "Just be careful. For all of our sakes."

The door closed silently behind him. *Great. More cryptic warnings.*

Something rustled in the restricted section. *Maybe rats?* Not to knock Jonathan's housekeeping skills, but it was pretty clear he didn't get back here very often. *He must have some kind of charm against pests though. Couldn't have anything munching the sacred pages.*

I checked under the table just in case. Nothing there.

No one in the hallway. Usually, when things moved on their own, I could pinpoint the active witch in the area. Nobody needed to hide what they could do when everyone in town could do it too. But the library wasn't exactly busy. I hadn't seen anybody else when we passed through the stacks. Only three witches in the whole place, and I'd never moved anything with my mind. Jonathan's Gift depended on his physical presence, and Giles had the same magical talent as my brother Ben. That was probably one of the reasons he'd agreed to train him. They both saw things that others didn't.

What did he see when he was here?

The grimoire shivered.

Not a rat, then. Just a nervous, self-aware text written by witches and bound by the remnants of mythical creatures. Giles's warning might have been less generalized than it seemed. I pushed back a shiver of my own. What damage could a book do? The only danger here would be if I somehow knocked it off the table and dropped it on my foot. Little chance of that since I could barely lift it.

"Hey there, book," I said. "I'm not going to hurt you. I promised Jonathan, remember?" Trying to soothe a book felt ridiculous, but I knew people who talked to plants, and they never even twitched.

The pages fluttered and stilled. It wasn't quite the glorious moment I'd hoped for, but at least the grimoire had accepted my presence. In retrospect, I was lucky it opened for me at all. I peered over the page, following the lines with a gloved finger. The handwritten words wavered.

"Help me out here. Is the boundary really coming down? Is that what's wrong with Alice? Or is it just the end of her turn? What happens if we don't have a Gatekeeper?"

The words shifted.

THERE IS NO GATE WITHOUT THE KEEPER.

Cool. "No Gate, but not No Boundary. So… if Alice dies and no one replaces her… what? No more Wakenings? No more messages to the outside world? We're just trapped?"

The room tightened around me. Too small and not enough air. I closed my eyes, pushing the walls back. *Don't panic. Ask the right questions.*

"How do we open the Gate?"

THERE IS NO GATE WITHOUT THE KEEPER

Yeah, thanks. I got that.

"What if we just leave it open? If I accept… If I am the next Gatekeeper, I control the Gate, don't I?" *Could I do that? Open the Gate and walk through it?*

THERE IS NO GATE WITHOUT THE KEEPER

So… no? The Keeper has to stay in the Gatehouse to keep it open? How is that fair?

"Okay, but why? Says who? Who made these stupid rules anyway?"

MARY

The first Gatekeeper? The one from history class who founded Queen's Creek? Are we seriously living our lives by rules set generations ago? How long did she think this could last?

Dates formed next to her name. Maybe they'd always been there. My eyes adjusted to the strange text. The name faded, the ink disappearing into the paper as if decades had passed in seconds. A new name rose to the surface. New dates. Then another. One every eighty years or so. *No. Every seventy-nine years, exactly.*

CLARA

MARTHA

ALICE

As the dates for Alice's tenure floated out of the paper, I squeezed my eyes shut. I could do the math. I knew what they would be. Each Gatekeeper, starting her duties on her twenty-first birthday, ended when she would have reached a century.

They knew. There was a pattern. Every one hundred years. They knew.

The boundary was coming down because Alice was too old to hold it. She'd used up a lifetime of energy keeping us safe, and now she was spent. But she kept trying to hold on a little longer. Why did she tell me we had time?

When I opened my eyes, Alice's name had started to fade. "No, no, no. Just wait right there. She's not dead. Don't you erase her."

The ink pulsed, but the Gatekeeper's name stayed on the page. I stared at it, half afraid it would disappear if I blinked.

I didn't want to see the next name.

"So, it really is her life that feeds it then. Her energy locks the boundary around the Creek. And when it's used up, that's it? We replace her like a used battery? What about Last Light? It powers the illusion to hide the boundary, couldn't some of that energy heal her, too?"

If books could sigh, I'd have sworn this one did. I flipped through the pages, careful not to leave any creases or tears. It had to include something about the nightly custom. The energy had built up for years. Surely there was enough to sustain the Gate without a Keeper by now.

I found sections on family and home maintenance, spells to build confidence and character, spells to mend fences—both physical and metaphorical. A section on healing laced with diagrams indicated which parts of the body responded best to different elemental potions. Lines covered the pages, twisting like balls of string, threads connecting injuries to their associated cures. All of them eventually led back to a triple moon, our symbol for the Source.

One section near the back of the book attempted to organize basic theories into a series of lessons for enhancing the Craft.

I considered ripping it out and taking it with me for future reference. *Jonathan would kill me. Dad would be so mad...* I almost did it just to spite him. *Don't like it, Professor Corey? Come back and stop me.*

Before the book could protest, I lifted the page.

It disappeared from my hand.

Shit. Now Jonathan really was going to kill me. "I'm sorry," I told the book. "I didn't mean it. I would never..."

The page was still missing. The grimoire didn't believe me. *How do you convince a book you mean it no harm?* Leaning back in the chair, something slipped out of my back pocket. My phone. I waved it at the book.

"Okay, look. I can take a picture of it. I don't need to rip anything. I was never going to do that, but you know, I definitely won't. Can I have the page back now? Please?"

I'm begging a book.

The page reappeared without fanfare. It was gone, and then it wasn't.

"Thank you," I said, snapping the shot. I flipped the page to get the back.

Another diagram. A bell curve? Then a graph. Energy over time. Population over time. More witches meant more magic. More magic needed a stronger illusion barrier to hide it. A stronger barrier needed more magic to fuel it. A degenerating cycle.

The Last Light ritual. Everyone in Queen's Creek sending energy to hide the boundary, putting more magic into the spell to hide magic.

The magic we were feeding the boundary spell was destroying it.

It was only a matter of time.

"How do we stop it? There must be something we can do."

The list of names began to glow as each one resurfaced, one below the next. A new name appeared at the bottom.

My name.

No. Why does it have to be me?

I tried to remember the exact words of Alice's prediction. She'd made her selection years ago, and the fog of childhood clouded my memory. I closed my eyes, drawing the memory back.

Just breathe.

It came slowly, but as I controlled my breath, things became clearer. I could see her standing in front of me, taking my little hands in a ritual that felt more personal than routine. A secret, just between us, while my parents waited outside. Her words fell softly, but I heard them, correcting my memory.

Not the next Gatekeeper.

The last.

The me of my memory knew that it was true. She was born a seventh child of a seventh child, fated to be Gifted beyond measure. But something happened. Something that still hid in the shadows. There was no Gift, and no amount of study had developed the Craft in its place. She didn't know it yet, but she would live an unmagical life.

And now I knew why. The bind. My curse.

Who did this to me? Why bind my Gift, if I had such a consequential destiny?

"All in time," Alice had said.

The vision wavered. The present reasserted itself.

Dad was right, and Alice knew it before I left. The boundary was coming down. The time of the Gatekeeper was ending. I still didn't understand why.

"Why me? And why am I the last?"

If the writers of the ancient book knew, they chose to keep it to themselves. The ink drained from the pages, leaving the past as blank as the future.

28

I had chores to do before the world as we knew it could come to an end. Alice's astral presence had assured me we had time. Besides, Thomas wasn't back from Ben's yet. Maybe they found something in Dad's notes that would help this all make sense.

In the meantime, the funeral was tomorrow. I hadn't seen Mom since yesterday. We hadn't talked since our last life-altering conversation.

"How's your head today?" she asked when I walked into the kitchen. "How are you feeling?"

Lost. Confused. Overwhelmed.

"Better. I'm sorry about yesterday."

"Why?"

"I feel like I'm making things worse."

She hugged me, and I put my head on her shoulder. "It was never going to be easy," she said. "I'm glad you're here."

I closed my eyes. *I'm sorry for blaming you for everything. I'm sorry for being angry when I should have been kind. I'm sorry. I'm sorry that I can't say it out loud. I don't know why.*

I sucked in a breath and pulled away. "How can I help you

now?"

Mom gestured to the table, once again covered in paper. We sat down in front of a creased paper map. She pushed it across the kitchen table to me. There were three possible sites circled for his memorial. She'd already spoken with Mrs. Kirk to get approval and schedule the blessing. We just needed to finalize the site. My brothers would be there. The Gosnalls would help, but most of the crowd from the Reading would leave us alone. We marked a passing as a family.

"This one is nice," she said. "We used to walk here in the fall. The view..." She took a trembling breath and looked up at the ceiling, shaking her head. She bit her lip and then smiled awkwardly. "This is hard."

I took her hand.

We sat silently, looking at the map. Then she started to hum a mournful tune, sweet and unrecognizable. The map blurred and came back into focus. The soft music drew us in. We still sat at the table, but we were also outside. The spot she'd chosen was on a small hill, an easy walk toward the back of our community. A wooded area that opened to a clearing. The Creek flowed on the other side. You might see the water through the trees once the leaves fell. The tune of her song blended with the birds, and the breeze, and the burbling water.

"It's beautiful," I said.

The trees swayed a little, the leaves lighting up with the shifting sun. The birds sounded like they were in the room with us. At least three different songs overlapped, alternating their solo parts. Mom's hum underscored it like a movie soundtrack. She sighed. As it faded, something rustled just out of sight, maybe deer. The birds went quiet. Before the vision ended, a hulking shadow spread across the clearing.

"What was that?"

"Hmmm?" The spell was over, and Mom rubbed her eyes.

Her elbows rested on the table. She folded her hands in front of her and blinked a little, coming back. "What did you say?"

I wanted to say that I had concerns about this plot of land, that there was something ominous in those last moments. At the very least, there might be bears. But she looked so tired. I had ignored what all of this was doing to her. The circles under her eyes dragged down the laugh lines. Her hair clung to her head. She tucked it behind her ears. She looked somehow both younger and older. I felt like I could see her whole life at the same time.

"Never mind. Let's take a break. I'm thirsty. Can I get you anything?"

"I'm fine." She wasn't. "But I will have some water if you're getting some. I just want this to be done."

I poured two glasses from a pitcher of well water in the ice box and brought them back to the table. The spring that fed our well drew from an underground branch of the Creek. It had a strong mineral taste. I imagined the water pushing its way through cracks in the clay, splashing over rocks, winding through a hundred tiny pathways to pool at the bottom of the well. It was determined, in constant motion. It took a hundred thousand years to get here, and in another hundred, it will have completely changed the landscape.

My mother smiled, but it didn't reach her eyes. "Where did you go?"

"I'm here," I said. I put the glasses on the table and sat down across from her. "Where to next?"

The other two sites were just as lovely, one just off a path leading to a mine that closed over a hundred years ago and one against a stoney outcrop on the other side of the hill. It might have been the exertion from raising the visions, but Mom seemed less interested as the afternoon dragged on. I could tell that neither of these sites meant as much to her as the first one.

"Will it be painful for you to go back to a place you used to go to together?" I imagined reopening wounds every time she went to renew the blessing on his memorial.

"It will all be painful," she said. "At least that one has happy memories, too."

I stood and carried the empty glasses to the sink. "I'll tell Mrs. Kirk that we've chosen the place."

"Thank you. I do have a few other things to get done. Then I need to get started on dinner. Your brothers will be here." She pushed in her chair and stood there for a moment to steady herself. The family photos on our ice box practically screamed for attention. She looked away.

"Let me help you with that. Just wait til I get back."

She nodded, but she'd have everything done without me if I was gone for too long. The light from the kitchen window settled around her. She closed her eyes and lifted her face to its warmth. Then, with a sigh, she shuffled down the hall to her room. The door clicked shut, and I hoped that she would get some rest.

In the meantime, I needed to see that hill in person.

There was no direct route from our house to the place my mom had chosen. As with most errands, I followed the winding path that uncoiled under shaded trees and opened into the town center. From there, I'd cross the market and choose another branch that meandered away. The foot of the hill was on the outermost curve, nearest the Creek on the far side of the community. It was about the same distance as the Gatehouse but in the opposite direction. The path spiraled up through the wooded rise, ending in a clearing where the trees had given up the climb.

Conversations buzzed in the market as people picked up the last few ingredients for dinner and refilled their supplies for Last Light. We had several more hours before sunset tonight, but no one wanted to risk being caught unprepared.

The air hummed with natural magic.

When I passed through on my way to the Reading, the square had been deserted, the empty market pergolas casting spiderwebs on the hard-packed dirt. Where merchants now spread food and home-made products on carefully arranged displays, the degradable remains had littered the ground. In an hour or so, they'd pack up their tables, the cloth wrappings, and any unsold fruits of their labors, but feed the unused organic materials back to the earth as they did then. By Last Light, it would all be gone, absorbed back into the land, feeding the energy of this place.

I wondered if Mrs. Kirk was back in the Tower yet. I should probably stop there first.

"She's not."

My second favorite brother's voice was in my head. He smiled at me from a vegetable stall where he waited in line with a basket of onions and mushrooms. Mom hated mushrooms. He must be having dinner with Elspeth again tonight. Caleb nodded to acknowledge this thought. "I'll be over to see Mom after Last Light."

The words appeared in my mind like my own thoughts. Although he could hear whatever came to mind before I said it, I walked over to have the conversation aloud.

"Have you seen Mrs. Kirk?" I asked, "How do you know she's not in the Tower yet?"

Caleb made no reference to the fact that I'd changed the venue for this discussion. His line moved forward, and he took another step toward the table. I inched forward with him.

"She came through a little while ago with Uncle Giles. They went that way," he said, angling his head away from the Tower.

There was nothing in that direction except the Gatehouse. I raised an eyebrow, but Caleb only shrugged. I got the impression that he might know a little more but that it would have to be a silent conversation. He nodded.

"Let's talk later." Caleb's telepathic abilities could be useful, but I always felt a little lost afterward. I wanted my mind to be clear when I got to the hill. I needed to be prepared for whatever cast that shadow. I'd try and catch Mrs. Kirk on the way back.

"What are you up to, Cate?" Caleb asked.

I attempted a reassuring smile, but I'd already left the vegetable line so far behind me that I wasn't sure if the question was in my ears or my mind. I waved and disappeared into the small crowd. Weaving through the market, I occasionally greeted my neighbors, who all seemed compelled to offer condolences or tell stories about their experiences with my father. I tried to honor their grief, but the sun was already shifting over the trees, and I had somewhere to be.

Once I broke free of the square, my breath came more easily. My pace slowed. The hard-packed dirt path narrowed and developed a spongy carpet of moss and fallen leaves. The breeze pulled the hair from behind my ears, and I absently pushed it back. I listened to the rise and fall of bird songs, insects chirping. Something small crashed through the trees behind me, and a squirrel ran through the undergrowth. My breath caught for a moment, but nothing chased him. I still had a ways to go before I reached the spot where the shadow crossed the clearing in Mom's vision.

29

I'd walked paths like this one since I was old enough to outrun my brothers. When the house started to feel small, and the guys seemed to take up all of the space, I'd slip out and get lost in the woods. Eventually, I knew every turn and tree, but not at first.

When I was still young enough to believe in fairies, I followed one from our garden. I thought it wanted to play.

Someone should have warned me about the wisps. Gabriel might have done it, but he and Matthew were already out on their Wakenings.

A little shiny spot, glinting in the afternoon sun, it darted around in my peripheral vision. I pretended not to notice, but as I half-heartedly tended the plants, I tracked its movements. I let my eyes relax, and it flickered a little brighter, drifting in and out of the middle distance. I reached out for it. The light blinked out. I pouted a little. Squinted. Blinked. Pushed my fists against my eyes until I saw spots, but no fairy.

Inside the house, my mom was singing again. Something with a cheerful beat and sad lyrics. She sang a lot when Thomas was around. Even then, I knew there was something special about Mom's music, but when she spent time with Thomas, her songs felt stronger, more meaningful. Sometimes she'd send him out to help me with my chores in the garden or remind him to do his own, but I was pretty sure she just needed a break.

Something crossed in front of me, a floating speck of light. I giggled. "Hi!"

The light blinked and bounced. I was a little disappointed by its silence. Shouldn't there be bells? It zoomed away over the fence.

"Wait!" I chased after it, climbing the fence, only getting caught on a loose board once. I stumbled and pulled my shirt free, spun around. The fairy was right there, at the end of my nose. I crossed my eyes.

"Hi!" I said again.

The fairy twinkled. It blinked and hopped away, barely keeping to the path. A few times, I had to climb over rocks and under drooping branches. I pressed my hand to the bark of a large tree. It was darker in the woods, but that made the fairy light shine brighter. It moved faster. I slipped on fallen leaves, caught myself, kept going. The light created shadows that danced across the sheltered path. We had gone so far that the sunlight barely broke through the canopy.

I tripped. The crash echoed as invisible animals startled through the trees. Birds left their hidden perches, rustling the branches and knocking leaves loose.

I squinted my eyes so tight that my nose wrinkled, and my mouth puckered. I sucked in cool air through my teeth.

"Owwwwwwwwwwwwwwwwwww!"

I froze on my hands and knees in the damp fallen leaves. My knees sank into the mud, but the real problem was my hand. My eyes still closed, I sat back on my heels, keeping my hands in place where they'd landed.

"Ow. Ow. Ow. Ow. Owwweeeeeeeee!"

I peeked through one eye, barely seeing more than lashes. Steadying myself on my knees and left hand, I slowly pulled my right hand out of the muck. Stopped. Bit my lip. Peeked again. As I lifted my hand, something thin and sharp came out of the dirt with it. Tears bubbled on my eyelashes, distorting my vision like a crystal ball. I seemed to have three right hands rotating in front of me, each of them dragging a splinter that was really more of a stick.

I felt the scream starting in the bottom of my tummy. It tied everything up in knots and fought its way up into my chest, making it hard to breathe. I squeezed my eyes shut. The tear bubbles popped and escaped down my face. Lights kaleidescoped in strange twirling patterns in front of my locked eyelids. I gritted my teeth. Somehow I knew I'd never catch that fairy if I let the scream out. I moaned, releasing air slowly until my lungs were completely empty.

I opened my eyes. The little ball of light hung from a tree branch, watching me. I had to be brave. I sat back, getting my butt soaked in the mud, and pulled my hand into my lap. My breath came quickly, flaring my nostrils. Bigger than a toothpick but not quite as big as a pencil, the splinter was wedged into the heel of my hand, just above the wrist. The less ragged edge pointed toward my fingers.

I blinked at the fairy in the tree. The light blinked back. Still panting through my nose, I bit down on my bottom lip and grabbed the splinter with my left hand.

"Ow. Ow. Ow. Ow. Ow."

It didn't budge. My stomach flipped again. I sucked in another breath and pulled harder. The sounds of the forest seemed louder. Frogs, in particular, had a lot to say that night. Crickets, who might have been wiser to be quiet with all those frogs around, chirped. The trees swayed, rustling branches. Things moved in the dark, making themselves known by the reaction of other things around them.

The scream didn't give me any warning this time.

When I opened my eyes again, the little light was gone. I should have been more scared, but without the light, the shadows had all disappeared. Blanketed in darkness, I whimpered and pulled my wounded hand close. Something crunched through the path toward me. I stood.

"Did you hear that?" someone whispered.

"You know we didn't," someone answered.

"What's that by the big tree?" asked a third voice.

"What's what?"

"Which tree?"

"That—oh, never mind. You never see things the way I do. Just come this way."

I must have known it was my brothers looking for me on the path, but I turned to run in the opposite direction. In the darkness, I smacked headfirst into the tree where the light had been.

"Owwwwwwwowowowww!"

"I heard that one," said Jonathan.

"She's over here, by the tree." Benjamin sounded closer.

Jonathan crunched through the brush. "Which tree?"

"Why is it so quiet?" asked Caleb.

He was right. The animals had gone still. I'd missed the change at first because of the ringing in my ears and the noise my brothers made. Caleb always noticed things like that.

I reached out slowly, with my good hand, and brushed my fingertips against the tree. Keeping my sore hand folded into my chest, I leaned into the tree and pushed myself up. The leaves crackled under my feet. The sound echoed in the woods. I knew Caleb would hear that.

My eyes struggled to adjust to the total darkness. I wondered where the fairy light had gone... Had whatever scared it away silenced the other animals too? A moment later, a light bobbed toward me. For a split second, I thought my fairy had come back. Then a shadow stepped in front of the light. I sucked in my breath.

"What's wrong with your hand?" Benjamin kneeled in front of me and gently pulled my sore hand away from my chest.

Jonathan arrived next, carrying a star torch. The light twinkled like the fairy, a small flame in a glass jar that gave off no heat. Caleb had one too. He held it over me to get a better look at my hand. He wrinkled his nose.

"That looks bad."

Jonathan handed his star torch to Benjamin and picked me up. I would have complained, reminded them for the thousandth time that I was a big girl now and didn't need help. But I was suddenly very tired, and it was still eerily quiet.

Benjamin passed the star torch to Caleb, who struggled a little, holding both of them. With his hands free, Benjamin climbed into the lower branches of the fairy's tree.

"What do you see?" asked Jonathan.

Benjamin looked down. The light from Caleb's torches bounced and flickered on his face. It barely reached Benjamin in the tree. "Nothing."

Jonathan shifted his weight, settling me easily on his hip. He looked down at Caleb. "What do you hear?"

Caleb tilted his head like a puppy. He closed his eyes and pursed his lips. His eyes opened wide. "Nothing."

Jonathan nodded and turned back toward the path home. "Bring the light. Let's go."

"No," Caleb said, "Listen! There's nothing! How can there be nothing? Benjamin?" He reached for our brother as he hopped out of the tree. "Where did everything go?"

Jonathan stopped.

"It's just black," Benjamin said. "Outside this circle.... Once you get past the star torches... it's just black everywhere."

"Are you sure?" asked Jonathan.

"There's nothing."

"Where did everything go?" asked Caleb.

"We're not sticking around to find out," said Jonathan. "Benjamin, take that other torch from Caleb. Let's go."

"I don't need it," Benjamin said.

"He can't carry them both. Look at him." It was true. Having trouble holding them each in one hand, Caleb was trying to balance one on top of the other. His eight-year-old fingers slipped.

Benjamin sighed and grabbed the top one before it fell. "I guess if the world only exists within the light of these torches, we'd better keep them lit. I'll go in front." He glared at his younger brother.

"You follow Jonathan, and make sure you shout if you hear anything." He started walking without waiting to see if anyone followed.

Jonathan walked carefully, stepping deliberately in Benjamin's footsteps. For a while, I watched his feet cover the smaller footprints, sink into the ground a little farther, and leave bigger prints behind us. The shadows started to come back as we reached the path. I snuggled my face into my brother's neck. As I closed my eyes, I heard crickets again.

I must have fallen asleep that night, swaying in his arms, because my next memory was of Jonathan tucking me in at home. In the morning, my hand had been wrapped in a sweet-smelling cloth. The sting was almost gone. Mom's remedies worked quickly.

30

The hill was a gentle slope, but the path wound around it anyway, taking me in circles when I wanted to get to the clearing directly. After a couple of turns, I paused to look through the trees uphill. They thinned out near the top, and I could almost see where I needed to go. Leaving the path, I hiked through the woods, occasionally pushing branches aside and stepping over fallen logs. It was darker than the path, but it was still early.

My glasses started to fog up, so I pulled them off and wiped them with the edge of my shirt. My breath left a little trail of smoke. The temperature dropped quickly, and goosebumps prickled my bare arms. I should have brought a sweater. The snowflakes at the Tower might not have been such a fluke after all. It was weird for this time of year, but the weather around here had always been a little weird—seemingly eternal autumns with a few days that got extra cold so the locals could call it Winter.

They don't know what Winter is.

I'd never seen more than a few flakes before I got to the Midwest. That was a rough transition... from checking the mail barefoot to wading through drifts up to my knees to get to class just a few days later. Apparently, our Winter Weekend had come a little late this year. Or maybe it'd come back? Did Dad's letters mention snow back in the first semester? I pulled my arms into my sides and took bigger steps as I climbed straight up the hill.

My foot slipped on wet leaves, and the next thing I knew, I landed in plank pose on the side of the hill. Something rustled near my face. I pushed back on my heels but didn't see whatever it was. Something dropped through the branches of a tree in the distance and crashed to the ground. A particularly clumsy squirrel, maybe. Or a snake. *Please let it be the squirrel.* Whatever it was, the sudden noise was enough to make other animals scatter. The forest was much louder for a minute or two.

That's probably how I missed his arrival.

I wiped my hands on my jeans and stood back up. The next switchback in the path was just a few feet in front of me. Someone else stood on it. He looked toward the other sound. *I wish I had his cloak.*

There wasn't anything inherently creepy about a man in a hooded cloak in this community, even one much taller and broader-shouldered than me. But still, I hesitated to make myself known. Maybe I'd spent too much time in the city.

Thomas had made some snarky comments about my haircut, and even Elspeth offered to lend me a dress if I "wanted to get out of those jeans." *I like my jeans.* I even liked the new holes I just put in the knees. More authentic. Brian's girlfriend would call them *vintage distressed.*

As a cloud crawled across the sun, and the woods grew darker, the guy in the cloak cast a longer shadow, and I felt a little *distressed* myself.

Another crash in the trees ahead, and the guy took off after it, his cloak lashing out behind him. I shifted my weight but managed not to lose my balance this time. The guy followed the path. It straightened out now that I was near the top of the hill. Without really knowing why, I jogged after him. *Not such a damsel in distress after all.*

At the top of the hill, the trees suddenly disappeared. The clearing Mom showed me came out of nowhere, a perfect ring edged in redcaps, surrounded by dense forest. Cloak Guy stood in the middle, his arms raised as if to hold up the sky. I stepped into the shadow of one of the last trees and held my breath.

The cloud covering the sun moved, and I could've sworn this guy was responsible if it weren't basically impossible. The sun peeked out of the torn cloud, its rays escaping and forming beams like a child would draw. They lit up the trees.

They lit up *my* tree. I jumped back, flinching at the sound I made. When I raised my eyes, the guy in the clearing dropped his arms and pulled back his hood. He looked over his shoulder and seemed to focus on a tree to my right.

Adam.

He wasn't wearing his mask under his cloak, apparently not on duty for whatever this was. What kind of shift did he have? He couldn't be Guardian all the time. Obviously. Not least because he was here now. I hadn't really thought about it until—

What was that?

Another crash came from the other side of the clearing, but this time he didn't chase after it. His arms came up in a defensive pose, his back to me again. Something rattled the branches.

"Go back!" Adam yelled. "You have no business here!"

Against my better judgment, I stepped out from behind the tree. I wanted to see what he was facing—the shadow that covered everything in Mom's vision.

But it wasn't just one shadow. The darkness was made up of a hundred moving parts, overlapping shades that rolled across each other as they pushed into the clearing. Where were they coming from?

Not this dimension. The air felt thin. *Not the air. Reality.* Like the bubble around our existence stretched thin, and something on the other side held a needle.

A tree fell in the distance. The noise was almost covered by a loud, mechanical rumbling.

Then, the shaking branches became still. Not taking any chances, I pulled a large rock out of the ground, hefted it in my right hand. Adam turned around. His face was red, and his eyes dark. He wasn't surprised to see me. "Didn't you hear me? Get out of here!" His voice sounded strangely hollow.

I can't believe he thinks I'll obey that order. When have I ever—

The shadows pulled back across the sun, and the temperature dropped again with the disappearing light. I shivered.

"What is that?" I yelled.

"Go!" A voice that was not Adam's echoed from where he stood as if it were coming a long way down a very dark tunnel.

Wind ripped through the clearing. The trees should have blocked it, but the air streaked through and around them, dragging leaves and sticks up with it. Adam's hands came up again.

I raised my rock uselessly.

Because I was sure now, something was here with us, and it didn't want us here. It had just used Adam to make that clear. He shook. The blown debris whipped around the clearing, making tighter and tighter circles.

I took a few steps forward to avoid the branches and leaves spinning past behind me.

It liked that. A laugh that still didn't sound like Adam came from Adam's throat. His eyes blazed, but he stayed where he was. His hands opened above his head, pushing against the sky. He blinked, and his eyes cleared for a moment.

He was winning. He shook his head free and lowered one arm, reaching out to me. I hesitated, but the whirlwind pulled debris closer, making the clearing less clear. I dropped the rock, closed the gap, and took his hand.

Everything stopped.

Like the plane, and the Creek, and the Reading, the world froze around me. *I've been here before.* The leaves hung in the air. In the moment before the clouds cleared, a tiny light flashed in the darkness of the tree line. It felt like the world ended at that tree line, nothing but darkness beyond the clearing. The floating light blinked out. *There's no such thing as fairies.*

Then the sky turned blue, and although it was weird to see the clouds frozen, this time the calm was soothing.

Adam's hair shone in a perfect beam of sunshine cutting through the clouds. His hand felt strong and warm and safe. It would have been romantic if it had been anyone else. I didn't know why he hated me so much, but this didn't seem like the moment to ask.

"Don't let go," he said, his voice softer than it'd ever been, and when he looked at me, my stomach flipped.

Okay, so maybe it's a little romantic. I cursed the Tarot card in my back pocket.

He looked away, up at the hand he still raised, and closed his eyes. He was shaking again, but so was everything around us.

The ground rumbled. The frozen branches and leaves started to shiver and then drop out of the air, suddenly regaining their weight.

I gripped his hand and widened my stance, balancing on my toes like I used to when the L took a fast curve. The same vibrations went through the soles of my shoes. The energy warmed my legs, then continued up through my gut, my chest, along my arm. My hand burned where it clasped Adam's, and I could have sworn sparks jumped the connection. The ground rose underneath my feet like the hill was getting taller.

The sparks from our fingers raced across Adam's chest and followed the line of his other arm.

Lightning struck the sky.

The clouds exploded in white light. My eyes burned in the direct sunlight. When I remembered to look away, I squeezed my eyes shut. Spots danced on my eyelids.

Most of the spinning leaves slowed again. When it stopped, I could tell it was over. Whatever started the cyclone had gone. We were alone in the center of the clearing, surrounded by spiraling piles of leaves and branches.

Adam lowered his arm and wrapped it around me, our other hands still clasped between us. He bent his head, and our foreheads met. With his eyes still closed, he took a long breath. My breath matched his. My glasses pressed into my face as his nose bumped mine. We may as well have been floating in space.

Everything else was gone.

I tilted my head back. His breath caught. When he opened his eyes, he dropped my hand and pushed me away. The familiar glare returned.

"What are you doing here?" he asked.

"What am I doing here? What the hell was that?"

"That—was none of your business. You shouldn't be here." He walked back toward the path, apparently done with whatever brought him here.

I wasn't. I held my ground, looking at the drifting leaves. "Where are you going? That thing—"

"It's gone," he said, "But it'll come back. You shouldn't be here when it does. I'm not strong enough to push it back again. I nearly wasn't strong enough this time." He looked at me curiously.

My stomach tightened. I waited for him to elaborate. A competitive staring contest in the clearing.

"Why are you here?" he asked again, but this time it sounded less like an accusation.

"My mother chose this place. She chose it. But there's something here that..."

"That doesn't care who chose it," he said. "It's not safe here. *You're* not safe here."

"Why not? What is it? And if it's not safe, why are you here? What kind of magic makes the earth move?" I stared at him across the clearing. His cloak rippled around him. I was a little embarrassed by how I phrased that, but I couldn't take it back now. Instead, I asked the question that'd been on my mind since I first saw his shadow in the woods. "What are you?"

"I'm the Guardian at the Gate, and I shouldn't have let you back in. Go home, Cate. Go back to school and the city and forget all about us. Again."

31

ait. What? Was that why Adam was all weird and hostile? Because I'd been on my Wakening? What did he care? I didn't know what to say, so I said nothing. Somehow that was worse than anything I might have said. He disappeared into the trees.

As I stood there watching the trees sway in the gentle breeze that was nothing like the chaotic wind that tore through the clearing a few minutes ago, I remembered... something. Before I left, three years ago, before Adam left on his Wakening, was there something?

It seemed so long ago. Walking with Adam, my hand in his again. Another memory fought its way forward. Sitting side-by-side, knees touching, talking about our plans. *Why is it so hazy?*

I squeezed my eyes shut, blocking out the present. Images flickered across my eyelids, half-formed. An argument. Another voice. *Just forget about him. He's not worth it.* And I had. I tried again to bring the memory back, but it wouldn't come.

I wiped my eyes, but no tears blurred my vision. My head hurt. I had goosebumps. When I rubbed my arms, my hands came away cold and wet. I looked down just as another snowflake landed on the back of my hand and slowly dissolved.

Since I couldn't keep standing at the top of a windy hill and staring into the middle distance like a Brontë heroine, I shook it off and made my way back down. I was cold and wet, and my insides felt just as soggy.

Family first, Thomas had said yesterday. One problem at a time. Even if new problems seemed to materialize at every step.

I needed to take decisive action. Brian once told me how he liked running because pounding his feet on the pavement felt better than pounding his face into a pillow. I didn't deny that there was a certain appeal to working out a chaotic emotional problem with something I could physically control. But if I ran down this hill, I was just as likely to end up back in the Healer's cottage as I was to emerge with a sense of inner peace.

Instead, I combined some of the meditation practices I grew up with and a mindfulness technique I learned in a kinesiology course at school. *See? Going away to college was totally worth it. Here I am using those Gen Ed classes in real life.* I concentrated on the placement of my feet on the path. One step at a time, consciously feeling the ground underneath my shoes. I timed my breaths with my movements, in through my nose, out through my mouth. With each step, I mentally scanned the next part of my body, moving up from my feet, relaxing the muscles by force of will. I loosened my jaw, pulling my tongue down from the roof of my mouth. I hadn't even realized it was stuck there. By the time I reached the bottom of the hill, I felt much more myself.

Unfortunately, taking this route burned off most of the afternoon. I needed to report Mom's choice to Mrs. Kirk as I had intended to do before the... snow. *Honestly, it's probably for the best that I go there now. I'm sure that if the thing I think I saw was really as bad as it seemed, Mrs. Kirk would know about it. She'll already be working on a plan to protect us. I'm sure it's fine.*

Just to be extra sure, I leaned my back against a tree and pulled out Nora's card. I closed my eyes and hid the card between my hands. It warmed immediately, and I wasn't surprised to see the knight raising his sword and charging ahead. *A man on a mission.* I chose to interpret it as confirmation of my plan rather than a warning.

So, that's it. I'll go straight to the Tower. I pushed off the tree and got moving again, already considering the route of least resistance. I shook my head. *Just stick to the path.*

The market was probably getting ready to close down by now. There would be fewer people wanting to ambush me with their grief. I was sure I'd given Mrs. Kirk enough time to return from wherever Caleb saw her going with Giles, but sticking to the path might give her a few extra minutes. If she was coming from the Gatehouse, she'd need it.

Adam must have reported what happened with Alice. The Speaker probably wanted to see for herself. If the Gatekeeper's health was failing, the coven needed to know. They needed to prepare the next initiate.

Do they still think it's me?

Nope. Not today's problem. Today's goals were entirely built around making the funeral happen as easily and peacefully as possible. For Mom. For all of us.

Whatever happened after that was going to happen.

I'm putting out positive energy. Everything will be fine. Everything happens in its own time, for its own reasons.

When I reached the Speaker's office, I knocked on the heavy wooden door, and the iron handle turned on its own.

"Ms. Corey, come in. I'm so sorry for your loss," Mrs. Kirk said, coming from behind her desk. Her office was immaculate, everything at right angles, oriented to the cardinal directions. A few books stood between stone bookends on a cabinet behind her, but her desk was clear. Her head would probably have spun if she'd seen Nora's office. *What was she doing before I came in, sitting at that empty desk facing the door? Was she expecting me?*

She was shorter than me, and when she took my hands and looked up at me with sympathetic eyes, I was reminded of a child who had done something wrong and hoped you won't notice. I'd forgotten she was so small. She'd seemed so imposing on the platform during the ritual.

I searched her expression but couldn't place my suspicion. She smiled, the fine lines around her eyes deepening for a moment. Then she squeezed my fingers and released them. She flicked her wrist at the door, and it closed gently behind me.

She smoothed a stray gray hair back to the dark bun at the nape of her neck. Like many of the women in our community, she didn't dye her hair, and although the top had gone almost completely silver, it was still growing in dark underneath.

I'd changed my hair so many times in the past couple of years that I couldn't say for sure what it looked like under the dark purple dye. I pushed my glasses back up and thanked her as she retreated behind the desk.

She gestured to a chair opposite her and waited for me to sit before settling into her own. It was like sitting in the dean's office back at school. She tilted her head a little and asked, "How's your mom doing?"

"She's doing the best she can right now. It's hard when there is so much... uncertainty."

She frowned. "Uncertainty?"

"Since we don't actually know what happened to him."

"Yes," she sighed. "We will probably never know why he chose to cross the Creek." She looked down meditatively.

I can't take it. "How can you be so sure that he did? Or that he did it willingly? Did you even investigate?"

Her head popped up. "What do you mean? You were at the Reading. You heard Detective Parker's report. He had no doubts."

It felt like a test. If Thomas was right about Shiri, she wasn't strong enough to have caused my blackout during the Reading. Was the Speaker?

If I admit that I can't remember what happened there, what will she do? Send me back to the Healer's cottage? I don't have time for mandated recuperation.

While I struggled to come up with a reasonable response, she mistook my silent anger for sadness. "He was very troubled," she said, shaking her head.

"What do you mean?"

"I'm sure you know. Some things changed while you were away."

"What things?"

"I don't like to get into anyone's personal life. Perhaps you should talk to your mother."

"My mother is mourning his loss, just like everyone else. More. Her sons are missing, her husband is gone, and you seem eager to erase his existence."

Shit. I've gone too far. Mrs. Kirk hadn't noticed Matthew and Gabriel were missing at the Reading, and Mom had kept them out of the investigation somehow. Whatever she'd been planning, it looked like I'd ruined it.

Mrs. Kirk pursed her lips. She sat back in her chair. *Was she humming?*

The Speaker's eyes unfocused briefly. Then, she nodded. "I think we need to take a step back. We're here to discuss your mother's plans for the ceremony. Not your father's...mistakes. Let's remember him before these troubles."

Frigga, Mother, bless me with patience. I could scream. This woman is actively destroying my father's reputation rather than admitting he was right.

But my mother wanted a blessing, and the Speaker was High Priestess. I folded my hands demurely in my lap. Maybe she missed what I said about my brothers. "I'm sorry. It's just such an emotional time. Please don't allow my disrespect to..."

She waved a hand as if it were nothing, but the corners of her mouth twitched, and I knew she felt like she'd won something. She pulled a map from her desk drawer and smoothed it in front of her. She placed her hands on either side. "What location has she chosen?"

For a second, I saw the clearing, not as a dot on the map, but real in front of me, swirling with a tornado of leaves and branches again. I blinked, and it was gone. Mrs. Kirk waited. I watched her eyes as I pointed to the place on the map where the green splotches of forest opened up. Her eyebrows rose just slightly.

"Interesting," she said, looking up at me, and her eyebrows were back in place. She smiled, her lips tight. "A lovely spot. Such nice views."

I waited.

"Of course, I'm sure that she also considered..." She pointed to a spot farther from the Creek, at the base of a hill. "This area has some lovely wildflowers. It would be so nice to visit. Peaceful."

Her eyes narrowed a fraction. When I didn't respond, I could've sworn there was another twitch, down this time. Then she straightened and smiled again. "Okay, so the clearing then? I'm sure that we can make that... work. If you're sure that's what she wants...?"

My turn to sit back. "It is."

"Then I can take care of the rest. Shall we plan for sunset tomorrow? That will give us the day to prepare." She folded the map and returned it to the drawer.

"Thank you." *That wasn't so bad. Awkward-as-aura-work, but could have been worse.*

"Perhaps afterwards, you and I can have a little chat about your future here. About your responsibilities."

Shit. "I don't think you understand…"

She stood. Once again, I got the sense that she knew more than she should.

"We'll talk again tomorrow. Please share my condolences with your mother, and let her know that if there is anything I can do…" The speaker waved her hand, and the door creaked open behind me.

I guess this meeting is over.

32

I caught my breath in the entry to the Tower. Mission accomplished, even though it was close there for a minute. What would have happened if she'd heard what I said about Matthew and Gabriel? Would she reopen the case? Start a new one? How many of my family members would be accused of tampering with the boundary? Was it worth it if we got my brothers back?

Why hadn't she heard me? Her reaction had been strange. The humming. And when she nodded, it was like she was resetting the scene. *Like she'd blacked out for a second.*

And now I know how Mom is keeping two missing sons off the radar. No wonder she was so exhausted. She'd used her siren song to distract anyone who started to think about them. She must have done it before I came home.

I sat on the floor and grounded myself with my back against the stone wall. Before I looked at Nora's card, I took a moment to set my intention. It wasn't much more than a vibe check, but I wanted to know how I was doing.

Will anything positive come of these awkward conversations and experiments in self-control? The Queen of Coins smiled down at the pentacle in her lap. Making progress. Despite the lingering feeling that the High Priestess was hiding something, I was confident that Mrs. Kirk would do what she could to protect my mother. *Maybe I can find a balance after all.*

The sun painted colored shadows on the floor as it passed through the stained glass window. It was getting late, but there was still some time before I needed to get home for dinner. Maybe it was the influence of the nurturing Queen of Coins, or maybe it was Mrs. Kirk's reminder that I was running out of time to get back through the Gate before the time of my Wakening officially closed, but I felt drawn to the Gatekeeper. Besides, I wanted to know what the Speaker saw. Was Alice awake again?

"No." Adam was in Guardian mode again, standing at the foot of the bridge to Alice's cottage with his mask in place, his staff in his hand, blocking my way.

"I just want to see if she's okay," I said.

"The next time I let you cross this bridge, it will be so you can take the door on the other side. Are you ready to leave?"

"You know I'm not."

"Then the Gate is closed to you."

I looked past him, half expecting the door to open on its own like last time. Maybe half wishing it would. But it seemed that Alice didn't want to see me now or wasn't interested in contradicting Adam's intention. I shouldn't have been surprised. The trust between the Guardian and Gatekeeper was essential to her protection and the safety of the Gate. I looked back at Adam, trying to make out his eyes in the shadows cast by the mask. The wolf's face was impenetrable.

"Can we just... talk?" I asked. "We used to be friends, I think."

"You think?" He shook his head. "I don't have anything to

say to you."

"Take off the mask and say that."

He slowly pulled the wolf mask away from his face. He took a deep breath before looking up, and his eyes were no more readable than they were before.

"That," he said solemnly.

I blinked. "Was that a joke? Did the Guardian at the Gate just make a joke?"

"I'm not the Guardian when the mask is off." He shrugged.

I considered grabbing the mask and throwing it into the Creek, but he had the leather straps looped around his wrist. "Adam, what happened to us? Why do you hate me so much?"

He crossed his arms, and the mask dangled from his elbow. "I don't hate you."

I didn't believe it, but his eyes softened when I looked up. "Why are you trying to get rid of me?"

"You don't want to be here." His arms fell to his sides. "You shouldn't stay. I'm trying to make it easier for you."

"By acting like a psycho?"

"By guarding the Gate." He lifted the mask again.

"Wait!" I reached out to stop him, but my hand came short of actually touching the wolf.

He hesitated.

"What are you not telling me?"

His eyes narrowed, "You know."

"I don't," I insisted. "You always know when someone is lying. Test me."

He closed his eyes. Static lifted the hairs on my arms. My skin tingled. The feeling passed when he opened his eyes. He looked confused.

"It's there," he said, "But it's not..."

"What?" I shifted my weight and put my hands on my hips.

He took a step closer. "What happened to you?"

My stomach flipped. "What are you talking about?"

"Nothing is gone. It's just... blocked. You're being honest when you say you don't know, but... it's all still there." He leaned to the side as if something blocked his view.

"What's all still where? You're not making any sense." I shifted my weight again to put myself back in front of him. Could he see what I'd almost remembered? Through the haze that blocked that part of my mind from me?

He tilted his head and squinted at me before closing his eyes again. The air around me charged. The push was stronger this time. A hum in my ears. A flash of memory. Walking in the clearing again. The edge of something different. Then it was gone. Adam looked at me like a wasp was circling my head.

"What was that?" I asked. "I almost remembered it before... after the... thing that happened when we were in the woods."

He smirked. "Right, before, after the thing that happened."

"You know what I mean. What would you call it?" I asked.

"An unnecessary danger," he said. "You shouldn't go there. Nobody should, but you definitely shouldn't."

"It isn't safe," I said, echoing his earlier warning. He wasn't wrong. Whatever had tried to come through the veil had felt... malevolent. I didn't believe in Evil any more than I believed in fairies, but those shades had definitely meant us harm.

"Right. It isn't safe."

"Are you going to tell me why, or is this a fun game of keep away for you? What's with all of the secrecy, Adam?" He'd known what he'd find when he got there. How? And who else knew? The Speaker's hesitance to approve the clearing as the site for my father's memorial took on new meaning.

"Look," he said, staring at a spot at least two inches behind my eyes, "You already know more than I do. I don't know why you can't see it, and I don't know what will happen if I tell you what we both know. Maybe nothing. Maybe you won't believe me. Maybe your head will explode." He tilted his head again, more like a curious puppy than the wolf.

I raised an eyebrow. "Ha," I said flatly, "there's that Guardian humor again."

"No, seriously, I don't know what will happen. I've never seen a block like that."

You're cursed, Elspeth had said. *It's a curse that's binding you.*

"So, you're just not going to tell me things... things that I already know... because you're afraid to get brains all over you? Thanks, man. You've been a great help. I feel safer knowing you've got my back." I punctuated my statement by turning my back and walking away.

"Cate."

I stopped but didn't turn around. It seemed like every time I talked to Adam, I just got more confused. *What if he's right? What if the Reading wasn't the first time someone messed with my memory?* Adam was probably the only one who could tell me.

"Cate," he said again. "I'm sorry."

Damn it. I don't have a choice. Who else am I going to talk to? Mom was grieving. Mrs. Kirk made her position clear. My brothers were... I didn't know. They'd want to protect me, and that was the last thing I needed right now when it felt like I was on the verge of finally understanding.

When I turned around, he stood so close to me that I jumped back reflexively and tripped over my own feet. He grabbed my arm, and I overcorrected, smashing my face into the folds of his cloak.

I froze. When I let myself breathe again, my eyes watered and my glasses fogged up. I inhaled the scent of rain and dirt and falling leaves. The ground dropped out from under me.

For a moment, I was falling.

Then I was back in the clearing again, but Adam wasn't there. I stood inside the ring of trees with my dad. He was talking about my Wakening. I didn't want to go, but he said it was important. I asked why it mattered so much to him, and he was about to answer, but the memory faded, and I couldn't hear him anymore.

"Wait!" I cried, even as I surfaced. Adam's arms tightened around me.

"I've got you," he said.

I looked up. As my glasses cleared, the memory disappeared completely. Adam's eyes were soft, but there was a bit of a playful smirk behind the concern.

"Don't let go," I said. I closed my eyes. Inhaled. Leaned in. The same smell of wet trees and earth flooded my senses and made me dizzy. This time the descent was less steep, but I gripped Adam's arms anyway, taking a step closer.

I was walking in the clearing, but this memory was older. I gritted my teeth in frustration—in both the memory and now, I wasn't getting what I wanted. In the past, I looked up at the person I walked with, and my present self was barely surprised to see Adam in the memory.

What did surprise me was the feeling underneath. *Why don't I remember this? I'm not sure what we are to each other, but Adam is... was... more than just my brother's friend.* "Don't go," I said, not sure if I was saying it in the past or present.

Past Adam did that annoying half-smile thing. He'd already made up his mind. I didn't know why he bothered to bring me here. If he expected me to yell, he'd be disappointed.

In the present, Adam held me close and rested his cheek on my head. I shrugged him off but didn't step away.

"Why are you doing this?" The question echoed in my memory.

"You know why."

Maybe I did, but this conversation was equally frustrating in both timelines, so both of me pushed him away at the same time. This time, when I stumbled back, I caught myself.

"You're an ass," I said.

He didn't even have the decency to look confused. Of course, he'd heard it before. We were still recycling that old conversation, even as the details faded.

"You left me," I said for the first time.

"You were supposed to be here when I got back," he said. "Why didn't you wait for me?"

I couldn't tell if he was angry or disappointed. Somehow I was sure that the me in that memory would have known. I was also sure that he was still an ass.

"My dad—"

Adam laughed. Angry, then. "It's always about him, isn't it? Even now. Well? What are you going to do now, Daddy's girl?"

33

The door to Alice's cabin swung open. *He's not the Guardian without his mask, he said.* I pushed past him and almost ran across the bridge. I slammed the door behind me. I saw him fuming through the window. He glared at the cottage door before putting his mask back on and resuming his stance at the foot of the bridge, his back to us.

Alice sat in the only chair in the room. She looked stronger than when I last saw her, but she didn't stand to greet me. The sun shone coldly through the windows on both sides. I couldn't tell if it was the glamour or just a nice day.

"You do not know what you do not know."

"Because no one will tell me! Why is everything a blessed secret? I can't even access my own memories without that," I waved in Adam's direction, "psycho earth wizard and his obsession with the truth."

As I said it, I realized that I was right. Adam's natural elemental magic must have enhanced the connection to my memory when I smelled his cloak. The same cloak he wore in the memory and in the clearing when we faced that spirit. It had to be a spirit to affect the air the way it did, but whose spirit could be so strong? My father's? I couldn't believe my father would be so violent, especially around me, but maybe that was why Adam held my hand. I protected him.

I couldn't be sure if I wanted it to be true, but I had to admit that I liked the idea of Adam needing me. It felt familiar and weirdly comforting. There was a connection there that I didn't know I had, but it was already slotting into place as if it had always been there. *What else am I missing that's right in front of me?*

"Are you going to explain...?" I asked, with very little hope that she would.

She sighed softly. "You will know when the time is right."

"Right," I said. "Thanks."

"The Queen of Coins is not finished with you." But Alice was. I wasn't even going to ask how she knew about my last reading. Of course she did.

"I'm glad you're feeling better." I meant it, but she might have questioned my motives. I did.

Her door opened again. Adam still stood across the bridge. He was wearing his mask and facing into the community, but something about his posture showed he was aware of the change behind him. As I crossed the bridge, he stepped to the side, enough for me to get by. He asked no questions as I passed. His bearing was regal, but I was looking for a Queen, not a soldier. I followed the path, feeling the eyes of the wolf on my back.

I was so lost in thought that I almost missed the most obvious next step. Literally. Following the spiraling path from the Gate led me directly past the Healer's cottage. I needed to get home, but who in this entire community was more connected to the Queen of Coins than Elspeth? Careful and caring, a practical female figure with both sense and sensibility. And she even read classical literature.

When she opened her door, she had her novel in the other

hand, a finger between the pages. "So, the Cat came back," she said. She smiled, drew an invisible X on the page and closed the book. She left the door open and walked back inside.

"The very next day," I said. I followed her in and closed the door behind me. "You didn't think I was a goner, did you?" The old song used to annoy me, but when Elspeth invoked it, there was comfort in the custom.

Elspeth gave me a pity chuckle. "How's your head?"

"Still attached," I said. "Only hurts when I think."

"Better stop that then. Let me take a look." She gestured to the cot. When I sat, she stepped back and crossed her arms. Her tongue stuck out a little as she considered waves of light that only she could see. "Had an interesting time, have you?"

"You could say that," I said.

She dropped her arms. "Well, you're a mess. But you know that. Your head is healing in spite of you. There are all kinds of knots," she waved at the area around me. "But you know, they're not related to the injury." She sat in her chair, glancing at the book on the table. "Do you want to talk about it?" she said, her mind clearly still in the Massachusetts Bay Colony.

"If you're not busy..."

Something flickered in her eyes as they adjusted to the present. It wasn't a small thing to come back to reality. The room was still lit by candles and filled with herbs that would have been at home in Hawthorne's time, but no one here would be shamed into their fashion choices. Good thing, too, since I doubted the Puritans would approve of my hair color or her neckline. "I know how it ends," she said. "I'm in no hurry to get there."

I wasn't sure what to ask her or what she might know, but Alice sent me here for a reason. I looked for connections. "You and Caleb have been together for a while now, huh?"

She frowned. "You didn't come here to talk about that.

What do you really want to ask me?"

"Are you happy here?" She might have been the only person who could understand even a little bit of what I was going through. That night when we snuck out to look at the Creek before Caleb and Duncan left for their Wakenings, she'd been so excited.

I mean, she was nervous because, of course, she was. It would be our turn next. Leaving everything behind to see what else is out there.

But as we sat in the shadow of the tree line and watched the moon glint off the ripples in the water, she'd smiled. When Caleb came back—early, without Duncan—the smile had been gone. In the days before I went to the Gatehouse, we barely spoke. Her parents had forbidden her to leave, and mine had almost pushed Thomas and me out the door. Now we might both spend the rest of our lives in Queen's Creek, whether we chose it or not.

She shrugged. "This is my home. Everything I need is here."

"You never wanted to see if there was more?"

"You saw. You still came back."

It wasn't the same, but that wasn't what I said. "It's not permanent."

She frowned, pulling her braid over her shoulder and twisting the ends around her fingers.

"What?" I asked.

"You're planning to leave again? To stay away this time?"

"I came back to find out what happened to Dad," I said, aware that I hadn't really answered her question. Every conversation lately seemed to move me further from the answers to my own.

Elspeth hesitated. "I can't tell you what to do, but that binding—"

"It blocks my Gift. And that bites, for sure. Somebody is

going to answer for my traumatic outsider childhood. But you know where I won't need a Gift? Outside." *Please let me have time for at least one ill-advised revenge plot before I get out of town. If not for my father, for my misspent youth.* I could still take pride in my unmagical existence while grieving all my losses.

"Umm. Can I take another look?" Before I could answer, she stood, pulling those half-moon spectacles out of her skirt again. Squinting at me, she found something by the side of my head. Pulled at an invisible thread until I winced. Nodded. "Yeah, no. You're stuck. I mean, you can go wherever… whenever you want, but yeah, you're always going to end up back here."

"What does that mean?"

"You can't leave and not come home. Not without leaving something behind. There are these… threads. Remember when I said you were all knotted up?"

"I thought you meant emotionally."

"That, too. But these…" she pulled the invisible thread, and I felt a little tug in my chest. "And these…" she pulled the one she found by my ear. My head tilted in that direction as if she was pulling my hair. "They're something else. You may want to leave now, but you'll always come back."

"My Wakening is almost over. How's that going to work when I'm in Chicago, and the Gate is closed?"

She pulled off her spectacles and tapped them against her palm. "I think that depends on what's under that bind. We're going to have to free your Gift."

I left the Healer feeling more broken than when I woke up from the head wound. For all her empathic intuition, Elspeth couldn't see who'd cast the bind or how to remove it. We needed more answers, and I had no idea how to get them. Whoever had done this to me was strong, and they'd hid it from me for a reason. *What would they do when they found out I knew?*

Following the curves of the path, I took the branch that led home. The spiraling dirt road had sometimes felt monotonous in its inefficiency, but I barely noticed. I tried to imagine what Elspeth saw, the twisting threads circling my head. I touched my face, but of course, there was nothing there that I could feel. I brushed my hands down my shirt, but nothing caught like when the Healer pulled an invisible string. I didn't know what I expected. I didn't have her Gift.

Or.

Maybe I do. I'm bound. Maybe I can hear things like Caleb or see things like Benjamin. Maybe my singing voice can... no. I have a terrible voice. That's not the curse. That's just genetics. Dad was a terrible singer. But who knows what I can do or how long I've been blocked from meeting my Potential?

Despite the way I'd embraced my normal life in the city, I had to admit I'd always held out just the slightest secret hope that I was just.... delayed. It was almost reassuring to finally have a reason. A name for what went wrong. Even if it didn't fix anything. I'd gotten used to living mostly magic-free during my time away. But if I was bound to our community, and my Gift was cursed, I'd have to go back to my study of practical spells. I needed to develop my Craft. At least until I could find a way to break free.

My independence had been hard-won, even if it was an illusion, and I refused to go back to the life I led before my Wakening.

34

I didn't know what started the fight. Maybe it was me. The last few months before my seventeenth birthday were cloudy. Dark, right before the worst storm of the year, shot through with burning lights and screaming thunder, cloudy. The garden was almost destroyed. Maybe that was it. Mom stopped it all with a word. My brothers dropped their hands, wiped out the sigils in the dirt. The game had gotten out of control. The magic was too strong, already glitching and unpredictable.

Someone lifted me up. I leaned against him, my head on his chest, his heartbeat drowning out whatever he said. Things faded after that. Someone said, "I'm sorry!" And someone said, "We didn't mean to..."

The memory was all mixed up like the ones Adam helped me see, connected to them somehow. My head hurt again, but I wasn't sure if it was the memory or the concussion. I tried to remember what happened next, but time was very wibbly-wobbly, and I couldn't get the order right. I argued with my mom. Or was that before? Which time?

Things had been awkward but mostly peaceful between us since I'd been back. I couldn't be sure what it was like before. There was a reason I didn't call home from Chicago. A reason besides the Gate. I pulled out Nora's card without waiting for it to warm between my hands. Zombies. Judgment came in the form of an angel raising the dead. The card called for reflection and suggested an awakening or a reckoning. I was more than ready.

Family dinner can wait.

I stepped off the path, almost home but still out of sight. A fallen log, just out of the trees, had been carved with a couple of seats, worn smooth by the years. I sat, rubbed my hands on my thighs, and rolled my head gently from side to side. Closing my eyes, I let my hands fall open on my knees and listened to my breath flow in and out. The rhythmic waves merged with the sounds of birds in the trees and squirrels rustling in the leaves. The light that made it through the trees played across my eyelids. I tried to clear my mind, but the questions kept pushing back. I concentrated on fading each one as it appeared. I needed to go back to that day in the garden.

Mom was so angry. "You could have been killed!"

"I'm fine."

"This time. What happens next time? And after that?" Mom was shaking.

"I will be fine. I can take care of myself," I said through gritted teeth.

"It isn't safe for you here." She stared into my eyes as if she would communicate telepathically, but neither of us was adept at that skill.

"What are you saying?"

She sighed. "Maybe it's time."

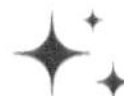

"Let me help."

That voice. It was happening again. The voices in my memory and in my ears said the same thing. I kept my eyes closed but nodded, sensing Adam sitting next to me on the log bench. He put his hand on mine, and I closed my fingers around it. He guided my meditation back to the memory.

"Let me help," he said back then. In my memory, we were back in the house. I sat at the kitchen table. My mom stood in front of me, gripping the back of a chair.

Adam.

Adam was nearby. As I gripped his hand, he became clearer in the memory. After helping me into the house, he'd backed off. He stood in the kitchen doorway and waited for my mom's response.

"We've had enough help from you," she said. "Encouraging her to put herself at risk."

"Mom, that's not fair!"

"It wasn't his fault," Thomas said. He inched past Adam to join us in the small space. "In fact, he—"

"Enough!"

"But, Mom!"

"No. Thank you for your offer, Adam, but it's time for you to go now." She looked at him for the first time since we came into the house, her fingers drumming a rhythm on the back of the chair. It was almost musical.

Adam nodded. "Of course," he said, holding her gaze for a moment before turning to me. "I'll see you later," he said. It was an invitation and a promise.

I smiled, but then he was gone.

Mom's hand stilled.

I opened my eyes.

Adam was looking at our hands, still clasped on my knee.

"She made you go," I said.

"It seemed like the right thing. It felt like my idea."

I squeezed his hand, adding one more thing to my growing

list of complaints against my mother.

He looked up at me. "And you agreed."

"I told you not to go." But that memory was still blurry, and I wasn't sure.

"We had a plan," he said. I could feel him waiting for me to make the connections.

"Help me remember."

He brushed the hair behind my ear with his free hand and then let his fingers rest on my temple. He closed his eyes.

I closed mine.

We were back on the path to the clearing. I was seventeen, and my boyfriend was leaving me.

"Don't go," I said then. The pain washed over me. It wasn't just a memory anymore.

He smiled a half-smile that was just enough to bring out the dimple in his cheek. I loved that dimple and hated him for weaponizing it. "You know I have to," he said.

"Why? Because she said so?"

"She's not wrong," he said. "You aren't safe here."

"Then stay! How am I safer without you?"

"It will only be for a little while. I'll find a job. Get us a place to live. In the meantime, you have Thomas..."

I laughed.

"And the rest of your brothers."

I rolled my eyes.

"And you are more than capable of protecting yourself for a few months." He smiled again. "Maybe just stay out of the garden when the guys get competitive."

"Take me with you."

"Your parents will never agree to that."

I wanted to say, "Who cares?" I wanted to run away and start our own kind of magic in another world. But I didn't. I wanted out so badly, but I wasn't ready.

"You promise you'll come back?" I said.

"You'll hardly even miss me. And then it will be your turn, and we can go together."

He would give up magic for me. Maybe not completely, because he'd always have his Gift. But leaving Queen's Creek, staying out after our Wakening... It would never be as strong.

Something had been missing from my unmagical life in Chicago, but it hadn't been my Gift. I'd never meant to go alone.

The clearing closed in until the path merged with the trees around us. Adam's hand dropped from my temple, but his other hand was still on mine, and his thumb traced the lines of my palm.

"When I came back, you were gone," he said. "They wouldn't tell me where you went."

"College. They sent me away to school."

"But why didn't you wait for me?"

"You left me first." It was childish, but the memory was still hazy, and I didn't have the answers he wanted. I wanted to explain, to wipe the pain from his eyes, but I didn't remember. Whatever I had with Adam was still there, but it was confusing to feel... the way I felt now, without the memory of the experiences that sparked it.

"We had a plan. You were supposed to wait for me."

With my eyes closed, I tried to go back to my memories of the time before I left. They were all out of order and still blurry, but they felt like more than fantasy, and a lot of them featured Adam. I felt his arms around me, his breath in my hair. I heard his heartbeat. I was lost in a haze of shifting scenes. Things I was sure I remembered blended in with the unfamiliar. Shadowy edges, blurry places that hid a presence I was starting to recognize. Sometimes, the shapes of things lost their focus entirely, and I was left with colors and sense memories.

Opening my eyes, I found the Adam from my memories there beside me. His hair had grown a little longer, and the mask of the Guardian leaned against the log, but this was the boy I left behind. My breath caught, and I looked down at our hands. I didn't know what to say.

It was a few minutes before sunset, and everything glittered. Frost coated the ground, glistening over the moss and stones. It crunched under my feet when I stood. The temperature must have dropped again. Our breath floated in the air. Adam draped his cloak over my shoulders and used it to pull me closer. My hands went to his chest. He was warm under his linen shirt, even though his arms were bare without the cloak. I leaned in and pressed my forehead against him.

"Cate." He said my name so softly that I felt the vibration before recognizing it.

My head rolled to the side. He smelled of leather, and wood, and dirt, the forest after the rain.

His arms tightened around me. A runic tattoo in blue ink flexed around his bicep. I wanted him to say my name again.

He did.

I raised my head, and this time, when he dipped his to meet me, our noses slid past each other, and our lips met. The kiss was a memory and an apology. I pulled a breath through my nose and parted my lips. Three years ago. He was saying goodbye. I didn't want him to go. I pulled his lower lip between my teeth as if this kiss would change his mind. His response was not quite a growl, low in his throat. I was reminded of the wolf's face on the Guardian's mask. His hands gripped my arms.

He pushed me away. He'd been pushing me away ever

since I came home.

We had a plan. He should have left on his Wakening when Caleb and Duncan did, but he wanted to wait for me. So we could go together.

But plans change.

There'd been a fight in the garden. My brothers' magic got out of control. I couldn't protect myself. Cate-the-Cursed with no Gift. I hadn't known I was bound.

It might not have mattered with the way their spells glitched and exploded. Early signs of the apocalypse. We didn't realize how unstable the energy was in Queens Creek.

Mom thought Adam was a bad influence. He never thought my missing Gift should hold me back. She just wanted to keep me safe.

When he left, she thought we were done, but he was just going ahead. We had a plan.

"Why didn't you come back?" My voice trembled.

"It wasn't safe. After what happened with Duncan. The hunters. I couldn't lead them back here. By the time I lost them, you were gone. So, I lost you, too."

"I'm sorry," I whispered. *Why didn't I wait for him? How could I have gone out there on my own and forgotten him?*

He stepped back. "I can't do this again. I don't know what's happened to you, but it doesn't change things. You have to leave Queen's Creek. And I have to stay. Go home, Cate."

Before I could say anything, he disappeared.

Pulling his cloak tighter, I finished the walk home slowly, my feet melting tracks into the frost.

35

I didn't want to see my mom after what Elspeth and Adam had helped me see. I wasn't sure I could forgive her, but I couldn't confront her about any of it. It was bad enough that she ruined my relationship, but she had the same Healer training as Elspeth, so by bell, book, and candle, she had to know about the binding.

We'd suspected Mrs. Kirk after Thomas found that list in her office, but she wanted me in the Gatehouse. *Why would she bind my Gift if she needed me to take over for Alice?*

Bound by someone close to you, Elspeth told me. *Someone very strong.* Mrs. Kirk had my Gift labeled on her list, and she was strong, but I would never have considered her close. And if she wanted me in the Gatehouse, it didn't make sense for her to leash my magic. The bind to keep me here, sure. But why announce me as the next Gatekeeper if she knew I didn't have a Gift to activate it?

The people closest to me had been the ones who sent me away. *"We couldn't allow you to be trapped in the Gatehouse for nothing,"* Mom had said.

Was Mom strong enough to create the bind herself, or did she just stand by while my father hid my Gift from me? Had she blocked my memories of Adam to keep us apart? What if she used her magic to make me forget again?

I hesitated at the door, listening to the voices on the other side. My mother laughed. At least one of my brothers had beaten me home. A moment later, Benjamin and Thomas rounded the corner on the path. It must have been Jonathan inside.

"Hey, Cate," called Ben. "Nice day for a walk." He grinned.

Shit. How far behind me were they? A hex on his stupid Gift of sight. I hope he trips on the stepping stones that lead from the path to our front door.

He didn't, of course, and neither did Thomas, who put a hand on my shoulder and smoothed the cloak. "Love this. It's perfect for this weather." He turned back to Ben. "Doesn't Adam have one just like it?"

Ben tapped a finger to his mouth, ever the pensive observer. "You know, I think he does. Very like."

I wanted to pull the hood up and melt into the shadows.

"Glad you approve of my outfit, guys," I said. "How was your day? Productive, I hope? Any news?"

Ben's face darkened. "Nothing good."

"Doom and gloom is an after-dinner conversation, I think," Thomas said. "Definitely after drinks." He pushed past me into the house. "Hey, Mom, we're back," he called.

"Ben, don't you think..." I said, but he shrugged and followed Thomas.

"There's still time," he said as he passed, but the shadows behind his eyes disagreed.

When I stepped through to the kitchen, it felt like an ambush or an intervention.

"Hi, Cate, how ya doing, hon?" said Jonathan. He patted Thomas on the back and gestured for him to take over whatever he was cooking. The fatherly expression on

Jonathan's face as he stepped away, wiping his hands on a dishtowel, almost undid me. I gritted my teeth.

Thomas stood by the stove, vaguely waving a hand in the direction of a spoon that stirred the pot on its own. He looked at Ben.

Mom was about to say something when Ben spoke up. "How's that head?" he asked, leaning back against the counter.

Mom tried again, "I could take a look..."

I held her eyes for a moment. "You know, I think I'm going to go lie down. I'm sorry about dinner. You all can eat without me."

The preparations went much faster once I'd left the room since they could magically complete multiple steps from the recipes at once. Soon, the chairs scraped the rough wood floors as they all sat down. How often had they done this, come home for dinner with Mom?

My stomach twisted at the thought of her eating alone, but if she hadn't bound my Gift, she might not have to be alone. Maybe I could have helped. I could have been here if my parents hadn't hidden everything from me. All of those letters and not one of them mentioned the danger. None of them gave any kind of warning about the risks they were taking to try and stabilize the magical energy of Queen's Creek.

And they were still doing it, acting like nothing was wrong. Most of the house wasn't shielded for noise control, and the walls were thin. Mom always liked being able to hear what was going on when we were home, even if it got a little rowdy sometimes. The dinner conversation was muffled by the two doors between us but still audible.

Mom asked Jonathan about his Equinox plans with the girls. They weren't old enough to participate in the ritual, but there were plenty of other games for them at the festival.

They'd already started making flower crowns. And they'd stay for the lighting of the bonfire, of course, but probably leave soon after. School night.

Sure. Yeah. They've got to rest up for the Apocalypse. I'm sure that will be a great teachable moment for them.

"What did you two get up to this afternoon?" Mom asked.

"Oh, not too much," said Benjamin. "Just going through some of Dad's stuff."

"We can talk about it later," Thomas said.

Right. Because why should the family have an open conversation about our father's last work? It's not like it might give us some kind of understanding about what actually happened to him or how to stop the boundary spell from imploding.

The conversation touched on happy family memories and plans for the memorial service. There was some discussion of who would speak, what readings should be given, which of Dad's personal items would be blessed. It had to be the most mundane discussion ever held by a roomful of witches.

Caleb arrived after dinner. He asked after me, but I didn't quite catch Thomas's answer.

I can't stay in this room forever.

I can't stay in this house forever.

I pulled out Nora's card. "Help me decide," I whispered. "What do I need to know to move forward?" I closed my eyes and felt the card stir. My fingers warmed where they touched the paper. I tried to slow my breath, but all of my muscles tightened across my back. The tension wrapped around my chest. My shoulders rose. I brought my head down, first one side, then the other, chin to chest, but it didn't help. Even with my eyes closed, I knew what it would be. No matter what I chose, something was ending.

The rider on a pale horse. Even though I knew the card only revealed a change I knew must happen, I shivered when I opened my eyes to the Death card. I'd reached the end of something significant, and things would have to be different from now on. There'd been a lot of change in my life in the past few days. This might have been what I needed to see to let it all go.

My Wakening was almost over, but there was no need to stay here and wait it out. Letting go of the past would help me move on to a new beginning.

I can't do that here. Everything around me is linked to a past that I can barely remember. Maybe it's better off forgotten.

I gathered my things and shoved them into my backpack. Coming here was a mistake. Dad was gone, and I'd probably never know what really happened. It was stupid to think I could change anything. The only thing coming home had proven was that I really was Cate-the-Cursed, and I probably always would be. I'd lived without my Gift for so long, I wasn't even sure I wanted to know what it was anymore.

Okay, that was a lie. I was desperate to know. But I couldn't trust anyone in this house to tell me.

My brothers had just accepted what they were told. Even Thomas, who was so adamant that we had to get back here and do something, had basically been going through the motions.

Maybe I don't know him as well as I thought I did.

36

W here are you going?"

Thomas stood in my doorway, one hand casually bracing himself on the frame.

I glanced around the room, the open backpack in my hand. "I don't belong here."

"You're ditching out before the funeral?" He raised an eyebrow and crossed his arms. He wasn't as intimidating as he'd like to be.

"You don't need me. I came to dissent the Reading. I didn't get it done. Mom's fine. Everything is planned. You guys have it handled. I'm going back."

"You're not serious."

I glared.

"You are serious." His eyes widened. "You're just going to take off, then? Leave the community for good? Were you even going to say good-bye?"

I rolled my eyes at the pained expression on his face. "Like you'd even miss me."

"That's not fair."

"How long were we out there before you came to visit?" I sat down on the edge of my bed and rubbed my eyes. We'd left at the same time, but after eighteen years in this house, we'd agreed to start our Wakenings alone to see who we were without a mirror. I hadn't expected it to last so long. I thought he'd gone home without me. "Why did you show up at the coffee shop? You didn't know about Dad until Adam called. But you were there every night for a week before that."

When I looked up, Thomas looked away. He stepped into my room, absently picking things up and putting them down again as if he hadn't seen everything in here a hundred thousand times, as if we didn't spend our childhood in each other's spaces.

"I wanted to see you," he said softly.

"What?"

He stopped and turned to face me, his eyes wet. "I wanted to see you," he said again. "Didn't you want to see me? Before... But I guess not," he gestured to my bag. "Our Wakening is almost over, and you just can't wait to get away." His expression dared me to deny it.

I couldn't.

He pulled the chair from my desk and spun it around, straddling it and folding his arms across the back. "I know it was rough when we left. It was hard not knowing about Adam. Thinking we lost him like Duncan. But he's back now, and we're back, and it looked like you guys were catching up. I know the world is maybe coming to an end, but can't some things go back to the way they were?"

"What do you mean, 'We lost him like Duncan?'" I thought back to the days before we left. They were still foggy, but Adam had loosened whatever was blocking the memories. I pushed further.

Adam was gone. I wanted to wait for him, but something happened. Caleb came back alone. He was scared. Duncan had been taken. He didn't know where Adam was. *Why didn't I see this before? How much of my memory was affected?*

Thomas frowned. "Please tell me you talked to Elspeth about that concussion."

"I'm serious. I don't remember. Do you think that bind she found is affecting my memory?"

He tapped the back of the chair, thinking. "Maybe. But she said you'd been bound for years. How bad is your memory? Do you remember growing up here? School? It's not like you have amnesia."

I closed my eyes, gripping the mattress on either side of me. *Where to start?* My earliest memories felt foggy, but that was just the passage of time, wasn't it? Things became clearer the older I got.

Until I was seventeen. The memories Adam helped me find slotted themselves into place, but others were still missing. Anytime I tried to reach out for more details about our relationship or what happened after he left...

I skipped ahead to just before Thomas and I left. We sat here in my room then, too. I cried. Fear and loss made me choke. More than that, I was angry. I felt betrayed and abandoned.

Forget him. It's going to be alright. You'll forget all about him once we're gone.

My eyes widened. "You did this to me!"

Thomas straightened as if slapped. "What? I did what?"

"I can't believe I didn't see it before. You did this. You made me forget him. Why? What's wrong with you?" I stood, sure I was going to hit him this time.

My brother backed out of the chair, holding his hands up. "Wait, wait, wait. What are you saying? You actually forgot about Adam? But I just saw you... and what exactly do you think I did?"

I rubbed a hand across my forehead. Images surfaced faster now that I knew what to look for. "You thought he'd ditched Caleb and Duncan when the hunters attacked. You told me someone who would do that wasn't worth my time. You told me to forget him."

"And you did? Holy Hera, Cate. What kind of girlfriend are you?"

I clutched the chair between us. "You. Used. Your. Gift."

His eyebrows jumped. "Oh, shit."

"You want to explain?"

He backed up against the desk. "No? I mean, I don't know. I didn't mean to? I definitely didn't do it on purpose. You know how messed up our magic was back then. Still is. Not yours, obviously. But the rest of us. The energy was all crazy and unpredictable. I didn't mean to *influence* you. I just meant, you know, to reassure you. I was trying to help. I figured it would all blow over while we were gone. He had to have some kind of explanation. And he did, didn't he? You guys looked pretty forgiving out there earlier."

"You made me forget my boyfriend."

"No. No. I gave you permission to do what you wanted. I didn't put a spell on you. I'm not a siren." He'd used the argument before. I was never really sure if he was offended by having his Gift compared to Mom's, or jealous of it.

"We left here without him. He probably thinks… I don't know. We had a plan, and I didn't follow it. And now his Wakening is over, and he can't ever leave again."

"But you're still planning to." He eyed my backpack on the bed behind me.

"We both know I was never meant to stay."

"I don't know that. You don't know that for sure. Maybe you were always meant to return." He picked up a poppet that had lain on my desk for most of my life. "We could go back to the way things were. Things don't have to change just because you left for a while."

"I hated the way things were, and everything changed when I left." I took the poppet from him and shoved it in a drawer.

"Not us. Not your destiny. This is a cannon event."

"You watched too many movies out there. It's fine for you. You're just like the rest of them. But I can't... I don't... What am I supposed to do here? We still don't know who bound me. Elspeth said only the person who cast it can remove it. What if it was Dad? I'll never have real access to magic. How am I supposed to live in a place where nothing I ever do will be good enough?"

"Good enough for what? You're part of this family. We'll take care of you."

Grabbing my bag, I zipped it shut and threw it over my shoulder. "Mom sent Adam away *to keep me safe*, but all she did was take away the one person who cared about me as I am. You made me forget him because you were *trying to help*, but you just made everything more confusing. And now he wants me to leave *for my own good*. But someone in Queen's Creek bound my Gift, and I'm bound to this place, and I still don't know why. I wish everyone would stop trying to take care of me before you all get me killed. I can take care of myself."

I pushed past him into the hallway.

For a split second, I fought the urge to turn around and apologize, but then my brother opened his big, stupid mouth and generously saved me from my better judgment.

"Ass-face," he said. The mundane insult had always been a touchstone for us. Recognition of an apology without apologizing.

I smiled and wiped my eyes one last time. "Jerkwad," I said, using the standard response. I shifted my backpack and rounded the corner, where I ran straight into my mother.

"Excuse me?" Mom said although she had to have heard this exchange often enough not to take it personally.

"Mom."

"Where will you go?" She sighed. It almost wasn't worth the fight I knew was coming.

"I'm going home, Mom," I said carefully. "Wasn't that what you wanted when you sent me away?"

"That was your dad's idea. I just wanted you safe. This will always be your home."

"Oh, is it safe now?"

She ignored my sarcasm. "You could at least wait a day. Show that much respect for your father."

"Like he showed me?" I asked. "Like you did?"

They did this to me. I have to get out before they take that choice from me too.

"You don't know anything," she said. "I know how you must be feeling. You miss your father, and things seem different than you left them. That happens sometimes when you go away. It's part of growing up." She gestured to the living room couch. "Let's sit down and talk about it. Ask me anything."

I'm sure she thinks she knows how I'm feeling, but she's no empath, and I'm not interested in more lies or excuses.

"I don't want to sit down." I tried to move past her, but she put up a hand, and as much as I wanted out, I wasn't ready to physically move her to make it happen. I slumped against the wall.

"What's wrong with me, Mom? Why didn't you trust me with my own Gift? What was it? Did I set stuff on fire? Block out the sun?" *Shit. Did I? Was I causing the storms? If my father bound me, and he was gone... was the bind already broken? Was my Gift coming back?* I slid down the wall to the floor, collapsing in on myself.

"Am I the reason our magic is unstable?"

Mom sat beside me, putting her hand on my knee. "It's not your fault. It was never your fault."

I don't believe you. We sat in silence.

"Please let me go," I said finally.

"No."

"No? Listen, Mom—"

She patted my knee once more and stood. "No. You listen. This is still my house, and while you are under my roof—"

I jumped to my feet. "I don't want to be under your roof. Don't you get it? I should never have come back here. My own parents couldn't trust me. The two of you bound my Gift and sent me off to live as a mundane. Or did you do it alone? Maybe that's really why Dad crossed the Creek. He couldn't trust you either. You thought he was crazy, just like the rest of them. "

She should have slapped me. I probably deserved it. I waited for it, but she didn't raise a hand. Her whole body tensed, but the explosion didn't come. She was crying.

"All I have ever done is love you," she said, barely moving her lips, "and try my best to keep you safe. The Mother knows you haven't made it easy."

It was as close to a confession as I was likely to get. She'd done it. Bound my powers and sent me to a mundane college hundreds of miles away. An unmagical life and an early Wakening. *To keep me safe.*

My muscles tensed, shaking in anger as the edges of older memories pushed against the ones I seen with Adam. I looked into her eyes for some acknowledgment that they were true. "You separated me from everything, everyone that mattered. You wanted me to live a life without magic. Congratulations. It worked. Now, let me go back."

"One more day," said Caleb from behind Mom. I should have known he'd overhear. Even without his Gift, our voices must have carried.

Please let Jonathan and Benjamin stay in the kitchen. This hallway is getting crowded.

"What?" I said.

"Stay for the funeral," Thomas said. "Just one more day, and then you can go back to forgetting all of us if that's what you want."

"That's not what I want." I looked back at my mom. Her shoulders sagged, but she didn't wipe away the hot tears running down her face. Her fingers clenched and unclenched at her sides. I couldn't tell if she intended to hug me or hit me. And that was really what gave me my answer. "I can't stay here."

"You don't have to," Caleb said. "Stay with Elspeth."

I shook my head. "Elspeth doesn't need me staying there, getting in the way…."

"Cate," said Thomas. He looked into my eyes, and I wanted to trust him. "We came home for a reason. The job's not done." I felt his energy rise. I knew what he was doing, and I resented it. But I also felt a little guilty about the way I'd been talking to Mom, and part of me appreciated the excuse to give in.

"Just give it a day," he said.

I knew it wasn't my idea, but it felt like a good one.

What will it hurt? I can still get out before my birthday. Maybe I can even help ensure this Equinox festival is not our last.

I couldn't look at my mom. My eyes found a hole in the rug, a streak in the wall, Thomas's dirty shoes tracking up the floor. Finally, I found his eyes. "One day."

37

Elspeth didn't exactly have a spare room at the healer's cottage, but she welcomed me anyway. She had shown no surprise when I arrived. There was no small talk or random chatter, but the quiet wasn't silence.

She put fresh sheets on the cot where she had treated my concussion, and we had dinner around a small table lit by fat, drippy candles. The stains on my side of the rough wooden surface indicated that it more frequently held potions and medical supplies, and the whole space smelled faintly of healing herbs, but it might have been the tea. It seemed to be the healer's favorite remedy.

The best thing about Elspeth's skills was that she knew immediately when to leave well-enough alone.

Usually.

"We're going to have to talk about it eventually," she said, clearing my plate and replacing it with another cup. This one smelled of lemon balm and lavender, a calming tonic to soothe my nerves.

"Are we, though? Really?" She was right, but I didn't have to like it. *Besides, why play polite when your friend has a Gift for understanding how you feel?* Inhaling the steam from my cup, I reminded myself that I owed her more than that. The guilt came out in a sigh.

She rolled her eyes. "Your aura is telling me enough already. I don't need Caleb's Gift to hear what you're thinking about, but it would help to have some context. You can start with the easy one. What did Thomas do this time?"

"My brother used magic against me." I sipped the tea and set the cup in front of me, warming my hands. My fingers shook.

Elspeth's eyebrow shot up.

"Unintentionally," I admitted.

She clasped her hands in front of her on the table and waited for me to elaborate.

"Thomas used his Gift to make me forget my relationship with Adam."

The healer frowned. "If that's true, I'm surprised he's not the one on my doorstep. But has his Gift changed since you guys left? Last I checked, a muse can't make you do anything you wouldn't do on your own."

"It was before we left. I don't know. Part of me must have wanted to forget him… But now that I have, I don't really know why."

"What do you remember?"

The taste of his lips. His breath in my hair. His arms around me. "Not much."

She reached across the table to touch my arm. Before she made contact, she pulled back a little. "Do you want my help with that? Or do you just want to rest? The tea should be taking effect soon."

I wet my lips, considering. Could Elspeth's Gift reveal what Adam's hadn't? Was it fair to ask? The boyfriend-shaped holes in my memory didn't hide what happened to her brother. Thomas hadn't erased everything that happened before we left.

Caleb had come home, panicked and exhausted, without Duncan. He told us the witch hunters found them in town. He didn't know how they'd identified them, but he heard them talking.

Duncan thought he could distract them. How could they resist a witch whose Gift was charisma? He literally led a charmed life.

Caleb didn't like it, but... something happened, and Duncan told him to run. It seemed like the only option. My brother had taken turn after turn to keep the hunters from following, but Duncan never caught up either.

Duncan's disappearance had been the reason Elspeth missed her Wakening. It had been a cautionary tale for any of us who left the community afterward. *Watch what you do, or the hunters will find you.*

What did any of it have to do with Adam?

Elspeth reached for my hand. "Close your eyes."

Flashes of light and two years rolled back behind my eyes. Three. Another month.

Caleb and Duncan leaving for their Wakening. We saw them off, a party in the clearing, just the youth of our two families and our friends. Elspeth's older sisters danced around a bonfire. Her brothers joked with mine. Our families would only do this one more time, next year when Elspeth, Thomas, and I, the youngest siblings, took our turn in the mundane world.

One of Elspeth's brothers teased Adam about not taking his chance at an extra year of freedom, but his arm was around my shoulders, and he pulled me close. "I can wait."

But he didn't.

I pushed for the next memory, and it came back all at once.

A year later, after Ben came home, and Caleb had left. It started in the garden. Jonathan, Ben, and Thomas played a game, something borderline mundane so that I could participate. Thomas cheated.

Gabriel and Matthew stood by the fence, deep in a conversation I didn't understand. Something about energy and time. There wasn't enough, or there was too much.

"Listen to me!" Gabriel vibrated, lightning sparking off him in short, bright bursts.

Jonathan stepped in front of me. He was always doing that. Protecting me when I didn't need it. Gabriel would never hurt me. I pulled at Jonathan's arm, but he didn't move.

Matthew's hand came up, using his Gift to shift the energy. The lightning fizzled and popped. Soap bubbles floated harmlessly away.

Thomas held up a hand, pushing his intention. "Whoa. Guys, it's all good."

His magic wavered in the air, almost invisible. The charged air made my arms tingle.

Gabriel's storm expanded.

"Shit." Not for the first time, Thomas's influence didn't go as intended. The vibes changed, but Gabriel's energy had to go somewhere.

Ben laughed as the electrified bubbles collided, shooting tiny fireworks over the garden.

I tilted my head back to watch and lost my balance, tripping over my own feet.

Jonathan caught me. "You want a closer look?"

He threw me into the air, laughing. I should have screamed, but he'd finally loosened up. And it did feel *all good*.

It felt like flying.

Lights exploded around me.

The view was amazing. I could almost see over the trees into the town center. Adam walked down the path toward our house. I waved.

And then gravity reasserted itself, which would have been fine if Jonathan had stuck around to catch me. Under the influence of Thomas's vaguely positive intention, my strongest brother moved on to separate Matthew and Gabriel, who had interpreted the muse's effort to calm them as some kind of approval of their battle techniques.

Adam ran down the path, his hands guiding the earth in front of him, lifting a hill beneath me as I fell. The elevated earth still looked pretty solid, and it was getting close. Faster now.

As the ground reached for me, I sobered enough to panic. My arms windmilled, and one connected with the wooden edge of a raised garden bed. Something snapped, but before I could register whether it was my arm or the rail, I floated back up.

Adam gathered me into his arms and raced to the house.

I shrieked when he braced my arm against his body. The place where I had hit the garden wall throbbed. *Definitely broken.*

He winced as though he felt the pain himself. "I'm sorry," he whispered. "I tried."

Mom met us at the door, eyes shifting from anger to concern in an instant.

"Stop." Her tone was stronger than magic. All of the boys froze, battles and games forgotten.

Inside, she healed my arm and broke my heart, all but banishing Adam from our home. It was an overreaction, and she'd probably reverse it later. But no one was going to tell her that now. Matthew or Gabriel would say something to her in the morning, protecting me, as they always did. And she'd give me some half-apology caged in an excuse about a mother's love and her desire to keep me safe.

I followed Adam out. "You don't have to do this."

"It might be for the best. I was supposed to go with Caleb

and Duncan anyway. I'll catch up with them. Maybe they already know somewhere I can stay while I find us an apartment. I'll have it all set up by the time you're ready to leave."

He said he was going to join them, but Caleb came back alone. Adam never lied, so what happened to him?

No messages came through the Gate. No one else brought news when they returned from their Wakenings. Months passed.

I couldn't live in a constant state of fear. Almost without noticing, my anxiety turned to anger.

How could he do this to me?

When the time for our Wakening finally arrived. I almost didn't go. Elspeth hadn't gone. Maybe her parents were right. Duncan and Adam had both disappeared. Who knew what was out there?

"Talk to her," my mother urged Thomas. She didn't have to push.

"What's the point of going out there without him?" I asked my brother.

Forget about him.

I opened my eyes, blinking away the dizziness that came with shifting from the past to the present.

"He didn't abandon you," Elspeth said.

"He came back after you left. He went straight to your parents' house, but you were already gone."

"What happened to him out there?"

She sat back in her chair, twisting the end of her braid around her fingers. "That's probably for him to tell."

"He's not exactly talking to me right now."

She threw her hands up, literally clearing the air. "The two of you. I swear, you live for the drama. Why you can't just have a conversation… He's still in love with you, you know."

"Then why didn't he come for me? When he came back,

and I wasn't here. Why didn't he come find me?"

Another hand wave. "Well, he couldn't, could he? Timing has never been your strength."

Adam's birthday. His Wakening had ended while he was still inside the boundary.

"I think he became Guardian so he could watch for you. But you were gone for so long. Honestly, I didn't think you were ever coming back." She didn't sound angry or disappointed. Just sad. I'd left her behind, too.

My birthday was three days away. I'd promised my mom I'd stay for the funeral, but afterwards? What would happen to them all if I left? *There is no Gate without the Keeper.*

"I don't know what to do," I admitted.

"It should be your choice." Elspeth stood and carried the empty tea service to her sink.

"It doesn't feel like my choice."

"What does that card say? Your charmed object? It felt like a positive influence. The person who gave it to you wanted to help."

I pulled Nora's tarot card out of my pocket. It hadn't changed. I held up the Death card where the healer could see it.

Her eyebrows twitched. She leaned back against the sink, crossing her arms. "You know that's not—"

"I know."

"It's a big change though. Something's coming."

"Can you see it?" I leaned forward as if proximity had anything to do with psychic sight.

"Just the way you feel about it. I'm an empath, not an oracle."

So I told her everything. Alice's prediction that I would be the last Gatekeeper. Dad's research into the boundary spell. Mom's explanation for Matthew and Gabriel's absence. Gabriel's notes on energy and wisps. My unsuccessful experience with the grimoire. Giles's warning in the library: Adam's reaction when I'd claimed my rights as Alice's successor.

"You read the grimoire." The statement hid questions, but I couldn't guess them.

"Not the part I thought you'd want to talk about, but yeah. It wasn't terribly helpful." Unless you counted confirming several of my worst fears.

"I thought you wanted to leave."

I do. "You told me I can't."

"Well, not anymore." She shook her head. "Why would you claim your rights if you don't want to stay?"

"I don't know. I didn't mean it. I was trying to get past Adam. He didn't believe me."

"But the grimoire did."

"What?"

"I think we need to go to the library."

38

Elspeth grabbed a couple of star torches, the flickering lights swinging from short handles. As dark as the library path had felt in daylight, it almost vanished at night. Without the torches, I would have stumbled past the turn.

There was very little chance Jonathan would be at the library this late, which meant we could explore the shelves without answering any questions. If we found the way in. The ivy draping the cottage may as well have been chain link. I raised my torch, peering between the vines for a door. A couple of lightning bugs winked.

"Here," called Elspeth from somewhere to my left.

My torch caught the edges of her movement as the door swung inside. Then she was swallowed by the darkness. A distant rumble warned of a coming storm. The wind pulled at my hair. *Hurry.*

The door swung closed behind me, probably more from balance than magical security. Inside, our torches put up a valiant effort to show the way, but only lit enough of the space to cast shadows. I knocked against Jonathan's desk, causing a small avalanche. The librarian hadn't returned the texts he'd been studying in the afternoon.

"Shhh." Elspeth lifted her torch to show her face. She did a fairly good impression of my brother. "Respect the books."

I held up my hands, remembering the promise I'd made him. *I'm not going to wreck the books. You can trust me.* "Sorry, Jonathan."

She put her torch on the desk and bent to pick up fallen tomes. I stacked them a little farther from the edge.

"Has he seen your dad's notes? What does he think? About the boundary coming down?" she asked.

"I'm not sure."

"You didn't ask?" She stacked the last book, running a hand over the embossed cover.

"We haven't exactly had a family meeting. I didn't even really know what questions I should be asking until last night."

"What did you tell him when you were here this morning?"

"That I wanted to see the prophecy. Why I was chosen." It occurred to me that I hadn't actually done that. The revelation that I would be the last Gatekeeper had come from me, not the grimoire. *Stupid book was holding out on me.*

I peered through the shadows toward the restricted section in the back of the library, but our lights didn't extend much beyond the desk. The drawer rattled open when I pulled. Paperclips, tape, notecards. Where did he keep the key to the cabinets in the back?

Elspeth flipped the pages of the book. "You guys should talk more."

"Sure. I mean, if I get stuck here, I imagine I'm going to be talking to all of them more often. Probably baby-sitting…" *I'll just tell him to drop them off at the Gatehouse. Are kids allowed in the Gatehouse?* Maybe Alice was alone by choice.

"No, look. Jonathan's been reading about the Gatekeepers,

too." She pulled a finger down the table of contents.

Time to Keep by Meghan MacDonell.

The book featured a rough timeline of the Gatekeepers' lives, when they'd taken up the mantle, and how long their turns had lasted. A chapter in each section detailed their family histories, and another included interview notes and journal entries on how they occupied their time. It was the kind of thing that should have been on a required reading list for future Gatekeepers. My parents really hadn't done anything to prepare me.

Last night, Mom said they sent me away because the boundary spell was breaking. Tonight, she'd said it was to keep me safe because I couldn't protect myself from my brothers' chaotic magic.

But they'd never intended for me to stay. Was that why they bound my Gift? To keep me from becoming the Gatekeeper?

I flipped to the back of the book, looking for the index. Surely, a history of the Gatekeepers would have a transcription of the prophecy we used to identify new ones.

There was only one line. *The next Keeper is chosen in accordance with prophecy*.*

"Go to the end notes." Elspeth tilted the book, fanning the pages.

**The Gatekeepers' prophecy is read from the grimoire by the previous Keeper as she reaches the end of her turn. She alone is responsible for choosing her successor, and she alone understands their qualifications.*

I groaned and pushed the book away.

Elspeth took a closer look. "She didn't tell you why she chose you?"

"No, you know. She's an oracle. It's all cryptic statements and riddles. Anytime I ask her anything, she says, *You will know when the time is right*, or *All in time*, or whatever. It's never the right time."

Elspeth flipped back to the index.

I knew what I wanted to ask, but I wasn't sure how to phrase it delicately. *Hex it. She'll understand.*

"What about you?" I asked. "You're a seventh. What did she tell you when they took you to see her?"

"No."

"I'm sorry. It's none of my business–" I tried another drawer for the key.

Elspeth laughed. "No. That's what Alice said when I went in. Just *No.*"

"Wow." The drawer stuck. I felt around to find what kept it wedged in.

"Yeah, I've never been so relieved to be rejected in all my life."

I sat in Jonathan's chair and rattled the drawer.

"Sorry," she said. "I'm sure you'll be great. It'll be fine. You know. Last Gatekeeper, yay…"

Her enthusiasm trailed off without even attempting sincerity, but I appreciated the support.

"I'm not mad at you," I told the empath. "This whole thing is just–"

The drawer came loose. I pulled the torch closer. Nothing. Why wouldn't it open if it was empty? I ran my fingers along the bottom and up the sides. The light flickered, glinting off something in the corner.

"Got it." I held a small key with brass filigree. The drawer slid back smoothly.

Elspeth took the book in one hand and her torch in the other, following me through the stacks to the restricted section. The tall shelves didn't shift on their own like they had when Jonathan brought me back, so it took twice as long to maneuver our way to the tiny room where the grimoire was kept. I only got lost once. Elspeth didn't mention it.

When we passed the archway of antique books, I reached up to tap the keystone text for luck. *Minerva guide us.*

Two pairs of gloves lay on the table.

"Damage nothing. Alter nothing. Take nothing." I repeated Jonathan's words for the benefit of any books that might be listening.

"The Librarian's Rules?" Elspeth asked.

"Yeah." I pulled on the first pair of gloves and unlocked the cabinet at the end of the row. Elspeth laid the other book on the table, taking up her own gloves and sliding them over her fingers.

The grimoire was heavier than I thought it'd be, even knowing my brother's strength. I winced as it thumped onto the table.

"This morning, I asked it about the Gate and the Keeper, and it kept coming back to me and my destiny. But now we have that one." I nodded to Elspeth's book. "So, I think we focus on the boundary. We've got to be very clear about what we're asking, though. The grimoire doesn't like broad questions."

If Elspeth had any concerns about talking to a book like it was alive, she didn't voice them. "Okay. What do we want to know? What's wrong with the boundary? Why is it coming down?"

I shook my head. "I don't think it knows what's happening now. It only knows what's already been written."

"Has this ever happened before?"

"I don't think so. I mean, I would hope if the boundary had a history of going all chaos magic, someone would have created a plan to stop it from happening again."

I might be giving our ancestors too much credit.

Elspeth sensed my doubt. "Maybe ask the book about the boundary's history."

The cover creaked when I opened it. I tried to keep my

voice low and calm. "Hey, book. I'm back. Remember me? Elspeth and I were wondering what you could tell us about the boundary? Maybe just start at the beginning. How did Mary set it up in the first place?"

Nothing happened, so I used a gloved hand to turn the page. Words shifted across the paper, overlapping as it swirled in runic patterns.

Elspeth gasped. "Can you read it?"

"Not yet." I straightened my glasses and let my eyes wander over the text, focusing and unfocusing as some of the words started to surface.

Stop showing off, book.

The words paused for a second, then shivered and settled into orderly paragraphs. "Thank you."

Elspeth frowned.

"It's more cooperative if you're polite," I explained. "See?"

"No. It's all just… It's almost like runes, but they're all written on top of each other. You understand these symbols?"

The page was laid out like a history textbook, with columns and headings in bold. "What do you mean? It's English. Kind of dry, old-fashioned English, but there aren't any runes on this page anymore."

The book took offense at this description. A few of the sentences shifted, the syntax updating.

I snickered. "It's okay, book. I got it."

Elspeth sat in the chair across from me. "I told you it believed you."

"What?"

"Didn't Jonathan tell you? That book is only legible to those who have written in it, their descendants, and those who will record the next entries. Are you related to any of the previous Gatekeepers?"

"I don't think so." Seemed like the kind of thing that would come up in discussions of community expectations and unavoidable destiny. But then, my brother could also have mentioned that there was a chance I might not be able to read it when he got it down for me. He must have had more faith in my destiny than I did.

"Then the only way you can read it is that the grimoire recognizes you as Alice's successor. You declared yourself, and the Source heard."

If the book could smile, it would have.

"Great." All the more reason to find out how the boundary worked. Because my birthday was less than three days away, and Goddess help me if I was going to spend the rest of my life in that Gatehouse. If I really was the last Gatekeeper, the boundary was coming down this week.

I skimmed the page, reading pertinent bits aloud for Elspeth while she cross-referenced them with the less ambiguous history text.

"Mary was a water witch. I guess that's why she chose the Creek for the boundary. Plus, you know, how often do you find water flowing naturally in an almost perfect circle? Had to be a sign. She made a sacrifice. This is like what they tell us in school. Gave up her life to the Gate so that we could be safe. But how does it work? What is the boundary?"

The pages shivered. The part about her life grew larger. I skimmed ahead to the end of Mary's turn.

"*It was her time. When the time of the first Keeper was coming to an end…*" *Shit.* Was that what Alice had been trying to tell me? All of this *it's-not-your-time* stuff. The boundary *was* Time.

Elspeth's eyes widened as she came to the same realization. "It's a time stream. Like, an actual, literal stream of time. That's why the Keepers don't age. Why no one can cross it. Because how would you leave your own timeline? The Gatehouse must be some kind of bridge between our Gatekeeper's time and theirs. The mundanes' I mean. Wait, do you think it can go the other way? Back to the other

Gatekeepers?"

I checked the grimoire for confirmation. "The boundary is time. The Gatekeepers regulate it with their lives. Their turn is the span of their natural life, how long they would have lived on the outside."

The book didn't move. So no real answer to the time travel question. Maybe it didn't know.

Although. That would explain a lot about Alice's cryptic and irritating nature. If the Gatekeepers controlled time? That would be a colossal secret to keep. Imagine what a town full of witches could do if they could manipulate time?

There had to be more the grimoire could tell us. "The boundary has been working for so long. Why is it coming down now? Have all of these lives not been enough?"

The words shimmered, rearranging themselves into the timeline of Keepers' lives again. Small triangular symbols like the ones we'd seen on the census in Mrs. Kirk's office glimmered by each name. Elements.

"After Mary, the next one, Clara, was an earth witch. Looks like she built up that hill with the clearing on it. Something about the high ground, but that might be figurative. No, book, it's fine. Don't shift until I'm finished. Sorry. It's trying to help. Okay. After Clara, there was Martha and then Alice. Martha was a fire witch, and Alice's element is air." *And mine is spirit.* Was that why she chose me? To complete the pattern? I pushed back from the table, chewing my nail.

Elspeth flipped a few pages in *Time to Keep,* checking the history's records against what I'd just read from the grimoire.

"That's all four quarters. They've completed a cycle," she whispered.

39

Something moved in the back of the room. My heart hammered.

You shouldn't be here, Giles had said. He'd made it sound like he was concerned about my head injury, but his eyes had kept shifting to that corner.

"Do you see that?" I asked Elspeth.

"What? Oh. Yes, I see it, too." She closed the book and pulled it to her chest.

My stomach twisted. The room tightened around us, the dark stretching along the walls to close us in. An electric charge made the hairs on my arms stand up like they had in the clearing before Adam faced the storm.

"You want to check these books out and finish our work back at your place?" I dragged the heavy grimoire to the edge of the table. In no version of this timeline did I see myself lifting it back onto its shelf in that dark corner.

The cabinet that had held the grimoire disappeared. Then half of the next one.

"But we're not supposed to take the grimoire out of the restricted section... oh." Elspeth scrambled out of her seat as the shadow in the corner started to spread.

Part of the table vanished.

I grabbed my star torch before the shadow swallowed the rest of the room.

We pelted through the stacks, stumbling over the rugs and knocking aside Jonathan's enchanted cart. It might have been my imagination, but by the time we reached the front door, the grimoire felt lighter in my arms.

Elspeth raised her arm, her hand twisting around an invisible handle. She pulled back as the door came into sight, and it flew open. We charged out into the night. I slammed the door behind us. The ivy dropped back into place. We backed away toward the path, waiting to see if whatever lurked in the shadows would follow. The door shook with an invisible impact.

Panting, I leaned against a tree.

Elspeth put a hand on the door. "You said you and Adam faced some kind of shadow in the clearing? Was it like that?"

"Pretty close." The door creaked.

"How did you stop it?" Elspeth whispered something to the vines, and they twisted around the door handle.

"I didn't. Adam channeled it, and then he pushed it back somehow." *When I took his hand.* Nora's card showed me the Knight of Cups when I thought about him, and he'd certainly seemed chivalrous on that hill. Calm and steady.

But there was more to that card. *Follow your intuition.*

I wanted it to stop, and it did.

I was chosen by the Gatekeeper.

The boundary is a time stream, and it's failing.

The time I've missed.

The blackouts.

Elspeth raised an eyebrow.

"What?"

"Nothing. I just never really thought of Adam's Gift as anything so... active."

I almost said something about the way she'd opened the door without checking how it felt about that first. Not all Gifted magic looked like its elemental affinity.

Adam held out his hand. The ground rose up beneath us.

But that was after everything stopped.

"You think I did it." Whatever was on the other side of that door wanted to get out. Could I stop it?

"Do you still have that card with you? The one you thought was charmed?"

"Yeah, but I can't really get to it right now." I shifted the grimoire, afraid to put it down in case I couldn't pick it back up again.

"I don't think it matters. As long as it's on you." She squinted at the door as it shook again.

Something dark peeked through the cracks around it. "It's going to get out."

Elspeth spoke quickly. "No, it's not. These blackouts you've been having, you feel like you're missing time, or everything around you freezes?"

"Both, sometimes."

"You ever do it on purpose?" She moved away from the door to stand beside me.

"What? I can't do that. I don't have a Gift." The fear came out of habit, but the excuse was a lie. I'd fooled myself for years.

"You do, though. It's just bound. But I think that card is a conduit. Somehow, it's helping you bypass the bind. Try now." She watched the door. "Try. Freeze time inside the library."

A roll of thunder punctuated her command.

I closed my eyes, remembering the darkness in the woods, the silence on the plane, the static at the Reading. I visualized the angry shadow from the clearing, the way it broke when the sun burst through the clouds.

We could use some of that light now. *Hecate help me.*

Short, quick breaths through my nose. I gritted my teeth. If it was me before, I could do it again.

Nora's card reacted in my pocket. My star torch flared, and I saw the flash through my eyelids. I imagined the darkness inside the library collapsing, banished by moonlight and stars.

Stop.

I opened one eye and then the other. Elspeth didn't move.

"Did it work?"

The ivy loosened, peeling back from the door, becoming less armor, more decorative. The whole cottage seemed to sigh in relief.

Elspeth whooped. "Yes! You are a goddess-blessed hero. Imagine what you'll be able to do when we cut that bind."

All of the air rushed out of me at once. I leaned back against the tree, hugging the grimoire to my chest. I blinked away tears. *I can do magic. I have a Gift.*

And I've had it all along.

My chest ached. Elspeth had been right, and part of me had never believed her. Too afraid to hope in case it turned out to be another mistake. Another failure. I'd been Cate-the-Cursed for so long, all I knew was an unmagical life.

But there was nothing wrong with me. Not cursed or unlucky. Bound.

They kept this from me. It's been just below the surface, fighting for air, and they held it down.

But not for long. I'd pulled the Death card. Time for things to change. "You really think we can?"

"I think you can do anything you want, Gatekeeper."

We walked back to the healer's cottage as quickly as we could. Her table groaned under the weight of the grimoire. I pulled Nora's card out of my back pocket and tucked it back into my phone case. If that was the conduit to my Gift, I needed to keep it safe until we found a way to break the bind.

Elspeth paced, still clutching *Time to Keep*.

I sat on the cot, crisscrossing my legs in front of me. "Does that book say anything about the boundary coming down?" *Is it coming down because I'm the last Gatekeeper, or am I the last because it's coming down?*

She shook her head. "It's mostly biographical information about previous Keepers. It ends with Alice taking on the mantle. That was almost eighty years ago."

She handed me the book, and I paged through it, looking for commonalities explaining why Alice chose me. They were all the seventh child of a seventh child like I was. But although each was guided by a different element, they all showed significant Gifts at young ages. Almost all of them had been seven years old when their Gifts emerged. Not a single late-bloomer in the bunch.

A tiny voice in the back of my head asked if I was wrong. The joy of accepting my Gift waned under a blanketing cloud of imposter syndrome. I'd worked magic at the library, but what if it wasn't mine?

"Do you think you can help me with my memory again? I need to go further back. Like fourteen years ago." The first blackout I could remember. The only one that happened before I got Nora's card. I needed to be sure it was my Gift and not hers.

"I can't show you anything you don't already know." But she was already pulling out those half-moon glasses she'd used last time she examined me.

I closed my eyes.

"Focus on what you do remember." Elspeth already sounded far away.

My vision blurred and cleared again.

I was a child. Seven years old. I followed a twinkling light into the woods. In the dark, I tripped and fell. The light went out. I was hurt and afraid. My brothers charged loudly through the brush to find me, and it should have been a relief, but I had left the garden without permission. Mom would be so mad.

I ran. I didn't see the tree in front of me until it was too late.

My head hurt, and my heart pounded. I wanted to go home, but I didn't want to get into trouble. I needed more time.

Please. Just stop.

I squeezed my eyes shut.

When I blinked them open, the world stayed dark. I heard my heartbeat in my ears, but no other sounds disturbed the woods. A leaf hung in the air, knocked free when I crashed into the tree. But it didn't fall. I reached for it and winced.

My hand throbbed where the splinter had broken the skin. "Owwwwwwwowowowww!"

"She's over here."

My brother's arms wrapped around me, and my head rested against his chest. I yawned, closing my eyes to a more welcome darkness.

I woke when we got home.

Jonathan tucked me in, but I didn't fall asleep again.

He left the door open a crack to let in the light, and I listened to my big brothers arguing with Mom and Dad in the kitchen.

"You have to do something. She's getting too strong."

"She's just a child."

"You didn't see what it was like. Everything stopped. If we'd been any closer, we might still be there."

"Oh, I doubt that. She didn't know what she was doing. It probably faded when she fell asleep."

"How far do you think she can reach?"

I tried to hear more, but my seven-year-old body had used up her energy. I slept.

Something tugged me awake, but I was lost between

memories. Flashes went by, blurs filled with sound. A voice separated from the white noise.

"There's more," Elspeth said. "I'm following a thread. Do you feel where it goes?"

The tug grew stronger, and I concentrated on finding the next memory.

In the morning, Matthew and Gabriel returned from their Wakenings. They were early. Or Gabriel was, at least. They had news to report from outside the boundary.

Mom sent me and Thomas outside. Something about little pitchers and big ears.

She wasn't wrong. While Thomas and I took turns spinning a top and balancing on the edges of the garden barriers, we caught snatches of the conversation inside. None of it meant anything then.

Gabriel had noticed an increase in the number of wisps outside the Creek. Matthew said things were disappearing from a construction site just outside the boundary. Materials glitched out of existence and back again, like a spliced recording. Time moved slower in the trees.

"They put a night guard on the site, and he said a few nights ago, everything froze around him. The very air stilled, and he couldn't move for a few minutes. He's telling people the place is haunted."

"There's no way she's affecting things on the other side of the Creek."

"Has she been evaluated?"

"It's too soon."

"She might be the answer."

"She might be the problem."

"She is a child."

"Then protect her, for all our sakes."

The image blurred again. Another tug, changing direction, pushing me through to the next memory. This one felt like a dream. My mother's hand on my head, healing the bump where I'd hit the tree. My father's voice urging me to stay calm.

"Are you sure?" Mom whispered.

"It's for the best." Dad brushed my hair from my face.

Mom hummed a soft tune. My eyes closed. The hum became rhythmic, the waves carrying me further from myself.

Dad wrapped something around my head, soft and fuzzy like my blanket, delicate as a spider's web. "Almost done."

His fingers traced a sigil at my temples.

The bind tightened, making me gasp.

"Shhh…" Mom brushed her hand through my hair.

I relaxed, but the tension didn't go away.

Mom started to sing…

The music faded into static. My eyelids fluttered, and when I opened them, the healer's cottage spun around me. I gripped the edge of the cot. My stomach twisted.

For all her talk of protecting me, how I wasn't safe in Queen's Creek, my mother was the reason I couldn't protect myself. I'd guessed it before. But seeing it, remembering it, was so much worse.

She'd stopped anyone from searching for Matthew and Gabriel because she was afraid of what the Counsel would do when they found out. The consequences of tampering with the boundary. Losing her magic.

But she'd done it to me.

It's for the best, my father had said.

My stomach heaved, and I coughed, choking on acid and betrayal.

They'd done it together.

"Tea? I think tea." Elspeth tucked back a strand of hair that had come loose from her braid. Her eyes darted from me to her kettle. I knew she'd seen everything I had.

I nodded, but the movement made me dizzy. *Good thing I'm already sitting down.*

While she steeped something with a distinctly medicinal smell, I opened the history book again. The beginning of my chapter as Gatekeeper might turn out to have more similarities with the others than I'd thought.

I'd stopped time that night in the woods when I was seven years old. I'd stopped time far enough around me to affect the construction site on the other side of the Creek.

We should have celebrated. They should have taken me to Alice to have my Gift evaluated. I should have trained with someone who shared an affinity for the same element. Someone who understood what I could do. *Was there anyone like me in Queen's Creek?*

Instead, they'd hidden it. *But not well.*

"It's ready," Elspeth said. "Are you?"

I set the book aside and gingerly pulled myself out of the bed so I could join her at the table. We sat in silence, alternately staring into the tea and glaring at the grimoire.

Until the candles went out.

40

When you lived in a cottage in the middle of the woods and didn't have electricity, the darkness when the candles went out was somehow both total and thick. The snuffed candles trailed a pale stream of smoke that barely burned your eyes as it dissolved in the air.

Usually, this sudden darkness was nonetheless peaceful because you had chosen it. Usually, you were close to your bed and planning to close your eyes anyway, so the immediacy of the darkness did not cause concern.

When Elspeth's candles went out, neither of us had breathed on them. The flash of lightning that burst outside her window just before we were plunged into the dark only emphasized the blackness. I blinked, stunned by the bright light that took ours with it.

Elspeth snapped her fingers a few times. Almost anyone in our community could relight a candle that way.

Nothing happened.

In the next flash of light, I saw the concern on Elspeth's face, but the rolling thunder drowned out her words. The walls creaked, and the shingles rattled in a wind that wasn't there a few minutes ago. Before my eyes adjusted, a loud noise came from the front room. Elspeth's door screamed under the combined pressure of the wind and a knock that sounded more like a battering ram.

I grabbed the sides of the table to keep from knocking it over as I jumped from my seat. Elspeth did something similar. Although she moved gracefully, the air pressure changed when she came closer. Magic vibrated off of her, yet we were still in the dark.

The rain hammered the windows. I took her hand, and we made careful progress toward the door. Someone shouted on the other side, but I could barely make it out over the howling storm. The door bent inward, straining under the rain, and the voice, and the fists that hadn't stopped pounding. I couldn't decide whether I intended to brace it or open it when we got there.

The choice was made for me when the door exploded.

Broken shards of wood flew past. There were splinters in my hair. Elspeth and I screamed. Well, I screamed. I assumed a similar sound was coming from the Healer, but as it was still nearly impossible to see or hear her, I couldn't be sure. Covering my face with one hand, I pulled her down to the floor with the other. Elspeth's hand tightened, and this time, I heard her cry out. I crawled closer and put my arm around her. Her side was wet. *Please, let it be the rain.*

A huge shadow filled the doorway, its edges lit by lightning flashing through the trees. When he turned to peer into the dark room, I recognized the wolf's profile.

"Adam?"

He couldn't hear me, but without the door in its frame, the lightning did its job for a few seconds at a time. The Guardian strode into Elspeth's home. He grabbed her and half-dragged, half-carried her out into the storm.

"What are you doing?" I yelled over the growling rain.

"What's happening? Where are you taking her?"

I wouldn't get any answers while he wore the mask, but even carrying extra weight, he was hard to keep up with. I hoped processing and ignoring my questions would slow him down.

It didn't.

I stumbled over every fallen branch and sometimes over my own feet, but I kept Adam in sight. The rain didn't stop either.

The Creek was running so quickly that it splashed over the planks of the little wooden bridge. Crossing it together this time, we both appeared to walk on water. I hoped to pass this test with fewer injuries. Elspeth leaned heavily on Adam when we got into the Gatehouse. He dropped her in Alice's chair and disappeared into the bedroom. Elspeth winced and peeked between her fingers at the wound in her side.

"How bad?" I asked.

"Oh, it'll do," she said. "Can you find me a cloth?"

I scanned the mostly empty room. The gauzy curtains were the only things that looked like they might be useful. I pulled one down from the window that faced away from the Creek. On the other side, the sunlight was blinding.

Before my eyes could adjust, Elspeth called my name, and I turned my back on the forest. She was about to pass out. Dropping to my knees beside her, I pressed the cloth into her hands. "What can I do?"

"Just... stay..." she said.

I put one hand behind her to steady her and one hand on her knee, to steady me. She peeled back her shirt and gasped when it clung to her skin. She pulled it loose. A sliver of the door the size of a pencil stuck out of her side. I closed my eyes.

"Cate?"

"I'm sorry." All of this potential she saw in me was

completely useless when it mattered. *What good is a link to the Source if I can't help my friend when she is bleeding in front of me?*

"This isn't... your..." she said.

And now, I feel guilty for wallowing in front of a wounded empath. I looked into her eyes and repeated my apology, knowing that she would read the different subtext. "I'm sorry," I said. "Let me help."

She nodded and pushed the curtain back into my hands. "Wrap it around. I'll need you to bind it when..." She took the sliver in one hand and held the other flat above the injury. She murmured words I couldn't hear. Her hand started to change. It wasn't glowing, exactly, but even I could sense the magic being concentrated there.

I stretched around her, pulling the cloth tight to cover the wound. I was ready, but she knew that before I said it. With a small cry, she pulled the sliver out. I pressed the cloth to the wound, but the blood was already slowing. I tied the impromptu bandage as best I could and took her hand just as she lost consciousness.

I knelt beside her with her head on my shoulder when I heard Adam behind me.

"You have to come in now," he said.

I couldn't look at him. I brushed Elspeth's hair back. "She's out cold. Maybe if you hadn't destroyed her door and impaled her with it when you brought Alice's invitation, she'd be more prepared for a visit."

"No," he said, taking a step toward me. "It's too late for her. I wasn't fast enough. She wants you now."

"It's too late for her?!" Elspeth would need some time to recover, but the magic was working. She hadn't lost that much blood. "What are you—"

"It's too late for her to help," he clarified. "Alice is dying."

I almost dropped the healer. Adam stood with his back to the uncovered window, and the sun still blazed outside of the community. I was blinded by his haloed silhouette. As I blinked at the black dots in front of my eyes, thunder crashed behind me. I heard the rain pounding the covered windows. Everything was backward. Usually, Alice's presence at the Gate kept things calm on our side, no matter what was happening out there.

"Help me," I said. Together, we lowered Elspeth from the chair and tried to arrange her comfortably on the rug. I took down another curtain and used it as a blanket, marveling again at the darkness that hid the Creek. Whatever was happening to Alice affected everything inside the boundary.

Adam opened the bedroom door and stood to the side. He wouldn't be coming in with me. At least Elspeth wouldn't be alone.

Alice lay in bed, golden hair and white dress trailing away from her delicate form. *When did she get so small?* Her skin wasn't gray, but it had lost the glow she had when she met me at the door a few days ago. Her eyes were hooded, and when she breathed, a quiet creaking sound caught every inhale. I knelt beside her, almost a reflection of the way I sat with Elspeth, but I knew that Alice was further away. She held my hand when I gave it to her, and her eyelashes fluttered.

"What's happening?" I asked. "What can I do?"

She struggled. "You're here. I'm glad that you are. It is not yet your time, but mine is ending."

"Tell me what I can do," I begged.

"Prepare yourself. You have what you need. You have always had what you needed. Remember that you have a Gift." She's said it before, when I first arrived. I'd thought she meant Nora's card, but maybe she'd been telling me the truth all along.

She took a shaking breath. "You still have time."

Double meanings again. Why did she have to be an oracle?

Hexing useless Gift that only made sense in retrospect. We couldn't live our lives backwards. "What can I do? Alice? You have to help me. I don't know what to do."

Alice's mouth moved again. I leaned in to hear her. "Reset the balance. Go back to the beginning to find the end. Call the quarters to call them home."

"Back from where? The beginning of what?"

"Find the one who was lost. Bring the outside in. Go now." Her eyes closed, and I knew I'd heard her last words. She was still breathing, but something important was gone.

I ran my fingers through my hair, wincing when they caught on some bits of Elspeth's cottage. The dust flew farther than I'd realized. I rested my elbows on the side of the bed and bowed my head in my hands, but it was too heavy. Interlacing my fingers on the back of my neck, I pressed my forehead into her quilt.

Find the one who was lost. But I'd lost so many.

My glasses hung for a moment and then dropped on the bed. I squeezed everything tight, held my breath, counted to ten, and—let it all go. The jagged breaths, the held-back tears, the fear and anger and sadness I'd been pushing aside rushed out of me and filled the Gatehouse. Acid tears burned my face as they ran through my eyebrows and into my hair.

When my heart rate slowed, I pushed my hair behind my ears and stood, wiping my glasses on my shirt. I could see again, but nothing much had changed.

If I had any doubts about the imbalance in Queen's Creek's magical energy, tonight's weather would have shattered them. The storm was too sudden, too strange, and the way it interfered with Gifted witches' spells...

Adam should have been able to heal Alice through the Gatekeeper's bond with the Guardian. He should have been able to blink to Elspeth's cottage and back instead of loping through the trees like the wolf. Even Elspeth's injury should have responded quicker to her self-treatment spell. According to Dad's notes, the energy from the community's Equinox festival would push the balance too far, but it might have already been too late.

At the door, Adam was shaken. *What is the Guardian at the Gate without the Gatekeeper?* "I couldn't heal her. The Gatekeeper's magic isn't responding to me," he said, confirming my suspicions. "What should we do?"

Find the one who was lost. Bring the outside in. I'd come here to find my father, but he wasn't outside. Neither were Matthew nor Gabriel.

The one who was lost. Not the one *you* lost. The one who was lost outside? Duncan?

Call the quarters to call them back. Call *them* back, not *him*. If I found Elspeth's brother, could I bring back mine? Could I bring them all back?

Reset the balance. You still have time.

But for how long? Outside the uncovered window, the moon dipped in the sky. One more day until the Equinox. Two until my birthday. If I was going, I had to do it now.

"You're the Guardian. Guard...." I gestured to both rooms. "Them."

I hesitated, watching Elspeth's labored breathing. What good would it do to bring her brother back if I lost her while I was gone? "I have to go back to the Healer's cottage. Stay with them. I'll go as fast as I can."

"But what if she..." he looked at Alice on the bed.

I followed his eyes. "She's not going to die."

He raised an eyebrow.

"Yet." I sighed. "Look, Elspeth is going to need medicine and bandages, and maybe there's something there that can help Alice, too." *Was the grimoire still on her table?*

"Just hurry," he said as I stepped into the storm.

March 19

Illusion, Fear,
Anxiety

Positivity, Vitality,
Success

41

The rain pelted my face as I pushed through the trees, cutting my way back to Elspeth's cottage. I pulled my useless glasses off and shoved them in my pocket to keep them from sliding off my nose and getting lost in the brambles. Looking for the open places in the blurry mess surrounding me, I saw a small ball of light winking in the corner of my vision.

If only I believed in fairies, they might make themselves useful. Light up the path, maybe, guide my way.

But friendships with fairies were for children, and a light in this storm was more likely to be a will-o'-the-wisp leading me astray like the one I chased all those years ago. Grown-ups have a much easier time believing in the bad stuff anyway.

Tonight the overgrown malevolent lightning bugs seemed drawn to the power of the boundary spell. Gabriel had been right — there were more of them near the Creek.

The storm eased by tiny but noticeable increments the farther I got from the Gate. Soon, I made it to the Healer's cottage and picked my way over the wreckage of her front door. I wiped my glasses on the first dry cloth I could find, a dish towel near her wash basin. When I put them back on, I was surprised by how little damage was done. The door lay in a million pieces, but the rain had barely puddled past the threshold, and the wind hadn't disturbed anything in Elspeth's workspace.

I grabbed my backpack from the floor and started loading it with first aid supplies. Bandages, a couple of jars of salve, and two or three potion bottles looked promising. Wrapping the grimoire in Elspeth's pillowcase, I tucked it into the bag, willing the seams to hold. It still weighed a ton, but it seemed less willfully burdensome than it had when we first met. *Look at me, personifying the book again.*

I pulled Adam's cloak from the hook by the door where I had left it and latched the collar around my neck.

The hike back to the Gatehouse went easier. At least this time, the wind was at my back. With the hood pulled over my head, I could shade my face from the rain and keep my glasses in place, no matter how hard the drops fell.

Adam and I worked quickly and almost silently to treat Elspeth's wound. Neither she nor Alice woke. Not even when Adam placed his hands above her head and heart and tried to summon the magic like he did before.

I unpacked the rest of the supplies and left the grimoire wrapped in the pillowcase by Alice's bed before zipping up my bag and pulling it over my shoulders. It dripped down my already soaking jeans, but it wasn't raining on the other side of the Creek, so hopefully, it and I would dry out soon. I left Adam's cloak hanging by the Creek-side door, feeding a puddle under the coat hook. The trees on that side bent toward us. The walls creaked, and the windows shook. The Gatehouse wasn't built for this.

I put my back to the storm and the rustling curtains and faced the unfiltered sunlight streaming through the windows on the other side. Adam stood in front of the door.

"I have to go," I said. I knew better than to promise that I'd be back this time. I wasn't even sure what I was looking for, much less how to find it. Did she really expect me to find Duncan just wandering by outside the Creek after three years?

He started to interrupt, but I didn't let him.

"If I'm not back in time," I said, "she's also a seventh." I pointed at Elspeth as if he didn't already know.

"She chose you." There was a time when he had chosen me, too.

"She told me to go." And so did he. Several times.

"Your Wakening—"

"Isn't over yet," I insisted. But it didn't matter. I wouldn't be stuck here before I had to be, even if the Gatekeeper was dying. *Even if I might be stuck out there for good.* I was leaving anyway, wasn't I? Threads or no threads. Nothing I'd remembered changed the fact that I didn't belong here. That it probably wasn't safe for me to stay. Maybe if Elspeth was the new Gatekeeper, she didn't have to be the last. She wasn't bound or cursed. I'd bet her energy would heal whatever was wrong with the boundary spell.

When I raised my eyes from the sleeping healer, Adam watched me. It was a good thing she lay between us because the look in his eyes was almost enough to change my mind. But he was the one who pulled away.

"I have to go," I said again. Even so, I didn't like leaving Elspeth this way. "Take care of her. She's important."

"I will," he said, still blocking the door. After a moment, he realized the problem and stepped aside.

Outside the Gatehouse, the sun dripped through the trees. Birds were having what I could only assume were several different extremely animated conversations. A hawk screeched above the trees, but it barely gave the birds pause.

There were too many of them, and the trees were too dense. I pushed through fresh undergrowth toward the clearing where we ditched Thomas's rental. I couldn't imagine it'd been found, but I crossed my fingers anyway. I would need the motor and the GPS to find my way out of here since I couldn't use the Craft to scry for a location I wasn't sure about.

It might've been luck or corporate negligence, but the car was exactly where we left it. I thanked all of my stars, the goddess in all her forms, and any other source of blind luck I could remember. My hand on the door, I closed my eyes for a second and willed the keys into the visor. I asked my subconscious to assure me that I had left them there when we ran for the Gate.

Hope was the only magic I really had, so I held on tight. I crossed my fingers with both hands, crossed my arms and whispered, "Please."

My eyes snapped open when something cracked behind me. The deer was just as startled when I turned around. I watched it disappear back into the woods and tried to shake the feeling that I still wasn't alone. The door creaked when I pulled it open. My backpack swung through to the passenger seat and fell over sideways. I sat behind the steering wheel and flipped down the visor. The keys dropped into my lap.

"Yes!" *Maybe we're getting somewhere after all. I just wish I knew where.*

Nora's card showed the Moon, an image linked to the subconscious, fear, and anxiety. It also represented illusions, things that are not what they seem.

Alice said I had what I needed. I'd always had it. *What have I always had? Come on, Dorothy Gale, where are the ruby slippers?*

The contents of my backpack spilled out on the seat. A few T-shirts, underwear, an extra pair of jeans, the tank and shorts I'd been sleeping in, the book I brought for the plane. My wallet and phone in the front pocket. When the bag was empty, I shook it upside down and tossed it on the floor in front of the passenger seat. A small blue envelope peeked out. *No.*

Nonononono.

It was just like all the others, except for the short note in Mom's handwriting on the back.

I found this yesterday, haven't read it. I hope it brings you closure. Love, Mom.

She must have slipped it into my bag before I left.

I melted back into the seat. The envelope was sealed and stamped. I chewed my lip.

Then I ripped it open. My dad's familiar handwriting filled the front and back of the small page. It was hard to read through the water in my eyes. The tears made the words curve and waver.

Dear Kitty,

This might be the last letter you get from your dad for a while. It feels momentous and fraught. Your Wakening is almost over, and if you return, we'll have no need of such formal communication. But I must say that I've enjoyed it, putting my thoughts to paper for you and reading yours. Somehow, there seems to be less of a filter between the mind and the hand than when thoughts attempt the more traditional route from the brain to the mouth.

And so I will be direct with you now, in case this is the last opportunity.

I hope that you don't come back. Please don't be hurt. I would never want that for you. In fact, that is why I so deeply hope you have found your place out there and have all but forgotten us back home.

Queen's Creek was never meant to be a permanent settlement. It was an expedient solution and a much-needed escape for witches at a time when there was nowhere else to go. But we've overstayed our welcome. Magic was never meant to be contained. It will not remain so much longer.

I think I've found a solution, but the Bridge will need support from both sides. Perhaps, if I succeed, we'll see each other again soon, without a need for crossing through the Gate.

If something goes wrong and you are drawn back here, my contact may be able to help. His card is enclosed. It may well all come down to you, but please remember that you are not your Gift, and your destiny is yours to choose.

Be well, daughter.

Always,

Your Dad

A small white business card rested in the envelope. Luke Williams, a local real estate agent. On the back, a date and time were scrawled in my father's handwriting. Both past.

I waited for a dramatic lightning flash or thunderclap, but it didn't come.

No wonder he didn't mail it. He said he didn't want me to come home, but this would have brought me back immediately. I rubbed the tears out of my eyes and put the letter back in the envelope.

I knew exactly where I needed to go next.

The little ball of light on the other side of the windshield said otherwise.

"Not today, wisp," I muttered. I threw the car in reverse and almost backed into a tree, turning it around. The will-o'-the-wisp reflected in my rearview. I switched gears before it could lead me astray. The GPS could wait until I got back on a paved road. The wisp wouldn't follow on asphalt.

42

A t the first sign of civilization, I pulled over and plugged the address from the business card into the car's navigation system. The office was less than ten minutes away. I was tempted to make it in five, but since I was the only witch who couldn't talk her way out of a speeding ticket, I kept it to a very conservative five miles over the speed limit. *Got to keep up with the flow of traffic, right? Not that there is much around here.*

It still took me longer than I'd hoped to get there, between tourists slowing down past every hotel and an accident in front of the Cracker Barrel. I checked the address three to five times, but it was completely unnecessary. There was a bench with one of those ads with the guy's name and number right out front. I pulled into the first available parking space, unnervingly close to the front door, and sat there with my hands on the wheel. The number painted on the door matched the address on the business card from Dad's letter.

My fingers were stiff, and I had to consciously unclench my teeth. I stared at the door, running my fingers through my hair, pulling out the knots. I adjusted my glasses and straightened my shirt. I stared at the door some more.

There might be answers behind that door. There have to be answers behind that door. Alice sent me here for a reason.
What if I don't like the answers?
What if I don't ask the right questions?
Why does it have to be me?
I wish Thomas were here.

The storefront windows were tiled with properties for sale, each featuring a blond man smiling his encouragement from the top left corner. He looked young, and his confident expression was both encouraging and grating in its repetition. Several fliers showed new construction homes in the wooded area I'd just left. The expanding mundane neighborhood was getting a little too close to the Creek.

The door opened, and a frazzled middle-aged woman came out. She laughed, blushing. She held the door open for a second longer than necessary and waved to someone inside.

"Let's go," she called. When the kid reached the door, she grabbed his arm and propelled him out onto the sidewalk. Smiling through gritted teeth, she mouthed "Thank you" to someone I couldn't quite see through the glass. As she walked away, her reflection cleared, and the blond man from all the fliers stood on the other side of the door, another copy of that confident expression.

I'll bet his teeth do that sparkly thing like Thomas's. How did Dad know this guy? What sort of contact did he have with someone living in the mundane world?

Adam said Dad broke the covenant.

The guy started to turn away, and I remembered, at the exact moment he saw me, that I was not invisible, parked right in front of his office. I pictured myself diving below the dashboard like a teenage private eye. Of course, I didn't do that, but I really wished I could.

I wish I had my phone out so I could buy some time pretending to text. Or actually calling someone. Instead, I smiled. He waved. I waved back. Goddess, why am I so awkward?

Grabbing the keys, my wallet, and my phone from the pile of crap I dumped out on the seat next to me, I managed to get out of the car and over to the door without tripping on the curb or committing any other graceless feats of embarrassment.

He leaned out, holding the door open, the wide smile still on his face. "Come on in."

The sign over the door just read Realtor, and when I came inside, there was only one desk. The office was comfortable, though small, with a couple of low leather armchairs and a coffee table spread with magazines. A glass-fronted mini-fridge full of water bottles sat in one corner with a single-serve coffee maker on top. All of it shined.

"Hey there," he said as if he had expected me. "I'm Luke."

"Cate."

"Welcome, Cate." He made unblinking eye contact as he shook my hand. Something in his smile felt familiar. It was both off-putting and reassuring.

I looked around the office as an excuse to break away.

"Make yourself at home," he said and motioned for me to take a seat.

I perched on the edge and flipped the business card through my fingers.

"So, what brings you in today?" He sat behind the desk. His tone made the generic question sound personal.

Destiny? A mission from an oracle? My father's last letter to me? *Go with that one. It makes you sound less crazy.* I put the card on the desk. "I think you knew my father. Marcus Corey?"

He nodded. "Yeah, we did some work together a while back. How's he doing?"

He's legally dead. Lost in a magical time stream. Beyond the veil. Unreachable. Maybe on his way home if all goes well. I swallowed.

Somehow, all of it felt equally true. "He passed."

He looked down, flipping the card and running his fingers over Dad's writing. *So, they did know each other.*

"I wondered why he didn't call." He smiled sympathetically this time. A shadow crossed his eyes. "I'm sorry for your loss."

"Thanks." Now what? How did you ask someone if they were a witch? Especially in a town that wasn't supposed to believe in magic. I studied my fingers.

He leaned forward as if sharing a secret. "Queen's Creek is a very special place."

Wait. What? Why does it sound like he's been there?

When I didn't answer, he continued. "Some people find it difficult to leave. I might be able to help. If you're ready for something new."

The same words from Dad's letter. Did he know what I needed help with? Who I needed to find? "Umm. Thanks. I have a few things to work out before I go. I'm helping my mom with Dad's estate. A lot has changed in the last few years."

"This area has had a lot of development recently. But I think we've managed to preserve the magic." He winked.

Goddess-bless-it, he winked.

"What did you and my dad work on together?"

"He was very interested in preservation. Creating a sanctuary for some… endangered species near the creek back there."

Endangered or enchanted? A wildlife sanctuary bordering the Creek would keep those developers back. It would create a buffer between us and suburbia. Fewer mundanes in the woods near the boundary might mean less of a drain on the energy that hid it.

Was it still breaking the covenant if you did it to save the community? What if the realtor was a witch? There were no vows of secrecy between members of the community.

He didn't look familiar, but I didn't know every witch in Queen's Creek.

Ugh. Curse the covenant of secrecy and whoever thought it was a good idea. This was how I went three years meeting with an academic advisor without realizing she was a witch. Would Nora ever have told me the truth if I hadn't been about to drop out of school and face self-exile in an electronically unreachable town in rural Virginia?

I needed some kind of clue that I wasn't reading into his words. Or that wink. Was he flirting or hinting? If he turned out to be a witch, I had to side-eye this entire conversation.

"Have you worked here long?" The leather chair squeaked as I shifted and leaned closer to the chrome and glass coffee table.

He didn't answer right away, but he didn't have to. One of the magazines on the coffee table was flipped open to its feature story: Rising Stars: 30 Under 30! He landed at number eight. "Luke Williams, 24, of Hawk Realty."

He was even younger than he looked. The same age as Caleb. The same age as Duncan. He could have started working here and still contacted my dad while he was on his Wakening. But he'd have been stuck out here since turning twenty-one.

Luke saw me looking at the magazine and grinned. "Nice, right? Such an honor."

"Yeah. Congratulations." It truly was an impressive achievement. *You'd have to be very skilled or very lucky. It would help if you knew someone.*

He leaned back, crossing his arms behind his head. He flexed.

I rolled my eyes, then coughed when his polo sleeve rode up, revealing a tattoo. Blue runes circled his upper arm.

Or if you knew magic.

"You want some water? You look a bit pale," he said, going to the mini-fridge.

I was always pale, but I thanked him and took the bottle anyway. After a few sips, I set it on the table, glancing at my phone but thinking about Nora's card hiding in the case. Invisible in plain sight. *Find the one who was lost.*

This supposedly mundane realtor had a runic tattoo. It might pass for an interest in Vikings or medieval fantasy fandoms among his clients, but the Celtic symbols had other meanings in Queen's Creek.

He was almost certainly a witch. He knew my father. I didn't know the story behind Adam's tattoo, but they were too similar for it to be a coincidence.

43

Umm. Nice ink."

"Thanks. Yeah, it reminds me of a friend of mine. We went through some things, but he got me out of a tough situation. He was a real solid guy, *salt-of-the-earth*, you know? You ever have a friend like that?"

I searched his eyes. They were warm brown, edged in green like Elspeth's.

My breath caught. It couldn't be this easy. Could Duncan be sitting right in front of me this close to the boundary?

Not that what he was doing was easy. This wasn't a simple style change like Shiri's rainbow hair. Sitting here in plain sight behind plate glass windows, this witch was holding together a glamour that changed his hair color, face shape, and skin tone.

But not his sister's eyes. And not the tattoo that connected him to Adam.

Magic was weaker outside the Creek. To hold a glamour like that for so long, you'd have to have a Gift.

Duncan's charmed life. The Gift of charisma. People trusted him. They believed in him. Even if he was lying.

But if he had a Gift, why did he live out here where no one

else used magic? Why didn't he come home?

30 under 30!

He'd hidden too long, missed the window for his Wakening.

He was still hiding.

What if he was in hiding from the witch hunters? Caleb and Duncan had been caught because they weren't careful. They said something or did something they shouldn't have in front of the wrong people. Caleb was lucky to get away.

I wanted to trust him, but how could I tell if that was my intuition or his Gift? How had he stayed safe for so long? Had he really lost the hunters?

My stomach sank. *Or had he joined them?*

Adam would know. Or Elspeth. *Why couldn't I have a Gift like theirs?*

I was taking too long to answer. Looking down, I pretended to read a message on my phone. Stood and stepped away from the desk. *Check out my acting skills.*

"Sorry, I need a minute." My phone warmed in my hand. Not my phone, the card in my phone case. *Shitshitshit.*

Luke—Duncan?—froze.

Hecate help me. I accepted my Gift less than twenty-four hours ago, and I'm already using it in public. I'm going to owe Thomas an apology.

I shoved my phone into my back pocket and gripped the back of the chair, watching the realtor. The room was utterly silent. *That's what happens when you put a pause on everything, including the a/c and the fridge.*

Only the light changed as a cloud passed in front of the sun outside the storefront windows. Time moved normally outside this office.

You still have time.

How much time did I need? What good did it do to freeze time in here, while it was still running out at the Gatehouse?

Go back to the beginning.

If this was Duncan, he knew who I was. He'd probably recognized me even before I'd asked about Dad. Why didn't he say anything?

How far did this disguise go? Dad called him his contact, but the card read *Luke Williams*. Did Dad know who he was working with?

He offered to help if I wanted to leave. What kind of help?

Elspeth could have read his aura or sensed his sincerity. Adam would have known if he were lying. If Thomas were here, he could have used the same influence that encouraged me to come home.

How did Duncan get here? What's he been up to?

I stumbled. My vision blurred in a way that was starting to become familiar. My heart rushed in my ears. The card warmed.

A translucent image overlaid the scene in front of me. The realtor didn't move, but at the same time, another version of him shifted in his seat.

He raised his arms again, flexing to show off the tattoo. This time, I saw him watching my response.

I was in the chair, fiddling with the business card. I stood, backing to the door.

He held it open.

The kid stepped into the office backward, followed by his mother.

Luke's afternoon appointments played in reverse, speeding up as it went. He'd met with a young couple before the mom, and an older man before them.

My stomach pitched, and I gripped the back of the chair. The days and weeks whirred by in a dizzying race. A pattern developed. Most days, he spent some time at the desk and met with a few clients. In the afternoons, he grabbed keys from the desk and left for a few hours, probably showing properties.

At night, the office sat empty and dark.

Until a few months ago. I tried to slow the rewinding images, pulling back some of my energy. Luke came in with a young woman. They didn't turn on the lights, but the moon shone through the big windows. She gave him a backpack, and he took it to a closet I hadn't noticed in the back of the office. He emptied supplies onto the shelves: toiletries, bottled water, a small mint tin almost exactly like the one that disguised my ritual altar supplies at school, packs of matches… Then walked her back to the door and sat behind his desk, where he flicked through a phone as though waiting for someone.

Wait.

The scene paused. If I played it over in the right order, Luke was waiting for that girl. When she came in, he gave her everything a young witch on the run would need to take care of herself.

Go back.

Similar scenes played every few months, always at night. The kids Luke met were all between sixteen and twenty. They all looked scared when they arrived and grateful when he offered a small talisman on a leather cord, slipping it over their necks.

I'd thought all of Dad's contacts on the outside were academic colleagues, but not every kid who left for their Wakening was going to college. Thomas hadn't.

I watched a few more scenes play out the same way, recognizing some of the kids. A neighbor, the younger brother of one of Caleb's friends. *Okay. Just because he's helping lost kids from Queen's Creek doesn't mean he's a witch. It doesn't mean he's Duncan.*

I had to know for sure. The covenant and consequences and all that. *Maybe he's just a good samaritan… who happens to have met a bunch of troubled magic users. Why don't we have a secret handshake or something?*

"You could just ask," said the young man who still sat behind the desk. Why hadn't I recognized his voice before?

The vision sped up, moving forward in seconds until the shadow play I'd been watching overlapped the real scene in front of me. The second Luke sat behind the desk and merged with the real one.

I gasped, blinking until the double vision cleared.

He tilted his head. "Are you alright?"

"Are you Duncan?" *Hex the covenant.*

He smiled. "Not here."

My heart raced as the prospect of reuniting Elspeth with her long-lost brother warred with the possibility that bringing him home might somehow fulfill my destiny as the last Gatekeeper. "You know how you said you might be able to help me? I think maybe we can help each other."

If I can get him there. He might not even be able to see the Gate anymore.

"In that case, I'll follow your lead." He grinned. Something about his smile made me want to trust him. Remembering the blush on his last client's face, I hoped I wasn't making a mistake.

44

We took Thomas's rental, and by some miracle, I successfully guided us back to the place where I found it. When the pavement turned to gravel, I pulled over.

We'd ridden mostly in silence, but I needed to get some things straight before we got back to the Gatehouse. For one thing, I'd rather cross the boundary with my friend's Gifted older brother than my father's possibly mundane contact.

I turned in my seat so I could look into his eyes again. Duncan's eyes were so out of place in this social media influencer's body. The disguise didn't hold up if you knew what to look for. Had my father seen it? Or had they done all their business by mail?

"Did he know?" I couldn't imagine Dad keeping Duncan's survival a secret from his family.

Duncan rubbed the back of his neck, ruffling the back of Luke's light hair. "I thought he might, sometimes. We did most of our work through messengers, but there were a few phone calls. It's so much harder to change my voice."

"Who did he think you were?"

Luke's hand came out for another handshake. "Luke

Williams, Hawk Realty. Your dreams are my reality. When I'm not at the office, you can find me at the Y, where I volunteer with the Big Brothers/Big Sisters program."

I held back a snicker at the cheesy tagline. "Those kids that you help, do they know you're a witch? What keeps them from spoiling your secret identity when they come home?"

"I tell them I came down from Salem, missed the return flight at the end of my Wakening, and I'm looking for a way to stay connected to the magical community. It's partly true, and they want to believe it, so…" He shrugged.

I unbuckled my seatbelt and played with the clip. "Why didn't you come back? If you were here this whole time…" I gestured to the clock on the dashboard. "It wouldn't take that long to get to the Gate from town. Did you miss your window on purpose?"

He sighed, leaning back in his seat and staring through the windshield. "What did Caleb tell you?"

"He said hunters got you."

Luke's eyebrow lifted.

"He said you guys were out somewhere, and he heard witch hunters talking about you. They sensed your Gift."

He smirked. "Oh, they sensed us. We were reckless. It was stupid. Party tricks. But the mundanes had never seen anything like what we could do. The best audience."

I tried to bite my tongue, but it got free. "You did magic in front of mundanes? And you didn't think there would be consequences?"

"I said it was stupid, didn't I?" It was more than stupid. More than reckless. But before Duncan disappeared, fewer stories about local witch hunters had trickled into the Creek. The threat had felt far away.

"So, what happened?"

"We ran. They followed us." He made the terrifying news sound obvious.

"But Caleb came home." My brother had been scared. The story of his close call burned through the community in days. Some people wanted to go after Duncan immediately. Others feared drawing more attention to the Creek. The Speaker sided with them.

"He wasn't as good at hiding as I was."

The air between us shimmered, and I saw Duncan through the glamour. His brown hair, the same shade as Elspeth's, had grown a little longer than Luke's. His skin took on a tan hue with warmer undertones.

"Don't get me wrong, Caleb was a great watchdog, the best early warning system we could ask for. But his glamour needed work. When I put on a disguise—"

Luke snapped back into place. "You see what I want you to see."

I see why he left you behind. Elspeth's older brother had always been a little full of himself, probably a side effect of the confidence his Gift inspired. "So, what then? You're saying Caleb lied? You didn't get kidnapped by witch hunters?"

He turned to face me, his back against the door. "He was never going to go home without me. And if he stayed out there with me, we were going to get caught. Dude can hear a pin drop in the next county, but he can't walk across a cotton rug without alerting the neighbors."

"You ditched him." *Left my brother to face witch hunters alone and—*

"I led the hunters away and then changed my appearance to slip them. I thought I'd catch up with him at the Gatehouse." His eyes widened, practically begging me to see what a heroic act he'd made of running away. I almost believed him.

"Why didn't you?"

"Adam."

I closed my eyes, forcing the memories I'd found with Elspeth and Adam into chronological order. He'd left after the fight in the garden. After Caleb and Duncan had left on their Wakenings. When Caleb came home, Adam was gone. Caleb hadn't seen him.

When I opened my eyes, Duncan continued. "He turned up in town, and the hunters were still watching for anybody new. I think they'd figured out what I can do. I couldn't let them take him when I was the one taking risks."

Still trying to come out of this story an honorable hero.

"So, I grabbed him, and we lay low for a while. But he didn't want to hide. Said he wasn't going to use magic anymore anyway. He had this whole plan to get a job and an apartment so he could come back for you."

I smiled.

"We met with a realtor. She helped us find a place, and then she offered to help me, Luke, if I wanted to start a new career. I barely had to push her at all. People like this guy. I don't know why it didn't work as well on the hunters. They must have some kind of totem. A charm against my charms." He frowned, genuinely confused about how anyone could resist him.

He might have been adorable in his innocence if he hadn't set a boatload of consequences in motion for the rest of us.

"Adam was much better at the undercover thing than Caleb. Might have been because he was telling the truth about his plan—he didn't use any magic. But the hunters kept sniffing around. He was afraid to go home in case he led them back to you."

I'd tried to wait for him, but Dad had been insistent. Now I understood why Adam hadn't sent any messages home.

"So, I talked him into doing a binding spell."

My skin turned cold. "A what?"

He rolled up his sleeve to show the runes on his arm. "The

tattoos bind us together. As long as one of us is hidden, the other can't be found. The longer I stayed as Luke, the safer he would be. We figured he'd go back, and as soon as he crossed the boundary, it would be safe for me to drop the glamour. Can't be more hidden than inside the boundary."

As long as one is hidden. But Adam was still inside. Either the bind didn't work as well as Duncan thought it would, or Queen's Creek wasn't as hidden as we thought it was. Was the boundary that weak?

Duncan didn't notice my panic, or maybe he confused it for engagement in his story. "By the time you two came out, I'd be on my way back in. But the trip took him longer than we planned, and I had no way of knowing why. It's completely stupid that we've been living in there for so long, so close to this town, and have no way to communicate across the boundary."

He's not wrong there. So much could have been avoided if there'd been a more reliable source of communication than snail mail.

"Then a kid stumbled out of the woods and blinked to the main road. She was lucky I was the one watching and not the hunters. I helped her get away."

Goddess, were all of us so dumb? Did anyone listen to Alice's warnings before they left? The Gatekeeper's messaging might have been wrapped in cryptic prophecy, but the whole "Don't use magic in front of mundanes" part should have been reinforced by our parents and families. It was incredible Queen's Creek had gone so long undetected. A testament to the early power of the boundary spell, really.

"By then, my time was running out. I decided it would be better for everyone if I didn't come back. My Gift has always worked better on mundanes anyway." He paused to give me time to appreciate his sacrifice.

And it wasn't that I didn't appreciate it, this double life

he'd been leading, but the sun moved through the trees, and I worried about how much time we'd wasted catching up. "So you took the real estate job and joined the Brothers and Sisters as an excuse to meet with kids on their Wakenings. How did Dad get your card?"

"I sent it back with one of the kids. I probably could have come to the Gate myself. I haven't seen any sign of the hunters in months. But, you know, my Wakening ended three years ago. I wasn't sure I'd be able to find it. Anyway, the kids told me magic was glitchy at the Creek, and I'd been keeping an eye on the construction. There wasn't much I could do, but an established community member, even one who did most of his business in absentia like the professor… He could start the process for a conservation space."

"But it didn't work," I said, remembering the piles of clay and cleared land I'd passed on the way in with Thomas.

"It's not a quick process." Duncan picked at an invisible piece of lint on his dark jeans.

Something rattled in the trees above the car, making the branches scrape across the roof. The first signs of a storm darkened the trees.

"If you still want to help, we need to get back." I opened the door and leaned out, checking for rain.

Duncan got out of the car but hesitated before shutting the door. "I know I've been gone a while, but the boundary still has an age lock, doesn't it? How are you planning to get me in?"

I pulled my backpack over my shoulders and studied the sky through the breaks in the canopy. A flash of lightning and a distant roll of thunder encouraged me to get moving. It was a massive relief to know we probably weren't leading witch hunters back to our home, but I shared Duncan't concern about what he might see when he got there. And whether he'd be able to cross.

For now, we'd have to literally worry about that bridge when we came to it. I didn't want to risk getting stuck in the woods during a storm while we tried to think our way through picking a magical lock. "I'm not sure the boundary will be a problem much longer. Can we continue this while we walk?"

Without waiting for an answer, I headed down the path. It was barely open, just a tunnel through the trees, more likely made by deer than people. A moment later, I heard Duncan on the gravel behind me. As the stones gave way to hard-packed dirt, I felt bad about his shoes. My sneakers were already coated in mud from running through the storm last night. Hopefully, the pointy dress shoes he wore under his dark jeans had better traction than they appeared to have.

"Watch out for roots. Some of them might be snakes," I warned, stepping around a suspicious one.

The trees cracked overhead. The sun hid. The temperature dropped. Further discussion of my half-formed plan could wait until we reached the shelter of the Gatehouse. Duncan seemed to understand and walked beside me silently. In the dark wood, lightning bugs flashed among the fallen leaves.

Or maybe that wisp from this morning brought friends to welcome me back. Ignore them and keep walking.

The clouds brushed the tops of the trees. My stomach tensed. What if the boundary collapsed before we got there? Where would the energy go?

This is how I die. That next thunderclap will announce the brightest flash of lightning I've ever seen. The trees will catch fire despite the water that hangs in the air. I'll suffocate on the smoke and burn with the forest.

45

Something popped next to me, a small explosion probably caused by a squirrel in too much of a hurry to stay in the trees. But I was equally sure that I should revise my imminent cause of death to an actual lightning strike. No need for secondhand burning. It would strike me down right here. Or a bear. There were bears in these woods, right? *The crashing to my right is definitely a bear, who's going to eat me and—*

And then the sky really did open up. The rain had been working its way through the trees *(an excellent sign, I'm sure)*, but now we were walking through a wall of water. I squinted and wiped my glasses, but my shirt was already soaked through. My soggy shoes made disgusting, squelchy sounds and threatened to stay behind at every step. I couldn't tell if we were still on the path.

Before I had time to place myself on my admittedly incomplete mental map, I fell. Duncan crashed into me, my feet slid away, and we both went down. *I can't breathe.*

He groaned and rolled away. I snatched a breath. I was breathing water because it was still pouring out, and we weren't under the cover of the trees anymore, but it was something. I pushed myself up, sputtering, and tried to find Duncan in the curtain of rain.

There he is. He'd gotten to his knees and tried to stand, slipping in the mud with his impractical shoes.

I pushed my drenched hair away from my face and made another impossible attempt to wipe my glasses. I needed windshield wipers. Or contacts. *Or, you know, the magical ability to see without them.*

I gave up and shoved my glasses back into place. The blurry colors reformed into the vague shapes of trees, and brush, and a gaping black hole just a few feet from where Duncan knelt. The space around it opened up, cleared of wood. I could almost see another road in the distance.

Wow, that's a big hole. Was that always there? No, right? I swear the woods went out farther from the Creek than this.

It could be a ravine. But this giant ditch wasn't cut out by shifting land over several decades. This was wider, deeper, and very man-made.

Duncan wobbled as he stood up. He was a little shaky and a little too close to the pit.

I tried to help him out before he became another problem. "Hey, Duncan? Don't back up."

"What? Have you seen my…" He'd lost a shoe in the mud, and his soggy polo hung heavily. He stepped back.

"Wait!" Too late. He was already slipping, that socked foot missing the edge. He scrambled to stay up but slid back over the side. I fell on my knees, grabbing his shoulders, bracing myself against nothing, digging into the red clay mud. I leaned back and looked behind me for anything I could hold on to. There was nothing.

The water in the bottom was just enough to give me flashbacks to my unintended plunge into the Creek a few days ago. I panicked as I slid under and the churning runoff closed over my face. I wouldn't call it another near-death experience, but it was definitely tragedy-adjacent. I came up sputtering, just long enough to suck in some air before I went back down. This time, I bounced off the bottom not far below me. I could probably have stood if I had gotten my feet under me, but I kept getting flipped around, and I couldn't tell which way was up.

I somehow managed not to hit my head again. My feet finally landed on something hard, and I pushed off. When my hands broke the surface, Duncan grabbed them and pulled me up. Before I could thank him, he collapsed. This time, I pulled him up. The water hit just above my waist, but the level dropped quickly. Duncan was taller, and once he stood, the water wasn't doing much to support his weight. He winced and leaned on my shoulder.

"Thanks," he said. "Sorry. My ankle. I think it's broken."

I squinted at him through the rain. It seemed to be letting up a little. The clouds overhead swooped across the sky. I'd never seen them move so fast. The water from my hair dripped down my forehead, rolled over my saturated eyebrows, and caught on the ends of my lashes. I used my free hand to push my hair back again and rubbed my eyes. Everything looked shiny and vaguely distorted. Because I'd lost my glasses. I groaned.

Duncan pulled back a little but couldn't afford to completely let go. "Sorry," he said again, "Am I hurting you?"

Great, now I've made it awkward. "No. It's not you... It's..."

He reached for something floating in the water around our knees. "Yours, I believe?" he said, shaking some of the muck off my glasses.

"Thanks." I made a solid, ineffectual attempt at putting them back on my face one-handed, my other hand kind of trapped, supporting him around his back. He smiled and squeezed my shoulder with the hand that was basically holding on for dear life. Then he used his free hand to loop one side of my glasses over my ear. He brushed the hair that stuck to my face behind my ear too. I tried not to read too much into the moment when his face came into focus. Because it was Duncan's face again—as if the storm had washed away his glamour.

"Thanks," I said again.

"You're welcome." He looked at the wall of the trench behind me. "It's pretty slick, but we can climb it." His tone was back to normal, confident, though concerned.

"Ummm." I wasn't sure. This trench was cut straight down, severing any plants that might have grown over the sides. I couldn't tell how deep it went, but neither of us would reach the top from here, even on our toes.

"Sure, see, this is all clay," he said, maneuvering to support himself against the side instead of my shoulder. "I'll bet we can dig out some footholds and—" With both hands against the dirt, he raised a foot and kicked at the wall. He immediately regretted it.

"Aaarrghhh!" he groaned in pain and frustration. Wincing, he pulled his leg back and leaned his forehead against the side. "Maybe not," he said softly.

"Hold on." I scraped out a step with my foot, the wet clay molding around the toe of my shoe.

He smiled sheepishly, the smudge of dirt on his forehead marring his otherwise glistening face. Somehow, the rain that was just making me soggier made him shine, even without the glamour. "I could probably lift you out..." he said, looking at me appraisingly.

I stopped digging to give him a similar evaluation. His polo shirt stuck to his shoulders and chest. His arms had the defined muscles of someone who considered the gym part of his job. He might have been strong enough.

"And then what?" I said. "I can't pull you up. That's how

we got stuck in here in the first place."

"You could go get help."

"I'm not going to leave you in a ditch and wander around the woods alone in a storm."

"I thought you knew where you were going? And the storm is over." He held out a hand to catch the last drops of rain.

He was right about the rain, but I was less confident about my sense of direction.

I promised to stay for Dad's service, and I need to make sure that Elspeth is okay. And I should help Adam read the grimoire so that they can complete the transfer. But that's the end of my checklist. As far as I'm concerned, my obligations end on my birthday, which I intend to spend outside of the community.

I put a hand on the clay wall, trying to decide where to put the next hold.

Looking at Duncan, I realized I'd already found the answers I came home for. If I had any hope of getting my life back — my normal, unmagical life in Chicago — I had to follow through on Alice's last request. My curse would be nothing compared to the consequences of ignoring her. Not to mention the guilt of leaving everyone unprotected. That meant going back to the Gatehouse, for a while at least.

But first, I had to get out of this ravine. I pushed my fingers into the dirt and pulled out a hunk of clay.

"Help me," I said, "We'll do it together." I refused to be trapped in a place where I didn't belong.

And time was running out.

46

I never wore a watch because I usually had a phone, and every piece of electronics in the mundane world tells time.

Of course, I was currently without all my stuff since it was sitting in a useless pile at the top of the ravine, where I dropped it when I fell. So I couldn't be completely sure, but it felt like climbing out of the ravine and helping Duncan drag himself out after me took somewhere between twenty minutes and an eternity. I was about 97% sure that the sun would set and possibly rise again before we reached the top.

"Man, come on!" I called down to him from my position at the treeline. I'd wrapped a vine around a tree and lowered it to him, but I could hardly hold on to it, much less get enough leverage to pull him out. "Doesn't your gym have a rock wall?"

He mumbled something about CrossFit and free weights. There was a lot of grumbling and grunting (on both sides, if I was honest) before his hand reached over the ledge. I grabbed it and started to drag him the rest of the way, but mostly, I just stood there and gave him a counterweight as he pulled himself up. He kneeled in the mud to catch his breath. He tried to stand. It didn't go well.

"Maybe take a minute," I said, aware of the irony after I'd rushed him to climb out. But we wouldn't get far if he hobbled himself permanently. "It's not like you can walk on that. You should be sitting down and elevating it, at least."

The edge of the ravine crumbled away where he pulled himself over the side. Big hunks of clay and stone tumbled down into the pit.

"Not here," he said.

"No," I agreed. I tried to work out how far we were from the path and how far down the path we had to go to get to the Gatehouse. The clouds started to clear, but the sky didn't get any brighter. I was afraid the hide-and-seek sun had gone behind the trees for the rest of the day.

"Let's get to that tree," I said, pointing to the one nearest where we came out of the woods. He wrapped his arm around my shoulders and hopped on his good foot. It was the most awkward three-legged race of all time, even accounting for the inherent clumsiness of the event.

The tree was blessedly carpeted with thick green moss, and I was grateful to be out of the mud, even if it was still caked all over me. We sat shoulder to shoulder against the trunk, facing the hole we'd just dug ourselves out of.

With a little luck, we might find the path and get back to the Gatehouse before the next storm passes through. I couldn't count on it though.

There was a crack in the sky. Jagged light burst through the branches in front of us and slammed into a thick tree that had probably stood there for several generations. Duncan squeezed his arm around my waist and pulled me to the side as the tree crashed to the ground where we had been sitting.

It definitely made a sound, but no one else could have heard it over my scream. The lightning strike ignited the dry wood chips that flew out of the places where the tree had come apart. The water from today's rain hissed as it evaporated, steam rising with the flames.

The sky darkened. A huge, low cloud hovered between us and the setting sun. The edges glowed orange and purple. I lifted an arm to shield myself as the sparks continued to fly around us.

The trees around us caught fire from the errant sparks.

"We have to go!" I dragged Duncan up beside me.

We moved through the woods as fast as his injuries would allow, ducking under branches and stumbling over roots. We managed to stay one step ahead of the fire, but the wind cut through the trees, knocking limbs loose and sending ash into our eyes. It was exhausting. I stumbled at the edge of a shallow trench. A thin rivulet of water wound through it. I knelt in the brook and splashed water on my face. When I stood up on the other side, Duncan blinked at me.

"Where did you go?" he asked.

"What? I'm right here." I raised an eyebrow and waved at him.

"But you were gone," he said. "You were there, and then... you weren't."

"But you see me now?" The fire behind him was slowing down. The demanding wind calmed to a breeze. Even the dark clouds seemed farther away.

"Yeah..." he said as if he didn't quite believe it.

"Now?" I said, waving both hands.

"Yes."

I backed up a few steps and waved again.

"What did you do?" he asked, squinting.

I waved again. "Right here."

"You're all... faded. Like I'm looking through a foggy window."

I backed up again.

"Stop!" He took a step forward. He tried, anyway. As soon

as he stepped into the brook, his ankle gave out, and he fell. I ran back to help him up, but he waved me off and sat on the bank.

"You really couldn't see me?" I said. "I was right there." I pointed to a bush on the other side. A tiny wisp darted through the leaves.

"Where?" He squinted. "How could you see anything through all of that?"

"All of what?" The bush was right in front of him. Why couldn't he see it?

"There's so much fog, or I guess maybe it's smoke from the fire... or steam from the rain. Do you not see that?"

I looked behind me. It still looked just as clear as where we'd come from. A little dark, a little damaged by the storm, but it was all there. "Come here."

I reached out to help him up, but no matter how far I stretched, I couldn't reach him. "Just, come over here, and I'll show you."

"I'm trying." He did. He was actively trying to get up and follow me, but something happened every time he touched the water.

I looked at the brook again. It was very narrow and rough and shallow, but it extended out into the woods in both directions. Now that the wind had slowed, I heard the water falling over rocks just out of sight.

"Shit."

47

At least we found the Creek. And we had a 50/50 chance of following it in the right direction to end up at the Gatehouse. But if he didn't see the Creek right in front of him, would Duncan be able to see the Gate? The Creek was so narrow here that I didn't recognize it at first, but there was only one explanation for why I could cross the water, and he couldn't. One explanation that was not without holes.

No one should be able to cross except at the Gate. That's why we have a Gate. Is this a weak point because it's started to dry up? Is the Source linked to the water? Or is the whole barrier really that close to failing because of what's happening to Alice?

I had to get back in.

Duncan sat awkwardly on the bank, his now familiar face crumpled in frustration. *Poor guy.* I couldn't just leave him all windblown and broken. If we got to the Gatehouse, Elspeth should be able to treat his ankle.

If she's recovered from her own injuries... I'm sure she's fine. By now, Adam would have sent word to my mom. There would be two healers in the cottage.

Okay. So. Right.

Having resolved to do the possibly impossible thing and lead a witch who couldn't see the boundary up to a Gate he probably couldn't cross, I stepped back across the Creek and helped him stand.

The storm returned so quickly this time that we were soaked through before we even got moving. The dark sky flashed, illuminating the heavy clouds that had blocked the sun, now hiding the stars. I led us a little away from the Creek, winding through the trees, where the wind was weaker, and the canopy blocked some of the rain.

Luckily, a few wisps seemed to have found something they liked near the water. If I kept their lights in sight, I thought I could keep us on track, if not completely dry. It might be the first time in history will 'o th' wisps actually helped guide someone home.

Duncan didn't question the change in direction. It took a lot of energy for him to drag himself along, holding his wounded foot out of the mud and clutching my waist to keep balance. My feet were so soggy after a while that it was almost as if I walked barefoot. My skin squelched against the sock, rubbed against the shoe, and pulled against the mud. My jeans plastered themselves to my legs, making them stiff and heavy. I used my free hand to pull at my shirt, but it insisted on twisting and riding up. Between the water flowing down from my hair and face and bumping against Duncan's side, it was a lost cause. We passed an opening in the trees and the wind managed to get through. I shivered.

"Are you alright?" Duncan asked.

I am so not alright. I might have been crying a little, but who could tell? Between the raindrops rolling down my face, and the blinking from the water up my nose, I could barely see.

"Cate?" Duncan said. "It's going to be okay. This rain has to give up sometime. Or we'll find... Something. The woods don't go on forever."

I rubbed my face and tried to look up at him. "How can you be so sure? Look around. Does this storm seem normal to you?"

Even as I said it, the wind picked up again. I leaned closer to Duncan. The trees around us were bending just a little too much. They creaked and popped.

"Maybe not..." he said, "But lightning never strikes—"

"SHUT UP!" I had enough bad luck without him jinxing us, too.

A bolt of fire crashed into a tree, and it fell in front of us, shaking the ground.

But Nora's card was still in my phone case, and the phone was in the backpack I was carrying. My Gift had gotten used to using the conduit to force energy after my intention.

For a moment, everything froze. Steam hovered silently above the cracked stump. The leaves stopped swirling through the air. The darkness was almost total without the lightning flashing above us.

I made an ill-fated attempt to wipe my smeary lenses on my saturated shirt. The trees around us were all familiar but also wrong, somehow. These trees had stood here since before I was born, before my parents were born, probably. But they might have just appeared.

Concentrating on slowing my panicked breath, I pulled back my energy, releasing time to its original flow. Nothing changed.

In my head, I unloaded all of the curse words. This adventure just lost its PG-13 rating. Words that, coming out the mouth of another member of my family, would cause dramatic reversals of fortune. People and things and weather: all doomed to eternity in dark, scary, dangerous places.

"Cate?" Duncan sounded far away. Maybe the words weren't all in my head.

"Wait!" I said, "Our eyes will adjust. Stay where you are."

He didn't answer. I didn't hear him walking away, but I didn't hear him at all anymore. Not a crunch of shifting weight or a ragged breath of exhaustion.

"Duncan?"

Silence.

Great. Silence in a forest full of living things, active living things, potentially magical, violently active, living things. This is going to end well.

I pushed my glasses back up my slippery, snotty nose. It helped nothing because even though I assured Duncan our eyes would adjust, as I stood there, dripping in the dark, they hadn't. I was shaking. I shoved my balled fists into my armpits. My shoulders hunched around my ears. The base of my skull throbbed. *I can't breathe.* My heart raced. *I might throw up.* My knees bent, and I slowly folded myself into a little muddy ball. The wet earth soaked through any remaining dry spots.

After all of those years growing up under my brothers' watchful eyes, I'd never felt so alone. Even when I left home, I found family in the theater and the coffee shop. Other people who were just a little bit weird, who came from someplace else, who were trying to find themselves as much as I was. Brian hadn't declared his major yet and seemed to change his mind about it every other week. Nyla, my roommate who was so academically driven that she scheduled out her life months in advance, had shown up at the dorm one day with a completely different style — natural curls and flowy skirts replaced by bright red box braids and overalls. Someone had been there, choosing what to do next, what to wear, where to go, just like I was.

I felt pathetic, crying into my knees, balled up on the ground, lost in the woods less than a mile from home. I'd failed at everything. I hadn't stopped the Reading. I had no idea how to get my father or my brothers back. And now I'd lost the person Alice sent me to find.

I rubbed my goose-pimpled arms and shook some of the rain loose from my hair. It slapped my cheeks. Stung.

I pulled a few sticky strands free from my glasses and straightened the frames. Sniffing, I wiped my nose with the back of my hand and looked up at the dark sky. It was barely brighter than the ground, but I could make out the moon through the clouds. It came out early.

There was something else. Smoke rose slowly, twisting and winding above the trees on the other side of the Creek. It came from a hilltop and glowed white as the last light faded into moonlight. The opposite of the dark waves that pressed us down during the storm. Although I was too far away to catch the scent of burning herbs, somehow, I knew what it was.

I'm missing my father's funeral.

48

I pushed myself out of the mud and wiped my hands on my jeans, smearing them with red clay. I was surprised to be able to see my hands after so long in the dark, but the storm had passed, and somewhere behind the trees, the sun was setting. Only in an enchanted forest could sunset chase away the shadows.

The clouds rolled back and the light spread slowly, tracing its way along the moss on the ground and up the trunks of trees. The sky eased back from purple to blue. The moon shone just as brightly. I put it behind me and followed the Creek toward the light and the rising smoke.

When Alice's cottage finally came into view, I was more confused than ever. This wasn't the adorable gingerbread house I left. The roof sagged. The windows were broken, and the door hung crookedly in its frame. The stone path to the porch was overgrown with years of weeds. The Gatehouse looked long abandoned.

"There is no Gate without the Keeper," said a soft voice in my head. The voice was familiar, and though it was unsettling to hear voices that weren't there, I was ready to accept guidance in any form after the day I'd had.

"Alice has passed," I whispered.

"The Gatekeeper's time has ended," said the voice.

"Merry meet," I thought.

"Merry meet," the voice echoed.

I stepped carefully around the uneven stones until I reached the door. There was no sense of the life that used to fill the other side. The shimmer of Alice's power was completely gone.

"Shit."

"Language," said my father.

"I'm sorry, Dad," I said, rolling my eyes. "What was the appropriate reaction to *there is no Gate*? And, by the way, when I wished for guidance, I didn't exactly expect the disembodied voice of my missing father."

He didn't answer.

Instead, a hesitant voice behind me called out, "Cate?"

My shoulders sagged. "I'm sorry, Dad. Please come back." I closed my eyes.

Duncan hobbled up beside me. Score one for adrenaline.

I wanted to punch him for interrupting possibly the most important conversation of my life. When he put his hand on my shoulder, my face burned, and I almost said... I don't know. Something horrible, probably. Something I wouldn't really mean.

But I didn't, and then the ground shook, and the sky screamed, and the dark clouds roared back, and it was too late for me to say or do anything except grab Duncan and drag him up against the rotting door that used to lead me home. The locked entrance shielded us from the storm.

"What aren't you telling me?" Duncan slid down the door to sit on the threshold.

There's so much to choose from. I sank down and sat beside him, leaning shoulder to shoulder.

"They're having my father's funeral right now." I knocked

on the door behind me. "Over there. This was the Gate, but it's gone. I wasn't sure you'd be able to see it, but I didn't expect it to be closed to me yet. I thought I still had time."

"So, you go across the Creek then," he said. "Back there, where you disappeared before. Must be a weak spot in the boundary."

"You know about those?"

"It's kind of hard to miss." He gestured to the purple clouds, the smoking forest, and a few lightning bugs that were a little too active during a storm.

"We think it's coming down."

"We?"

"Adam, your sister, and I. Before my dad disappeared, he was studying it. Did he tell you?"

"Not directly, but that would explain his dedication to getting the sanctuary approved. He wanted to move people farther from the unstable magical energy. Nice of him to look out for the mundanes. Who knows what's going to happen when it comes down. All that energy has to go somewhere."

"I think that's why we needed you."

"What do you mean? What can I do?"

"I'm not sure. But Alice told me to *find the one who was lost* and *bring the outside in*. If that's not you, who is it?"

He frowned. "What else did she say?"

I rolled my head back on the door. *"Reset the balance. Go back to the beginning to find the end."*

"Cryptic," he said.

"And irritating."

"The balance." He drew an X in the dirt.

"Yep."

"Inside and outside. The beginning and the end." He added a circle around the X.

I nodded.

"Sounds like she sent the right girl, though."

"How's that?"

He chuckled. "Who else do you know who can cross the Creek without the Gate and hit stop and rewind on time itself?"

She kept reminding me that I had a Gift. At least as often as she told me I still had time. It was the same message. The Gate was time-locked, linked to the Gatekeeper's age. *Back to the beginning.*

She didn't think I could go back to the first Gatekeeper, did she? And what was I supposed to do when I got there?

She wouldn't be able to tell me now. But maybe the grimoire could.

You were chosen for a reason, Thomas had said. Maiden-mother-crone was I sick of taking destiny's calls. But Duncan was right. *Who else could do it?*

I exhaled a sharp breath and pushed myself back to standing.

"I'll wait here." Duncan shifted a little, making himself more comfortable. He winced when he moved his foot.

"If we can get you inside, Elspeth might be able to help with that."

"You'd better get going then."

"I'll be back soon."

"You'd better," he said. "I'm not going to wait around forever." He flexed his foot and grimaced.

It took some time to hike back to the shallows where I had crossed before. I might have been able to cross beside the cottage, but I didn't want to relive my near-drowning experience of a few days ago. I had no idea what to expect on the other side. When I accidentally stepped over the boundary and left Duncan on the rainy shore, the difference had barely been noticeable.

Wading across the Creek this time, the change was almost instantaneous. While the sky had been clearing on the outside, this side was still gray from the storm. The sunrise filtered through an unending sheet of dirty clouds. The smoke on the hill disappeared as it rose.

I walked toward it.

By the time I reached the clearing at the top of the hill, Dad's funeral had long since ended. My family had paid their respects and returned to their homes to grieve in their own ways. A circle of stones in the center of the clearing bore the remains of their offerings, small reminders of who he'd been.

"Dad?"

He didn't answer, but something stirred in the air. The energy of this place vibrated. I felt a presence. More than one.

"Show me." The clearing blurred and the shades returned. Shadows of the past, recent and distant. Figures overlapped, oblivious to each other. Like when I had followed Adam, the space between this existence and the next stretched. Last time, I'd thought something pushed through the veil. Maybe spirits. But now I recognized the bubble.

Queen's Creek was bound by time, and as the boundary failed, so did the distinctions between our time stream and all those that had come before. In the thin spaces, like this one, time collapsed in on itself, folding over and over until everything that had come before us occupied the same space.

Some of the shadows had more depth than others. I reached out with my Gift to separate the double exposures. *There was my mom with my brothers. They walked into the clearing with Giles and the Speaker. Their words distorted into the wind. The vision reversed, and they walked backward down the hill.*

I picked at the threads of other shades, releasing the ones I didn't recognize.

Matthew and Gabriel trudged up the hill, carrying boxes of tools and notebooks. They settled in the center where the stone circle now lay. Matthew lit candles, but the wind blew them out. Gabriel held up an astrolabe, marking the measurements on a clipboard.

Gabriel returned several times on his own. No. He'd come on his own before bringing Matthew to help verify his findings. The longer I watched, the better I understood the flow of time, recognized the small clues in the sequences.

Once, he brought Dad with him. Our father nodded as he checked Gabriel's notes. He clapped him on the back. Gabriel beamed.

Further back, I saw myself come up the path, walking with Dad. Even from the outside, I sensed the tension between us. He was telling me I'd waited long enough. It was time to leave. I didn't want to go. I'd promised to wait for Adam.

I'd been so mad then, I hadn't seen the lines by Dad's eyes or the exhaustion behind them. He'd been working ridiculous hours, trying to develop the elixir Mrs. Kirk wanted to extend Alice's life.

Tears pricked my eyes. At first, I thought that was why I lost focus. The visions blurred again, one becoming indistinguishable from the next. Darker shadows oozed into the clearing, blanketing everything in darkness.

Everything and nothing cannot coexist.

Reset the balance.

I had to get back to the Gatehouse. The boundary was already coming down, and if Queen's Creek was going to survive, I needed to get help.

I ran down the hill, slipping on wet leaves and narrowly avoiding falling on my face. At the base, I stumbled through the brambles until I came to the edge of the shallow Creek. My foot sank in the mud, and I scrambled back.

I pushed through the weeds, keeping the Creek in sight but hoping for firmer ground. I was too far to hope for the path, but walking in less sticky mud for a while would be nice.

I kept waiting for the Creek to widen, for the Gatehouse to come into view. It didn't take this long to get to the place where I crossed. Where was it?

"You're not ready," said my father's voice in my head.

I stopped. "What?"

"You won't find it this way. You're not ready for what has to happen next."

"Which is what, exactly?"

"You know what your future holds. I tried to stop it. I should have known better. I didn't understand. You will. You can save us all. But you have to be ready."

"So, no pressure then." I rolled my head from one shoulder to the other, but it did nothing to loosen the tense muscles.

"When you're ready."

"How?" My chest tightened.

"Breathe."

I closed my eyes. Took in a ragged breath and screamed.

March 20

Progress, Opportunity,
Confidence

Assertive, Direct,
Driven

Choices, Stalemate,
Hidden Information

49

I'm done. I'm done with cryptic advice, and impossible expectations, and rules that keep changing, and not knowing what's going on, where I am, what I am. I am done. There is too much uncertainty, too many unanswered, unanswerable questions. I keep moving forward and not making progress, and it's time to call it. I quit. I'm done. They can find someone else.

When I opened my eyes, it was raining again.

"Prepare yourself," said my father.

A flash of light.

When it faded, I stood in Alice's bedroom.

Still alone.

On the floor, someone had cast a circle around me with candles and stones. The edges of things wobbled. Not seeing double, exactly. Maybe seeing one-and-a-half. I blinked a few times, but it didn't go away. None of this was real. *Call the quarters to call them home.*

I sighed. I'd have to complete the ritual to leave it. I lifted the chalice and stepped to the west. Bowing my head, I called on the powers of water to release my frustrated emotions. My tears fell into the cup. My anger drained away. I put down the cup and lifted a stone. I turned it over in my hands, running my fingers over the rough spots and sharp edges. Stepping to the north, I called to the earth. I asked for grounding. *Help me to heal, and bring me strength.* In the east, I used a feather to call on the power of air. *Bring me inspiration. Let my memories and dreams guide me.* I held my breath and let it out slowly, fluttering the feather. When I stepped to the south, I lifted a candle. *Fire, light my way. Give me the energy to complete my task.*

I blew out the candle and closed my eyes again. I knew I'd be back out by the Creek when I opened them. Because obviously, I wasn't done. Now that I'd cleansed myself of the negative energies that threatened me and my mission, I'd have to get moving. At the very least, I couldn't stay here in this sad drizzle, feeling sorry for myself while Duncan waited outside the broken Gate, and Adam and Elspeth waited for answers on this side. They still needed me.

Cursed or not.

The Gatehouse had changed again. From inside the boundary, the cottage appeared old but well-kept, with wildflowers and herbs climbing out of the window boxes. The curtains floated in one window. The other window was bare, the curtains I stripped probably still binding Elspeth's wounds. With no idea how much time I'd burned away between the shadows on the hill and the impromptu mediation ritual, I hurried across the unguarded footbridge and pushed open the door.

Elspeth sat alone on the floor, bent over a large, old book. Several more lay stacked on the floor beside her. She frowned.

I crossed to the far door and said a silent prayer with my hand on the knob. When I opened it, I faced the same footbridge I had just crossed on the other side of the Gatehouse instead of the stone threshold where I left Duncan. I slammed the door.

"There's no Gate without the Keeper," Elspeth whispered

to the book. "There will be no more Wakenings. No one can cross until Alice is replaced."

"You're wrong," I said.

Elspeth tapped the page. "Possibly, but I don't see how. I've been through these backward and forward. You were gone a long time." She said it without accusation, just a fact to explain her knowledge. At least she was feeling better.

I waited for her to catch up. Slowly, she raised her eyes and saw me. She looked back over her shoulder at the door where I came in. "How did you...?"

"I crossed the Creek," I said.

"You didn't."

"I did."

"But you're here. And you didn't use the Gate. It's not possible."

"And yet..." I spread my arms and did a little turn to demonstrate my presence.

"It's not possible," she mumbled, turning back to the book. "I must have missed something."

I sat down next to her. "Elspeth, we need to open that door."

She nodded, wincing as she shifted her position to get a better look at the page. She absently pulled the curtain bandage tighter. The color had returned to her face, and the fact that she was sitting up, poring over a book, was encouraging, but the wound hadn't entirely healed.

"Did Mom come and look at that?" My head throbbed. I'd hoped she would be here.

"She did." Elspeth sat back. "She's pretty upset you missed the funeral."

"Me too," I said, rubbing my head.

"What happened out there? And how did you get back in without using the Gate? I've been over every part of this book that has anything to do with the boundary, and what you're saying is impossible. There's only one person who should be able to cross." Her eyes widened as her mind caught up.

"I'm not the Gatekeeper yet, El. If I were, that door would have opened to reveal Duncan sitting on the stoop outside instead of bouncing me back into Queen's Creek." *I guess in a Gatehouse with no Gate, both doors lead back to the community.*

Her hand covered her mouth.

I bit my lip. Maybe not the best reveal of her brother's apparent resurrection. "I'm sorry. I'm so sorry. I didn't know how to tell you. You were unconscious when I left, and I wasn't even sure he was really the one Alice sent me to find. Or how I was ever going to find him at all."

I sucked in a breath. "But he's here. Duncan is here. He's been in town this whole time pretending to be a blond real estate agent. The hunters didn't get him, but he was afraid to come back in case he led them here. He's been helping kids who get lost on their Wakenings."

"He's alive." Her eyes filled with tears.

"Yes."

"And you brought him home?"

Before I could answer, she threw her arms around my neck. I hugged her back, squeezing gently to avoid her injury.

Adam came in through the door on the community side. He had a canvas sack slung over his shoulder and a loaded basket in his arms. It looked like he'd cleared out anything I'd left at Elspeth's place. The supplies landed heavily on the floor.

Elspeth sat back and grinned at him.

He closed the distance faster than I could stand and pulled me to him. His voice was muffled by my soggy hair. "You're back."

I wanted to freeze time right there and stay locked in his embrace. But the world kept turning, and time was running out. I pulled away.

"I did what she asked. I found Duncan. He's outside. But we can't open the door."

Adam raised an eyebrow, then walked past me to the outer door and opened it. The footbridge he'd just crossed lay empty in front of him.

"Whoa," he said. He glanced over his shoulder at the door he'd just come in, reassuring himself that he had, in fact, walked all the way across the cottage.

"There is no Gate without the Keeper," Elspeth said.

Adam closed the door somewhat less dramatically than I had. "So. What, then? There's no way out?"

"Not until we have a new Keeper," Elspeth said, tilting her head at me.

"I haven't taken on the mantle." *I don't know how*. There was no use fighting it anymore, but accepting a destiny and fulfilling it were two separate things.

"Who else is it going to be? After what you did with your Gift at the library? It has to be someone with a strong connection to the Source. Someone bound to the community." She started flipping through the book again.

"No, I get it. That all sounds like me, and Alice chose me, and it's my destiny. I'm the Chosen One, whatever. But that door didn't open to the outside either. You said it yourself: There's no Gate without the Keeper."

I waved at the failure of a door that should have led to the outside world. "No Gate."

I flung my arms out to indicate myself. "No Keeper. So what do we do now?"

"Are you saying you're ready?" Adam asked.

"Does it matter?"

"Yes," said Elspeth. "If you're going to do this, it has to be now. See?"

She pointed to a graph in her book. The title line read *Physics of Magic*. "There's a balance to the boundary spell.

Energy goes in, energy comes out. But the community has built up too much on this side. We're not releasing enough to balance the pressure. We have to open the Gate to let it out."

There had been fewer Wakenings since Duncan disappeared. Fewer witches leaving Queen's Creek, taking their magical energy with them, even temporarily. Families grew bigger every generation, putting more strain on the boundary.

I'd never gotten to talk to Thomas about what he and Ben figured out, but it made sense. All of those little spells added up, from the tiny things at home to community-wide efforts like Last Light. It was supposed to strengthen the boundary, but all it did was apply more pressure to the cracks.

And now… Dad's notes with the date circled. The graphs in Gabriel's journal.

"The festival. Shit. Are they doing the Equinox ritual right now?" Queen's Creek was about to exceed the capacity of the boundary spell to hold in the magic we produced. We were already pushing against the bubble. What would happen when it popped?

Elspeth chewed her nail. The light from the window cast a soft glow across the floor, the late afternoon sun breaking through the clouds. "Soon, I think. At Last Light, when the day and night blend together."

"How bad is it?" Adam asked. "What's going to happen if we don't open the Gate before Last Light?"

"There's too much energy inside the boundary. Without the Gate to release some of it, the spell will implode." She looked down at the book again. "I don't know what that means, exactly, but it doesn't sound good, does it?"

Adam ran a hand through his hair and sat in Alice's chair.

"So we open it, then. What do those books say about initiating a new Gatekeeper?" I pulled Adam's basket closer and shifted through the contents. I had no idea what I was looking for.

Adam squinted at me. "How did you get in?"

Here we go again. "I crossed the Creek."

50

Nobody crosses the Creek."

"Wasn't that my line? I've been saying that for days, but you said I was wrong."

"This is different." He crossed his arms.

"Everything is different. There's no Gate. There's no Keeper. Cate crossed the Creek. The Source is in chaos, or haven't you noticed?" Elspeth slammed the book shut, wincing.

"El—" Adam softened.

"No, she's right. That storm last night? The snow? That thing on the hill?"

"The veil is thinning," Adam said as if that explained everything.

It wasn't so much that it hadn't occurred to me, as I never expected anyone else to draw the same wild conclusion. I felt like I was living out a mundane horror movie.

Elspeth nodded. "The veil between worlds, between us and the others, it's thinner at the Equinox. If the Source is unbalanced, it might draw their energy."

"You're telling me those were ghosts?" Ghosts, memories, displaced energy. Maybe it was all the same. What if all those ghost stories were really just people with my Gift who didn't understand the echoes they were seeing? It would be easy to mistake overlapping timelines for a supernatural veil between the living and the dead, especially if one of the timelines showed people you knew to be long gone.

"You don't believe in ghosts," Adam said.

"Please tell me more about what I do and do not believe," I said.

"Guys?" Elspeth said, "We don't have time for this."

"Sorry," Adam mumbled.

"No, sorry. You're right." Why did everything have to end up in an argument with us?

The spell Elspeth found might not have been from the original creation of the Gate, and certainly wasn't as strong, but the components aligned with our goals. To open that which was closed required an active presence on each side, a key to connect them, and a keeper in between to hold it open. We slipped into our roles with minimal argument.

Adam would be the presence inside the Gate, reclaiming his role as the Guardian. Duncan would be the presence on the outside, and I would be the key since I was the only one we knew could safely cross over. As a seventh, Elspeth should be able to become a Keeper long enough to open the Gate. I just hoped she was strong enough. She didn't complain, but her hand went to her side sometimes, and although I knew she'd had extra time in the Gatehouse to mend, I wasn't sure she'd fully healed. I promised myself I'd relieve her of the mantle as soon as we got the Gate back open. We only needed her to hold it long enough to let Duncan inside.

When I got back through the shallows and around to the front of the cottage, Duncan was unconscious. Poor guy. The day I'd put him through... and we weren't done yet. The only justification I could make was that Gatekeeper or not, his sister was still a healer, so getting him inside was the next best thing I could do for him if I couldn't get him to a hospital. I sat next to him and nudged his shoulder.

"Rise and shine," I said.

His lashes fluttered, and he grumbled a little, turning and dropping his head on my shoulder. I tried not to laugh, but I couldn't hide the way the giggle shook my shoulder. Duncan started and sat up.

"Sorry! Sorry," he said. "I didn't. I don't. You're back."

"No," I said. "I'm sorry. We're going to have to do something here, and we're going to have to do it quicker than I have any right to ask. But they're already waiting, and I'm not sure how much time has passed in there."

"So, you made it in. That's wonderful," he said with a genuine, though pained smile.

"I need you to stand up now."

"You want me to walk on this?" he asked, pointing to his swollen foot. It looked like a baseball was attached to the front of his ankle.

"It's not far, and Elspeth's inside."

"You could have led with that." He put his hand on my shoulder and braced himself to stand.

Bring the outside in. It was what Alice told me to do. It had to work. I knocked to make sure Elspeth was ready on the other side. She knocked back. I turned the knob and closed my eyes.

When I opened them, light spilled out around Duncan, and at first, I was blinded. I blinked as Duncan pitched forward. Wrapping his arm around my neck, I put mine around his waist and helped him inside. Once the door closed behind us, Elspeth's light softened to a more manageable glow. Like Alice, she seemed otherworldly and mysterious, even though I'd known her my whole life.

And then she spoke, "Get him in the chair. Let me get a

better look at that leg."

She worked quickly, cleaning his wound, bracing and wrapping his ankle. He watched with wide eyes as his sister worked her magic. She used a combination of tinctures from the basket Adam brought to anoint the injury and a potion of fresh herbs. Before long, Duncan was comfortably sedated on a blanket on the floor with his leg elevated. Elspeth held his hand.

The Gatekeeper's glow faded as she expended her energy healing him. There was a reason the Keepers never held another position, why they lived simply and depended on the Guardians instead of using magic to conjure anything they might need in their solitude. Holding the Gate took everything.

It would take more than a temporary lock-picking spell to reopen the Gate permanently. We had to tap into the time stream and wake the ancestors, linking me to the Gatekeepers that came before. And we had to do it before it drained Elspeth's energy completely.

"Where's the grimoire?" I didn't wait for a response. The ancient tome wasn't in the stack Elspeth had searched. She couldn't read it. But I knew where to find it. I'd left it with Alice.

Her room was the same as I had left it, but the body on the bed was unfamiliar. The Gatekeeper I'd known, the one who'd sent me to find Duncan, had been preternaturally young with smooth pink skin and radiant hair. The woman in her place wore the same long white shift, but her hair had gone silver, and the ashy skin on her face and hands crinkled like tissue paper. She'd aged from twenty-one to one hundred in the span of a day, no longer sustained by the boundary spell.

"Oh, Alice, I'm so sorry." None of what happened to her was my fault, but I felt the weight of complicity with all of

Queen's Creek for what we'd done to the Gatekeepers.

A tiny voice in the back of my head told me to run. This was my last chance while the door still opened to the outside. *Your destiny is yours to choose*, my father's letter has said. But the time for choosing had passed.

As I stood there, the body faded. The Gatekeeper was leaving this mortal plane for the next one.

"Merry Meet," I whispered as I turned away, though she was already gone.

There was only one way out now. *Call the quarters to call them home.*

I lifted the grimoire from the floor, where it was still wrapped in Elspeth's pillowcase. It no longer weighed more than any of the books she'd been studying, although I wasn't sure anyone else should try to carry it.

So when Adam offered to take it from me as I shifted it to close the bedroom door behind me, I shook my head.

51

I set the grimoire on the floor in the middle of the Gatehouse. Silently apologizing to Jonathan for not thinking to bring gloves, I reached my bare hands inside and pulled it out of the pillowcase, laying it carefully back on the cloth.

"How did you get that?" Adam asked.

"I checked it out of the library." The cover was still stiff.

"The grimoire belongs to all of us," Elspeth said without taking her eyes off Duncan.

Adam raised an eyebrow. "Yeah, but…"

I turned to the section on the Gatekeepers. "We needed it. We have it. Best not to ask questions you don't want to know the answer to, Guardian."

He did it anyway. "Why did you come back?"

I stared at him. He wasn't asking why I'd completed the Gatekeeper's quest. "You called."

Adam tightened his lips. "You didn't answer. You never answered my calls."

"I was at work," I said, but that wasn't the whole truth. I'd been avoiding calls from this area code for months. I wanted to be left alone. To disappear into my new, unmagical life.

And I didn't remember him. How many calls had I missed?

"Guys?" Elspeth brushed back Duncan's hair and pushed herself up so she could join us around the grimoire. "Maybe save the relationship after we save the community? If this works, you're going to be colleagues for a while.

"You don't want this," Adam said.

"Not everything is about what I want." I'd been doing exactly what I wanted for three years. It was time to put someone else first. *Look at me grow.*

"You'll be trapped." He looked at the door as if it were already sealed. As if he were the one who longed for a life on the other side. Maybe our escape plan had failed us both.

"Maybe not." It had to be near this page. *Back to the Beginning.*

He sat across from me on the floor. "What do you mean?"

"We're going to bring down the boundary." Elspeth eased down to the floor beside me. A broad grin stretched across her face as she realized that she could read the pages now. The grimoire recognized the Gatekeeper.

"We're what?"

"After we unbind Cate so she can fully access her Gift. She's going to need it to take on the mantle." Elspeth smiled as though this were obvious.

"You were right. Dad was lying about trying to protect the boundary spell. But only because it's beyond protecting. It's what we've been saying. There's too much magical energy inside the boundary. It's pushing at the edges of things, causing all this chaos magic, glitches, weather. You said yourself, the veil is thinning because of the Equinox. The energy from our rituals is pushing it further. What happens if we rip a big hole in it?"

"Wasn't that why Elspeth opened the Gate? To vent the energy?"

I looked at her. She shrugged.

"It wasn't a permanent fix," I said.

Alice claimed being the Gatekeeper was my purpose. Elspeth saw my connection to the Source. Adam believed in me, even if he didn't like me very much right now. *I'm the seventh child of a seventh child. My father is gone, and I'm here.*

"It has to be me." I pointed to a page I knew they couldn't read and recited the instructions for transferring the Gatekeeper's mantle.

"Now, the hard part." Elspeth turned the grimoire to face her.

Adam sighed.

"Luckily, the Equinox is already thinning the veil," she said, paging through the book. "Makes contacting the dead easier."

Adam's eyes went to Alice's door. "Is that a good idea?"

"We're not going to disturb Alice. She means my dad. Only the person who cast the bind can break it. But it's okay." I put my hand over Elspeth's. "He's not dead. I've been talking to him all day."

They both looked at me with concern. I sounded crazy, even having done six impossible things since breakfast.

"He's not dead. He went into the Creek, but he didn't drown. It's the boundary spell. The time lock. The history of Queen's Creek is holding the magic inside. The intentions of our ancestors stacked one on top of the other. The spell isn't just being fed by the Last Light ritual. It's layered over with the energy of everyone who's come before. He's not dead. He's lost, and he's trying to find the way home."

"He's lost in… time?" Adam crossed his arms.

"Yes."

"But you've been in contact with him."

"Yes."

Elspeth twisted her braid around her fingers. "It might be enough."

"It has to be."

We set up the cord-cutting spell quickly. A length of ribbon, a pair of scissors, a candle to focus my meditation. There wasn't much Adam and Elspeth could help me with, but I appreciated their presence. I laid the ribbon out in front of me and stared into the flame, listening to my breath and waiting for my father to make himself known.

Elspeth crushed some herbs in a small mortar and sprinkled them over the candle, where they sizzled and sparked. The scent made me drowsy, and I closed my eyes.

When he spoke, I barely heard him. There were too many voices. I bit my lip and pulled my knees to my chest. *My head is full of spikes.*

Scenes surfaced out of order. Sometimes the memories were mine, sometimes Alice's, sometimes Elspeth's. There were others too, whispering warnings about a protection spell. The way that everything had an opposite. Building a fence could trap the guard dog. *Energy needs an escape. Nothing lasts forever.*

I squeezed my eyes shut and sorted the visions like a deck of cards, assigning suits to each of the Gatekeepers: cups for Mary, pentacles for Clara, wands for Martha, and swords for Alice. Mentally stacking the piles, I flipped through Alice's suit first. Through her eyes, I watched the Crone walk the border with the Sage. They talked about news from outside.

Mrs. Kirk was worried about sending our Youth into the world. The danger was coming. She worried about Alice. The Gatekeeper was weakening, and there was no Gate without the Keeper.

Giles wanted to recast the spell. Mrs. Kirk met with my father and begged him to call me back home. She set a deadline for completing the elixir of life. Threatened dire but undefined consequences.

Alice had other plans. She could regain her strength. She could wait until I was ready. She called out to my father, invited him in.

The border is fading. She gave him the card and watched him make a call. *The Gatehouse existed both inside and outside of the boundary. It was the only place a call like that would go through.*

Luke sounded happy. He'd love to help the community.

The memory changed.

Dad came back, made another call.

Luke found the deed for the land. He could help with the paperwork. We'd be protected from the development. They met at the Gate.

For a while, Alice seemed stronger. The border stood.

But protection comes with a cost. *The outside moved farther away. Without the new development, there was no need to maintain infrastructure. No local cell towers meant no service. The next calls didn't go through. Alice felt the distance growing. Maybe the delay was a mistake.*

The balance was not repaired. Time is collapsing.

Time. Through someone else's eyes, I watched the Creek flow past my window. The bank changed, rising and falling as the water cut its way around our community. But it wasn't just water. The magic that affected everyone here flowed with it.

I remembered how it trickled through the dry clay when I was on the other side with Duncan.

The border wasn't physical. Anyone could walk across a brook like I did. The water wasn't what kept people out. The Creek was bound to the Source of magic, and the magic of the Source was infinite. My father told me that time moved differently here. I hadn't understood.

"Now, do you see?" asked his voice in my head.

Still bound in the visions, I looked with my third eye. The boundary at the Creek didn't just slow time. *It was time.* In my vision, the Gatehouse shimmered. Alice smiled from the open doorway, still glowing, still young and strong.

There is no Gate without the Keeper. She was frozen in time, holding a space where the time stream was interrupted. It wasn't natural, but it was the only way out. This was why Wakenings ended at 21. *That's her age. Was her age.* She held the Gate, but the Gate also held her. When the Gate weakened... *why did the Gate weaken?*

I fell back into my own memories, fighting the storms in the woods. *The smoke in the clearing. Adam fought it because he was the Guardian, but it was here because of me. It stopped because of me. I was connected to the Source, even if I couldn't see it. It wanted me back. It pushed me here. I am needed.*

"You always have a choice," said my father's voice.

What choice did he make? Holding the deed to the land around us should have been enough. No more development, no more danger to the Source. The Creek should have flowed freely.

"But it didn't," he said. "We were too late. It was all going to be for nothing."

I remembered the trench in the woods and how close the new construction seemed. The Creek encircled our community, but the water had to come from somewhere, even if the Source of magic was inside. Maybe it had been diverted, blocked like I had been. What would the Elders do then? I'd seen the argument twice already in my visions. I knew how it would end.

Oh, Dad, what did you do?

I watched through Alice's eyes. There was a haze on the Creek. The boundary was failing again.

"It's time we end this, Giles," said the man on the bank.

The wind ruffled the other man's gray hair. "You're out of your mind! End this? It will end all of us. The border protects us, or have you forgotten the Trials?"

"The world has changed. We've got to change with it. We can't keep holding them off. They're too close now. At least we can meet them—"

"You had your chance to meet them when we were younger. We

all did. We all chose to come back. Some of us are happy here," said Giles.

"We have to move forward," my father said. "The border is coming down. It's just a matter of time." There was something about the way he looked at the water when he said it. He took a step back, getting his feet wet.

"Let's just talk about this," said Giles.

"We've talked, the Council has talked. It's enough. We're running out of time, but maybe I can buy us a little more." He took another step into the water. He closed his eyes for a moment. When he opened them, he looked up and called to the god and goddess in all their forms. "May the Youth inspire us, Warrior protect us, Sage make us wise, Maiden bring us hope, Mother show us your love, Crone accept my sacrifice."

Giles reached for him, but he pushed him away.

He stepped back one more time, and the current took him.

"It's going to be okay," said the voice in my head. "You have time now. I'll always be with you."

I opened my eyes, but the feeling of his presence lingered. Adam held the ribbon taut as I lifted the scissors.

A single snip completed the ritual. Energy rushed through me, effervescent as my Gift escaped the bind. I felt whole in a way I never had before.

52

When I caught my breath, I told them what I'd seen in my visions.

The overlapping timelines at the Creek and in the clearing gave me an idea. I'd played back scenes in the office when I met Luke, before I knew he was Duncan, and I'd guided my own memories with Adam's help. If I could reach back further, maybe I could manipulate the time stream.

I'd stopped time even when my Gift was bound. Now that it was free, what else could I do? The prospect of not only freeing my father from the time stream, but finding Matthew and Gabriel as well made my heart race. I coughed.

Call the quarters to call them home.

What if we were one ritual away from saving everybody? Bringing them all back. Stopping the boundary from imploding. Keeping the shades on their side of the veil. Separating the timelines.

It was a lot to ask of a wounded real estate agent, a weakened healer, an unmoored guardian, and a recently unbound witch.

But Duncan's leg already looked better under his sister's

ministrations, and we could recover her strength and Adam's direction at once if I became the Gatekeeper.

So, two rituals away from saving the world. First, accept your destiny. Then, tear it all down.

Adam cast a circle around me and Elspeth. I sat cross-legged in the center and laid the book open on the floor in front of me. With my back to Alice's hearth, Duncan on my left, and Adam on my right, I faced north. Elspeth faced me.

I sat up straight and filled my lungs with the scents of the candles and herbs burning in their quarters. I rolled my head to loosen my neck. My hands fell open at my sides. I concentrated on making my breath rise and fall like waves. In the quiet room, the others matched the rhythm with their own breath.

I reminded myself that magic was a craft, and bound or not, I had practiced for years. I didn't have to create the magic here. I only had to release control and let it in. I cleared my mind. Doubts immediately flooded in to fill the empty space. I pushed them away.

Breathe in. Breathe out.

Every bad, stupid, frustrating, idiotic thing I'd ever done crowded into my head.

Breathe. Let it go.

The things I should have done and said in the last few days were suddenly so clear that I couldn't believe I didn't say and do them when it would have made a difference.

Breathe in. Breathe out.

The doubts returned. This time, they floated away on their own. I focused on the way the light flickered through my eyelids. My breath loud in my ears.

I started to make shapes out of the shadows. Water closing over me.

Breathe in. Breathe out.

The water receded, and I stood on the footbridge. I felt

light. A soft glow surrounded me, and I realized I wasn't alone. The other figure asked me to stay, but I couldn't. I was already fading away. I lost sight of the bridge, wrapped in golden white light.

Breathe in. Breathe out.

I was inside again, and the room was warm. The quilt soft underneath me. The figure beside me still needed me. I gave her something before I disappeared.

Breathe in. Breathe out.

The man in front of me handed me a card. It was another key. It would bring him back when the time came. He'd need help, but he'd have it.

Breathe in. Breathe out.

Someone was yelling outside. Accusations. From the window, I saw a figure fall. The Creek washed him away. The figure on the bank looked familiar. The gray hair ruffled in the breeze.

Breathe in. Breathe—

Wait! It faded too quickly, someone else's memory. An older woman stood on the bridge with the figure who fell. The danger was near. It threatened us all. I caught my breath. The light flared.

Breathe in. Breathe out.

Each time, I went further back, deeper into the Gatekeeper's history. I caught glimpses and heard voices, but never enough. The picture was fuzzy, the sound muffled like I had a blanket over my head. I started to feel that it was all adding up to something, but each time, the scenes faded, and the sounds were replaced by the rhythm of our breath and my heartbeat in my ears. I didn't know if Adam and Luke could see what I saw, but I didn't think so. It felt too personal, like living someone else's life. I wondered if this was what Elspeth's empathic skill felt like. I couldn't explain it, but I felt her with me, too. It was getting crowded in my head, hundreds of years of Gatekeepers showing me their lives. A weight settled around me, but I felt stronger for it.

And then it was gone. The room fell silent, and I floated on bright white light. I couldn't see anything else.

It's time.

I lifted my head and raised my arms. I inhaled the perfumed air and reached my right hand toward Adam in the east. "I call to the powers of air to restore our memories and give strength to our dreams."

My left hand reached toward Duncan. "I call on the powers of the water that surrounds us to protect us and provide us with the wisdom to make the right choices."

I brought my hands together in front of me and bowed my head. The heat from the hearth warmed my back and I knew that the powers of the south were with me. Finally, I opened my eyes and reached both hands toward the north. Elspeth reached across the grimoire to take them. I grounded myself through her grip. "I call on the powers of the earth to bring life to the spell and make it real. As above..."

"So below," the others said with me.

All of the air went out of the room. My head flew back, and my arms fell back to my sides. I let the magic take me, and when my breath returned, all I saw was the bright white light.

I had the worst hangover. My head throbbed, and my mouth may have been stuffed with cotton balls. I squeezed my eyes and threw an arm over my face to block out the sunshine streaming through the window.

I rolled onto my side and edged my hand down my face so that I could peek between my fingers and a shield of hair draped across my eyes. Everything beyond the purple and black strands was a blur of neutral colors.

Where are my glasses? I groaned and closed my eyes again, reaching out to feel around for the missing frames.

Elspeth pushed them into my hand. Even without my glasses, she looked as lost and dizzy as I felt.

"Can you stand?" asked Adam.

For the first time, I opened my eyes fully, and my vision cleared behind the lenses. I pushed my hair back and looked up. Adam stood over me with a hand outstretched.

When we touched, overlapping images flooded my mind. I remembered everything. The spell we'd just completed, hiking through the storm with Duncan, fighting the shadows in the clearing with Adam, all of those awkward conversations with Mom, the drive with Thomas, my life in Chicago, my childhood... it all flashed by with memories that weren't mine. Everything that'd ever happened in the Gatehouse. Everything every Gatekeeper ever saw through the windows. I moaned and closed my eyes again. Had it been like this for Elspeth? No wonder she was still sitting down. *I might throw up.*

Adam lowered me back to the floor.

"We can wait," he said.

Duncan stood by a window, leaning against the sill. "Do you think it worked?"

In answer, a wave of light shimmered across the room, outlining the edges of everything in sparkling energy. When it shifted over me, my skin burned cold.

I pushed myself up slowly and walked to the exterior door. *Ready or not...*

When I opened the door, the sun was shining on the path that led into the woods. I closed it again. "The Gate is open."

They're staring at me again.

I looked down at my body, still muddy and bruised but now glowing like a hexed wisp in a dark wood. Just like Elspeth and Alice had.

"You get used to it," Elspeth said, still rubbing her eyes. "And I think it fades if you're not concentrating on it."

"Cool. I'm just going to…" I let myself into Alice's deserted bedroom and found her wash table. The cool water in the basin soothed my head.

I sat on the bed in Alice's room alone. *In my room, now, I guess.* I pulled my backpack off the floor where Adam had left it and patted the pockets. I didn't bring much, but there was only one thing I needed right now. When I found the card, it warmed in my hand. *The Knight of Swords. A quick-thinking man of action.*

After all that we'd accomplished, I did feel driven. The Gate was open. It had a new Keeper. But we weren't done.

What's next for us? The border is still failing. How long can the Guardian stand against the coming danger if the border comes down?

No one out there believed in magic now, but the trials were real. Our ancestors fled for a reason. How could we go back to that? The sanctuary Dad had started with Luke's help wouldn't be enough. The new development was already affecting the Creek.

The warmth of the card intensified against my skin. A woman in a white robe held two crossed swords, blindfolded.

I know how she feels. I want to charge forward, like the knight, but I'm not sure which direction to go. I could finish what my father started, find a way to safely drop the spell that had protected our community for generations, open the border to whatever was coming, allow my friends and neighbors to freely come and go. Or I could try to reinforce the boundary, to keep everyone safe, the way it was before.

It felt awfully convenient that the outcome I wanted seemed the more probable of the two. Nothing I'd read in either Dad's notes or the grimoire suggested I could safely do as the Speaker wished. I put the card face-down on the bed in front of me.

The room, where Alice lived peacefully for so many years, closed around me, trapping me. I'd done what was asked of me, but when would it be enough? Were these four walls the last I would ever see? I knew the answer before I picked up the card, but I couldn't help but smile at what it revealed.

A man stood on a cliff, facing out over a large body of water. Three ships floated by. Three wands grew out of the ground around him, tall and strong. Challenges ahead, but the sea was an opportunity. If this man could cross the water, so could I.

53

In the front room, Duncan, Elspeth, and Adam had gone back to the books. The candles burned out, but with the late afternoon sunshine still streaming in through the uncurtained windows, they weren't needed.

Elspeth bent over the grimoire.

Duncan held a stack of my father's notebooks. He looked up when I opened the door.

"Where did you get those?" I asked.

Adam answered instead. "I was sent to find what we needed. Whatever happened before he disappeared, your father was studying the boundary. Seemed like we might need to know what he found."

"Does Mom know?"

"She brought them herself. When she came to heal me," Elspeth said.

She'd been here last night after the funeral. What was she doing now?

"Adam, I think I have another mission for the Guardian."

He stood as if pulled by an invisible thread, but he didn't reach for his mask. He waited for a direct order from the Gatekeeper.

"We've got to stop the Equinox festival, but I can't leave—"

"You had a chance to get out. I thought that was what you wanted." His eyes blazed.

"I do!" My heart raced, and I felt sick to my stomach. *What if it was all a mistake?*

"Well, it's a little late now, don't you think? This is your life now, Cate. You gave us your life. Why would you do that?" His hand started to reach for me and then dropped.

"Maybe she doesn't have to," Duncan said. "I think the professor found a way. There's a spell here, but you'd have to be a Gatekeeper to read it."

"How can you tell? There are notes over notes," Adam said. He turned the notebook and looked at it sideways. "See? It goes up the margin and in between the lines."

The page Duncan had been studying was like so many of the others Thomas and I had read through at home. But the longer I stared at it, the more easily I could separate the layers of text. *There it is.*

The symbol for the Gate.

Elspeth saw it, too. "Wait! I think… Look, it's here."

She flipped through the grimoire until she found a page with similar markings.

I tilted my head, trying to see what she saw. For a second, squiggles ran over and through the spell, but when I blinked, they cleared. I hadn't read this page, but somehow, I had an impression of what was written. The lines that were still there had fuller meaning like each word was a story by itself. The other Keepers interpreted the text for me. Their experience informed my reading.

Elspeth and I shared what we read from the grimoire, and Duncan and Adam nodded when they found the same ideas in Dad's notes. Almost all the pages were covered in literal subtext, sometimes in conversation with the original text, sometimes responding to other voices. The history of magic in our world. Written by all of us. It was constantly changing, like we did.

Reading over one of the oldest pages, Elspeth found diagrams and runes drawn around the edges. Layers of text, lines, and arrows connecting notes to images. Instructions for the Last Light ritual. A biological study of will 'o th' wisps.

"It's all connected," I whispered. We turned the book around, tracing the text that crawled over the page. I kept coming back to references to the Creek, to the flow of magic through our community. Not around us, but through. The magic didn't come from the water.

It came from us. We were stronger together.

I'd been using Nora's card for days, but now I thought about her life as a witch for the first time. How had she stayed connected? Professors could choose their mentees. How many of Nora's students were linked to the Source? What about the students from Massachusetts? I bet their community had its own Source, a power that went back centuries like ours. Would those relationships be enough to charge her spells? If she could practice outside, maybe we all could.

Maybe my father was right—we didn't need the boundary after all. If we finished his plan to create the sanctuary, there would be a buffer between us and the new development. It might be enough to give the people who stayed the privacy to live as they chose, even without a magical invisible fence to protect them.

This is the land beyond the sea. We can have a future of freedom and still protect our home.

The boundary spell was failing because it was elemental. It was cast on the water, making the Creek merge with the stream of Time, a concept made literal. The Source of the magic was still strong because it came from the people, the descendants of the generations who cast it.

"We don't need a Gate anymore," Elspeth said.

"What are you saying? Everyone will be trapped. There'd be no more Wakenings. No one would even get the chance—" Adam tried to explain. But he still wasn't listening.

"She's not saying we close the Gate," I said. "We take it down. The Gate. Open the boundary permanently."

Adam ran a hand over his face. "We'd be exposed. There'd be nothing to contain the magic."

I nodded. "It would flow freely. With our people. Wherever they chose to go. They could take it with them."

Adam shook his head. "They're all going to panic. Some of our people haven't been outside in years. They won't know how to live out there."

"They don't have to go," Duncan said. "That's the beauty of the professor's plan. We build a Bridge. It's wide enough to vent the energy, and it keeps the boundary from collapsing. Then people can choose. And if they leave, they can always come back and be protected by the spell."

Adam looked at me. "The mission you have for the Guardian. Is this what it's about?"

"We can do this, but it's going to take all of us. And we're going to need help. We have to represent all of the elements to complete the spell. We have two water witches and one earth." I pointed to Elspeth, Duncan, and Adam in turn.

"You want me to bring back your brothers?"

I shot Elspeth an apologetic look. I didn't want Caleb here when I told his girlfriend what we needed her to do. We should probably try to hold off on the tearful family reunion between Duncan and their parents, too. "Just Thomas. And Mom."

A cloud crossed the sun, shading the room. It would be Last Light soon.

"They'll be gathering for the festival." Elspeth twisted her braid around a finger. The tip turned pink.

"Right." I bit my lip. If anyone could convince them the threat was real, Adam could. "You're going to need to talk to Jonathan, Ben, and Caleb, too. Tell them to stop the Equinox celebration. Now."

Adam pursed his lips but didn't argue with the Gatekeeper. He stepped out onto the footbridge, blinked, and disappeared.

"Hurry," I whispered.

"If we're really going to do this, you need someone on both sides." Elspeth had read all the same pages I had. She'd felt the same connection to the previous Gatekeepers. Of course she would come to the same conclusion.

Duncan ran a finger over the page in Dad's notes listing the Gatekeepers. "There were four of them. Four Keepers. Four elements. It's a completed cycle."

Elspeth had said the same thing back at the library.

"We need to contact them," I said. "Let them know it's time to release their hold on the energy for the boundary spell."

"You're talking time travel, not spirit work." Duncan put the notebook down.

"Yes. We need to reach them when they were still active in the time stream."

"Like what you did at my office?"

"It's going to have to be a little more direct. Someone's got to go into the time stream and come out at each of these points." The diagram in the grimoire depicted time as a circle. Five points of a pentagram linked the present with each of the previous Gatekeepers.

"Four someones." Duncan looked to Elspeth for confirmation.

She nodded.

"Our community has already sent three. Dad, Gabriel, and

Matthew are in the time stream somewhere. If I can reach them with my Gift, I can guide them to these." I tapped the dots.

"And the fourth?"

I chewed my thumbnail. *Goddess, I am such a coward.*

"It's got to be one of us," Elspeth said.

Duncan rubbed his face. "Of course it does."

"But we'll bring you back. That's why we need Mom and Thomas. We can bring everybody back if we have an anchor for each element. Mom and Dad both use air magic. Thomas and Gabriel both use fire. Adam and Matthew are earth witches. And the two of you…"

"We both receive our Gifts through the element of water," Duncan said.

"Exactly."

"You better bring me back," Elspeth said to Duncan, standing.

"Who says it's going to be you?" Her brother leaned back on his elbows.

She went to the window. "I think we're going to need your Gift here."

54

iles stood on the other side of the Creek, Mrs. Kirk beside him, looking more like a despotic school principal than an elected representative of an enchanted community.

I stepped out onto the Gatehouse threshold. The hair rose on my arms, some kind of static in the air.

"Dad, wait." Adam blinked in behind his father.

The Watch Commander's lips tightened.

"Well," said Mrs. Kirk, folding her hands in front of her. "This has been an unusual transfer, to be sure. Thank you for accepting your responsibility, Ms. Corey. I'm so sorry that we weren't able to prepare you better."

"*Sorry, Cate,*" Adam mouthed from across the Creek.

I shrugged my forgiveness. It would have been too much to hope that he could get the message through to my brothers at the festival without alerting his father and the Speaker.

"Do you understand what's happening here?" I asked. "Alice is dead, and—"

"And you've taken on her role, as you were destined to do. You had us all worried for a while. Some of us weren't sure that you'd come back at all." She tilted her head back so that she could look down at Giles, even though he stood several inches taller than her.

He looked away, pretending to be distracted by a small flickering light near the bank.

"But I knew we could count on you. You were always such a good girl, even if your father had some unusual ideas." She beamed in triumph.

"He was right." I balled my hand in a fist at my side. "He warned you, and you ignored him. Look around you. The Source isn't stable. Replacing the Gatekeeper isn't going to fix it this time. It's coming down."

Another wisp bobbed its way along the bank, fizzing and twinkling the closer it got to the water. It wasn't the only one. The Creek sparkled with flares of light that couldn't come from the setting sun. Even as we stood there, the boundary spell became more visible in the air between us, the illusion shifting to make the energy known.

It would have been beautiful if it hadn't been a harbinger of its own violent expiration.

Adam hadn't stopped them in time.

Her face darkened. "The Equinox ritual—"

"Is going to overpower it. Look at this! Does this look normal to you?" I threw out my hands at the shimmering boundary between us. "The Gate is barely containing the energy. If we don't let it out—"

"We can't let it out," she said. "Magic belongs to us. It belongs to Queen's Creek."

"It belongs to the people." Elspeth stepped out behind me. "All of the people. On both sides of the boundary."

I turned and took her hand. In the window, Duncan closed his eyes, and for a minute, I wondered if the pain was getting to him. Then he disappeared.

A second later, he popped into being on the shore beside Giles.

Duncan held out a hand, all charm. "Hi, you might not remember me. I've been gone a while. Duncan Scott."

Giles shook his hand, his eyes a little dazed. Duncan took Giles's hand in both of his and smiled. "It's good to see you again."

And that's why we needed him. The Gift of Charisma. Duncan projected an air of confidence, even after living among mundanes for the past five years. You had to trust him.

Recognition brightened Giles's face. He dropped Duncan's hand and slapped his back. "The prodigal son returns! Good to see you. How've you been?"

No questions about where he'd been, why he'd been gone so long, or how he managed to cross the Creek after his Wakening ended. *If I had his Gift, I would have had straight answers and caught the next plane back to Chicago on my first day back.*

Mrs. Kirk raised her eyebrows.

The wind picked up, rippling the water under the bridge

When Giles turned to present Duncan to the Speaker, she stepped back, hands still folded in front of her. "Young man, I don't know what you think is happening here. You must be very confused. I don't think anyone's ever come back from their Wakening so late. Perhaps we should get you to the healer's cottage and let Mrs. Corey get a look at you."

"She isn't there," I said.

"Excuse me?" said Mrs. Kirk, almost over her shoulder as she gestured for Giles to take Duncan away.

"Mom's on her way here." The threads that connected me to the Source now connected me to everyone. It made sense now that we knew the people were the Source of our magic. I felt their presence before they blinked in, just a few steps down the path. They carried star torches that did more to draw attention to the growing shadows than to light the way.

Another Gatekeeper secret. Why didn't they tell us we were the Source of our magic? Wouldn't it have strengthened the community to know we were literally stronger together?

The answer came as soon as I asked, floating up through generations of memories. *Protect the timeline.* Our community's belief that we drew the Source of magic from the water prevented anyone from questioning the protections on the Creek. People stayed away from it. No accidental time travel, no messing with the multiverse.

My mother and Thomas jogged the short distance from the edge of the woods to the Creek, their eyes wide.

Thomas reached out a hand toward the glowing boundary but came short of touching it, clearly having second thoughts about what might happen if he did. "Shit. Are we too late? Dad was right. It's coming down."

"No!" Mrs. Kirk's voice was shrill. "It has stood for hundreds of years and will stand for hundreds more."

The sky over the Gatehouse had grown dark again while we talked. Tiny lights flickered at the edges of the trees. More wisps drawn to the energy of the broken boundary.

"What are you so afraid of?" I asked. "Things have changed out there. Ask Duncan. The hunters are gone. No one is looking for us."

I crossed my fingers behind my back. Duncan said he hadn't see them in years, but if they'd bought his disguise, they might have focused their attention on another part of town.

"But they will. When they see what we can do. The Trials will start all over again, and we'll have nowhere to go." Mrs. Kirk searched for an ally but found none.

Fire streaked across the sky, flashing across the Speaker's face.

"Ailbhe," Giles said. I'd never heard anyone call her by her first name. It did not have the calming effect he'd hoped.

"Detective Parker," she said, narrowing her eyes. "Do you stand with these rebels? Against your Speaker? Against the community you serve?"

He held up his hands. "They are the community. They're Queen's Creek's future. They should have a say in how they live."

"They don't know what they're doing. They don't understand the risk," she said.

"Do you?" Thomas asked.

The air pressure shifted with the coming storm. Goosebumps rose on my arms. Adam appeared at my side, having blinked the short distance across the Creek.

"We have to release the energy, Speaker." Elspeth stepped out onto the bridge as she attempted to pacify Mrs. Kirk. "The community won't survive otherwise."

The wind whipped across the Creek, sending waves over the narrow bridge. I gripped Adam's arm to keep from being swept over. Elspeth wobbled, taking another step closer to the bank. The strobing lights of the wisps gathered at the far shore, dancing like psychotic fireflies. My skin vibrated with the energy of the boundary spell.

Another wave splashed over my feet, the water sparkling as droplets rose into the air. Tiny white sparks, too small to be wisps, floating in the wrong direction for snow, lifted out of the Creek, building into the wall of magic between Elspeth and the bank on the other side. The veil shimmered, more opaque by the minute.

"What are you doing?" Giles squinted, invoking his Gift. He saw something I didn't. Something emanating from the Speaker.

"We can stop it. Don't you see?" Her fingers twitched, and she muttered words I couldn't hear.

Mom stepped closer to Mrs. Kirk, surprise tempering the anger in her voice. "She's resetting the parameters of the boundary."

"The boundary would work better as a barricade. Don't you think?" Mrs. Kirk lifted her arms, raising the water of the Creek out of its bed, an impenetrable wall between the shore and the Gatehouse. Elspeth scrambled back, sitting hard on the stone in front of the Gatehouse where I'd hit my head the day I first came home.

"El!" Duncan disappeared from the shore and then reappeared in the same place, unable to blink past the Speaker's wall.

"You're blocking the Gate," Thomas said. "We won't be able to reach them."

She wouldn't cut us off completely… she's not that horrible.

"The best way for them to protect us is from the outside. The Guardian can hold back the hunters, and the Gatekeeper's energy will continue to feed the spell, as it always should have done."

Shit. She is that horrible. Maybe worse.

"What about Elspeth? She's your healer," Duncan said.

"Sarah can train another."

"This is wrong," Giles said, but he didn't move against the Speaker. *Typical.*

"It's not going to work." Mom could almost reach her.

Mrs. Kirk snapped her head to really look at her for the first time. "What are you saying, Sarah?"

Mom stepped between Mrs. Kirk and the bridge. "Marcus warned you that this was coming, and you ignored him. Are you really so afraid of what's out there that you would risk the lives of everyone in Queen's Creek? Or are you afraid of sharing magic with the rest of the world? How much power will you have if witches are free to come and go, if magic spreads outside this town?"

"Magic isn't meant for them! They rejected us, hunted us, killed our people. Why should their descendants know our secrets?"

I pushed my hair back from my wet face. "The secrets are destroying us. Don't you see that? Alice, my father, Matthew, and Gabriel. They're all lost because you didn't want anyone to know the boundary was failing. We can't keep hiding. The magic wants out."

Lights flashed in the wall of water. The wisps. As if to prove my point, the tiny magical creatures waded into the chaos. They soaked up the energy that hovered over the Creek, expanding as they drew off the power of the boundary spell and Mrs. Kirk's Gift.

She staggered, weakening from the expense of holding her new boundary. The wall of water dissipated into mist but didn't disappear. She stepped closer, one foot on the bridge, in an effort to assert her authority over the energy. The shimmering boundary spell closed around her, separating her from the shore. It recognized her connection to the water. No wonder she'd thought she could fix it herself. Her Gift was strong, but the energy feeding into the boundary almost overwhelmed her.

The wisps floated along the Creek, rising and falling through the waves of magic. Some of them flickered as they crossed, zooming into the woods outside to join the ones I'd seen when Duncan and I were lost. Tiny cracks glimmered in the air where they broke through the boundary. Thunder crashed overhead, the shock shaking the bridge. Mrs. Kirk lost her balance on the slick wood. She faltered but kept moving forward, pressing the boundary against the Gatehouse shore, locking us in.

The energy built in the air. It tore at my skin. A vision flared behind my eyes. An explosion.

"No!" My hands came up, and for the first time, I saw the magic of my Gift. Around me, everything froze. The water droplets hung in the air, static instead of flickering in the light. Even the wisps stopped their antics.

I saw it all now, the flow of everything, branching in a hundred different ways into the future. In none of them did the Gate still stand.

I stepped onto the bridge.

Breathe.

The tension of my Gift radiated up my fingers, holding everything in place. When I'd been lost in the woods all those years ago, the darkness had been absolute, but my brothers and I had moved through it, through the silence of a forest frozen in time. Even bound, I'd stilled a plane in the sky for a moment. I'd crossed the Creek on my own. More than once.

The Gatekeeper was bound to the Gatehouse, but it was the boundary spell that held her… me… and it was failing. I pushed it back. If I could get to her. If she had to look me in the eye.

Maybe she would see reason before it was too late.

The energy buzzed around me. I couldn't hold it much longer. My foot slipped, and I flung out my arms to steady myself. *What happens if I fall in now? If Mrs. Kirk does?* I'd almost drowned when I came back, but the time stream hadn't taken me.

What was different for Dad and my brothers?

Set an intention.

Magic was just energy manifested, directed toward your intentions. Dad had intended to give himself up to the spell, to sacrifice his potential energy like the Keepers to help the boundary spell stay open just a little longer. From what I read in the journals, Gabriel had projected the same intention. What about Matthew? Had Gabriel convinced him they could save the boundary?

Well, shit, I have no intention of doing that.

The clouds above the Gatehouse darkened. My reach didn't extend that far, and the time bubble I'd created was shrinking. I had to stop Mrs. Kirk from putting any more energy into the unstable boundary spell, and I couldn't risk letting her fall into the Creek. Who knew when she would turn up or what damage she could do if she had access to the Gate in the past?

55

I walked farther out onto the slick slats of the footbridge, concentrating on holding time in place and trying not to think about how deep the Creek went. Far above me, lightning streaked the dark sky. The wisps that hadn't been trapped by my Gift whizzed across the Creek, creating larger and larger holes in the boundary spell. The air crackled around me. A few of the trapped wisps flickered in place. The trees in the distance swayed in a wind I couldn't feel. Something cracked.

Suddenly, everything came back to life, wisps and wind moving at once. I'd almost reached Mrs. Kirk when the time bubble popped. I'd lost control of my Gift.

Lightning cracked the air.

"Look out!" Adam yelled behind me.

I ducked. My feet slid out from under me, and I reached for anything that might keep me on the bridge. Mrs. Kirk overbalanced, her face still turned up to the sky. We collided and fell. For a moment, everything went black. *Not again.*

I woke to chaos, explosions of light raining like sparklers above the Creek. Adam pulled me back into the shelter of the Gatehouse threshold. His wide eyes dazzled, reflecting the lights of the wisps and the cracks they tore in the boundary spell.

Giles sat on the shore near the washed-out bridge, cradling Mrs. Kirk's head on his folded cloak. The wind ruffled his shirt collar.

"Is she?" I couldn't bring myself to finish the sentence. She'd made horrible choices, but she believed she'd done it to save lives. And even if it wasn't my fault, I felt responsible for what happened to her on the bridge.

"She's unconscious, but she needs a healer."

Mom shook herself and knelt beside him.

Thomas looked from her to the bridge to Duncan, frowning. His hands went to his head, tangling in his hair.

"Where's Elspeth?" Duncan charged up the bridge, no longer blocked by Mrs. Kirk's spell.

It was as if time sped up and slowed down all at once. Everyone scanned the shore, the bridge, and the water. There was no sign of her.

No. This was not the way we'd planned it. She must have fallen. The wind is so strong now. Goddess, tell me she set an intention.

I pushed my hair behind my ears, but the wind whipped it back out, the strands tangling in my glasses.

The next bolt of lightning struck the roof, igniting the wooden shingles. Adam and I backed out onto the bridge.

The flames licked the Gatehouse, growing as they devoured the earliest shelter in Queen's Creek. The water flickered with the red and orange reflection, making it look like the cottage burned from both sides. The glow mesmerized me until I remembered my bag, Nora's card, and the goddess-blessed grimoire were still inside.

All of our hopes for venting the boundary spell safely are going up in smoke.

Panic froze me in place more surely than my Gift ever had.

Then Adam ran into the burning Gatehouse. Duncan

directed water from the storm over the fire, but his Gift wasn't as strong as Mrs. Kirk's, and the rain hissed instead of dousing the flames.

Before I could process what he'd done, Adam emerged, carrying my backpack. I breathed again.

"Thought we might need this," he said, revealing the heavy grimoire in my bag. "What do you want to do now?"

I looked at Duncan, who hadn't given up putting out the fire.

"There's still a chance we can bring them all back and keep this storm from destroying Queen's Creek. We have to open the boundary spell wider than the Gate," I said, remembering something from Dad's letter. "We have to build a Bridge."

The storm clouds finally burst, a downpour drenching the fire and leaving the ruin of the Gatehouse smoldering on the other side of the Creek. Mom and Duncan managed the storm. Between her connection to air and his to water, they directed the clouds away. Smoke rose from the husk of the Gatehouse.

Over the Creek, the wisps continued to dart in and out of the time stream, cracking the boundary a little more each time. Showers of sparks erupted like fireworks up and down the shore.

I hefted my backpack over my shoulders and turned to Adam and Duncan, still waiting near the Gatehouse. "We do this now, and we do it together. When this is over, we won't need the Gatehouse anymore. This bridge will guide the flow of magic in and out with our people. Like breath."

Duncan nodded, but spoke slowly to make sure I wouldn't miss a word. "You said we could bring them all back. I hope you're right. We have to find Elspeth. My family will be happy to have me back, but not at the expense of losing her."

Caleb will kill me.

"We'll find her." The previous Gatekeepers flooded my

mind, insisting that it was true. I swallowed. Communicating with the past made me dizzy.

Adam reached out to steady me, but I shook my head. "Stay where you are. For this to work, we need the elements represented on both sides. A beginning and an end. Adam, I need you to pull Matthew back. He'll be with Clara, the earth witch. I'm going to contact her through the time stream, but he'll need an anchor."

He sighed as if he wanted to argue but stood where I placed him.

"Duncan, Elspeth will be drawn to Mary, the water witch who created the boundary spell. You guide her back."

He nodded. "I'm trusting you."

Thank you seemed inadequate. I only hoped that I'd followed Alice's clues correctly. The footbridge was still slick, and I turned carefully. I walked through a constellation of flashing lights until I reached the midpoint. From there, I directed Thomas to anchor Gabriel and guide him back from Martha, the Gatekeeper who'd been aligned with fire.

Mom gave Giles one last instruction for Mrs. Kirk's recovery before joining Thomas at the end of the footbridge. "I'm ready. Call him back, Hecate."

Dad had written the spell we were about to perform, basing it on notes from Gabriel's research. It closely matched what Elspeth and I read in the grimoire. He must have spoken with Alice about it. They shared the same affinity for air magic, so he would be with her now. Was she less cryptic in her own time? How long ago had her Gift turned her into an oracle?

As I fought another wave of visions and voices from the previous Gatekeepers, it occurred to me that her confusion and uncertain advice might have come as much from hearing all of her predecessors as it had from her intuition and premonitions.

I sat on the wet wooden slats and crossed my legs. Dragging the grimoire out of my bag, I settled it into my lap. I used Nora's tarot card to mark the page, just in case I needed an anchor of my own. I wouldn't need to use it as a conduit now that we'd broken the bind on my Gift, but I still felt connected to it after all we'd been through together. I visualized Nora sitting at her desk with the rest of the deck, wishing me well, if not actively sharing her energy.

Call the quarters to call them home.

"I call to the powers of the air. I call to the powers of the fire. I call to the powers of the water. I call to the powers of the earth." The manic lightning bugs floating over the Creek flashed their approval at each invocation.

"I call to the ancestors, to those we have lost, to those we love, and those who are yet to come. I call to the beginning and the end. Help us restore the balance. Return what was lost. Let the outside in." I closed my eyes and focused on Alice, not wasted and fading on the bed as I had last seen her, but vibrant in her earliest days after taking the mantle.

The vision rose quickly. Alice smiled and a cool breeze marked her release of the energy she fed the boundary.

My heartbeat crashed like waves in my ears, a panicked rhythm easing to white noise.

Breathe.

My father stepped into sight beside the Gatekeeper, and my mother gasped. I wanted to run to him, but I had to hold the anchor. It was enough to have found him. Now, I had to find the others. Trust Mom to bring him home. *I must not turn back. Don't make Orpheus's mistake.*

I pushed through the time stream, dragging Thomas, Adam, and Duncan with me. My Gift finally worked the way it was always meant to.

I took another ragged breath, seeking Martha and Gabriel further down the time stream. The temperature rose. *There.*

Almost one hundred years into the past, the Gatekeeper meditated in front of the hearth, watching images that danced in the flames. Gabriel stood beside her, wearing a vest and a newsboy cap.

Martha acknowledged me, shared my vision as all the previous Gatekeepers had shared theirs with me, accepted what had to be done. The warm air around me tickled my skin.

"Nice look, Gabe." Thomas laughed. "How's Gatsby?"

"Thomas," I started through gritted teeth.

"Yeah, yeah. I got you. Take my hand, man." As his hand, and then his arm, reached through the hearth, I pushed away, following the time stream and trusting Thomas to save our brother.

Finding Clara required more concentration. She'd lived through the Battle of Williamsburg, hiding Queen's Creek when war brought mundane violence nearer than ever. I needed to meet her earlier.

At the turn of the nineteenth century, the Gatekeeper tended a small garden on the bank of the Creek. Matthew worked beside her, his sleeves rolled up and his trousers muddy. The ground trembled in response to our presence. Clara nodded her acquiescence.

"I'm here," said Adam. He reached for Matthew.

One more stop. I searched through a blur of images, tuning out everything but the sound of my breath. The Mary I found in 1730 shook with fear. Elspeth leaned over her where she lay on the floor, wiping her back with a cool cloth.

My stomach turned. The first Gatekeeper founded Queen's Creek after suffering thirty-nine lashes for practicing witchcraft.

"You're too soon," Elspeth said, stepping away from her patient. "She's not ready."

"El, I don't—"

"You have time. Come back for me later. I'll be fine." She returned to Mary's side, raising her hands over the wounds, stitching the skin back together with her magic.

I felt Duncan catching up to me. No way would he leave her here. But I needed the Gatekeepers' blessings to pull back the energy of the spell, and Mary was in no condition to help us. I backed into the time stream again, letting it carry me forward.

It only felt like a few seconds before I stepped back into Mary's Gatehouse, but years had passed for her.

"Elspeth?" Duncan stepped in behind me.

His little sister smiled as she took his hand. They disappeared into the time stream.

Mary sat in the chair by the window. A shawl draped her shoulders and gray hair escaped her bonnet. I knelt beside her. The air shimmered around me, reminding me that we were still in the time stream. This was a liminal space, outside of time. Here, her spirit held onto the energy that powered the spell, just as she had in life. She had to release it now to free us all.

"You should not be here," she murmured.

"I need your help."

"What more can I do?"

"You can let go. Your time has ended. Rest now."

"There is no Gate without the Keeper." She raised her eyes to mine, and I saw the warning. Flashes of her life outside the Gate, the fear in her vision of the future. I tried to show her mine, hope mingled with caution.

"Thank you for protecting us for so long. Because of you, your descendants have a chance to live their lives on their own terms."

"It will be a dangerous life," she warned.

"I accept the risk." Pain lanced across my back, her memory of thirty-nine lashes as real as if I'd experienced them myself. I cried out, tears streaming down my face. *Breathe.*

Her eyes bored into mine, testing my resolve. Gritting my teeth, I straightened, pushing back the pain. "It is my life, and I accept the risk."

Mary nodded. She stood, pulling her shawl tighter, then raised her hands in a blessing.

"Be well, my girl." She closed her eyes, and I felt the energy of the boundary spell release.

March 21

Clarity, Authority, Truth

56

reathe.

B I followed the flow of the time stream back to my present, dragging my consciousness to my body on the bridge. Lights flickered and images flashed by, the history of Queen's Creek through the eyes of the Gatekeepers.

I almost stepped out so many times, but none were more tempting than when I saw my father confronting Giles at the Creek and watched him fall into the time stream again. *I could stop all of this.*

Alice whispered in my ear, "This is not your time."

"It is though. I'm right here." But of course, I wasn't. I was in Chicago, working at the coffee shop with Brian, arguing with Thomas. What I saw now was all just shadows.

The stream sped up, pulling me along.

I opened my eyes. Mist rolled across the Creek, obscuring my vision of either shore. *How will I know if it worked?*

A breeze ruffled my hair, nothing like the gale that had whipped through during the storm. The foggy air above the water sparkled with tiny specks of light. The wisps drifted among the low-lying clouds, their bellies full.

The grimoire lay heavy in my lap. My legs had gone to

sleep. I heaved the book closed and lay it on my dry backpack. Straightening my legs, pins and needles ran all the way down. I pushed myself up, staying close to the center of the bridge, unsure how much of it existed beyond the few feet I could see.

Gabriel found me first, pushing through the mist with an arm around Thomas.

"Wait!" Duncan called out. A thump on the other side of the bridge.

My brothers and I moved as quickly as we dared back toward the Gatehouse. Duncan had sunk to his knees. Adam and Matthew kept him from falling over.

"Where's Elspeth?" It was so hard to see anything beyond where we stood.

"She was right behind me." Duncan covered his face in his hands.

Adam put a hand on his shoulder.

We had her. I'd seen him take her hand. Hex it all, Elspeth. Why couldn't you come the first time?

A buzzing in my head rattled my teeth. My heart beat in my jaw. *Is this what a panic attack feels like?*

Thomas rubbed a circle on my back. "Has anyone seen Mom and Dad?"

They could be anywhere. Any when. My legs gave out.

Gabriel and Matthew were arguing again, but it all just sounded like bees.

"Marcus!" My mother's voice rang out from the shore.

"Mom?" My stomach sank. *I've failed again. Cursed even with a Gift.*

Thomas and I pelted back across the bridge, but something pulled me faster.

"What happened? Where's Dad?" The mist clung to my skin, and the air in my lungs turned to ice.

"We were so close, and then... I don't know. He faded

away, and I couldn't see him anymore."

Behind her, Mrs. Kirk stood with her hands raised and her eyes closed. Her fingers called to the mist.

"What are you doing?" But I already knew.

Her fingers plucked the water from the air, weaving a new spell even as the energy from the old Gate dissipated. Invisible threads wound around my head, familiar discomfort. Elspeth had told me I'd never leave Queen's Creek. A bind like the one that hid my Gift, but this one kept me here.

Mrs. Kirk always knew she'd need me to complete her plans to strengthen the boundary. I was chosen by the Gatekeeper, but I was also the only name on the list in her office with a round elemental symbol. Aligned with the element of spirit.

She pulled the strings tighter, tying me to the spirits of the Gatekeepers, to all the ancestors who'd gone before. *No wonder the shades responded to me where the veil was thin.*

The Speaker had been weakened by the storms she created. Now, she drew energy from our spell before we could complete it. We'd lost Elspeth because the energy to draw her out had been redirected.

My father couldn't cross over because the energy that guided his return was being used to trap me once again.

My heart raced and my breath caught. My head pounded against the pressure and my own panic.

A shadow rose on the shore.

The Watch Commander stood shakily behind the Speaker, a new determination in his eyes. He grabbed her wrists, pulling them behind her back. Her eyes widened, and she struggled against him. But he was physically stronger, and his career had given him experience in subduing agitators. He whispered something in her ear, and she sank into him, her eyes closed again.

The threads she'd used to hold me slipped away. I shivered, and the last of them shook free.

"We'll try again," Thomas said. "You can call them back. We haven't closed the circle."

"I don't know if I can." Already, my connection to the Keepers felt more like a memory. The Gate had come down. The Gatekeepers had released their hold on the boundary. There was nothing to tie me to this point in the time stream anymore.

Bell, book, and candle. I could still use the grimoire as a link to the Keepers and the card as an anchor to the present.

All anyone can ask is that you try. Something Dad used to say. The words came through the buzz in my head. Was he trying to reach us?

"Stay here." *I can't lose anyone else.* I walked back down the bridge, stepping slowly along what I hoped was a path straight down the middle. Mrs. Kirk had raised the storm, but the unstable energy of the failing boundary controlled it now.

I nearly stumbled over the edge of the book. Mist shrouded most of it. Once again, I sat crosswise on the bridge and closed my eyes. I hugged the book with the card still between its pages. *Help me find them.*

The sound of waves washed over me so quickly that I clutched the book like a life preserver and willed myself to stay on the bridge. The mist darkened, lit by a quarter moon. *Where are they?*

"Cate!"

I turned my head toward the sound of Elspeth's voice.

A shadow with her shape formed in the mists. My astral self reached for her, and she took my hand. I pulled her closer. Elspeth had not escaped the mist unaffected. My friend, Duncan's younger sister, appeared old enough to be his mother. Laugh lines creased her face and silver streaked her braid, still trailing over her shoulder almost to her waist.

"I'm so sorry." I hugged her.

"For what? I lived my life as I chose. Wasn't that what you were trying to do?"

Before I could answer, another shadow appeared in the mist.

"Dad!"

He spoke, but I couldn't make out the words. The mist refused to clear. It closed around us despite my efforts to push it back. I held Elspeth's hand, dragging her with me as I tried to reach him. He faded in and out of the mist, a shadow surrounded by darkness.

Something pulled me back like the strings Elspeth had found with the bind. Whispers called me through the mist.

The sun broke through, burning away the clouds. The shadow disappeared.

Elspeth and I stood on the bridge. The mist drifted, taking the sleepy wisps with it. They'd lost interest in the Creek without the energy of the boundary spell.

As soon as the way cleared, Duncan ran to his sister, embracing her. He stepped back, gently touching the new creases at the corners of her eyes and running a hand over her graying hair. She ignored his confusion and hugged him again. "I've missed you."

Mom's eyes filled.

"I'll go back," I said, sitting back down with the grimoire. I squeezed my eyes shut, reaching out with my Gift. I sensed the flow of time, but it thinned. Where it used to fold back over itself in endless layers, now I felt only the immediate future and past. I turned back, rewinding time like I had at Luke William's office. The vision blurred, showing me nothing more than what I already knew—my father was missing.

My eyes stung. I'd lost my connection to the time stream. No Gate. No Keeper. My Gift alone couldn't reach far enough to find him.

Try anyway. I closed my eyes.

When I opened them, I lay on the cot in the healer's cottage. Elspeth sat in the chair beside me, a cup of tea on the table and a book in her hands. *No. I refuse to live through this week again.*

"She's awake." Elspeth didn't look up from her book, but as she shifted in her seat, the sun shining through the window flashed off her new silver strands.

Oh, praise Kore. I'm still in the present.

Mom appeared at my side, then Thomas.

"Welcome back, kiddo." Mom brushed the hair back from my face.

Thomas handed me my glasses.

"What day is it?"

"Did you hit your head again?" Thomas quirked an eyebrow.

Mom knocked him with her elbow, giving him a look of disapproval.

My brother grinned. "It's our birthday! How do you want to celebrate? I hear there's a deli in town that serves alcohol."

Our birthday marked the end of our Wakening. We were full members of our community if we chose to be. Exiles if we chose otherwise.

But the Gate that would have kept us trapped on one side or the other had burned down last night. The years of secrecy were coming to an end, along with the illusions that hid Queen's Creek from the rest of the world. I was the last Gatekeeper, just as Alice had told me.

The others had given their lives but would give no more of their energy. The storms had passed, and sun shone. The bridge would maintain the balance now, allowing magical energy to pass through the boundary spell, even as the spell continued to protect the witches who remained inside. No one could enter who intended harm to Queen's Creek or its people. After all, our magic was energy plus intention. It wouldn't support its own destruction.

"I'm sorry I couldn't bring him back."

Mom shook her head. "He's alive, and we'll find him."

My father was an alchemist, and his work was as much science as magic. There wasn't much I could do here. The rest of my family had the magic side covered. But if I went back to school, professors might be able to help with the science. Maybe Brian could introduce me to the Physics department.

I tried to avoid a *Wizard of Oz* lineup of goodbyes on the bridge and almost managed it when Thomas offered to run into town and pick up a few things. "Hear me out, Mom. Cellular Hotspot. We could bring your medical practice into the twenty-first century."

Mom rolled her eyes. "My practice is just fine, thank you."

"Okay, but, like, what about research? Or social media? You could communicate with healers from anywhere in the world."

Duncan nodded. "I can help you set it up if you like. We'll have you surfing the web in no time."

Duncan planned to continue his real estate business as Luke Williams. His face was already on fliers all over town. He was practically a household name. But now he'd come home whenever he wanted, spending weekends in Queen's Creek.

Giles repaired the Gatehouse, magically transforming it into a more functional way station. It would be no one's permanent home. Mrs. Kirk reluctantly approved the revised use proposal. But it didn't really matter since she retired to avoid the scandal of her actions at the boundary.

Before I left, I visited the Gatehouse to check out the renovations. In the updated bedroom, I took out Nora's card one last time. It flickered in a way it'd never done before. Judgment. Death. Finally, it settled on the King of Swords. Change after a period of reflection. New beginnings based on an awakening. Move forward with clarity of mind and purpose.

Adam came in hesitantly while I was sorting through my backpack. He seemed a little lost. It must have been strange to be the Guardian with no Gate.

"What will you do now?" I asked.

"I'll ask the Watch for reassignment."

"Still guarding something?" I smiled.

"People are going to be scared without the boundary. We need to make them feel safe."

I nodded. It was the right thing to do. Adam would always do the right thing. Still. "You could come with me…"

He smiled. "It's not my time. Call me when your Wakening is over."

Before I could make a snarky comment about the inevitable end to that arcane practice now that the borders were open, or the fact that technically it would have ended today anyway, he kissed me. With his fingers in my hair and my arms around his waist, it was both new and familiar. I was dazed when he pulled away.

"So you don't forget me this time," he said.

As if I could.

Thomas called after me from the front door.

"Better get going." Adam tapped the doorframe on his way back to the bridge. "And Cate? Happy Birthday."

About the Author

Jenn Lessmann is the author of three stories on Amazon's Kindle Vella and a contributor to *Indie Author Magazine*. *Unmagical* is her first published novel.

A former barista, stage manager, and high school English teacher with advanced degrees from impressive colleges, Jenn continues to drink excessive amounts of caffeine, stay up later than is absolutely necessary, and read three or four books at a time. She lives in Virginia with her husband and their two boys and writes snarky paranormal fantasy whenever their dog will allow it.

Want more news from Queen's Creek?

Read a FREE bonus story from Thomas's point of view when you subscribe to my newsletter at **www.JennLessmann.com/Thomas.**

About *Street Muse:* Thomas Corey has twenty four hours to convince his twin sister to come home before the Gate closes, and she's locked out of his life forever. Unfortunately, Thomas's Gift is... unpredictable, and he's about to find himself the unexpected center of some very unwanted attention.

Acknowledgments

From the outside, writing a book seems like a solitary task, and in some ways, it is the most alone I've ever been. But in so many ways, writing this book has made me a part of some of the most supportive and giving communities I've ever known.

Writing during lockdown was much less lonely after I discovered virtual writing groups like: 20 Books to 50k, Authors of IFA, several Maggie Stiefvater FB groups (and Discord servers), and the Indie Cover Project. Later, being about to meet in person with my local NaNoWriMo chapter and the James River Writers gave me the confidence to introduce myself as an author.

Thank you to Steph O'Neil for believing in me and encouraging me to dream. This book would never have gone beyond a lockdown diversion without you cheering me on.

Thank you to the authors of Kindle Vella, who were just as excited as I was to publish new work on an untested platform. In particular, thank you to Julie Gilbert, Rose Sinclair, and Ashley Marstaller, who read some of the earliest versions of Cate's story on Vella and offered advice. Much appreciation to Tess Combs, Azrielle Lawless, and Gage Greenwood, who made supporting other authors part of their brands, and who created safe spaces for new writers to talk about their work and share what they learned.

Thank you, Cristina Alvarez, who read my story on Kindle Vella as I posted it and left my first review. Some weeks, knowing you were waiting for the next episode was the only thing motivating me to publish it. I am beyond grateful that you follow my work (even though I teased you about *Twilight* when you were my student).

Thank you, Chrishaun Keller-Hanna, for your mentorship and friendship.

This book would not have been published without the help of my beta readers, who loved Cate's character, even when they didn't understand her motives. Thank you for showing me where I was lost, and helping me find the way out again: Davida De La Harpe Golden, Sherry Schafer, Jennifer Ragsdale, Heather Saliba, and Tess K. (and the Newbie Writers Group).

Thank you to my editor, Sharon Stogner, for helping me untangle dropped threads and fill dangerous plot holes.

Thank you to the Moms Who Write group on Facebook, who introduced me to my critique partners: Kat Keenan, Mariel

Hesley, and Elena James, and my mastermind group: Kat Keenan, Kristen Tassin Vallot, Holly Fyfe, and Sarah Mace.

Kat, you helped me find Cate's voice, made me think about my writing as a business, and shared so much of my process that you probably know this book as well as I do. Thank you from the bottom of my heart for your friendship and leadership!

There is a dedication going around social media in which an author thanks his family, without whom, he says, the book would have been published two years earlier. While it might be true that this book could have been completed faster, it is as much my fault as theirs, and neither the book, nor my life, would be the same without my husband and kids. And I wouldn't have it any other way. I love you George, Freddie, and Nate. (And Poe, who dragged me to the library every morning. May every author have such a dedicated familiar.)

Resources

Authors are always asked where they get their ideas. Here are a few of the many resources I used when writing this novel.

I hope you find them as inspiring as I did.

Tarot:
- *Everyday Tarot Deck* by Brigit Esselmont of www.Biddytarot.com
- Labyrinthos.co
- *Illuminating the Prophecy [Raven's Prophecy Tarot]* by Maggie Stiefvater
- *Anima Mundi Tarot* by Megan Wyreweden

Witchcraft:
- *The Dabbler's Guide to Witchcraft* by Fire Lyte
- *A Spell in the Wild* by Alice Tarbuck
- *Busy, Gritty, Inked and Witchy* podcast with Morgan from Inked Goddess Creations

Writing:
- *Save the Cat! Writes a Novel* by Jessica Brody
- *Fearless Writing* by William Kenower
- *Bird by Bird* by Anne Lamott
- *Rebel Author Podcast* with Sacha Black